MEDICAL

Life and love in the world of modern medicine.

Forbidden Fiji Nights With Her Rival
JC Harroway

The Rebel Doctor's Secret Child
Deanne Anders

MILLS & BOON

FORBIDDEN FIJI NIGHTS WITH HER RIVAL
© 2024 by JC Harroway
Philippine Copyright 2024
Australian Copyright 2024
New Zealand Copyright 2024

First Published 2024
First Australian Paperback Edition 2024
ISBN 978 1 038 93520 5

THE REBEL DOCTOR'S SECRET CHILD
© 2024 by Deanne Anders
Philippine Copyright 2024
Australian Copyright 2024
New Zealand Copyright 2024

First Published 2024
First Australian Paperback Edition 2024
ISBN 978 1 038 93520 5

® and ™ (apart from those relating to FSC®) are trademarks of Harlequin Enterprises
(Australia) Pty Limited or its corporate affiliates. Trademarks indicated with® are
registered in Australia, New Zealand and in other countries.
Contact admin_legal@Harlequin.ca for details.

This is a work of fiction. Names, characters, places, and incidents are either the
product of the author's imagination or are used fictitiously, and any resemblance to
actual persons, living or dead, business establishments, events, or locales is entirely
coincidental.

MIX
Paper | Supporting
responsible forestry
FSC® C001695
www.fsc.org

Published by
Harlequin Mills & Boon
An imprint of Harlequin Enterprises (Australia) Pty Limited
(ABN 47 001 180 918), a subsidiary of HarperCollins
Publishers Australia Pty Limited
(ABN 36 009 913 517)
Level 19, 201 Elizabeth Street
SYDNEY NSW 2000 AUSTRALIA

Cover art used by arrangement with Harlequin Books S.A.. All rights reserved.

Printed and bound in Australia by McPherson's Printing Group

Forbidden Fiji Nights With Her Rival

JC Harroway

MILLS & BOON

Lifelong romance addict **JC Harroway** took a break from her career as a junior doctor to raise a family and found her calling as a Mills & Boon author instead. She now lives in New Zealand and finds that writing feeds her very real obsession with happy endings and the endorphin rush they create. You can follow her at jcharroway.com, and on Facebook, X and Instagram.

To writer friends, especially the CC ladies.

CHAPTER ONE

ENTERING THE ARRIVAL hall of Fiji's Nadi Airport, Della Wilton sighed happily. Despite coming for a working holiday, the minute she'd stepped from the plane's metal staircase onto the sun-baked tarmac, her problems had dissolved, one by one.

Della hefted her overstuffed suitcase onto the airport luggage trolley, stubbing her toe in the process. She winced in pain, but not even a fractured digit could dispel her buoyant mood. Two whole weeks of sun, seminars and pro bono surgery at Pacific Health Hospital on Fiji's main island, Viti Levu. Just the boost she needed after the stagnation of the past three and a half years since her divorce.

With her cases secured, Della sought out the exit, already dreaming of snorkelling the coral reefs of the clear, pristine waters and lounging in a hammock strung between two coconut palms. She knew from previous family holidays and, more recently, her ill-fated honeymoon marking the start of her three-year marriage that there was a taxi rank outside. But she'd barely taken two steps in that direction when her laden trolley jammed to a halt, the wheels locking. Della grunted, momentarily winded from her midsection colliding with the handle bar. Trust her to choose the duff trolley. She reversed, hoping to free the sticky wheels, to no avail.

Another jerking halt sent her carry-on case tumbling to the floor with a loud clatter. Della bent to retrieve it. The back of her neck was already clammy from the heat and humidity and the battle with her luggage. Frazzled, she straightened. Came face-to-face with the last person in the world she expected to see in Fiji: Harvey Ward.

'Della...' he drawled, an amused smile tugging at his sexy mouth. He eyed her big case suspiciously, as if it was full of sex toys, chocolate and tequila—the sad single woman's survival kit. 'Hasn't anyone ever explained the principle of travelling light?'

Before Della could articulate a single stunned word in reply, Harvey swooped in and pressed a kiss to her cheek. Della gaped, disorientated, speechless and instantly and inconveniently turned on by the foreign contact, which zapped her nerve endings as if she'd been pleasantly electrocuted. He'd never done that before. Their usual form of greeting was a reluctant nod of acknowledgement or a terse *hello*.

'What on Earth are *you* doing here?' she snapped, abandoning the polite indifference she usually produced when addressing this man—not quite a friend, although they'd known each other for years. Not a full-blown enemy, although, as the more experienced trauma surgeon, he *had* stolen Della's dream job in Melbourne. And definitely not a lover; apart from that one reckless night after the granting of her divorce order three years ago, when, feeling rejected and embarrassed, she'd drunk too much rosé and had temporarily lost her mind.

On cue, Della's body helpfully recalled every detail

of how it felt to be naked in his strong arms. They'd had sex one time, and she still couldn't forget.

'It's good to see you, too.' Harvey laughed with infuriating composure, by-passing Della to select a new trolley, one that appeared to have perfectly behaved wheels.

Hateful man was good at *everything*. How dare he look so cool, relaxed, and indecently arousing in his casual linen shorts and polo shirt which showed off his light tan and lean, athletic build, when Della felt decidedly in need of another shower, preferably a cold one.

'I'm here to pick you up,' he stated simply.

Della pushed her damp, frizzy hair back from her flustered face, her skin crawling with head-to-toe prickly heat. 'Oh, well, that explains everything,' she muttered, her stomach taking a disappointed dive. The last person she wanted to *bump into* on her holiday was her professional rival and personal nemesis, Harvey. Especially when he'd obviously come all the way from Australia to goad her and point out her failings, as usual.

'I heard that,' he said with an amused shrug, effortlessly transferring her suitcases from *her* wonky trolley to *his* better one. 'What…? Not pleased to see me?'

At his flippancy, Della pressed her lips together stubbornly. That was another thing that got under her skin—just like her older brother, Brody, Harvey's best friend, the man had a competitive streak a mile wide. Probably why Harvey was so at home with her family, an overachieving clan of medics. Della's parents were GPs and Brody one of Australia's top renal surgeons. As the youngest sibling, Della had grown up scared that she'd never quite make the grade, a feeling that only intensified when self-assured, arrogant Harvey had been welcomed into the family as an honorary Wilton.

With both suitcases now perfectly balanced on the replacement trolley, Harvey shot Della a triumphant smile, commandeered the handle bar and began to stroll towards the exit, as if assured that she'd follow.

'So you're still bearing a grudge, I see,' he said, glancing over his broad shoulder, his stare brimming with the hint of challenge that never failed to raise Della's hackles.

Ever since Brody had first introduced them to Harvey— Della had been eighteen and about to leave for medical school—there'd been something about the newly qualified doctor, a hunger in his eyes, that had left Della mildly threatened. It was as if Harvey knew some big secret she was too stupid to see. She'd fancied him, of course, despite being in a relationship with her engineering student boyfriend. Harvey was a good-looking man. Even then, at twenty-three, before he'd become a surgeon, he'd possessed that air of supreme confidence. But only minutes into their first conversation, it had become glaringly obvious that they would never get along. Their mutual contempt had been instantaneous, their first impressions of each other terrible.

Brody had regaled Della with the tale of some poor woman Harvey had slept with the night before but wasn't going to call again. Harvey had merely shrugged, saying, "I told her it was nothing serious". Meanwhile, Della had been upset to leave her boyfriend and do long-distance, and Harvey had joined in with Brody's teasing, throwing out an insensitive "it probably won't last". Still dreamily in love at the time, Della had taken instant umbrage to Harvey's dismissive attitude to relationships. He'd acted as if the pursuit of love and commitment was beneath him and only for fools.

'I am not bearing a grudge,' Della said, hurrying after him, although at six-two he towered over her five-foot-six, his long stride giving him an unfair advantage. 'But I should point out that you *did* actually steal my job.'

She hated the bitter whine to her voice. Of course she was bearing a grudge. Technically, the position of head of trauma surgery at Melbourne Medical Centre wasn't *her* job. Technically, Harvey had just as much right to it as Della. But having already moved from her native Melbourne to Sydney for her ex-husband a couple of years earlier, and after the humiliation of her divorce, she'd desperately needed the professional win to boost her confidence. To lose a position to Harvey, of all people, especially after she'd slept with him, had been a bitter pill to swallow, leading Della to flee *across the ditch* to New Zealand for a consultant position in order to get away from Sydney and Ethan.

'Is it my fault that they wanted the best surgeon for the job?' he said with a wink. He passed through the automatic exit doors, where a blast of conditioned air bathed Della in his sexy masculine scent.

His casual comment nudged awake her highly evolved competitive streak. 'No, but it *is* your fault that you're an arrogant control freak.' She didn't notice he'd come to a halt until she'd collided with him, her breasts brushing his arm. She looked up, her face and her body on fire. He was too close and too tall and too... Harvey.

She stepped back, ignoring the playfulness in his dark eyes, because all she could see was the intense way he'd looked at her *that* night when he'd made her sob out his name.

'Come on, Della,' he cajoled, flashing that dazzlingly confident smile as if already certain of his powers to charm, 'it's been three years since the Melbourne job. Don't you think it's time to forgive me, to bury the proverbial hatchet, preferably somewhere other than in my skull?'

'If only…' Della muttered, fuming. She reached for the trolley, yanking it away from his control. Just because he liked to be in the driving seat didn't mean he could commandeer *her*. She caught another waft of his subtle cologne, the fresh laundry scent of his clothes and the warmth of his body, and fought the uninvited and intimate memories of that one night.

Sleeping with him had served to remind her that, despite being in her mid-thirties, she'd still been an attractive woman. Who better than love 'em and leave 'em bachelor Harvey to show her a life-affirming good time free of any strings? Because when it came to sex, he'd had plenty of practice. She'd heard the stories from Brody.

'Why *are* you here?' she demanded, coming to a defiant halt. 'Not at the airport, manhandling my cases, but here in Fiji?' More importantly, why had she meekly followed him outside when she'd always done her best to steer clear? From that first disastrous meeting, they'd rarely seen eye to eye, instead bickering like a long-suffering married couple. Harvey liked nothing better than to goad both Della and every boyfriend she'd ever brought to a family event, and Della could never seem to help rolling her eyes at his latest sexploits, affronted by his attitude towards commitment on behalf of all women.

'I was invited here by Dr Tora,' he said with a casual shrug, 'head of surgery at Pacific Health. Didn't they tell you?' He took a set of car keys from his pocket and dangled them from one long, elegant and capable finger, his easy smile further fuelling her irritation.

'Tell me what?' Della's blood chilled a few degrees, despite the hot tropical air clinging to her skin. Her voice carried a whiny pleading quality that hurt her eardrums. But whenever Harvey was around, she felt wrong-footed. Unstable. On her guard. But she couldn't show any weakness.

'That like you, I'm here to run a few seminars and have offered my surgical skills pro bono.' He dropped the bombshell and sauntered towards a nearby open-top Jeep with the hospital's name emblazoned on the door.

The hairs on the back of her neck rose. Floundering, *again*, Della hurried after him with her trolley. 'What do you mean? I don't understand.' *Please let it be a mistake.* She couldn't spend her holiday with Harvey. They might actually kill each other.

'We'll be working together for a couple of weeks,' he said in confirmation, as if in no way concerned. Effortlessly, he lifted her cases into the back of the Jeep, parked the empty trolley and walked to the driver's side, pulling his sunglasses from where he'd tucked them into the neck of his shirt.

Della wobbled on her feet, disoriented and overheated as if she was spinning inside a tumble dryer. Working together? They'd never done that before. It would be a disaster. She'd have to see him every day at the hospital with no hope of avoiding his arrogant swagger or his potent sex appeal? How was *that* fair?

'You have got to be kidding me,' she muttered, a string of swear words running through her head as she yanked open the passenger door and reluctantly climbed inside the Jeep.

'I'm afraid not,' Harvey said, starting the ignition and then leaning close to add, 'Love me or hate me, you're kind of stuck with me for a while.'

Oh, how easily they slipped into their respective roles, their game of one-upmanship, even here in beautiful Fiji. But as usual, Della felt one step behind. 'No, you're stuck with *me*,' she snapped childishly, crossing her arms and staring out of the window as Harvey chuckled and pulled out of the parking space, heading for the airport exit.

Della's lovely fortnight of sun and surgery, of giving something back to her Fijian counterparts before returning to her job in New Zealand refreshed and re-invigorated, dissolved before her eyes. Oh, she'd stick it out—she'd never allow Harvey Ward, of all people, to chase her off. If he could put up with her, she would put up with him.

But two weeks working with her professional rival? Two weeks trapped on an island with a man she knew intimately? Two weeks reminded of that incredible night in his bed when she hadn't had so much as a chaste peck on the cheek since...?

It sounded more like a prison sentence than a holiday.

CHAPTER TWO

A SOLID THIRTY MINUTES. That's how long it had taken
Harvey to calm down after the brief but silent car journey
to the hospital with Della. Even now, after a close shave,
a cold shower and a fresh shirt and chinos, he could still
feel the itch of her under his skin. The infuriating woman
needled him like no other and always had. Of course, she
was also mind-blowingly sexy.

'...and this is our emergency department, as you
know,' said Dr Tora, Pacific Health Hospital's clinical
chief of surgery, drawing Harvey away from memories
of that one night three years ago when, after socialising
with her family, Della had shocked him with a goodbye
kiss to the cheek that had turned...explosive. As explosive as the back-and-forth bickering that had always been
their main form of communication.

Forcing his head back into the game, Harvey waved
hello to a few of the ED staff he recognised from his
previous visits. He was proud to continue his support of
this hospital. The last thing he needed was for his long-
standing discord with Della to tarnish the reputation he'd
built over the years.

Just then, Dr Tora's pager sounded. The older man silenced it and read the display. 'Oh dear. I'm afraid I have

to go. Can I entrust Dr Wilton's security pass to you? I'm sure she'll be here soon.'

'Of course.' Harvey took the lanyard as if it were a live snake and slipped it into his pocket. Where was Della? His entire reason for meeting her at the airport was to try and mitigate any awkwardness. Since that night they'd had sex, they'd seen each other maybe six times, always in the presence of the other Wiltons. Instead, she'd fried his brain with that sexy little sundress she'd been wearing. Her blond hair was longer that the last time he'd seen her, the cut somehow softer so it fell in waves around her stunning heart-shaped face. But roaring attraction aside, they'd slipped so effortlessly into their respective roles— hers of barely concealed annoyance and his goading out those flashes of fire from her blue eyes—that clearing the air before they headed to the hospital had completely fled his mind. Images of her naked on top of him and under him, her defiant stare judging him even as she cried out in pleasure, had flashed before his eyes. They'd never once talked about that night, simply pretended that it hadn't happened. But as he'd said to her in the car, like it or not, they were stuck with each other. They'd need to find some way of putting all of that aside to work together. Harvey winced, braced for a very long fortnight.

A rushed patter of feet caused him and Dr Tora to turn around. Out of breath, Della appeared. Still flustered. Still scowling at Harvey. Still sexy as hell. Harvey groaned silently, calling to mind how she always looked at him as if he was something unsavoury she'd found on the bottom of her shoe to manage the constant temptation.

'Sorry I'm late,' she said, addressing Dr Tora and completely ignoring Harvey. 'I got a little lost.' She laced her lovely smile with apology as she stuck out her hand. 'I'm Della Wilton from Auckland's Harbour Hospital. Thank you so much for having me here at Pacific Health.'

Like Harvey, Della had obviously showered and changed since he'd dropped her at the staff bungalows an hour ago. She smelled fantastic, like an ocean breeze, her simple sleeveless dress doing nothing to hide her sensational body, not that Harvey needed a road map. He possessed an excellent memory, and he'd had nearly twenty years to study Della's abundant plus points.

'Bula, Dr Wilton,' Dr Tora said. 'I'm afraid you've just missed the tour of the surgical department, and I must excuse myself. I have an urgent referral patient to see. But I'll leave you in Dr Ward's capable hands. He knows his way around like a local after all these years.'

With a warm smile, Dr Tora departed, leaving Harvey and Della to what would no doubt be another polite and impersonal conversation, as was their norm.

'After all these years?' she asked, eyeing him suspiciously, as if he'd deliberately ruined her holiday with his presence. Her cheeks were flushed from rushing, the pale freckles on her nose a major distraction. He had intimate knowledge that they matched the ones across her shoulders and chest. Thinking about her freckles led to thinking about her naked, her gorgeous curves revealed for his greedy stare and hands. Her shockingly wild passion that, no matter how hard he tried, or how fiercely they argued, he just couldn't forget. They were like oil and water, incompatible but still flammable.

Harvey silently counted to five before opening his mouth in the hopes that he wouldn't say the wrong thing that would lead to another bickering match. The day they'd met, he'd still been grieving the death of his one and only girlfriend, Alice, sleeping around to numb the pain. Then, reeling from his instant and inconvenient attraction to his best friend's sister, he'd made some clumsy, thoughtless and cynical comment that Della and her long-distance boyfriend likely wouldn't survive them studying in different cities, in different states. Della had never forgiven him. Over the years, she took every opportunity to point out that, when it came to relationships, they wanted very different things, and her way was better.

'I come here every year,' he said, leading the way to the emergency department staff room. 'I usually run a few update seminars for our Fijian colleagues, do a few surgeries to help out.' It wasn't like he had a partner or family to holiday with, and he'd always preferred to keep busy.

'Of course you do,' she scoffed, her kissable mouth pursed with irritation. 'Why is it that you're everywhere I look, Harvey—invited to *my* family functions, working *my* job in Melbourne and now hijacking *my* holiday?'

'I could say that you followed me, Della,' he pointed out, his stare drawn to the elegant slope of her neck, a place he remembered the skin was soft and fragrant. 'It's not like I came to Fiji this year with the sole purpose of rattling your cage.'

'I wouldn't put it past you,' she muttered, walking off.

Harvey dragged in a deep breath. How would he survive two weeks in her company when they could barely make it through one conversation before she took umbrage or he goaded her? Should he remind *little miss high and mighty* how she'd used him for rebound sex three years ago, after her divorce?

Following, he caught up with her outside the occupied staff room where several nurses were taking a break. 'So, this is the ED staff room,' he said, biting his tongue for the sake of harmony. 'And this is the doctors' office.' Across the corridor, they found the office empty and stepped inside. 'Computer terminals, printers, photo-copier, etc.' Harvey slipped his hand into his pocket and pulled out her security pass. 'Use this to log in to the computer and printer.'

She took it, her expression wary.

Harvey scanned his own pass over the digital display in pointless demonstration. Della was a consultant trauma surgeon in New Zealand's leading hospital. She was per-fectly capable of figuring out how to use a photocopier. Enough procrastinating. Time to have that tricky per-sonal conversation.

'So, how have you been?' he asked, shoving his hands in his trouser pockets to appear relaxed and non-threatening. Better to get the sex talk out of the way before they started work.

'Oh, you know...' she said, moving around the room, away from him, as she pretended to scrutinise the post-ers on the notice board. 'Still the same old Della—still divorced, still working in Auckland.'

She always did that when she felt threatened—pointed out what she considered to be her worst failings, as if saying them aloud first, before anyone else could, was a defence mechanism. Not that Harvey had been about to raise either of those touchy subjects. He wasn't stupid.

'Look, Della,' he said, pushing the office door closed to give them a bit of privacy. 'I collected you from the airport because I wanted to clear the air.' He stepped into her line of vision so she couldn't ignore him. 'I know we've never talked about that night, but it was just sex.'

Just sex. The kind that had forever altered his perception and awareness of this woman. For sixteen years he'd successfully fought his attraction to her, thinking of her only as the untouchable sister of his best friend, a feat for which he surely deserved some sort of gold medal.

'There's no need to allow it to interfere with us working together for the next two weeks,' he finished, keeping his stare locked with hers. Because to look at her body was to remember that night and the way it had lit some sort of primed fuse and changed everything. Since then, there was no ignoring Della, his only defence to keep reminding himself that she was a relationship person and he was the opposite.

'As if,' she scoffed, a telltale flush creeping up her neck. 'I'm a professional, and it wasn't *that* good.'

'Liar,' he said simply, daring her with his eyes to argue the point so he could bring up how they'd set the bed ablaze, how she'd come twice and left his place looking sexily satisfied, if a little dazed. But then she'd confessed he'd been her first since her marriage had broken down six months earlier. Thinking about how she'd used *good old Harvey* to get over her ex that night, his stomach twisted. He hadn't realised how much it had bothered him until the next day when he'd awoken with the scent of her perfume on his sheets. He'd wanted to call her so badly, he'd locked his phone in the filing cabinet at work.

But Della hadn't finished insulting him.

'Well, there's no need to worry that I'll tempt you to break your *one time and done* rule,' she said, her expression withering.

She'd always made it clear what she thought of Harvey's commitment avoidance, always judged him and stuck up for the women he slept with and looked at him as if he was some kind of dirt bag. Of course, she had no idea that keeping his brief relationships superficial was how Harvey dealt with the losses in his life. Both his mother and Alice had left him in their different ways, and he never wanted there to be a third woman who made him feel powerless. He was better off alone and in control.

Harvey shook his head in disbelief, her jibe predictable but no less offensive. 'I'm not worried, and I don't have a *one time and done* rule.' He almost wished he did. That way he absolutely wouldn't be thinking about sleeping with Della again.

And was it his fault that Della was a relationship person, and with the exception of Alice, he was a bit of a loner? Was it his fault they shared a competitive streak, that they were professionally similar but personally opposites? She'd grown up surrounded by the loving but boisterous Wilton family, whereas Harvey's mother had abandoned him when he was eight years old. Was it his fault that, over the years, Harvey had deliberately stayed single whereas Della had fallen in and out of love with several unworthy men who'd one by one broken her too-big heart?

'And yet you're forty-two and have never been in a relationship that lasts longer than a bottle of milk,' she said, that curl of contempt tugging at her gorgeous mouth.

'Why do you always do that?' he asked, once more questioning the wisdom of coming to Fiji as planned once he'd discovered from Brody that Della would also be there.

'Do what?' She put one hand on her hip as if deliberately taunting him with her spectacular figure.

'Insinuate that my sex life bothers you?' He took a half step closer, his pulse accelerating as her pupils dilated, as if their bickering was a kind of verbal foreplay. 'Being sceptical about love isn't a crime, Della. And it didn't seem to matter when you needed a quick roll in the hay to celebrate the granting of your divorce order.'

She might despise his lifestyle, see him as some sort of threat because their views on commitment were so dissimilar, but she couldn't deny their rampant chemistry.

'It *doesn't* bother me,' she said, her breaths coming a little faster and her cheeks reddening. 'And don't act as if you hoped us sleeping together three years ago would be the start of something more. That's not your style.'

She was right. Just because they were trapped there together, he'd be a fool to act on this, a fool to do anything but ignore it as usual.

'So? You knew what you were getting into that night and wanted me anyway,' he pointed out. 'Perhaps because you needed a safe bet, and good old Harvey was available.' It was a low blow, but he couldn't stop himself from taunting her, not when she was acting so...holy. Not when she'd used him and never mentioned it again. Had she even given that night a second thought over the past three years?

Her mouth hung open and she blinked up at him, maybe searching for something cutting to say. But Harvey had already exposed too much. He didn't want her to know he'd been aware that he'd served a purpose that night. That her using him had stung. Maybe he could exact a little revenge now.

Stepping closer, he lowered his voice. 'Perhaps you like the idea of spending another night in my bed, Della. If that's the case, you only have to ask. For you, my bedroom door is always open.'

'Of course it is,' she muttered, triumph glittering in her wide stare. 'Same old Harvey. You never change.'

'Neither do your judgements,' he said, tempted to exaggerate stories of his past philandering for maximum effect. 'But as you've raised the subject of relationships, you obviously want me to ask. So, are *you* seeing anyone? Is husband-to-be number two waiting for you back in Auckland?'

Harvey clamped his runaway mouth shut. He didn't want to upset her any more than he already had just by being there. But a twist of envy gripped his gut. He shouldn't care if she was dating again. It was none of his business. All he needed to do was get through these two weeks in one piece.

Della raised her chin, her eyes dipping, but not before Harvey spied a flash of doubt. So that was *no* then. Hell… it would be so much easier for him if she was dating and therefore untouchable again.

'I've been busy…' she confirmed, glancing away. 'Moving countries, starting a new job, travelling home to Melbourne to visit my family every chance I get.'

Another dig about the Melbourne job… But now, fingers of unease slithered up Harvey's spine. Was she talking about the past three and a half years?

'So no dating at all since your divorce?' he pushed, the pitch of his voice changing to incredulous. Did that mean she hadn't slept with anyone else since she'd slept with *him*? Surely not. But now he was aflame with curiosity.

'My love life doesn't concern you,' she said primly, her stare bold.

Harvey saw red. 'Not even when you used me for sex, knowing that you were safe to walk away and never mention it again, despite the fact that we see each other all the time?' Now why had he said that? Why couldn't he have handed over her security pass, ignored how badly he wanted to kiss her and kept his mouth shut? Why was it these days, since that one hot night, he and Della always seemed to have some sort of unfinished business?

Her mouth agape, she blinked up at him, breathing hard.

His own heart rate thundering, his gaze dipped to the lovely curve of her lips. He knew how those lips tasted, recalled how they parted on breathy sighs. Had felt them against his skin as she'd cried out in passion. The metallic taste of fear coated his mouth. Forget the awkwardness; it wasn't their biggest problem. He wasn't going to survive these two weeks, fourteen long days, in Della's company without cracking and doing something stupid. Perhaps he should just kiss her now, suggest they sleep together again and get the sex out of their systems so they could go back to bickering over nothing.

Just then, as they faced each other, head-to-head, stares locked in defiance, there was a knock at the door. They stepped away from each other as Seema, one of the ED nurses, entered the room.

'Harvey, we've just had a walk-in casualty, and it looks bad—can you come?'

'Of course,' Harvey said, rushing to the trauma bay in the ED with Della at his heels. All the adrenaline he'd prepared for sparring with Della fuelled him now as he joined the man being wheeled on a stretcher into the resuscitation bay.

'His work colleagues literally carried him in,' Seema said about the patient, who was conscious and groaning in pain, his breathing harsh behind an oxygen mask. 'He fell from second-floor scaffolding, a drop of over twenty feet. His name is Warren.'

Harvey glanced at Della as he reached for a stethoscope. Their reckoning would have to wait. As if they were used to working together, she took up position opposite Harvey, on the other side of the patient, reaching for a second stethoscope, as the nurses cut away the man's clothing to expose his chest. Harvey noted his vital signs. His blood pressure was on the low side, his heart rate rapid but regular.

'He has an open fracture of the left humerus,' Della said, her eyes meeting Harvey's in silent communication.

Their casualty would be heading to theatre, but first they needed to eliminate anything more life-threatening than a broken arm.

'Any loss of consciousness or seizures?' Harvey asked Seema, testing the man's pupillary reflexes with a pen torch. They needed to exclude a head injury. Fortunately someone had fitted a neck brace to immobilise the man's cervical spine.

'No,' Seema said. 'One of the work colleagues who brought him in was on the ground and got to him pretty quickly.'

'I just need to examine you, Warren.' Harvey palpated the trachea above the breast bone before placing his stethoscope over the lung fields to listen to the breath sounds.

'He's got a pneumothorax on the left and tracheal deviation,' he told Della, knowing she would understand the urgency of the man's condition. In cases of tension pneumothorax, if they didn't drain out the escaped air from his chest and reinflate the collapsed lung, he could go into shock.

Della nodded, reaching for a sterile wide-bore cannula from the trolley at the head of the casualty. They needed to relieve the pressure on the heart by allowing the trapped air to escape before they could organise X-rays or they risked cardiac arrest.

'I think he might have a flail chest on this side,' Della said, adding to the list of problems. 'There's a lot of bruising of the chest wall and some surgical emphysema.' She peeled open the cannula as the blood pressure monitor emitted an ear-piercing alarm.

'His blood pressure is dropping. Let's decompress and then review,' he said to Della, who quickly swabbed the skin and inserted the needle into the man's chest cavity to allow the trapped air from the punctured lung to escape.

Harvey drew up some intravenous analgesia and, as the blood pressure rose, administered it via a cannula in the patient's arm. 'Warren. We think you might have some fractured ribs that have punctured the lung. We're going to organise some X-rays to be sure.'

'Let's get a chest drain kit ready, please,' Della said to Seema. 'And we need an urgent cross-match for blood transfusion.' She quickly labelled some blood vials and handed them to a porter, who would run them around to the haematology lab.

With the patient stabilised for now, Harvey and Della

moved aside to talk, their personal grievances and the constant pull of attraction set aside.

'That humerus will need to be internally fixed,' Della said with a frown of concern, shifting to make room for the radiographer, who wheeled in the mobile X-ray machine.

'We might need to surgically stabilise the fractured ribs, too,' Harvey said, his mind racing through the worst-case scenarios for the patient. Often, a flail segment, an area of ribs fractured in more than one place, was treated with mechanical ventilation and analgesia, but in some instances, surgery was required, especially if there were other complications like chest wall damage, haemorrhage or rib dislocations.

Della nodded in agreement. 'I'll call the anaesthetist and theatre. Either way, he'll need to be admitted to ICU.'

'And I'll speak to Warren's next of kin and consent him for surgery,' Harvey said, impressed with the way they'd forgotten their personal differences and their competitive natures and worked together for the first time.

'I didn't expect to operate on our first day.' She looked up at him, a flicker of surprise and respect shining in her eyes. 'Do you want the humerus or the chest?'

'Let's figure it out together when we get to theatre,' he said, confident that Della and he could set aside everything else when it came to their work.

'Sounds like a plan,' she said, her expression registering relief.

Before they found themselves trapped together in Fiji, he'd have been convinced they would squabble over the decision or over who was the better surgeon. But when it came to the safety of their patient, there was no room for ego, despite how he'd teased her earlier at the airport.

As they set about their different tasks, putting their patient first, Harvey wondered how long their enforced truce would last. Their sexual chemistry was obviously going nowhere. They would need to revisit the conversation on how best to manage it, providing they could tolerate each other long enough to talk.

As predicted, it was going to be the longest fortnight of Harvey's life.

CHAPTER THREE

LATER THAT NIGHT, after a full afternoon of surgery, Della took her frosty glass of beer from the barman and headed outside. Savu's, a beach bar a short walk from the hospital, had a handful of tables set on the sand. What better way to unwind than watching the stunning Fijian sun set. After her eventful and unexpected first day, she desperately needed time to put everything into perspective. Like how she'd almost kissed Harvey Ward earlier in the emergency department doctors' office…

What the hell had she been thinking? She'd had her 'roll in the hay', as he'd put it. The shameful memory of his hurt expression returned. He'd accused her of using him for sex that night, which she probably had on some level. But surely Harvey wouldn't have cared, would he? The man was a walking one-night stand. But maybe tomorrow, she should apologise.

Della stepped outside and instantly spied Harvey sitting alone at one of the tables near the water's edge. Her stomach swooped at the sight of him—long legs stretched out as he relaxed, his fingers casually gripping a beer bottle, his gaze trained on the ocean view. Della froze, her first instinct to forget her apology and avoid him, as usual. She could duck back inside the bar, down her beer and scurry home to her accommodation without having to analyse just how badly she still wanted the annoyingly arrogant man, despite the fact she had to work with him for the next two weeks and he still knew how to push all of her buttons.

For you, my bedroom door is always open... Right—for her and every other single woman on the planet.

As if he'd heard her scoff, he turned, and their eyes met. Della's body flushed from head to toe with that familiar jolt of attraction. Dammit, she couldn't run away now that he'd seen her, but nor did she particularly want to talk to him. If they somehow managed a conversation without bickering or hurling insults, she might feel compelled to admit that she'd found new respect for him as a doctor.

They'd spent hours in theatre with their fall casualty, internally fixing the man's fractured humerus and multiple rib fractures. To her confusion, she'd learned that Harvey was far from arrogant in the OR. When it came to surgery, he was meticulously thorough. He'd even shown humility, asking for her preferred surgical technique when it came to wiring versus plating of rib fractures.

Harvey casually raised his hand, beckoning her to join him, an easy, perfectly amicable smile tugging at that delicious mouth of his. How could he be so unaffected by her when she was all over the place? Hot with resentment that, when it came to getting over that night they'd slept together, Harvey had easily cruised into first place, leaving Della second best, she begrudgingly crossed the sand in his direction. Maybe she was simply stressed out by the idea of having him around 24-7. They'd spent more one-on-one time together today than they'd spent in the preceding nineteen years of their strained relationship. Normally, they tolerated each other for an evening maximum, and the social contact was always diluted by the presence of the other Wiltons.

As she arrived at his table, Harvey stood, pulling out the second chair. 'Great minds think alike.'

His smile, the way he swept his gaze over her, tripled her pulse rate. Why was he always so comfortable in his skin? Why did everything he did and said annoy her, so she came out fighting? Why did he have to go and show her what an all-round good guy he was, regularly donating his time and expertise here in Fiji? It was seriously messing with those preconceived assumptions she'd always clung to in order to keep Harvey in a nice, neat box.

'Yes, that was quite the first day.' Della sat and took a hasty sip of her drink, struggling anew with the surge of undeniable attraction. 'I needed to unwind.' Fat chance of that now...

'No place better than Savu's.' He smiled and raised his bottle in a toast. 'To beautiful Fijian nights.'

See, there he went again, being...nice. Della reluctantly clinked her glass to his bottle, her stomach fluttering as his stare held hers while he took a long, lazy swallow. He was so sexy, it wasn't fair. Perhaps she should sleep with him again and get it out of her system. Three years without sex really was too long—maybe when she returned to New Zealand, she should seriously consider dating again.

Jealous that she couldn't feel as unaffected by him as he appeared by her, Della scrabbled around for something to say that wasn't *I'd like to take you up on your offer and push open that bedroom door.*

'I checked on our fall patient before I left the hospital,' she said instead. 'He's stable and comfortable on ICU.'

'I checked too.' Harvey's eyes narrowed a fraction, that smug hint of amusement touching his lips, telling Della he could easily read her mind and sense her discomfort. 'But do you really want to talk shop when we could be enjoying the sunset?'

He inclined his head towards the pink-orange streaks in the sky, which deeply contrasted with the blackening sea and the patch of white sand illuminated by the lights strung overhead from the rear of the bar. Della pressed her lips together defiantly. If they couldn't talk about work, what the hell were they going to discuss? Maybe simply getting physical again was the *only* answer.

'How's Brody?' she asked, chugging another gulp of her drink, irritated by how effortlessly he could turn her on. Yes, talking about her family would smother the flames of their chemistry. Especially when it reminded her that, if not for Harvey, she would be working in Melbourne, where she belonged.

'Don't you know?' he asked, that mocking little half smile keeping her on her guard. 'He's *your* brother.'

'But you see more of him than I do,' she whined, dragging her stare away from the open neck of his shirt to where she knew his chest and torso was an anatomist's dream of sun-bronzed skin and delineated muscle. She offered him a tight smile. 'Since you stole my Melbourne job.'

She really needed to let this feud go; it was childish. And if he hadn't hijacked the lovely working holiday she'd planned, if he hadn't goaded her into talk of their sex lives, if she hadn't almost kissed him again, maybe she could have.

'Brody is good,' Harvey said with a small sigh. 'He and Amy are busy with work, but looking forward to baby Jack's naming day celebration.'

Della nodded, her heart full of longing to see her baby nephew again. She didn't need to ask if Harvey was invited to the Wilton family gathering in a month's time. He was invited to most events. Like she'd pointed out earlier, there was no escaping him.

'Look, Della, about the job...' he continued, turning serious. 'I wanted to explain. I don't know if Brody mentioned it, but my dad hasn't been well these past couple of years. I applied for that position because I really needed to stay in Melbourne. I'm all the family he has.'

Stunned by his vulnerable admission, Della shook her head in confusion. 'I didn't know. Brody never mentioned it. What's wrong with Bill?' She knew Harvey's parents were divorced and that he was close to his father. But Harvey had never opened up to her before, nor vice versa, as if they'd made an unspoken pact to keep each other at arm's length. Brody was adamant his friend had *hidden depths*, but until this very moment, she'd always doubted their existence.

'He's fine.' Harvey shrugged, clearly worried about Bill Ward but downplaying it. 'He's been diagnosed with multiple sclerosis,' he continued, his voice emotionless but his fingers picking at the corner of the beer label.

Shocked, her face heating because of how petulantly she'd acted when she hadn't known the full story, Della's throat tightened. Poor Bill. Harvey's dad was often included in family get-togethers at Christmas or on Australia Day. Della liked him a lot.

'I'm so sorry to hear that, Harvey.' Before she'd even realised she'd moved, Della found her hand resting on Harvey's warm, muscular forearm. Her comforting gesture spread tingles up her own arm. She pulled her hand away. Touching him was a no-no if she hoped to keep their sexual chemistry under control. And if Harvey could successfully ignore it, so could she.

'You must be worried about him,' she pushed, instinct telling her that control freak Harvey was probably in denial. Not that she could blame him. No one wanted to think of their parents ageing or becoming sick.

Harvey shrugged, pulling a deep drag of beer from the bottle. 'Dad's a proud man. He doesn't want pity, and he hates me fussing. But you can understand why I wanted to stay close at hand, in case he…needs me.'

'Of course…' she said, yet another of Della's rock-solid assumptions where this man was concerned disintegrating. 'Is he badly affected?'

He looked away, focused on the setting sun, as if he no longer wanted to talk about it. 'He's still managing his activities of daily living, but he struggles with the stairs. I've moved his bed to the ground floor, but ideally, I'd like him to sell up and move into an adapted bungalow.'

Della stayed silent, understanding both sides of the argument. Bill would fiercely cling to his independence, and as an only child, Harvey just wanted peace of mind that his father was safe.

'Anyway…' he said, dragging out the word to herald a change of subject. 'Back to my earlier question, before we were interrupted by our emergency. No dates in three and half years? How's that working out for you?'

Della sighed. Jerk Harvey was back. Only she could no longer hate him for beating her to her dream job, and she still needed to apologise for using him for sex. At this rate, with her justifications dissolving before her eyes, she risked becoming his...*friend*. No, the attraction would always get in the way of that. But now that she had to let go of her bitterness over losing the position to Harvey, she realised how she'd used it as a shield from thinking about that incredible night when she'd learned the stories about Harvey were true. He *was* good at everything.

'No need to sound so astounded,' she said haughtily. 'It's not fatal. I'm not ready for another relationship yet.' The last thing she wanted to discuss with Harvey was the breakdown of her marriage, the mistake she'd made in trusting Ethan, the humiliation of her divorce, when all she wanted was to be like her brother: happily married and starting a family.

'Who said anything about relationships?' Harvey asked, his stare holding hers the way it had in the ED doctors' office before they attended to the emergency, as if he could see straight through her to all her failings and weaknesses. 'I'm talking about sex.'

He took another swallow of beer and licked his lips the way Della wanted to. She swallowed, her throat bone-dry with lust. Harvey was the last man on Earth she wanted to discuss her sad lack of a sex life with.

His stare narrowed, his scrutiny making her flustered. 'So, are you saying that *your* last time was *our* last time?' he asked, incredulous.

'What if it was?' Della snapped, all the empathy she'd

felt for him a moment ago evaporating. 'You can't make a competition out of my personal life, Harvey.'

Because he'd win that argument, too. With that single exception, when she'd succumbed to Harvey Ward's charms, she'd lived like a nun since her divorce. It wasn't healthy, but Della had always needed an emotional connection to even think about being intimate with someone. That didn't make her a prude, just a woman.

'But you can make a joke out of *my* personal life?' he asked, his expression as calm as the sea before them. 'I like sex. Don't you?'

She felt his observation all over her body. Of course she liked sex. Why was that question so arousing and tempting, as if it was an offer?

'Don't goad me,' she snapped, 'just because we're different. I'm not like you.'

She looked away, hot and bothered. Why did she always allow him to get to her like this? Why couldn't she simply ignore him the way she'd tried to over the years? Because when it came to Brody's best friend, it had always been easier to dismiss and avoid him than to admit his relationship self-sufficiency, his easy-breezy attitude to dating, his cynicism about love only highlighted their differences and made Della feel somehow inadequate, reigniting those fears that she was being left behind in her family. She'd always wanted a loving, committed relationship and a family of her own, whereas Harvey didn't even believe in love.

But there was no chance of ignoring him now that they had to spend the best part of the next two weeks working together. No wonder she was feeling volatile.

'In what way are we different?' he asked, appearing

genuinely curious. 'I think we have a surprising amount in common, considering we're always arguing.'

Della dragged in a deep breath. She wanted to point out that *he* was responsible for their bickering, but she held back. They were finally going to have a meaningful conversation, after all the years of avoiding it with polite smiles and impersonal comments and, on Della's part, cowardice and self-preservation.

'Oh, come on, Harvey,' she said warily, 'we're total opposites, especially when it comes to relationships. And don't pretend that we could ever get along. You've never even liked me.'

Harvey took another lazy swallow of beer, his eyes on hers. 'I like you just fine, Della.'

The husky drawl of his voice turned her limbs molten with desire. Was that true? Did he like her? Admitting that he might be telling the truth, that Harvey did have another, deeper side, sat like a rock in her stomach, reminding her how she *had* used him for sex that night and he'd probably not only known it but also felt hurt.

'If you like me so much,' she said, on the attack, jittery with nerves from his admission, 'why take the moral high ground when it comes to our differences? To relationships? It's as if you see the kind of commitment most people want, the kind *I* want, as some sort of threat. As if you're too smart to fall in love like the rest of us, or you think love is a joke.'

'I don't think that at all,' he said, looking mildly uncomfortable for the first time. 'We've just always wanted different things. But you've done your fair share of judging, Della, right from the moment we met.'

'Well, you insulted me,' she said, aware she was overreacting and dragging up ancient history. 'We'd just been introduced, and you felt comfortable enough to point out my relationship at the time was doomed. In fact, you've objected to every one of my past boyfriends for some reason or another,' she continued. 'You didn't even like Ethan, as if *you,* the great relationship expert, Harvey Ward, were somehow privy to inside knowledge that our marriage wouldn't last.' She hated that he'd been right, *again.* That unlike Della, he'd shown good judgement when it came to her ex. No wonder she wasn't ready to trust her intuition and risk another relationship just yet. Perhaps she should take a leaf out of Harvey's book and enjoy a casual sexual fling.

'And you've always objected to *me,*' he said, eyes glittering. 'As if I wasn't a good enough friend for Brody or good enough to be associated with your family, just because I prefer to be single.'

Della sat back in outrage. 'See, this always happens. We're fooling ourselves if we expect to make it through two weeks of working together. We're too different, too competitive to ever get along.' She glugged a mouthful of beer, looking away from him in disgust. The Wiltons were an ambitious bunch, and Harvey fit right in. Della had struggled growing up in golden boy Brody's exalted footsteps, and then, just when she'd started to make her own mark by getting into medical school, he'd brought home driven, talented Harvey.

'We can do it if we have to,' he said calmly, where Della was braced for another battle. 'We didn't argue that night in bed. Or have you forgotten?'

Despite her temper, Della's body incinerated. She scowled at him. 'How could I forget when over the years

I've heard so many wild stories of your sex life from Brody?' She leaned forward, needing to win this argument. 'The threesomes. The heartbroken women past their expiration dates. Your rotating bedroom door and your untouchable heart.'

Harvey's lip curled, his stare narrowing as he watched her with curiosity. 'It was *one* threesome, and that was years ago.' His dark gaze rested on her lips. 'But you sound jealous, Della. We can rectify that.' He spread his arms wide and relaxed back in the chair in a *come and get me* gesture.

Every cell in her body perked up, his offer beyond tempting. How would she fight this physical compulsion for two whole weeks? Not even them bickering seemed to douse the flames. 'Oh please...' Della scoffed, her body temperature high with irritation and fierce desire. 'I am *so* done with men.'

Of course, he was right; they were good together. Great, in fact. A big part of her wanted another go at Harvey if for no other reason than to wipe that smug look off his face.

'Hey,' Harvey said, holding up a hand to ward off her unfair comparison, 'don't go bringing your ex into this again.' He took another swig of beer, cool, calm and collected.

Della dragged in a ragged breath. She was being overemotional. She didn't care one jot if Harvey slept with every other woman on the planet *but* her. Time to change the subject.

'Why didn't you like Ethan,' she asked, a lump in her throat, 'just out of interest?' She shouldn't care; her marriage and divorce were *her* business. But the part of her that had always compared herself to golden boy Brody and then later to carefree Harvey was scared to completely trust her own judgement. Had she missed some sign that others had seen? Ethan had wooed her with a whirlwind romance, proposed after a couple of years and then slowly changed once they were married. And Della hadn't seen the divorce coming.

'Let's not go there.' Harvey instantly sobered, glancing away. 'It's in the past, and it's nothing to do with me.' He clenched his jaw as if he had no intention of answering her question.

'Come on, I want to know,' Della pushed, her curiosity so wild, her heart rate went through the roof. It must be bad if he was refusing to say. Hot shame washed through her. It was bad enough that she'd failed at something Brody had nailed—a successful marriage and a family. Even worse that Harvey, of all people, had witnessed Della's defeat and now seemed to have some kind of insider knowledge.

'Leave it, Della.' Harvey frowned as he made eye contact, warning in his stare. 'You won't like what I have to say. We'll end up arguing again.'

'Tell me anyway,' she demanded, embarrassment a head-to-toe itchy rash. 'I insist.' Had there been some glaringly obvious flaw in her and Ethan's relationship? Had outsiders deduced what Della herself hadn't seen coming? Had Harvey correctly predicted that her marriage had been doomed?

With a sigh, Harvey reluctantly surrendered. 'I've known you since you were eighteen, Della. You wear your big heart on your sleeve. Fall in love and dive in, as if... I don't know. As if you somehow have something to prove. As if you're in competition with every other couple out there.'

Della gasped, mortified. 'I've also grown up since you first met me, Harvey.' Although she couldn't help but compare herself to her brother. She shrank inside, feeling sick. How dare untouchable Harvey, her nemesis, know her so well. How dare he see her need to be loved and to be accepted as she was so effortlessly when he didn't know the first thing about the emotion. Could he also see her deepest fear, that by pushing for a family, she'd pushed Ethan away?

'Trust me,' she continued with a scoff, bluffing for all she was worth, 'I have no interest in exposing my heart or diving into another relationship until I'm certain the lucky guy wants exactly what *I* want.'

She'd learned her mistake with Ethan. At the end, he'd accused her of being *baby obsessed*, even though when they'd met, he'd said he too wanted a family. But next time she was ready for a relationship, it would be with someone who, like her, wanted it all: commitment, marriage, a family. Yet how could she ever be certain they were being truthful when Ethan had managed to dupe her?

'Good…' Harvey shrugged, his expression full of regret as if he hated what he was about to say. 'Because sometimes…little things he said… I just got the impression that Ethan was… I don't know…holding something back.'

Della froze, wishing she hadn't asked but some sick twisted part of her willing him to continue.

'When you got engaged,' he said, his stare searching

hers, 'I genuinely hoped for your sake that I was wrong. That it would work out. That you'd be happy.'

Her eyes stung. She absolutely must not cry in front of Harvey. *Never ever.* Because he was right. When they'd met and fallen in love, Ethan had claimed he'd wanted the same things. But once they'd married, once they'd fallen into a routine of work and sharing a home, he'd started putting off their conversations about starting a family, made her feel as if the dream was suddenly one-sided. He'd used her desire to have it all to make her feel that *his* job was more important. Shamefully, she'd followed him to Sydney so he could pursue *his* career, reasoning that someone had to compromise. But even after his big promotion, he'd continued to put off talk of kids. Della had given the marriage her all, and delayed becoming a mother while Ethan established himself in an orthopaedic consultant role, but it hadn't been enough. He'd come home one day and said he wasn't ready to be a father and left. And Della had been blindsided. But *Harvey*, a man who knew nothing about relationships, had somehow predicted it.

Returning to the present, Della blinked, shivered, chilled to the bone. Harvey's concerned face came back into focus, something like pity in his stare. Her stomach turned with sickening humiliation.

'Well, bravo, Harvey—you were right, again,' she said, shame and failure a fire in her blood. 'You, who don't even believe in love, saw my marriage the way it truly was. But then, you'd know all about holding back, wouldn't you? You've never had a relationship. Do you even possess a heart, Harvey? Or are all those messy human emotions for the rest of us poor misguided fools?'

How could she have been so stupid as to consider sleeping with him again? They were polar opposites, too competitive and threatened by each other to ever see eye to eye. They couldn't even have one simple conversation.

'I don't think that,' he said, reaching for her arm.

But the damage was done. Della snatched it out of his reach. Rising to her feet, she shoved the seat back so hard, it toppled to the sand. 'I'll see you tomorrow,' she said, for once her voice staying impressively calm. 'Can I suggest that, for the sake of harmony, to make the next two weeks even remotely bearable, that we restrict our conversations to work, after all.' Without waiting for an answer, she stomped off.

CHAPTER FOUR

DELLA ENTERED HER staff bungalow on the hospital
grounds and slammed the door. The reverberations jolted
through Harvey from his position across the street. He'd
followed her, of course. He'd never have been able to
sleep if he hadn't made certain she'd arrived home safely.

He dragged in a shuddering breath, guilt making him
cringe. He should never have allowed himself to be lured
into a personal conversation. They couldn't be trusted not
to bicker, insult and upset each other. Then she'd forced
him to talk about her ex, demanding he be honest, before throwing his reluctant observations back in his face.

Why could they never have a nice, normal chat? Maybe
because the attraction was always there, bubbling away
beneath the surface. Harvey *hadn't* liked any of her boyfriends. She was right. None of them were good enough
for her, not even Ethan. She was funny and smart and
would do anything for anyone, and after today, Harvey
had gained a massive amount of respect for her as a surgeon.

Harvey crossed the road, regret a weight on his shoulders. What the hell did he know about committed relationships anyway? He'd been alone by choice for twenty
years, after Alice had died in a car accident. He'd as-

sumed he'd get over her death in time and want another relationship, but as the years had passed, he'd become increasingly convinced that he should have known better than to pin his happiness on another person. After all, if his own mother hadn't loved him enough to stick around, what hope did he have of finding someone with whom he could share his life?

Harvey tapped on the door to Della's bungalow, his gut twisting. The last thing he wanted to do was hurt Della. Why would she care what *he* had to say? But maybe she saw her divorce as some sort of failing, even though it was her ex who chose to leave the marriage.

The door flew open, as if she'd been standing and fuming on the other side.

'You left your sunnies at the bar,' he said, wearing an apologetic expression as he held out the sunglasses.

'Thanks.' She took them, dropping them onto the table just inside the door. When she looked at him again, her stare brimmed with hurt that he'd inadvertently put there because, ever since that night three years ago, he couldn't seem to manage this attraction.

'I'm sorry, Della,' he said, contrite. 'I didn't mean to hurt you. My comments were…thoughtless. I don't think you're a fool for falling in love. The opposite, in fact.' He stared into her blue eyes, forcing himself to open up in order to repair the damage. 'It's not that I don't believe in love. It's more that making yourself vulnerable with another person is a brave gamble. But then, I'm hardly an expert. As you pointed out, what do *I* know about relationships?'

She eyed him hesitantly, still wearing a frown.

'You shouldn't listen to me,' he went on. 'I just

wouldn't want you to be hurt again, that's all. If I'm honest, I didn't like your boyfriends because none of them were good enough for you.'

He shut his mouth, suddenly exhausted. He'd already given away how protective he felt of her, when he had no right. Her love life was none of his business, and *he* wasn't the man of anyone's dreams. At least she was brave enough to put herself out there, whereas he simply avoided the risk of letting someone close, of giving them the power to cause pain. When it came to matters of the heart, *she* was the experienced one.

Della sighed, her body relaxing. 'I *did* push for your honest opinion,' she said, shaking her head with regret. 'And I threw my fair share of insults your way. Maybe I just hate that you're always right. That, like Brody, you're better than me at *everything*.' Her lips twitched with amusement, telling him he was forgiven.

Harvey's pulse pounded with relief, but his stare raked hers. Did she compare herself unfavourably to Brody? Harvey was an only child, so he had no reference when it came to sibling rivalry.

'Not everything,' he said, a cautious smile forming. 'Definitely not relationships.' Harvey's parents had split when he was kid, so as far as he was concerned, relationship breakdowns were inevitable. Maybe it was time to tell Della about Alice, about his mother, about why the cynical twenty-three-year-old she'd met had been so down on commitment and still was, if pushed.

'Only because you've never had one,' she said, rolling her eyes. 'If you had, I'm sure that, like Brody, you'd have made it work. You'd probably be living *my* life by now—successful career, happily married, a houseful of adorable children.'

Harvey hid a wince, wishing he could say something to help reassure Della that she still had time to achieve her dreams, but he'd already overstepped the mark once tonight. He hated that she wanted what Brody had, but had been let down by her ex. Maybe once, a long time ago, Harvey might have harboured that same dream, back when he'd thought he was in control of his life and his heart. But growing up abandoned by his mother, the only woman who should have loved him unconditionally, had taught him that feelings, entrusting your happiness to another person, was a big risk. And he'd re-learned that same lesson the hard way when Alice had died.

'Well, if it's any consolation,' he said, steering the conversation back to the relative safety of work, 'having seen you in action in the OR today, I'd say you can hold your own as a surgeon with both me and Brody.' Respect for her bloomed anew. She was a good doctor and a talented surgeon, damn sexy qualities. But then, everything about Della was sexy and always had been. Probably why he goaded her. Nothing worse than forbidden fruit to increase ardour. And apart from that one lapse, when he'd kissed her back, one thing leading to another, Harvey was smart enough to stay well away. They wanted different things in life. Della wanted that marriage, husband, a houseful of kids dream, and Harvey liked being in control of his life and his emotions. So why was he struggling to walk away now?

'Careful, Harvey.' She smiled, eyed in him in that way that heated his blood, but also told him she could laugh at herself and at him. 'That sounds suspiciously like another compliment.'

He dragged in a shaky breath. 'Good. It is. Will you be okay?' He hesitated on the doorstep, needing to know that their stupid fight hadn't caused lasting damage to Della's self-esteem. He should leave. Let her get some sleep before their seminars in the morning. But he cared about her and genuinely wanted to see her happy.

'Of course.' She blinked, watched him with curiosity as if seeing him for the first time. 'I'm a strong, independent and resilient woman. It will take more than one little divorce to keep me down.'

'I know you are,' he said, seeing through her bravado. Those old protective urges resurfaced. The Harvey that had first met this woman had known all about the pain of heartbreak. It had been hard to stand on the sidelines and watch big-hearted Della go through break-up after break-up and finally her divorce. Not that looking out for her, back then or now, was his place.

'Okay… I'll…um…let you get some rest.' He took a half step back, his feet dragging. Being trapped with her in Fiji had forced him to admit how badly he still wanted her, how the grip he thought he had on his attraction was weakened because he couldn't avoid temptation and walk away the way he had three years ago, the way he did every time he'd seen her since. Nor could he shake the knowledge that she hadn't had sex with another man since him, that she still wasn't ready for a relationship. And if he needed one more sign that this trip had been sent to test him and his belief that Della was out of his system, she was looking at him in *that* way again.

'Thanks…' she said, touching his arm. 'For the sunglasses *and* the compliment. It means a lot coming from you.'

Her touch burned his skin, her words an acknowledgement that they might be different, but when it came to work, they respected each other.

'You're welcome.' His voice was scratchy. His feet didn't seem to want to move.

'You know,' she said, blinking up at him, 'I'm sorry, too.' Her breathing came faster. 'I *did* use you for sex that night. You were right about that, as well.' She blushed and Harvey shrugged it off, his pulse roaring because she was still touching his arm.

'That's okay. Truth is, I was happy to be used.' What kind of idiot would turn down sex with someone as gorgeous as Della, even if he had been her rebound? He'd never forgotten that night, probably because Della Wilton, like the rest of her loving, boisterous family, was a massive part of his life. But they really shouldn't discuss sex any more tonight or he'd never make it off this doorstep.

'I wanted to feel attractive again after, you know, being rejected,' she said, looking down and then meeting his stare. 'But it's not okay that I hurt you in the process.'

Harvey understood rejection, but were they declaring a truce? 'You're beautiful, Della. And I'm a grown man. I wanted you too much to care about your motivations.' Adrenaline rushed through his system. It felt good to admit that after all these years of pretending he didn't find her incredibly attractive. But this was dangerous territory.

Her eyes widened. Time slowed as they stared. What was it about this place that completely altered the nature of their relationship? It was as if for the first time ever they were being honest. Finally, Harvey tilted his head in resignation and stepped back. If he didn't leave now, he was going to do something stupid. And this time, there'd be no walking away, no pretending it hadn't happened, at least not until they left Fiji.

'Wait,' she said, reaching for the hem of his shirt and tugging. 'Don't go.'

He crossed the threshold. She closed the door, pulled him closer.

'Della...is this a good idea?' His hands found her waist, neither drawing her close nor holding her distant. Their bodies were inches apart. The heat of her, the subtle scent of her perfume, called to that part of him he'd always needed to lock down in her presence.

'It's just sex, Harvey,' she argued with a shrug, tossing back his earlier words. 'Best to get it out of the way so we can move on and work together, don't you think?'

Think...? All of his blood had left his brain. Thinking was impossible. But his instincts were still firing. 'I want you, but I don't want to hurt you again or give you the wrong idea about us. You know me.' They were too different for more than sex. Under all her bluff and bluster, Della was a funny, caring and wildly passionate woman any guy looking to settle down would be lucky to have. But Harvey wasn't that guy, and they both knew it.

'Come on, Harvey.' She blinked up at him, her stare dark with desire and unspoken challenge. 'I'm an intelligent woman. I'd never be stupid enough to expect anything but sex from a man like *you*.'

Reassurance dressed as an insult, but she was right. She knew him the way he knew her. He wasn't relationship material, and Della wanted it all. Of course, she didn't know everything about his past—some ugliness was too uncomfortable to share—but she knew enough to have realistic expectations.

'Are you worried that I'm using you for sex again?' she asked, a playful glint in her blue eyes. 'Because if it helps, I totally am.'

Harvey fought his instincts. He should have felt relieved that they were on the same page. That just like last time, Della wasn't looking for anything serious. But somewhere deep down, her words—*a man like you... using you for sex again*—also stung. Despite what she believed, Harvey *did* possess a heart. He'd just trained it to have very low expectations.

'I'm not worried,' he lied, clinging to reason as she inched closer, her breasts grazing his chest. He gripped her face, tilted that lovely mouth up to within a whisper of his. 'I just want you to be sure. Eyes wide open like last time.'

'I want you.' Della held his stare as she surged up on tiptoe and sought his mouth with hers. She gripped his neck and pulled him down, closing the distance. Della knew what she wanted, and she was right—this was the best way to break the tension so they could get through two weeks of forced proximity.

Too late to overthink it, Harvey crushed her close. The first touch of their kiss flooded his strung-out body with energising endorphins. Their lips parted. Tongues met, surged, tasted. A sense of déjà vu struck, as if he recalled every detail of the last time they kissed. As if they aligned perfectly.

'Harvey...' Della moaned as he slid his lips down the side of her neck.

His name on her lips shifted something primal and urgent inside him, so he pressed her body closer. Selfishly, on some level, Harvey needed to know that Della wanted him for no other reason than this fierce, immoveable attraction. This time, there was no ghost of another man to chase off. This was about *them*.

'Why is it that we get on so much better without words,' she panted, sliding her hands inside his T-shirt, her palms branding his skin.

'I have no idea.' Harvey backed her up, pressing her against the wall to increase the contact between their bodies. Maybe it was because words were open to misinterpretation, whereas physically, they just clicked. Harvey ground his hips against hers, urgency to be inside her pounding through his veins. Della angled her head, exposing her neck to his kisses. Then she shoved up his shirt, yanking it over his head and tossing it before removing her own.

He looked down to where her breasts were encased in sexy black lace. 'I swear you get sexier each time I see you.' And he was only human. Della was too sexy to ignore when she was on the other side of the room shooting him disapproving looks. Like this, seductive, needy in his arms, saying all the right things, he'd had no hope of resisting.

Kissing her again, he hoisted her from the floor so she wrapped her legs around his waist, her fingers demanding in his hair. She moaned as he cupped one breast through her bra, kissing his jaw, his neck, the notch between his collarbones while her hips undulated against his. Harvey's eyes rolled closed, the friction between their writhing bodies almost unbearable.

'Hold tight,' he said, slinging his arms under her butt and striding to the bedroom. He placed her on her feet, and she unclasped and removed her bra.

'Hurry,' she said, tugging at the waistband of his shorts. 'It's been three years.'

'Whose fault is that?' Harvey smiled as he popped the button on her sexy denim cut-off shorts, then scooped her back into his arms. Their naked chests pressed together, and he walked them back towards the bed. 'Besides, that's all the more reason not to rush.'

Ducking his head, he captured first one of her nipples in his mouth and then the other.

'See,' she gasped, her head falling back, 'you always need to be right, even now.'

'And you always need to have the last word.' He grinned, laying her down on the bed. He unzipped her shorts and slid them and her underwear down her shapely legs.

For a second he simply stared, swaying on his feet. She was glowing, beautiful, her stare heavy with desire. A knot formed under his ribs. This might be just sex, but Della was precious, almost family, as much a part of the furniture in his life as the rest of the Wiltons. He couldn't afford to mess this up just because he wanted her and the feeling was mutual.

'Don't overthink it, Harvey,' she said, holding out her hand for his. 'Just come here.'

Before he got too carried away by temptation, Harvey removed his wallet from his pocket, took out a condom and placed it on the bed. Then he kicked off his shoes and took her hand, lying down at her side.

'Kiss me,' she demanded, wrapping her arms around

his shoulders and hooking one leg over his hip so his doubts were silenced.

He cupped her backside and pushed his tongue against hers, laughing when she rolled him onto his back and sat astride him.

'So it's like that, is it?' he asked, toying with her nipples as she leaned over him to kiss him once more. He didn't mind her being on top or making demands or using him for sex. He'd grown accustomed over the years to the power play in his every interaction with Della, and he liked her playful side. She groaned as his hands skimmed her waist, her hips, guiding them to rock against his hard length.

'Stop teasing me,' she ordered, kissing him with renewed desperation.

When he rolled them again, tore his mouth from hers and trailed kisses down her neck, chest and stomach, she sighed in surrender. Going lower, he spread her thighs and covered her with his mouth. She cried out, her fingers spearing his hair. He wanted to take his time, to savour her, to unleash more of that wildly passionate Della that had blown him away three years ago. Her moans intensified. He pushed his fingers inside her and groaned as she tensed, gasped, climaxed, crying out his name once more. Triumph expanded his chest. If she'd waited three years, he wanted tonight to be memorable. She was right; this was their best form of communication. They didn't need feelings or hurtful words or one-upmanship. Just touch and honest desire.

'You are so sexy,' he said, shoving off his shorts and briefs. He rolled on the condom and kissed his way back up her satiated body.

'Don't be smug,' she whispered, smiling and breathless, drawing his mouth back to hers as she wrapped her hand around his erection.

'I'm afraid you can't stop me.' He grinned, gripped her thigh and drew it over his hip so he sank between her legs. 'Three years *is* a long time. Did you think about us?' He had.

'I might have done, on occasion,' she admitted begrudgingly, her pupils dilating as she snagged her lip with her teeth. 'But you don't need your ego stroking.'

Too late. With his heart thudding triumphantly because he hadn't been alone in reliving that night, Harvey laughed and swooped in for another kiss. Even after her orgasm, when admitting that they were hot together—that, like him, she'd struggled to forget—Della needed to come out on top. But with them naked and pleasuring each other rather than fighting, there was no point hiding how good they were together physically.

'Go slow,' she whispered, spreading her legs, inviting him into her body with a teasing tilt of her hips.

He pushed inside her, their stares locked. 'I thought about us, too,' he admitted, fighting his instincts to move.

Her eyes widened, a small gasp leaving her throat.

'Every time I saw you, I wanted you again, even while we fought and bickered and tried to pretend it hadn't happened.' He moved inside her body, his heart banging against hers.

'I wanted you, too,' she gasped as he thrust faster. Della tunnelled her fingers into his hair and drew his lips to hers, pushed her tongue into his mouth so he groaned. They'd never stood a chance of ignoring this attraction, this connection. They were too good together. Their sparks were exceptional. Fighting it was almost a crime against sex.

As he found the perfect rhythm, Harvey fought his own need. He wanted her with him, a tied race. He wanted her as consumed as him, so that they might move on, but they'd never forget.

'Harvey,' Della gasped, and he kissed her, cupped her beautiful breasts, thumbed her nipples erect and watched as desire darkened her blue eyes to navy.

'Come with me,' he said, picking up the pace so Della cried out and crossed her ankles in the small of his back, her fingernails digging into his arms. Harvey bent one knee for purchase, driving harder and faster. As fire raced down his spine, Harvey sent her tumbling over the edge once more, finally following her with a harsh groan, his body racked with spasms. He buried his face in the crook of her neck, sucked in the scent of her skin and wrung every drop of pleasure from their bodies.

Finally he released Della to collapse, satiated, at her side. They stared at the ceiling, both panting.

'Why did I wait so long?' Della asked, a satisfied smile stretching her lips.

'Beats me…' Harvey grinned. He'd been absolutely right about their unfinished business. But as the oxygen returned to his brain, awareness returned. Reason. Sense. Yes, their chemistry was still explosive, but it was also still something to be very wary of. Because neither of them had changed in the past three years. They still wanted different things when it came to relationships.

As he scooped a breathless Della into his arms, Harvey gritted his teeth, prepared for a fierce internal battle of desire for her, for *this*, versus self-preservation. Two weeks didn't feel like a long time, but if they kept being intimate, it was long enough to form a habit. When it came to relationships, he'd spent years fighting that kind of trap, keeping people out.

Surely he could survive thirteen more days until he could put some distance between himself and the temptation of Della?

CHAPTER FIVE

THE NEXT MORNING in the seminar room, Della tried to focus on Harvey's talk on sports-related trauma, but her mind kept wandering. Had last night really happened? How had they gone from arguing in Savu's to sleeping together again? Oh, she'd instigated it by asking him to stay. The minute he'd stood on the doorstep and apologised, the minute he'd opened up, let her in, hinting at his beliefs on love, the minute he'd alluded to the fact that, despite appearances, he'd always had a thing for her, all the anger and humiliation inside her had drained away.

How could she stay angry with Harvey, when she'd always had a thing for him too? When she'd seen another side to him? And how could the sex between them have been better than the last time? They'd had sex three times—the second time in the shower and again in bed before finally collapsing into a state of replete exhaustion. She'd awoken at dawn to the unfamiliar heat and sounds of a tropical island and nudged Harvey awake. He'd untangled his limbs from hers, kissed her, dressed and rushed back to his own bungalow, giving Della a brief reprieve to come to terms with the fact that Harvey seemed to be hotter than ever before.

How was that even possible, let alone fair? And what

did it mean for her attempts to resist him? Dragging her gaze from the man in question, Della glanced around the room. A small audience, predominantly doctors and physiotherapists from the hospital with a handful of local GPs, listened to Harvey talk. Della zoned back into what he was saying, their eyes briefly meeting, before he looked back down at his notes.

Shivers of both delight and dread danced down her spine. What was he thinking? Did he want this physical fling to continue for the duration of their time in Fiji, or was he done? He was giving little away, although he could hardly look at her the way he had last night in front of an audience. Della herself was horribly confused. On the one hand, having incredible sex with Harvey was better than two weeks of arguing. They were trapped there, after all. But was it wise? She'd never known Harvey to see a woman more than a few times. Would he even be up for a holiday fling? Or should they agree to put the sex behind them again and simply focus on working together? Her stomach sank at the thought. But just because she still wanted him, just because she'd witnessed a deeper side to Harvey she hadn't known existed, she'd do well to remember that when it came to relationships, they were total opposites. She sighed; she was talking herself around in circles.

The audience broke into a round of applause, and Della joined in. Harvey's talk had obviously concluded, although she'd missed most of it with her lusty daydreams.

'Thank you, Dr Ward,' Dr Tora said. 'A very informative update. We'll take a fifteen-minute break. Refreshments are available out on the veranda.'

While Harvey was approached by an audience member with a question, Della stepped outside and helped herself to a glass of iced water. There was no point trying to eat. Her stomach was too full of butterflies, her head too full of the dilemma. In theory, a little holiday sex hurt no one, especially when she and Harvey understood each other so well. At this moment, Della wasn't ready for more than sex, and even when that changed, she'd never consider Harvey. He didn't do relationships. So where was the harm in a brief sexual fling? But could she spend all this time with him, explore a sexual relationship that was obviously heading nowhere, and keep emotional boundaries in place?

'Thanks for the wake-up call,' a deep voice said over her shoulder, jolting her out of her thoughts.

Della hid a delicious shudder of anticipation, turning to offer Harvey a tight, professional smile as if they were no more than colleagues. 'You're welcome. The sunrise woke me.' Finding Harvey's big, manly body sprawled in her bed, taking up more than his fair share of space, she'd watched him sleep for a few indulgent seconds, carefully sniffing the scent of his shampoo and memorising the small scar on his shoulder. Even asleep, he was outrageously handsome.

'So...how are you feeling today?' he asked in a low voice, taking a sip of what smelled like strong black coffee, his favourite. 'Any regrets? I know I'm not your favourite person.' His voice was light as he watched her intently over the rim of his cup, his playful reminder well-timed. They'd been adversaries for so long. Could they truly be lovers, even temporarily?

'Hmm...' Della kept her expression serious and pretended to think about it. 'I guess I can live with what happened, given *I* was the one to instigate it.' She didn't want him thinking last night was his idea. 'How about you?' she asked, with a twitch of a smile. 'Have you booked the first flight out of here and deleted me from your contacts yet?'

Just because he'd admitted he'd thought all of her boyfriends including her ex-husband unworthy didn't mean their very different views on commitment and love had changed. What had he called it? A *brave gamble*? But why?

Harvey shrugged, his stare flirtatious. 'Not quite yet.'

Della fought a smile and looked down. There was a perfectly professional distance between his body and hers. To the outsider, they might be having a medicine-related conversation. Instead, her body was aflame. How could zero physical contact generate so many sparks?

'When you think about it,' she said, emboldened but her heart galloping with nerves, 'holiday flings are pretty harmless.' A safe, casual sex fling might do her a world of good. She searched his stare for any sign that he was done, although this was Harvey—short-lived flings were his forte. But if he was waiting for her to beg, he'd be waiting a long time.

'Hmm… They do have considerable benefits.' Harvey nodded, his expression thoughtful. 'A nice, neat end date when you fly home to the real world.'

Holding her nerve, she waited. She refused to crack until he cracked first. But surely they were on the same page? Surely them sleeping together benefited them working together harmoniously?

Flushed from her shameful justifications, Della held her breath as Harvey inched closer and dipped his head.

'As long as both parties use the other for the same thing, of course.'

Heartened, she caught a flicker of excitement in his eyes. Mentally, she raised a victory fist. She was willing to be used for sex, as long as she could use him in return.

'Of course. And this Fiji. Different rules apply,' she added, looking for his agreement. 'Once we leave this island, usual business resumes.'

'I agree,' he said, a small frown tugging at his mouth. 'Because we *will* see each other again.'

Della nodded, the warning clear. It was the same debate she'd been ruminating on all morning. Yes, their affair would end, but they couldn't ghost each other. Harvey would still be Brody's best friend, and Della would still see him at Wilton family functions.

'But by then,' she went on, reassuring herself as much as Harvey, 'we will have each moved on. Melbourne has a very active singles scene, I believe.' Harvey would find ample casual distractions once he returned to Australia. As they said, a leopard never changed its spots.

Harvey's stare intensified with that flicker of challenge she was used to. 'And maybe you'll find everything you want in Auckland—that devoted husband, a houseful of adorable children. You already have the successful career part.'

See, they knew each other so well. Uninvited, his words from the night before rushed Della's mind... *It's not that I don't believe in love...* Last night, she'd been too upset with him to give the statement much thought. But now it niggled at her. Was this another of Harvey's hidden depths? Was there some reason he'd sworn off relationships beyond his general cynicism following his parents' divorce?

'So, where does that leave us, I wonder?' she asked, dismissing the idea, because his motivations for staying single changed nothing. Harvey would likely never cancel his membership to the singles club, and Della still wanted it all with the right man. She wasn't stupid. There was no way she and Harvey, of all men, could be anything serious. She'd already made one big mistake with Ethan. Next time she risked her heart, she'd make sure the man was all in.

'I guess the door is still open to possibility,' he said cryptically, his stare sparking with heat, the expression doing silly things to Della's pulse. How could she still want him after last night? She'd lost count of how many orgasms she'd had, but it would be so easy to become addicted to sex that good.

'Speaking of possibility,' he said, stepping back so they were once more that respectable distance apart, 'I wondered if you'd like to explore one of the smaller islands with me later, as we have the afternoon off? We could rent a kayak and some snorkel gear. There's no point wasting the fantastic downtime opportunities.'

'That sounds good,' she said, visualising other opportunities—them alone and naked. 'As long as it's not Mallau Island,' she added with a mock grimace. 'I spent my ill-fated honeymoon there.' She offered him a wry smile, shoving all thoughts of Ethan from her mind. She'd moved on, her biggest regret that she hadn't seen through him sooner and saved herself both time and heartache.

But Harvey sobered, a small frown lodging between his brows. 'I wouldn't want to bring up any painful reminders for you. Why don't *you* choose our destination. A clean slate.'

'I will,' Della said breezily, hoping to reassure him, while enjoying that he was…protective. 'Don't look so worried. Mallau isn't the only stunning island in the archipelago.' There were over three hundred.

'In that case,' Harvey said, leaning in a little closer and dropping his voice, 'I'll do my best to keep your mind very much in the present and help you make some new memories.' The innocently phrased promise dripped with suggestion, filling Della with the thrilling fizz of anticipation.

'No, *I'll* help *you* make some,' she breathed, already looking forward to exploring Fiji with Harvey. Despite a worrying start, her working holiday had taken a very unexpected but pleasurable turn. Maybe two weeks trapped with Harvey in paradise wouldn't be so bad after all.

Just then, Dr Tora appeared from the seminar room, his face tense with concern. 'Excuse me, everyone,' he called. 'There's been a vehicle collision off the King's Road north of here. A minibus full of backpackers left the road and ploughed downhill into the dense bush. There are multiple casualties expected in the emergency department shortly. Can everyone who's available please head there to help where they can?'

As he spoke, multiple pagers sounded around them, urgent calls to their Fijian colleagues coming thick and fast.

Della and Harvey glanced at each other and abandoned their drinks. Their afternoon off, their downtime together—exploring, snorkelling, falling into bed— would have to wait. Duty called. They took off running, making it to the ED a few minutes later, in time to intercept the first wave of casualties.

'We have a twenty-three-year-old male with a penetrating abdominal wound,' the paramedic handing over a patient said as he wheeled the stretcher into a vacant resuscitation bay.

'He was flung from the window and impaled on a broken tree branch,' the paramedic continued. 'He has IV access, and I've given him morphine and IV fluids. Blood pressure is on the low side, but he's been conscious throughout.'

The casualty groaned in pain. Della sprang into action, listening to the young man's chest and abdominal sounds as nursing staff connected him to heart monitors and oxygen and began cutting away his clothing. A junior ED doctor drew blood from the man's arm to cross-match for a blood transfusion.

Harvey removed the dressing and exposed the wound in the patient's abdomen. A five-centimetre-diameter tree branch protruded from the wound just under his ribs on the right.

Della met Harvey's stare, seeing her concerns mirrored there. The risk of internal haemorrhage with injuries of this nature was high. This patient would need an urgent laparotomy to assess the internal damage and remove the branch. But if he was bleeding internally, first he must be stabilised.

'Let's get four units of blood cross-matched,' Harvey called to the junior ED doctor. 'Any sign of pneumothorax?' he asked Della, reaching for his own stethoscope.

'No,' she said, drawing up some more analgesia, 'but it will be a miracle if this has avoided his liver.'

Harvey nodded, his expression grim. They needed to operate on the man as soon as possible.

'I need an infusion of intravenous antibiotics, please,' Della said to Seema, the ED nurse, keeping one eye on the blood pressure monitor. Before her eyes, the pressure dropped. Her stare darted to Harvey, a different kind of adrenaline flooding her system. As if making a joint decision, Harvey nodded to Della and unlocked the wheels of the stretcher.

'Send the blood round to theatre,' he said, his voice calm but full of authority. 'Dr Wilton and I are taking him straight to surgery.'

It was the same call Della would have made. There was no time to waste. But as they rushed round to theatre, wheeling the patient with them, what shocked Della most was how good it sounded to hear Harvey automatically refer to them as a team.

CHAPTER SIX

IN THEATRE, HOURS LATER, Harvey sutured the abdominal drain in place and released the clamp, initiating the suction. The drain would remove any residual blood or peritoneal fluid from around the liver laceration, which he and Della had spent the past three hours patching, having slowly and steadily removed the offending tree branch and its splinters. With the exception of two additional nicks in the small intestine, which Della had meticulously repaired, this young man had been incredibly lucky. The internal damage could have been way more extensive and life-threatening.

'Are you happy for me to close?' Harvey asked Della, his back stiff from standing in the OR for so many hours.

Instead of the afternoon off they'd planned, they'd worked together on the complex surgery. Harvey was grateful for the second pair of eyes when it came to the areas of haemorrhage and the fragments of the broken branch they'd found in the man's abdominal cavity. He and Della worked together as if they'd been doing it for years, leaving all of their petty arguments behind, although not their sexual chemistry. Who'd have thought they could get along so well?

Della shifted a retractor, taking one last look at the repaired liver contusion. She wasn't going to be satisfied until she'd checked for herself, and Harvey respected her for that. As a consultant, he'd do the same. Della was an astute and thorough surgeon who didn't allow Harvey's slight seniority in years to deter her from making suggestions or questioning his technique.

'Looks as good as we can expect,' she said finally, her eyes meeting his over the top of her mask.

Harvey nodded in agreement and reached for a needle to close the abdominal wall layers one by one. 'Right, let's close him up. He's certainly not out of the woods yet, but we've done the best we can.' The biggest risk for the patient now that they'd stopped the bleeding was a postoperative complication, especially an infection. Hopefully the cocktail of IV antibiotics Della had started would help, but the young man's recovery would need to be closely monitored.

'I hear they've admitted three more casualties,' Della said, reaching for a second needle to help him close up the laparotomy wound. 'One head injury and two with multiple limb fractures who have been picked up by our orthopaedic colleagues.' She started her sutures at the other end of the vertical surgical incision so they would meet in the middle.

'Busy day,' Harvey agreed, glancing her way. 'We certainly had our hands full with this case. I'm grateful you were here.'

Before Fiji, he'd thought he'd known Della pretty well, but working so closely with her, not to mention their physical connection, was forcing him to take a second and third and fourth look. It was as if he was finally, after all this time, seeing the *real* Della, not the woman he'd spent twenty years avoiding looking at too closely in an attempt to manage his attraction. And it was freaking him out. Especially when she'd all but propositioned him this morning to continue their holiday fling until it was time to go home. Not that he'd needed any persuading.

'No,' she countered, flicking him a challenging look, 'I'm grateful *you* were here.'

Under his mask, Harvey grinned. Just because they'd slept together again, just because they'd agreed on a brief, physical fling, didn't mean their rivalry was completely over. And a part of him wouldn't have it any other way. He'd never felt bored in Della's stimulating, often challenging, company.

He dragged in a breath, his movements with the suture needle and forceps automatic. Now that their patient was stable and out of immediate danger, his mind wandered back to more pleasurable thoughts. There was no point trying to pretend that he was in control of their sexual chemistry, not here where they couldn't walk away from each other as they normally would. Having spent last night reacquainting himself with Della's body, Harvey would be fooling himself if he thought he'd be able to resist her while they were trapped together in Fiji. And as she'd said, a holiday fling was pretty harmless. They knew each other well. They were each invested in a future where they would see each other socially. They understood that when it came to relationships, they were complete opposites: she wanted one and he didn't. But a niggle of caution lodged in his brain. He didn't want to hurt Della. But she knew what she wanted, and for now, it was him; he'd be stupid to pass that up.

'But more compliments, Dr Ward,' Della said when

he'd remained silent for a while. 'Careful, Harvey. There must be something in the Fijian water.' She glanced his way with that playful glint in her eyes.

Harvey chuckled, relieved that the events of last night, first their row and then spending the night together, hadn't affected their relatively new working relationship. That they could respect each other professionally after he'd been appointed to the Melbourne job gave him an enormous amount of satisfaction.

'You'll have my head swelling,' she went on, her movements as practiced as his as they sutured the wound. 'As you know, the Wiltons are such a high-achieving family, it's hard to feel as if you've distinguished yourself.'

Harvey looked up, her comment giving him pause, as if he should have realised she had self-doubts, as if they'd spent twenty years misunderstanding each other. He'd never considered it before, but it must have been hard for her, growing up the youngest in a family of medics.

'But you *have* distinguished yourself,' he pointed out. Was that why Della always seemed to have something to prove? Harvey could relate to that. For a while, during his teens, he'd been determined to show his absent mother what she'd given up on, a part of him striving to be a son of whom she could be proud, as if he'd hoped she'd want to renew their relationship. But the phone had stayed silent. He'd worked hard at school, earned a place at medical school, and become a leading surgeon in one of Australia's top hospitals, but some days, when his mind wandered to his mother, he still felt...inadequate.

'There's no question,' he added, dragging his thoughts from his own upbringing.

She shrugged. 'I guess. Although growing up in Brody's

shadow, nothing I achieved was ever that extraordinary. And then, along came *you.*'

'Me?' Harvey tied off his last suture and cut the ends, his discomfort building.

Della looked up and nodded. 'Yes, *you.*' Her voice was playful, but he sensed she was about to offer information he hadn't known. 'I was just about to leave home for med school,' she continued, 'when Brody brought you home for the weekend that first time. Remember?'

'I remember I upset you with some immature comment about your boyfriend.' If she'd doubted her abilities back then, could that explain her sensitivity to criticism, especially when it had come from some guy she'd never met before?

Della ignored his reference and went on. 'You and Brody had just qualified, just started work as *real* doctors, and you were both insufferable. Strutting around, patronising me with warnings of how hard med school was, teasing me because I was moping over—' She froze. 'Oh, I can't even remember his name...'

'Oliver,' Harvey said, shame and regret hot in his veins as he recalled that weekend when he and Della had made such bad first impressions on each other and the part he'd played.

'Of course, Brody is such a great guy,' she continued as if he hadn't interjected, '*and* he's my brother, so I couldn't hate him for being better than me at everything. But you... You were fair game, I'm afraid.'

Harvey tried to find the humour in the story, but instead, his protective urges for Della fired. 'No wonder we hit it off badly,' he said. It shouldn't matter. The past was in the past, and they were just having sex. But the idea that she'd struggled to believe in herself among her competitive family, fearing she was second best to Brody, the idea of Della displacing her resentment for Brody onto Harvey, left him strangely flat.

Having closed the peritoneum and abdominal muscles, Harvey reached for a staple gun to close the skin. 'You know, I'm not sure if the appointment panel at Melbourne told you this, but you came very close to getting the job they offered me.'

Della stilled. Her eyes met his, full of questions. 'I appreciate you telling me that, Harvey, but I'm a big girl. I can live with second place, and I think they appointed the most experienced candidate at the time.'

Della's confidence in her abilities was attractive, but it was suddenly important to him that she knew of his regard. 'Credit where credit is due,' he said as he placed the final staple and reached for a dressing to cover the wound. 'Surgery is a competitive field. We're all vying for the same positions. Just because I got that job doesn't make me a better surgeon.' With the operation complete, Harvey gave the nod to the anaesthetist to wake the patient before stepping away and removing his mask and gloves.

'I know that—I'm heaps better than you,' she teased as they tossed their surgical gowns in the dirty laundry hamper.

'Well, I wouldn't go that far,' Harvey said as they left theatre to wash up. It was good to have their light-hearted banter back, but the more time he spent with Della, the more he realised that he hadn't really known her before, and he couldn't help but feel he'd missed out.

'You don't have to worry about me, you know,' she said, pausing at the sinks and turning on the taps to wash her hands. 'Despite the fuss I made over your job being rightfully mine, my ego wasn't really dented.' She looked up, met his stare. 'I was just in a bad place at the time, with the divorce. I needed a win. Any win. There's nothing better equipped to make you feel like a big fat failure than a divorce, trust me.'

Harvey reached for a wad of paper towels to dry his hands, a little lost for words that she'd confided in him. He was out of his depth with relationship advice, but he hated the idea that Della blamed herself for her marital breakdown. Harvey didn't know the details, but he was certain it wasn't Della's fault.

'Why would *you* be the failure?' he asked, defensive on her behalf.

'Oh, you know, because I should have seen it coming.' Della switched off the taps and yanked some towels from the dispenser.

Harvey struggled to find the right words. Della had never opened up to him before. 'Do you…want to grab a beer at Savu's?' he asked, wishing they were anywhere but at work so he could touch her, steal the kiss he'd waited all day for, make her smile. 'I'm happy to listen if you want to vent, although, as you know, relationships aren't my strong point.'

He didn't want to put his foot in it again. He watched doubt flit over her expression. He could understand that if she'd grown up feeling second best to Brody, the fact that she was now divorced, whereas her brother was happily married and a dad, might heighten her sense of failure.

'Don't worry, Harvey. There's no relationship to advise on. It's over. Forgotten.' She tossed paper towels in the bin and faced him with a brave face. 'I'm well shot of a man who, by the time we split up, had pretty much convinced me that his career was more important than mine, just because I wanted us to have a family.'

'What?' Harvey scowled, his flare of anger on Della's behalf hot and sharp. 'That's ridiculous.'

She shrugged, looking embarrassed. 'I know relationships are about compromise, but by the end, I felt as if he'd used my career as an excuse to put off talking about us starting a family, as if I couldn't possibly have both. As if I had to make a choice, a family or a career, but why should I? *He* didn't have to. *Brody* didn't have to. *You* wouldn't have to.'

'Why indeed?' Harvey frowned, shocked by the ferocity of his empathy. Had her doubts of being overshadowed by Brody bled into her marriage? Had smart and caring Della settled somehow for her ex's excuses? It was none of Harvey's business, but Della deserved so much better. She deserved someone who would raise her up, not tear her down. She deserved whatever white picket fence dream she chose.

They passed through a door and paused outside their respective changing rooms. It was after hours, their surgery clearly the last one of the day. The place felt deserted. Because it had been too long since they'd kissed, at least nine hours, not that he was counting, Harvey pressed his lips to hers, scooping his arm around her waist. She sighed, gripped his arms and returned his kiss. His thoughts silenced, his body relaxing. Normally he kept people at arm's length, but with Della, because he knew her so well, because she was a big part of his life, because she'd opened up to him, he couldn't help but feel invested.

Before things turned too heated, Harvey pulled back. 'I know we haven't always seen eye to eye over stupid things,' he said, cupping her face, his thumb gliding over her cheekbone, 'but for the record, I think you're amazing.'

He needed to shut up. He was straying out of his comfort zone, but he cared.

'Thanks.' She blinked, clearly touched by his uncharacteristic praise. 'Another compliment. Aren't you scared by the potency of the water?' She smiled, playful, and his heart thumped erratically.

He *was* scared, but not of the water. The real Della, the one he couldn't escape here, the one he was uncovering like an archaeologist exposes a dig, was addictive. It was as if last night had broken some sort of internal restraint. He couldn't seem to keep his hands off her or stop thinking about her and the new things he'd learned.

'I guess you're not so bad yourself,' she said. 'But if we can't trust the water, perhaps we should go for that beer. I'm parched over here.' She was returning to humour as if she could sense the shaky ground on which he was standing and wanted to toss him a lifeline, or perhaps she was also wary of exposing too much. After all, this was about sex.

'Right. Savu's it is.' Harvey released her reluctantly. 'I'll meet you back here in five minutes.'

They parted ways, ducking into their respective changing rooms with matching goofy grins. Harvey removed his scrubs and headed for the shower, using the time to straighten his head. Just because he knew Della well, understood her dreams, had begun to see glimpses into her fears and regrets, didn't mean he could be her confidant. He'd been alone so long, he wasn't even sure he was capable of having more than a casual good time. He certainly knew nothing about the kind of lifelong commitment Della wanted.

Next time she looked sad over her failed marriage or compared herself to Brody, he would do well to remember that not only was he ill-qualified to give relationship advice, but he couldn't be responsible for her happiness. As she'd pointed out, when it came to a man like him, Della was smart enough to have zero expectations.

CHAPTER SEVEN

THE FOLLOWING AFTERNOON, sitting at the front of the two-person kayak with Harvey behind, Della sliced her paddle through the clear sapphire-blue water, a sense of relaxed contentment flooding her system. Maybe it was the warm sun on her back or the salt in her drying hair after their swim. Maybe it was the wonders of the coral reef marine life, the clownfish and the butterflyfish they'd seen while snorkelling. Maybe it was the thrill of beating Harvey back to the kayak in a swimming race and the steamy victory kiss she'd claimed when he'd finally caught up.

Della glanced over her shoulder and caught Harvey's eye. A goofy smile tugged at her cheeks. Maybe it was all those things combined with extreme sexual satisfaction.

'It's so beautiful here,' she said, steering the kayak back across the lagoon towards the white sandy beach of Tokuma Island, a picture-perfect tropical oasis accessible by water taxi from the main island and home to an adults-only holiday resort.

'Hmm,' he agreed, his superior strength propelling the kayak forward. 'Better late than never.'

Della nodded, a small part of her wishing they'd spent their postponed afternoon off in bed. She couldn't seem to get enough of Harvey Ward. The minute he'd arrived to pick her up for their island adventure that morning, she'd dragged him inside her bungalow and kissed him sense-less. One thing had rapidly led to another. They hadn't even made it to bedroom this time, simply collapsed onto the sofa, tugging frenziedly at each other's clothes.

'I've had the best afternoon,' Della said, sighing hap-pily as she recalled burying her face against the side of Harvey's neck and crying out her orgasm while Harvey had groaned, crushing her in his arms as he climaxed. Was there any better way to relax than sun, sea and sex? But no matter how hard she tried to compartmentalise their physical relationship, she couldn't help but enjoy Harvey's company—his dry sense of humour, his geeky encyclopaedic knowledge of most subjects, the playful challenge he brought to everything like a dash of spice, keeping life interesting.

Reminding herself to also embrace caution—she couldn't get carried away and forget that he was still the same old Harvey—Della steered the kayak into the shal-lows. They climbed off and tugged it up onto the sand near the rental place—a palm-roofed shack filled with paddles and snorkel gear. They returned the masks and snorkels to the *used* bin and headed up the beach for the shade of one of the palm leaf umbrellas dotting the shoreline.

At her side, Harvey took Della's hand. She smiled over at him, the breath catching in her chest. She'd been ner-vous about spending too much time with him, but Fiji Harvey seemed like a completely different man to his Australian counterpart. He was fun and caring, and she had to constantly remind herself that he'd never actually been a boyfriend. His romantic gestures were merely a pretty irresistible form of sexual foreplay.

'I brought some snacks,' Harvey said as they sat on the warm sand. He opened his small backpack to reveal some crackers, a pack of nuts and two apples. 'We need to keep our energy up.' He winked, his suggestive smile sending Della's body molten.

'See, no matter how hard you try to hide it, you *are* a good guy,' she teased, opening the roasted almonds and popping one into her mouth, touched by his thoughtfulness.

'It's true.' Harvey shrugged and took a giant bite from one of the apples. 'That must be why Brody and Amy have asked me to be Jack's mentor for his naming day. I wasn't sure if they'd told you yet.'

He watched her carefully. Obviously *he knew* that Della had also been asked to mentor Jack, the equivalent of a godparent. Della nodded, not in the slightest bit surprised by Brody and Amy's choice. Harvey was Brody's best friend. Of course he would ask him to be there for his only son. But that meant, like it or not, she'd definitely see him again in three weeks' time. By then, their holiday fling would be a distant memory, although it would be hard to forget days like today, when they'd not only had great sex but also had fun and laughed together, making brand-new memories.

'I can't wait for Jack's naming day,' Della said, taking a long drink from her water bottle. 'As his aunt and his mentor, I'll have two excuses for cuddles. Don't tell my brother, but I might even steal him and smuggle him back to New Zealand.' She laughed, but a niggle formed a knot in her chest. She was happy for Brody and Amy, but newly divorced, it had been hard to hear their pregnancy news and not feel a massive pang of longing, as if yet again she was being left behind.

'I'm looking forward to it, too,' Harvey said with an easy smile combined with that hungry stare of his.

'Really?' she asked, trying to picture Harvey holding her baby nephew, who was coming up to six months old. Jack had one bottom tooth and an adorably gummy smile. 'You've never struck me as the kids type.'

Harvey glanced her way, his expression unreadable. 'I like kids just fine. Small, cute humans—what's not to love?'

Della's pulse pounded with excitement as she watched him polish off the rest of the apple. There was something sexy about the way Harvey ate. Of course, there was something sexy about his every move, but she'd never have guessed he'd be comfortable around kids. But thinking about Jack's naming day left her wondering if she and Harvey could successfully ignore their fling once it was over, as they had last time. The idea that they'd revert to bickering strangers doing their best to ignore each other left her unsettled. She didn't want that. Maybe they'd finally become friends once this sexual chemistry had run its course?

She watched a droplet of water trail a path down his toned and golden abs. Nope, having Harvey as a friend seemed unlikely. Or would they still hook up every now and then, before Della moved on to a new relationship?

'Contrary to what some people believe,' he said, distracting her from how exactly their relationship would work in the future, 'I even possess a heart.' He shot her a teasing glance, and stowed the apple core in a paper bag.

Guilt left her flushed. 'I guess we didn't really know each other very well before Fiji,' she said, lying down beside him on the sand, where he was propped up on his elbows. She rested one hand on his chest, brushing at the grains of golden sand that glinted on his skin.

'I guess we didn't,' he said, lying back and pillowing one bent arm under his head. 'I'm glad we finally got the chance to know each other better.' His other hand came to rest on hers, his intense stare shifting over her face.

Della's belly fluttered as if he'd hungrily scoured every inch of her bikini-clad body. She recognised that look, and his touch, no matter how innocent, never failed to turn her on.

'You know,' he said, falling serious, 'I *did* have a relationship once, a girlfriend, before I met you and Brody. I wanted you to know, because...you know, relationships aren't easy, for anyone.'

Della stiffened, gaped, completely at a loss for what to say. Her fingers stilled in his dark chest hair, the rapid thud of his heart under her palm telling her this was hard for him to confess. And was he reassuring her again because she'd told him how her divorce had made her feel like a failure? But Harvey...a girlfriend? He was *Harvey*. Never short of offers but always alone at couple times— Christmas, birthday celebrations, holidays.

'Did you love her?' she asked finally, her raging curiosity an uncomfortable gnawing in the pit of her stomach. Was that what he'd meant when he'd said being vulnerable with another person was a *brave gamble*? Had Harvey had his heart broken and subsequently turned his back on commitment? How had she never known this about him? And why should it matter? She wasn't jealous. It was just that the more time she and Harvey spent together, she realised that she didn't really know him at all.

As if he regretted the impulse to share this with her, Harvey sat up, rested his arms on his bent knees and looked out to sea. 'I don't know...maybe.'

Well, that was vague. The easy, laid-back vibe they'd enjoyed all afternoon while they'd swum and snorkelled the reef departed. That jealousy she'd denied a moment ago slid through Della's veins like fire. Harvey in love? A secret relationship he'd kept from her. Did Brody know?

'What happened?' Della softly asked, scared to pry but even more scared to miss this opportunity to know him better, because in light of his revelation, they seemed like strangers again. 'Did she break your heart?' Was that why he was slow to admit he'd loved this girl? Was that why he'd avoided relationships all these years? It seemed like an extreme reaction, but she didn't want to judge.

'Kind of...' He sighed, keeping his back turned.

'Well, I can understand why you'd be reluctant to confide in me,' Della said. 'After the way I've judged you in the past. If it's any consolation, I regret that now.' Della lay stiffly on the sand, shame holding her tongue. She'd assumed that he was happy with casual sex, but now it seemed that the reality might be much more complex. He *had* been in a relationship once. He'd probably loved someone and had his heart broken. Brody was right— Harvey *did* possess hidden depths.

'It's not that,' he said, turning to face her, his expression stoic. 'It's just hard to talk about. She died in a car collision aged twenty-two. She was a medical student like me. Her name was Alice.'

Della sat up, covered her shocked gasp with her hand,

her heart twisting painfully at the tragic news. 'I'm so sorry, Harvey. I had no idea.'

'It was a long time ago.' Harvey shrugged, returned his gaze to the sea. 'Brody knew that I didn't like to talk about it. I know he's a know-it-all as a brother, but as a friend, he's very loyal.'

Della's mind reeled. She understood that Brody would keep Harvey's secret, but she wished she'd known this vital piece of information sooner. In context, it painted tortured Harvey in a whole new light. He must have really loved this girl. Were heartache and grief the reasons a younger Harvey, the man she'd first met and taken an instant dislike to in a love-hate kind of way, had played the field? Had loving and losing Alice had a profound effect on him, so he avoided further pain by avoiding commitment?

Della swallowed, her throat burning with regret and jealousy. 'Is Alice the reason that you don't date?' she asked in barely a whisper, some part of her needing to know if he was still in love with this woman. Still grieving. Still heartbroken.

'It's not that cut and dried,' he said, keeping his back to her. 'I didn't wake up the next day and make a conscious decision that I was done with relationships for good. It just kind of happened that way.' His shoulders tensed. 'We'd been together a couple of years,' he continued, his voice tight. 'And although it probably wouldn't have lasted, I was devastated to lose her like that, so... suddenly. So pointlessly.'

'Of course you were. Who wouldn't be?' Della reached out and placed her hand between his shoulder blades. Yes, their relationship was about sex, and this Harvey, a complex man hiding a vulnerable side, was a stranger to her, but she couldn't help but comfort him the way he'd tried to do for her at Savu's last night after she'd admitted details of her divorce.

But why wouldn't it have lasted? She desperately wanted to ask, but maybe she'd pried enough. Instead, she pressed her lips to his sun-warmed shoulder, her eyes stinging with emotion. Everything she'd assumed about this man had shattered like glass. He wasn't arrogant and competitive; he was dedicated and driven. He wasn't carefree and single; he was protecting himself. He wasn't two-dimensional; he was complex.

'I guess when the shock and grief faded,' he went on, 'it seemed easier, less effort, to keep my relationships superficial. No need to tell a one-night stand about your sad past. I didn't want to talk about it anyway, even if someone had asked.'

Della caressed his shoulder, too emotional to say anything. Why hadn't *she* asked? Instead, she'd taken him at face value, ridiculed his choices and used him for sex. Twice.

'I focussed on work,' he said, shooting her a wry smile. 'Before I knew it, one year had turned into another and another. By the time five years had gone by, I'd developed casual dating habits—keeping it light and impersonal, having a good time and moving on—that didn't seem to have any downside.' He glanced over his shoulder. 'You know that saying—"if it's not broken, don't fix it"?'

Della nodded in understanding.

'Well, that encompassed my personal life.' He shifted, lay back down on his side, pulling Della down too. 'I guess I just never found a good enough reason to change,' he said, although Della wondered if he might be holding something more back.

He propped his head on one hand, and she mirrored his position so they faced each other in the shade of the umbrella. 'Because relationships are risky,' she said flatly, knowing all about the pitfalls of loving someone and having your heart broken. But whereas Della hoped to find love again in the future, Harvey had found the perfect solution to protect his heart—staying single. He'd never met a woman it was worth risking the status quo for, or he just didn't see that anything was lacking in his personal life, or he was happy with the sacrifice if it meant avoiding pain.

'Don't you ever get lonely?' she asked cautiously, looking down at their clasped hands where his thumb slid against her skin, raising goose bumps on her arm. She doubted she could do what Harvey had done, stay alone all these years. She loved being part of a couple, having someone to share things with, someone who just understood you. Until it went wrong...

'How can I be lonely surrounded by Wiltons?' he said with a small smile, distancing himself from the question and the heavy turn in the conversation.

Della couldn't blame him for putting up emotional barriers. She'd done the same last night when he asked about Ethan.

'So you see,' he said, a twinkle of humour coming into his eyes, 'I'm not heartless. I'm just stuck in my ways. Lazy.'

Della entwined her fingers with his, desperate to ask all the questions building inside. By avoiding long-term relationships, he was keeping himself safe, yes, but wasn't he also missing out on connection, on knowing someone on a deep level as much as they knew him?

'Lazy or scared?' she asked, looking up. She could fully relate to the latter. Putting herself back out there in search of a relationship, of the right man, often seemed too monumental to contemplate, but unlike Harvey, she didn't want to be alone forever.

'You're probably right,' he said. 'Although my explanation puts me in a better light.' As if he wanted to draw a line under the topic, Harvey leaned close and pressed his lips to hers, the heated kiss almost enough of a distraction to end the conversation.

His hand rested on her waist, his tongue sliding against hers. Della sighed, turned on by his touch but still reeling from everything she'd learned about him in the past few days. It was as if she hadn't known the real Harvey at all, as if she'd filed him away in a mislabelled box to keep herself safe from her feelings, and now she needed to re-examine them in the cold light of day. No, there were no feelings beyond attraction and respect. Feelings had no place in their fling.

Pulling back, she rested her forehead against his, breathing hard. 'I understand the fear, you know, the emotional gamble of being vulnerable with another person. Why do you think I haven't bothered with dating since the divorce? I've had my fingers burned, and I'm in no rush to go through that again. It's as if my instincts, my judgement took a massive hit.' That part of her that hadn't seen her marital problems coming was terrified to let another person close, terrified to get it wrong, again. Although her time for meeting *the one*, for falling in love and starting a family, was running out. She'd be forty in two and half years.

'I can understand that.' His searching stare flicked between her eyes, so Della wanted to hide behind her sunglasses. He cupped her face. 'But you deserve to be happy. You deserve to have it all, Della, if that's what you want.'

Della nodded, her throat hot and achy. To be seen for the first time since her divorce, and by Harvey of all people… She *did* want it all, but having what she wanted wasn't straightforward.

'Knowing what you want is the easy part,' she said with a sad laugh, looking down at their clasped hands to hide her eyes from him. 'It's finding someone who wants the same as you that's tricky. I've already got that wrong once.' She didn't want to think about her ex, not lying here hand in hand with Harvey, when they were finally sharing something personal, when she felt so close to him. But now that she knew his reason for avoiding relationships, their differences were more obvious than ever. It wasn't that Harvey wanted to be single. It was that he didn't ever want the risk of a relationship, and to eternally romantic and hopeful Della, that was the most depressing thing she'd heard for a long time.

'It will happen,' Harvey said, an encouraging smile in his eyes. 'You have everything going for you—a great career, an awesome personality, this sexy body…' His smiled stretched, but then he sobered. 'Just don't settle for less than you deserve, okay?'

Della nodded, confused that Harvey, of all people, understood her so well. Had she compromised too much and settled with Ethan? Had she, over time, allowed her ex's dreams to eclipse and squash her own? It hadn't felt that way at the time, but by then end of their marriage, he'd changed. He'd sold her a fairy tale and rewritten the happy ending.

'You deserve to be happy too,' she said tentatively, too scared to know if he was still in love with Alice. 'What does that look like for you? Being alone forever?' Her pulse pounded so hard, she feared he might feel it in her fingers. This degree of emotional intimacy was uncharted territory for them.

'I don't think about forever.' He shrugged, his stare untroubled. 'I just know that right now, my life is good. I'm in control. Why would I mess with that?'

'Ah…the control freak again,' Della said, trying to make light of it even as her heart sank. She told herself she was disappointed for Harvey, because surely everyone wanted to be in love? To share their life with someone? To feel deeply connected to another human being? But maybe for Harvey, control of his emotions was more valuable. And a part of her could understand.

'Don't feel sorry for me,' he said, tugging on her hand and steering them back to playful territory. 'I do all right with ladies, as you know.' He winked, drew her close, captured her lips in another searing kiss that fogged her mind and silenced all her questions.

Bewildered by what she'd learned, Della surrendered to his kiss, her lips parting, their tongues gliding. There was no point stressing Harvey's choices. The two of them were there to have a good time, not to build a relationship, even a friendship. If nineteen years of casual sex hadn't helped him get over Alice, what chance did Della have in two weeks? He wasn't hers. He wasn't anyone's. If she became distracted by the real Harvey, the man she was coming to understand more deeply every day, she might forget to focus on their physical relationship. She might forget how they still wanted different things, and likely always would.

She gripped his biceps and lost herself, her body sliding closer to his until her breasts grazed his bare chest and their thighs touched. As their kisses built in intensity, she grew aware that she was only wearing a bikini and Harvey board shorts. They were on a public beach on an island popular with snorkellers. They might be in paradise, but they weren't alone.

Breaking away, she calmed her excited breathing. 'We should, um, head back. The last water taxi is at seven.'

Harvey nodded, sliding his legs from the tangle of hers with a wince. 'Just give me a second.'

She smiled, glancing at the bulge in his shorts. When he was ready, they gathered up their belongings and walked hand in hand towards the resort and the dock for the water taxi. As she sat snuggled into him on the boat, her back to his front and his arms around her waist, Della was stunned by how little she'd known Harvey before and how much they had in common beyond their jobs. This man, the dedicated doctor protecting his vulnerable heart, was way more dangerous to her than the carefree ladies' man she'd easily dismissed for close to twenty years.

But Della still wanted the future she'd been denied—love, marriage, a family. And when she finally overcame her fear, when she was finally ready to risk her heart again, she couldn't afford to make another mistake. Next time she fell in love, she needed to get it right.

CHAPTER EIGHT

THE NEXT DAY in the ED was hectic. Harvey and Della had no planned operations, so they'd split up to help the local doctors with the surgical admissions. Harvey had just finished seeing a six-year-old there on holiday with suspected appendicitis when a text came through from Della.

I have a patient who needs a second opinion if you're free.

Harvey washed his hands, his eagerness to reunite with Della leaving him jittery. Yesterday had been a big day. After their kayaking adventure at Tokuma Island, after he'd opened up to her about Alice's death and she'd hinted again at her regrets over her marriage, she'd spent the night at his bungalow. They'd wordlessly showered together, lazily washing the sand and salt from each other's body before falling into bed. They hadn't talked about their pasts again. It was as if they were each processing what they'd learned. The trouble was that by spending so much time with her, by discovering new things about Della, by constantly needing to touch her, Harvey was struggling to keep his emotions in check. He felt out of

control, and that was a huge concern. Her words from
the day before looped in his mind.

*You deserve to be happy too... What does that look
like for you? Being alone forever?*

Distracted anew by the power of that question, Harvey
went in search of Della. He'd never seriously considered
it before, but now that she'd raised the idea, now that it
was out there in his consciousness, he couldn't seem to
put it out of his mind. Nor did he know the answer. Maybe
he shouldn't have let Della in yesterday, but he'd wanted
her to know that most people had relationship regrets,
that she wasn't alone.

Harvey found Della in a nearby bay with an anxious-
looking couple in their thirties. As always, his pulse
banged at the sight of her, his fingers restless to touch
her soft, sun-kissed skin, his lips eager for those passionate kisses that always escalated out of their control.

'Dr Ward,' Della said, her expression both apologetic
and relieved. 'Thanks for coming. Mr and Mrs Beaumont
would like a second opinion, and I told them you're Melbourne's top trauma surgeon.' Her stare carried questions,
as if checking he was okay after his confession yesterday. But he'd rather she look at him with desire than pity.

'Only because they were too stupid to appoint you,
Dr Wilton.' Harvey smiled at the patient, Mr Beaumont,
who was lying on the stretcher, supporting his left arm
in a sling.

Della was a compassionate doctor, a talented surgeon
and a good listener. She would be a catch for any man.
Harvey hated to see the threads of doubt she carried. Yes,
she knew what she wanted, but she also felt that she'd
compromised too much in her marriage.

'The Beaumonts are here on their honeymoon,' Della told Harvey. 'Mr Beaumont is a fit and healthy thirty-year-old who fell off a jet ski this morning travelling at approximately fifty kilometres per hour. He sustained a mild concussion on hitting the water and has an anterior dislocation of the left shoulder.'

Harvey listened as Della pulled up the shoulder X-ray on the computer, which clearly displayed the dislocation. She angled the screen so the newlyweds could also see the results. Harvey quickly examined the man's arm and then scrutinised the X-ray and read the report, in no doubt of Della's diagnosis. It was a standard case of shoulder dislocation, but some patients needed a second opinion. That didn't mean Harvey was better equipped to treat this patient than Della. He trusted her clinical acumen unreservedly. In fact, he realised with an internal jolt, he trusted her, full stop.

That was why he'd told her about Alice. But when had that change happened…?

'So I'm afraid, as Dr Wilton pointed out,' Harvey said, standing side by side with Della in solidarity, 'you have a dislocated shoulder. I agree with her diagnosis.'

Harvey glanced Della's way, hoping she saw his absolute faith in his stare. But standing close without touching her left him restless to drag her into his arms and chase off all her doubts. The same fiercely protective urges he'd experienced yesterday at the beach when she'd told him about her ex-husband flared anew now. What was going on with him, and how could she make him feel this way when he'd effortlessly avoided it for twenty years?

'The good news,' he added to Mr Beaumont, 'is that there doesn't appear to be any fracture or significant tendon or muscle damage, so you won't need surgery. But I concur one hundred percent with Dr Wilton's clinical assessment and the treatment she's suggested.'

Tearful, Mrs Beaumont dabbed at her eyes with a tissue and gripped her husband's hand on his uninjured side. Harvey could sympathise. Of course the wife would be worried. No one wanted their honeymoon marred by injury, but these things happened when you came off a jet ski at speed. The man was lucky the injuries weren't more serious, particularly the concussion.

'Once we put the shoulder back in place,' Della said, her voice reassuring, 'and once the pain and swelling have gone down, you should make a full recovery. If you're happy for us to proceed, we can quickly pop your shoulder back into the joint. The sooner we do that, the less the risk of surrounding tissue damage. Why don't you two chat about it for a moment.'

Harvey and Della left the bay and moved a short distance away so they wouldn't be overheard.

'Thanks for sticking up for me so heartily back there,' she said, looking up at him with a curious smile, perhaps because in the past, when Brody teased her at family gatherings, Harvey had always kept quiet or joined in. If he'd known back then how Della's feistiness was a shield because she compared herself to Brody, how she felt the need to prove herself, how she considered her divorce in particular a personal failure, he'd have been way more tactful.

'Any time, Della.' Shame for how he'd behaved when he'd been focussed on keeping a lid on his attraction for Della coiled inside him. 'You know it's not personal—some patients just like to question everything.'

'Of course.' Della nodded, a flicker of amusement in her stare. Then she sobered and frowned. 'Are *you* okay?' she asked, glancing around the department to make sure they were alone. 'You know...after yesterday. You were gone when I got out of the shower.'

'I wanted to get in a run before work,' he said, shaking off the unfamiliar swarm of emotions that yesterday's confessions, both his and hers, had churned up. 'But I'm fantastic,' he said, staring intently. 'I had a great sleep and woke up feeling...energised.' He'd kissed her awake, as if reaching for her naked body next to him had become the most natural thing in the world, and he wanted her to look at him as she had when he'd pushed inside her and rode them both to orgasm. Would he still reach for her back in Melbourne? Would he crave the scent of Della's perfume on his pillow? Would he acclimatise to having an empty bed again? The idea was mildly depressing...

Della flushed and shot him a censorious look. 'I remember,' she said. 'No need to brag.'

Harvey reined in his smug smile. 'Shall I leave this to you?' he asked about the shoulder dislocation. 'You don't need me.' Although he'd somehow grown used to them working together. They made a great team. Another thing he'd have to get used to when he returned to Australia.

Della shrugged, her ego clearly undamaged. 'I think the wife just expected a prescription for some painkillers and to be sent on their way.'

Harvey bit his tongue, mildly insulted on Della's behalf that her skills had been questioned. A junior doctor could reduce a shoulder dislocation, whereas Della was an experienced consultant trauma surgeon.

'If you have a moment,' she went on, 'I could use your

assistance. I prefer Matsen's traction to reduce a shoulder dislocation, and it's a two-person job.'

'Really? Matsen's?' Harvey asked about her choice of technique mainly because he enjoyed evoking the sparks of challenge in her eyes.

'Yes, Matsen's.' She smiled a mocking smile, clearly onto him and in no way intimidated.

'You don't use the Milch manoeuvre?' he pressed, questioning her to bring out the barely disguised amusement in her stare. 'That's what *I* prefer...' These days, since they were getting along so much better, they weren't sparring as much. Part of him missed it, and maybe Della did, too.

'Well, it doesn't surprise me that we're different,' she said calmly. 'But my technique is better. And it's *my* patient.'

Harvey grinned, glad to see Della wouldn't let him get away with anything, despite the fact that she might be starting to trust him too. After all, she had opened up about her ex. 'Then it's your call,' he said, happily yielding.

'Good. Matsen's it is.' She shot him a victorious look. 'Come on. That shoulder isn't going to right itself. I'm sure the Beaumonts want to get back to their honeymoon.'

Dutifully, Harvey followed her back to the bedside. A week ago, when Della and he only knew the superficial things about each other, they might have more fiercely argued the point on whose technique was better, although there were many. But it didn't matter. They both knew the important thing was to quickly put the head of the humerus back into the joint.

After some time to consider, the patient was happy to

proceed with the treatment. With Mr Beaumont lying on his back and the bed lowered, Della and Harvey took up their positions opposite each other, Della taking hold of the injured arm and Harvey standing next to the man's opposite shoulder. Harvey gripped the ends of a sheet passed around the man's chest and under his affected armpit, while Della held his dislocated arm in position, bent to ninety degrees at the elbow.

'Ready?' she asked the patient, who nodded and then closed his eyes, squeezing his wife's hand.

Della held Harvey's eye contact, silently mouthing *one, two, three* so they were in sync. She leaned back, applying traction to the patient's bent arm, while Harvey pulled on the sheet, applying counter-traction in the opposite direction. With a slight pop, the dislocation reduced, and the patient released a long sigh of relief.

Della flashed Harvey a grateful and triumphant smile that made him want to kiss the living daylights out of her. Instead, he beamed. 'Good old Matsen's. Worked like a charm.'

Della carefully hid her smile, clearly trying to stay professional in front of the patient. They thought differently on many subjects, but when it mattered, they'd proved time and again this week that they could compromise. Would they remember that when they saw each other in the future, or would they revert to bickering over nothing? Had this fling in Fiji forever altered their relationship? Harvey hoped so. He didn't want to go backwards where Della was concerned. Did that mean he wanted to be her friend? *Friends* seemed inadequate after everything they'd shared. But he couldn't seriously be thinking they could be more than friends, could he?

'Who's Matsen?' Mrs Beaumont asked, confused, interrupting the disconcerting turn of Harvey's thoughts.

Della flushed and shot Harvey a disapproving glare. 'It's the name of the technique we just used to relocate your husband's shoulder. Dr Ward and I differ on most things, so we'd discussed our preferences outside.'

Funny how those differences of theirs seemed less important here in Fiji. Harvey excused himself to the couple, quietly addressing Della before he left the bedside. 'Don't forget we have that bilateral laparoscopic acromioplasty to get to.' The made-up medical procedure was their secret code for a coffee break.

'I'll be there shortly,' she said with a straight face, turning to the patient with instructions. 'You'll need to wear a sling for the pain, and to help the swelling go down. I'll prescribe you some analgesia for the discomfort, but an ice pack will help too. And needless to say—no more jet-skiing.'

Harvey headed to the break room and flicked on the kettle, the euphoria of working with Della eclipsed by the return of his unsettled thoughts for the future. He made hot drinks, coffee for him and tea for Della, and then crossed the corridor to the deserted doctors' office to check his emails as a distraction, which was where Della found him a few minutes later.

'Thank you for your help back there,' she said, coming into the room. 'And thanks for trusting my technique. I know it's hard for you to take a back seat, control freak that you are.' She pursed her lips playfully, but all Harvey could think about was kissing her. Maybe then he would remember that this was about sex, not friendship or…feelings. Because when it came to relationships, to more than a casual good time, he had no idea what he was doing.

'For you, I'm always happy to take a back seat,' he said, dipping his head closer and dropping his voice in order to distract them both. 'Especially when we're so good together, in and out of work.'

Della laughed, a tiny shudder passing through her body, so he knew she was thinking about last night and this morning, about their near insatiable physical need for each other. Harvey pushed closed the door before drawing her into his arms. 'Is it wrong that I find your bedside manner incredibly sexy?' Without waiting for a response, he pressed his lips to hers, groaning when she speared her fingers through his hair and deepened the kiss.

This was under his control. Feelings had no place in what they were doing. Harvey was most likely having a wobble because he'd opened up to Della about Alice yesterday. Letting someone that close felt...unnatural. But Della had a way of sneaking under his guard.

'It could be considered mildly perverted,' she teased, tugging his lips back to hers.

Harvey gripped her waist and pressed her up against the closed door, pinning her with his hips. 'How can I want you again?' he asked, his lips sliding down the side of her neck. 'I'm seriously concerned for my own health. I feel like that Aussie marsupial mouse, antechinus, that commits reproductive suicide, literally dying from sex-fuelled exhaustion.'

Della laughed, gasped, tilted her head, exposing her neck to his lips. 'Don't be so dramatic. You know very well that the ultraviolet in sunlight increases testosterone levels. You're just holiday horny.'

He laughed and she brought his mouth back to hers, her body writhing restlessly as his hand delved under her blouse to feel bare skin. Thank goodness he wasn't alone. They couldn't seem to keep their hands off each other. Forcing himself to pull back, he rested his forehead against hers. 'I didn't just lure you here for this, you know. I made you a cup of tea.'

'Thank you, but you can lure me anytime.' She kissed him one last time and then pushed him away. 'That being said, we have the entire afternoon of work to get through.' She wiped at his mouth, presumably at the traces of her lip gloss, and straightened her blouse. 'Are you going to Dr Tora's barbecue tonight? We could walk to his place together if you are. It's not far from the hospital, apparently.'

'I'd love to walk with you,' he said, reaching for her hand, his restlessness building now that she was no longer in his arms. Touching her had become a compulsion, one he was trying not to overthink. Their days in Fiji were numbered. With him back in Melbourne and Della returning to Auckland, the necessary break would happen naturally, and Harvey would surely shake off this feeling that, for the first time in twenty years, a relationship that went beyond sex might not be so bad.

'We'd better get back to work,' she said sheepishly. 'The ED is filling up out there.'

Harvey nodded, his hands reluctantly slipping from her waist. 'If I don't see you before, I'll call for you at seven tonight.'

'It's a date.' She smiled, and he felt instantly lighter. She opened the door and ducked out of the office.

Harvey lingered for a few minutes more, trying to

straighten his head. Could he and Della really go back to their former relationship after sharing so much? Could he see her at Jack's naming day and not want her? Could he watch her date and fall in love again without being eaten alive with jealousy?

But what was the alternative? Trying to have more than a physical fling with Della would surely put important areas of his life at risk—his newfound truce with her, his friendship with Brody, his valuable place in the Wilton family. Was he seriously considering taking those risks, not to mention the personal risks to him: that powerlessness he detested so much?

Because if he wasn't careful, if he overstretched and tried to have more than a fling, he might hurt Della and damage his relationships with all of the Wiltons. With those stakes, Harvey had the most to lose.

CHAPTER NINE

LATER THAT EVENING, after a family barbecue at the beautiful beachside home of Dr Tora, Della and Harvey waved goodbye and set off for the stroll back to their hospital accommodation. As soon as they were out of sight of the older man's elegant wooden villa, Harvey reached for Della's hand.

She smiled, shuddered, his touch now familiar but still new enough to affect her entire body with tingles. Because for Della, what had begun as *just sex* was now way more complicated.

'You okay?' he asked, picking up on her strange mood as they headed along the sand. 'You seem a bit quiet.'

'I'm fine—a little tired maybe.' Della faked a big smile, too confused by the way she felt to say more. She'd never in a million years have predicted that her and Harvey's previously strained relationship would turn so harmonious and confusing. Working together, sleeping together, discovering new things about him; it was intense. And now, where Harvey was concerned, she could no longer easily untangle her feelings. She only knew they were dangerous.

'That was a lovely night,' she said to take her mind off the rush of panic. She stepped close, holding on to his arm with her other hand so they could walk side by side along the beach. 'Watching you get thrashed at footy by Dr Tora's grandchildren was a particular highlight for me.'

Harvey smiled, and Della relaxed. She didn't want to drag the evening down with her solemn mood, nor could she explain herself anyway. It wasn't like she could tell Harvey that uncovering his *hidden depths* had changed how she saw him and cracked open the lid on feelings she'd spent years denying. She knew it was ridiculous, but a part of her, the part she was scared to examine too closely, wondered if, in another life, they might have stood a chance of something more than just physical. But Harvey didn't want more.

'That little wiry one kept cheating,' Harvey said, the humour in his dark stare setting off another cascade of longing in Della. 'I caught him literally moving the goalposts more than once.'

Della chuckled, although in truth, the sight of Harvey, playful and sporty, engaging with the group of differing aged kids had made her mouth dry with lust and something else. Fear. Was she at risk of developing real romantic feelings for Harvey?

Her stomach tight with unease, Della clung to the lighter topic. 'I guess that's easily done when the goal is an imaginary line between two coconuts, but well done for being a good sport. I'm not sure Brody would have let them win. He's too competitive.'

And right now, as befuddled as she felt, she really needed Harvey to be rubbish with kids, rubbish at *something*, although if he'd sworn off relationships, he obviously had no burning desire to become a father.

'Speaking of kids,' he said, glancing her way as if he

somehow knew the path her mind had wandered, 'it's Mother's Day tomorrow. Don't forget to message Mrs W.'

Della watched him curiously, her hormones firing once more. Harvey really cared about her mother. Why had she never noticed that before? It was as if, when it came to Harvey, she'd been walking around with her eyes closed.

'If you don't mind,' he added, pulling his phone from his pocket, 'I was going to send her this picture of us.'

Della took a closer look. They were standing together on Dr Tora's veranda with the sea behind them, smiling into the camera, looking tanned and relaxed, Harvey's head tilted in Della's direction.

'Of course not,' Della mumbled, shocked by the contentment she saw shining in her own eyes. Would her mother recognise it? Would Jenny Wilton have awkward questions for them when they were next all together for Jack's naming day? No, she too knew Harvey well enough to know that any sort of relationship would be the last thing on *his* mind. It should be the last thing on Della's mind too, but perhaps this fling had simply proved she was finally ready to move on and start dating again.

Della passed the phone back. Everyone looked happy on holiday, especially if they were also having oodles of awesome sex. Her look of contentment didn't mean anything.

'Do you always wish my mother happy Mother's Day?' she asked, surprised. It just occurred to her that Harvey rarely talked about his own mother. Della knew his parents were divorced, but she'd always assumed his mother must have died.

Harvey shrugged, slipping his phone back into the pocket of his shorts. 'Your parents are like family to me.

Mrs Wilton is the closest thing I have to a mother. She's always been so warm and welcoming. I send her flowers on her birthday, too.' He shot her a smug smile, and Della's pulse fluttered at his thoughtfulness.

'You complete and utter suck-up,' Della said in mock outrage. 'Show up me and Brody, why don't you.' But her rampant curiosity flared into an inferno. 'What happened to *your* mother? I've never heard you talk about her.'

A week ago she wouldn't have dared ask him such a personal question. But she and Harvey had come a long way since that first day in Fiji. Now he was her first thought when she opened her eyes. His appearance brought excitement, not annoyance. With every day that passed, with every new revelation she learned, she felt their deepening emotional connection. Perhaps that was the problem. It was time to go home and leave their holiday and their fling behind... She swallowed that metallic taste of fear. It would be a relief to leave Fiji next week, so she could feel back to normal.

'My parents split up when I was eight,' Harvey said, stiffening slightly at her side. 'She wasn't around much after that.' He kicked at a seashell, sending it skittering along the sand.

Della held her breath, a knot forming under her ribs. Brody often said that Harvey didn't like to rake over the past, but there was obviously more to the story. 'But she's still alive?' Della gently pushed, wondering if his estranged relationship with his mother shaped him. How could it not?

He nodded, keeping his face turned away, his gaze trained on the ocean and the setting sun on the horizon.

'She visited for a while after she left my dad. But soon, her visits dwindled.'

Della's stomach clenched with empathy. Why? Surely she'd want to see her son? 'I'm sorry, Harvey,' she whispered. 'That must have been hard for you and Bill.'

Why had she never asked about his mother before? Why had she never bothered to scratch the surface of this complex man? Out of fear, maybe, because she'd been trying to keep her distance? Falling for twenty-three-year-old Harvey Ward would have been younger Della's stupidest move. If the timing had been right for them both when they'd first met, she suspected that she would have fallen hard.

He shrugged, but now that she knew the real man so much better, Della tensed, instinctively attuned to his vulnerability. 'I was lucky,' he said, almost as if persuading them both. 'I got to live with my dad. He's a great father who always made time for me.'

'I have a lot of respect for Bill,' Della agreed. 'But as a kid, you would have loved both your parents.' She couldn't seem to let this go, as if finally she'd caught a glimpse of the innermost layer of Harvey Ward. The missing piece of the puzzle that would put everything into perspective and maybe help Della untangle her conflicted feelings.

Harvey winced, and Della's heart broke for him. 'I was torn in the beginning,' he said simply, but she felt him stiffen. 'Being happy to stay with my dad felt wrong, as did begging for my mother to take me with her every time she visited and then left again.'

'That's a horrible position to be in.' Della blinked away

the sting in her eyes, grateful for the failing light. 'No kid should feel as if they have to choose a parent.'

What had his mother's repeated abandonment done to intelligent, caring Harvey? He must have felt so confused. Yes, he was close to his father, but that wouldn't wholly make up for his absent mother. No wonder he'd kind of adopted *Mrs W*, as he affectionately called Jenny Wilton, as an honorary mother.

'In the end, my mother made the choice for me.' He turned to face her, a sad, bitter smile touching his lips and his eyes hard. 'By the time I was ten, she'd remarried a man who had two little girls and moved out of state. I didn't really hear from her again after that. She chose her new life, her new stepdaughters, over me.'

Della's chest ached, her sore heart racing. Harvey had grown up feeling rejected by the one woman who was supposed to always be there for him, to love him unconditionally with a mother's special brand of love. Had that abandonment strengthened his reaction to his girlfriend's sudden death, made him the self-confessed loner who didn't believe in commitment and love?

'I wish I'd known this sooner,' Della said, her world rocked by his confession and what it meant. Did he want to be alone forever, or was he, like Della, simply scared to risk his heart again because life had taught him that the women he loved disappeared or let him down, or chose someone else?

This past week, buffeted by revelation after revelation, she'd just about managed to cling to their carefree and casual sexual chemistry. But how could she keep her feelings for Harvey in check, knowing what she now knew? How could she fit him back inside that box where she was safe from the way he made her feel—as if they might actually stand a chance?

'I don't like to talk about it,' he said, his voice gruff. 'It's bad enough to remember how powerless I felt at the time, to admit how many years I spent pushing myself, trying to be a son she could be proud of in the hopes that she'd one day come back for me.'

Della squeezed his hand. 'I understand.' Of course he would feel powerless, never knowing if or when his mother might visit, wondering if he'd done something wrong, grieving and confused. Driven, intelligent Harvey would hate feeling that way. And then history had kind of repeated itself when Alice too was suddenly and definitively ripped from his life. No wonder he chose to keep his relationships superficial after that to avoid the risk of being hurt again. Harvey liked to be in control, and there was nothing worse than love for turning your world upside down.

Della reeled as they walked in silence for a few minutes. But she couldn't stay quiet for long, not when Harvey's pain was palpable. When the real Harvey, scarred and battle-weary, called to her, because they had so much in common. When it would be so easy to fall for the man she was getting to know, but for one giant obstacle: he wasn't the right man because they still wanted different things.

'You know,' she said, gripping his arm, 'you're not powerless now. You said it yourself—your life is good. You're successful and hot and, despite trying to hide it from me for the past nineteen years, a really good guy. *I'm* proud of you, especially given I used to think you were just a jerk.' Della tried to smile, clinging to humour to keep things light, desperate to feel the way she used to feel about him, before they'd come to Fiji. With that Harvey, she'd known exactly what to expect. She'd known she was safe.

Harvey returned Della's smile, dragging her close and pressing a kiss to her forehead. 'I see the need to offer compliments is catching. Maybe we should get off this island before we fall madly in love with each other.'

Della stiffened, his joke falling flat. There was something about it she just couldn't find funny, as if one more revelation, one more day working at his side or night in his arms would push her over the edge towards deep, deep feelings.

'It's not magical water, Harvey.' Retreating to their usual banter, Della forced herself to remember that it had been twenty years since Harvey had so much as thought about a relationship, let alone love. His mother's rejection was as heartbreaking as his girlfriend's death, but whatever his reasons for staying single, it meant that Harvey was seriously inexperienced when it came to commitment. She might like, respect and empathise with him now, but she'd still be a fool to fall for a man with so little relationship history, who only wanted to be in control of his feelings. *She* wanted more, so much more.

'Phew, well, that's a relief,' he said, casting her a playful smile and slinging his arm around her waist, the subject closed.

Della walked at his side on shaky legs, glad to have the conversation back on lighter topics. She *wasn't* stupid. When she was ready to fall in love again, she needed a man who knew what he wanted, whose dreams of commitment and a family matched her own. She wouldn't make the same mistake—falling for the wrong guy—twice.

But later, just before she drifted off to sleep in Harvey's bed, her mind returned to the idea that, with the exception of him being so rusty when it came to relationships and having very good reasons for protecting his heart, Harvey ticked an awful lot of boxes.

CHAPTER TEN

THE NEXT DAY was Sunday. Harvey suggested a walk to Vatuwai Falls, the relatively remote waterfall Dr Tora had recommended to them the day before. They'd spent the past hour walking inland from the nearest village, holding hands when the width of the track through the forest allowed. Of course, with Della wearing her sexy denim cut-off shorts, which made her backside look great, single file also had its advantages.

'There it is,' Della called excitedly over the sound of tumbling water. She shot him an excited smile and rounded the final bend in the forest track ahead of Harvey, disappearing out of sight.

Harvey lengthened his strides to catch up, Della's enthusiasm contagious. But she made everything better, brighter, richer. They laughed together. He slept more soundly with her in his arms. She even made the workday pass quicker. What was he going to do without her back in Australia? And how had she sneaked so close that he'd opened up and told her about his mother?

'I'm going in,' Della said as he joined her at the edge of the water.

The falls were nestled in the shade of the island's lush rainforest, the pool beneath ten feet of cascading water, cool and inviting. And they had the place to themselves. Della dropped her backpack and took off her T-shirt and shorts to reveal her gorgeous bikini-clad body, her stare full of that familiar challenge that boiled his blood. Harvey's mouth, already thirsty from the heat of the day and the physical exertion of the trek from the car, dried further with longing. How could he want her again when they'd had sex at sunrise? How would he ever switch off this ravenous craving? How would he see her in the future and not want her the way he wanted her now?

It was crazy, but since they'd started to get to know each other on a deeper, personal level, since he'd seen her fears and insecurities and felt comfortable to open up to her about his past, he'd started to imagine things. Terrifying things. Things that took the control he loved and snapped it clean in two.

Could Della and he have something more than a sexual fling? Could she ever take him seriously? Could she ever want a man like him? Della dreamed of the whole fairy tale, and he was not only severely rusty when it came to feelings, he was also scared that he might be broken. Maybe it was just the magic of Fiji, the dreamlike bubble away from reality. Perhaps it was that until they'd been forced to spend time together, he hadn't really known the real Della at all, and it was just messing with his head.

'Careful,' he called as she gingerly traversed the rocks at the edge of the pool before stepping into the ankle-deep water. They were at least an hour's walk away from the nearest village and further to proper medical care. If one of them slipped, had an accident out here, they'd be in serious trouble.

'Come on, Harvey; it's lovely.' Della ignored his warning and waded into deeper water, the surface lapping against the tops of her thighs, wetting her coral-pink bikini bottoms. Before his brain could re-engage, she dived under the water and surfaced closer to the plunge pool at the base of the waterfall.

Harvey dropped his backpack next to hers and quickly removed his T-shirt and shoes. He was already wearing board shorts, so he followed Della into the pool, the shock of cool water on his skin a welcome reset to the fire she'd set in his blood. When the water reached his hips, he dived in and swam in swift strokes after Della.

'Keep up,' she said, turning onto her back and laughing.

Della was a strong swimmer—she'd told him it was the only sport Brody wasn't good at, because he didn't have the patience to train—and she loved to throw out challenges. Normally he was happy to accept them. But today, maybe because he'd told her about his mother last night, maybe because he'd been reminded how Della's family was also his, how he needed the Wiltons more than ever what with Bill's diagnosis, he was feeling exposed. Needing to get his hands on her to switch off that part of his brain focussed on reason and problem-solving, the part wondering if they could possibly work in the real world, when Harvey had abandoned the things Della wanted years ago, he powered through the water, catching up to her at the base of the waterfall. Della laughed, tried to get away, splashed him in the face.

She might be a stronger swimmer, but Harvey was faster. He snagged her around the waist, treading water as he dragged her nearly naked body against his, so she was all soft curves and slippery skin, taunting him with

JC HARROWAY   113

the things he couldn't have. Because soon, he'd have to give her up, give this up.

The minute they touched, Della back in his arms where she felt way too right, need roared through his blood. 'You always keep me on my toes, do you know that?' He dipped his mouth to hers, captured her smiling lips and kissed her.

She draped her arms around his shoulders and kissed him back, her lips parting, her tongue sliding against his so his arousal flickered in his shorts. 'Well, just because you like to be in control, we can't have you growing complacent.' Laughing, she wriggled free of his arms and kicked away.

Complacent? How could he ever feel settled around Della? She made him unstable, as if he was spinning at the centre of a whirlwind, caught between opposing emotions—fear that he could never be what she needed and an almost overwhelming desire to let her in anyway. But he'd spent twenty years keeping people, including Della, out.

Needing her touch to dampen some of the panic, Harvey caught her again, gripping her waist. 'No chance to be complacent with you around,' he mumbled against her lips, stealing another kiss. To douse the heat they generated when they touched and to pay Della back for the splash to the face, Harvey kicked his legs, guiding them both under the cascading wall of water. The force and shock of the water hitting their heads broke them apart, gasping.

On the far side of the falls, Della laughed, reached for his shoulders and kissed him playfully. 'You always have to win, don't you?'

'Of course.' He grinned, his stomach hollow. There

was one aspect of his life where he hadn't excelled: relationships. Even if Della wanted more than these two stolen weeks in Fiji, with him of all men, was he capable of giving her more than sex? He didn't want to let her down or cause her pain. She'd been hurt enough in the past, and hurting her would mean disappointing, possibly losing, all the Wiltons. But could he really walk away, knowing that this attraction between them had always been there, knowing that he would see her again and again, knowing that now he had nowhere left to hide? She knew all his shameful secrets.

She kissed him, her tongue surging against his as her legs wrapped around his waist under the water. Her bikini-clad body scalded his skin, driving him from memories to the present. Harvey gripped her waist, his toes touching the rocky bottom of the pool. Behind the waterfall, the sunlight was dappled, and the natural pool of shoulder-high water extended into a cave carved from the rocks of the overhanging cliff. Some primal urge shifted through him, a feeling that they might be the only two people on the planet. Nothing seemed to matter beyond how her touch, her kisses, her saying his name made him feel... invincible.

'Why can't I keep my hands off you?' he groaned, growing harder inside his swim shorts as she dropped her head back, exposing her neck to his kisses.

'I know what you mean.' She gripped his waist tighter with her thighs, her breasts bobbing on the surface of the water, their creamy curves teasing him, as if begging for his touch, his mouth. Harvey cupped one breast, his hand sliding down her bikini top and raising the nipple to his lips.

'Harvey...' She sighed and slipped her fingers through his wet hair, releasing her hold on his waist so she slid a little further down his hips.

The heat of her bathed his erection through his shorts. He was struggling to think again, his only instinct to bury himself inside her and chase the mind-numbing oblivion that was never far away when they touched. If he could focus on this, on pleasure, for just a few more days, surely his perspective would return once he was away from the temptation of Della.

Harvey untied the top of her bikini so the cups fell. He switched sides, his grip on her waist tightening as he laved the other nipple. He looked up. Della was watching him, her eyes heavy with desire.

'I want you all the time,' he said, turning them around and backing up against the rocky ledge at the edge of the pool so he could hold her there with his hips. 'What are we doing to each other?'

'I don't know, but let's not stop yet,' she said, gasping when his hand slid between her legs and inside her bikini bottoms.

He was out of control for her, a rage of hormones and terrifying feelings. Fear gripped his throat. What if this all-consuming need for each other didn't fade once they returned to their respective lives in Australia and New Zealand? What if a part of him always pined for Fiji, for Della? What if seeing her back in the real world brought the nice, neat life he'd constructed for himself crashing down around his head? What if she was the only person who could fix it, but she didn't want him?

Before his thoughts could disappear down that blind-ending tunnel, Della slid her hand between their bodies, inside his shorts, and cupped his erection, massaging him in her tight fist so his mind blanked. Harvey dragged his mouth from hers, the last thread of reason strung taut to the snapping point. 'We don't have a condom.'

'I'm okay without it if you are,' she said, kissing the side of his neck while she continued to stroke him under the water.

Harvey groaned, capturing her lips once more. They trusted each other. Knew each other. Neither of them would put the other at risk. Because he was consumed by desire, because she was looking at him as if he could give her everything she needed, Harvey untied one side of Della's bikini bottoms so the fabric slid away from between her legs.

She braced her arms around his shoulders as she sank a little lower, her stare holding his. 'I want you, Harvey.'

Triumph rocked him. He gripped her waist and pushed inside her, the heat of her fanning the rampant flames in his belly. Could she want him for more than sex? Could he give her what she deserved, what she craved? Commitment? But what if he failed, let her down, ruined things for them and for himself?

'Yes,' she hissed as he filled her, her lips parted on her soft gasp, distracting him from thoughts that had no place in what they'd agreed to: a fling.

He cupped her face, bringing her mouth back to his, pressing his tongue against hers, overtaken by an uncontrollable sense of wildness to focus only on this physical connection they'd found and moulded into something unfamiliar but so meaningful.

'Don't stop,' she said when they parted for air. She spread one arm and clung to the rocky ledge at her back while Harvey gripped her waist under the water, held her close to the rhythmic thrust of his hips.

'You're beautiful. I've never wanted anyone this much,' he choked out, watching arousal darken her eyes. 'You know I've always felt this way about you, don't you, since that first time we met?'

She gasped at his honest declaration, something in her stare telling him she too had denied their attraction. But there was no point hiding it. She made him crazy and always had, this possibility there between them since the start, as if waiting for the time to be right. But was *right* enough? As soon as Della was ready to date, she'd be looking for *the one*. Whereas Harvey was so far behind when it came to relationships, he might never catch up. They might never be on the same page. What if he tried and failed?

Because he didn't want to think about where that would leave him once they returned to normality, Harvey dived for her breast, raising it to his lips and sucking. Della cried out, one arm around his neck, holding him close.

'Yes, yes,' she moaned, so he picked up the pace, driving her higher, even as he fought off his own release. He could give her this, give her a part of himself he hadn't given anyone in twenty years. He'd let Della in emotionally. It was no wonder he felt bombarded by unfamiliar impulses.

'Della…' he groaned, his hips jerking erratically, faster and harder, his need for her boiling over.

She gasped, her fingernails digging into his shoulder as she shattered in his arms, holding him so close as her orgasm crested that all Harvey could do was crush her to his chest, bury his face against her neck and follow with a harsh cry.

'Are you okay?' he muttered, his lips against her skin, as he held her tight and came down from the high.

She nodded, retying her bikini top at the back of her neck. Slipping from her body, he helped her retie the bottoms, his insides trembling. What was she doing to him? And how would he return to his solitary life when he'd allowed her so close he feared she might be able to see through him as if he was made of glass?

Silently, they swam back under the waterfall to the main pool, holding hands as they waded ashore. Harvey glanced her way as they sat on the rocks in a shaft of tree-dappled sunlight to dry off and rehydrate. Was she, like him, moved by the intensity of what they'd just done? Was he being a fool to think she could ever take him seriously when it came to more than sex? Della was a practical, intelligent woman who knew exactly what she wanted. Could he ever be enough?

'Just to reassure you,' she said, leaning against his arm, 'because you've gone suddenly quiet—I'm on the pill. No need to worry about an unwanted consequence.' She looked up at him, the way she'd looked at him last night when he'd told her about his mother, as if he finally made sense.

'Thanks for the reassurance.' Harvey snagged her hand, raised it to his lips and pressed a kiss there. 'But I was thinking how we only have a few more days left, and how it will be extra hard to leave Fiji this time.' Because as soon as the real world encroached, they would be over. Did she still want that? Was there any part of her that wanted to see where this could lead?

She nodded, releasing a small shuddering sigh. 'I know what you mean.' She smiled at him, her expression relaxed. 'Best holiday ever.'

Harvey pulled on his T-shirt, needing to be less exposed. 'But you still want a baby, right?' he said, some inexplicable force in control of his words. 'Just not mine, obviously.' His gut twisted. With fear or some foreign ache? But he wanted Della to be happy, even if he couldn't be the man to make her so.

Della stilled, glancing over at him as if he'd asked some sort of trick question that required a considered answer. 'I do,' she said, looking down at her feet, flexing her toes in the water. 'But perhaps when I'm ready, I'll... I don't know...go it alone. Use a sperm donor. After all, I'm nearly thirty-eight. My time for finding Mr Right is running out.'

Jealous at the idea of Della with another man, Harvey pressed his lips together. Her lifestyle choices were none of his business. He certainly wasn't qualified to be the man of her dreams. It had been many years since Harvey had allowed himself to think about wanting a family. But would she truly be content to go it alone?

'That's certainly one way to go,' he said, keeping his voice light, although his throat burned. 'But isn't the adoring husband a crucial part of your dream life?'

Could he bear to watch Della walk down the aisle again now that they'd become...not friends exactly. In fact, there was no label for what they'd become. But for Harvey, it was the most meaningful connection he'd ever had. Why else would he have confided in her about his mother's abandonment? Why else was he constructing wild and improbable imaginings where he was a different man, a man worthy of Della? Especially when those imaginings put a huge part of his life—his valued place in the Wilton family—at risk.

'He was crucial...' Della rolled her eyes, looking mildly embarrassed. 'But I've kind of had my fingers burned. Maybe pushing so hard for a family was what scared off Ethan. Perhaps it's better to have part of my dream than to push for it all and end up with nothing again.'

Pricks of unease tensed Harvey's shoulders. 'Didn't he know you wanted a family before he proposed?' If Ethan had known the first thing about Della, surely it was that she'd always wanted to be a mother.

'Of course he did,' Della said, ducking her head so he could no longer see her eyes. 'But obviously he wasn't ready, or I asked for too much and ended up losing everything.'

Harvey gripped her arms, turning her to face him, his heart racing. 'Why shouldn't you have everything you want? It's not that you asked for too much, it's that Ethan sold you a lie or said one thing and then changed his mind.' His protective instincts built to a frenzy. He didn't want Della to ever doubt herself, or be scared to risk another relationship, scared to trust her judgement.

Despite being out of his depth, Harvey cupped her chin and raised her gaze back to his. 'Don't make that about you, when it was clearly his issue. You shouldn't have needed to convince him, Della. He should have understood your dreams and supported them. That's the promise he made when he married you. I was there; I heard the vows.'

Della stared, speechless, blinking up at him. Then she

dropped her gaze. 'Marriage is complex, I guess…' She shrugged, a small, vulnerable smile on her lips. 'Despite the way Brody makes it look easy.'

Harvey winced, hearing the hint of dismissal in what she left unsaid. Of course Harvey had no right to offer advice, knowing so little about commitment and nothing about marriage. She knew it. He knew it. Just because they were good together, just because he'd started to wonder if they had a future together, didn't make him some sort of instant relationship guru.

'You're right,' Harvey said, reaching for his towel to dry his legs. 'I'm the last man in the world qualified to give relationship advice. I'm not even sure I'm capable of being in one after avoiding them all these years.' He shoved his feet into his walking boots, withdrawing because he was so obviously out of his depth, and she could see right through him. She wanted a husband, a baby, and he was ill-qualified to make her the promise of even a real date.

'Maybe you're right to go it alone,' he added, stowing his towel in his backpack. 'Why wait around for some perfect guy to sweep you off your feet? If you want a baby, you should have one. Cute tiny humans. What's not to love?' Harvey shut his mouth. He had no idea what *he* wanted. But the idea of Della being a solo parent was almost as unsettling as the idea of watching her date men who were better qualified than him to be in a relationship.

Feeling powerless again, he reached for her hand and pulled her to her feet. 'Come on. Let's head back to the car. It's getting late.'

Eyeing him with curiosity, Della dressed and pulled on her backpack. They set off along the track through the forest, hand in hand once more. Harvey took some deep breaths, willing the storm inside his chest to abate. He needed to be careful. His thoughts, his imaginings were writing cheques he wasn't certain he could afford. He was the last man on Earth who should make Della any sort of promise. In a few more days, and they'd be back to their real lives. All he needed to do was silence the crazy possibilities in his head, enjoy the rest of their time together and try to ensure that their new close relationship survived once they'd each moved on.

CHAPTER ELEVEN

MONDAY MORNING, the day after their trek to Vatuwai Falls, Della awoke to find Harvey's note on her pillow.

Gone for an early run. See you at work x

She smiled, her heart fluttering with longing but her head slamming on the brakes. She headed for the shower, mulling over the intense conversation from the day before, when they'd talked about babies and her marriage and her dreams to have it all. It must have been her imagination, because Harvey had seemed...wistful? But she'd likely still been high from the way he'd touched her under the waterfall, as if he had no choice. The way he'd consumed her with his kisses and that hungry stare as he'd pushed inside her body. The way he'd confessed to always wanting her that way.

But that was just sex. Attraction. She'd felt it too, simmering away between them all these years. So why was she torturing herself with rumination when he'd also soon after warned her that he wasn't capable of being in a committed relationship? Just because she understood his heartbreaking reasons for being single didn't change the fact that he was essentially a relationship virgin, and

Della was a veteran with one failed campaign, next time searching for *the one*. And she couldn't afford to get it wrong again.

Quickly dressing, Della drank a cup of tea and dried her hair, her feelings a confused mess. But feelings, whatever shape they took, were irrelevant where Harvey was concerned. Anything beyond respect and lust was ridiculous. This was *Harvey*. Single for the past twenty years Harvey. Even if, through some major transformation, he wanted to temporarily continue their fling when they left Fiji, not only was it was physically impossible—he lived in Australia and she lived in New Zealand—it was also a huge risk to Della. If she was sleeping with Harvey, she wouldn't be dating someone else, someone who wanted to settle down, to fall in love and start a family. That was a lot to give up for *just sex*.

Trying and failing to forget about Harvey, Della arrived at the hospital. She'd barely made it to the department of surgery when an urgent call came through. She hurried to the ED, finding Harvey just ahead of her in the corridor, his hair still damp from a shower.

'What do we have?' Della asked, meeting his stare as a flurry of butterflies shifted inside her.

'Suspected stabbing, I think,' he said, shooting her a secret smile and then switching on his game face.

That's what Della needed to do. Pretend she had everything under control. Then, maybe by the time she arrived home, it would be true. Her feelings would shift into perspective and life would go back to normal, without Harvey.

Seema, the ED nurse, met them inside the resuscitation bay. 'We have a fifty-six-year-old man presenting with acute shortness of breath,' she said, handing over the ambulance report. 'Paramedics found what looks like a stab wound in his left chest wall. Erect chest X-ray results should be through any second.'

Della and Harvey rushed to opposite sides of the patient. The man was conscious, pale and sweaty and unable to talk for breathlessness. On autopilot, Della checked his vital signs on the monitor and then reached for a tourniquet. While Harvey palpated his abdomen and listened to his chest, Della drew blood from the man's arm.

'Reduced breath sounds on the left,' he told her and then added to Seema, 'I need a chest drain, please, and an urgent echo. We need to make sure the knife hasn't penetrated other structures in the chest.'

Keeping one eye on the blood pressure monitor, Della quickly labelled the blood tubes for the lab, passing them to a hospital porter. 'I've ordered a cross-match for blood transfusion,' she informed Seema. 'Have the police been called?' This obviously wasn't a self-inflicted wound.

The nurse nodded and set about replacing the empty bag of intravenous fluid feeding the drip in the patient's arm. Harvey tapped at the computer keys, bringing up the digital chest X-ray, which showed a white-out of half the left lung, indicating the presence of blood in the chest.

'Haemorthorax,' he confirmed, glancing at Della. She joined him at the monitor and took a closer look, scouring the image. 'Looks like some free air there under the diaphragm, too.' It was subtle, but free air in the abdominal cavity suggested a puncture of the stomach or intestine. 'The knife must have passed through the diaphragm.'

Harvey gave a nod, clearly on the same wavelength. Stabbing injuries to the chest, while clearly life-threatening, could also enter the peritoneal cavity and damage abdominal organs. And given the man's blood pressure was dipping dangerously low, the best way to assess trauma to the spleen, liver or kidney was an exploratory laparotomy. There was no time to hesitate.

'I'll call theatre and the anaesthetist,' Della said, reaching for the phone. 'You insert the chest drain.' The sooner they operated, the sooner they could stop any haemorrhaging and repair the perforation to the gut.

With the man booked in for an emergency laparotomy, Della quickly washed up, pulled on sterile gloves and joined Harvey on the patient's left side. Harvey swabbed the skin of the man's left chest wall and administered some local anaesthetic. Chances were there was a partial collapse of the lung along with blood inside the chest cavity. The chest drain would drain the blood and help the lung to re-expand. While Harvey carefully but expertly inserted the chest tube to drain the blood and escaped air, Della explained the man's injuries to him and consented him for theatre.

Thirty minutes later, with the patient anaesthetised and his abdomen opened up, Della found the puncture to the stomach along with a two-centimetre laceration of the liver.

'There's the hole in the diaphragm,' Harvey said, repositioning the suction to clear the operative field of blood.

'Thanks,' Della said, reaching for a suture. 'Let's sew up the liver first. Then we'll tackle the stomach.'

Harvey turned to the scrub nurse. 'Can we have a laparoscope, please?' He turned back to Della. 'We can take a look inside the chest before we close the hole in the diaphragm, make sure the pericardium is intact.'

'Good idea.' Della nodded, her eyes meeting his for a second. The echo had shown the heart and the sack around it appeared normal, but it didn't hurt to double-check while the patient was under anaesthesia.

Without getting in each other's way, they repaired the liver laceration and stitched up the stomach perforation. Operating together had become so intuitive now, Della worried that she might forget how to do it alone when their time in Fiji was over. But she couldn't rely on Harvey for anything. Reality was calling. By the end of this week, he'd go his way and she'd go hers, and this, *them*, would be over.

She waited for the rush of relief, but it didn't come. Perhaps that was simply because they still had one more test to get through before they were truly out of the woods when it came to moving on: Jack's naming day. She would see Harvey again in a couple of weeks. It was hard to believe that she wouldn't want him still. But indulging would only delay the inevitable, and she'd be foolish to endlessly pursue a dead end. She couldn't have Harvey forever, so it was best to make a clean break after Fiji. To try and switch off the constant need for him. To fill her thoughts with something other than Harvey and how he made her feel as if she'd been alone for long enough, that as long as she kept her eye on the prize, she *could* achieve her dreams.

An hour later, with the surgery complete and the patient headed to the surgical ward, they de-gowned, washed up and headed for the staff room.

'I need tea,' Della said, flicking on the kettle. Maybe it was a good idea to start weaning herself off Harvey now, before she became any more attached.

Harvey passed Della the tea bags, his stare distracted. 'Let's sit down for a few minutes. I have something to tell you.' He busied himself with making black coffee, his expression serious so Della's nerves fluttered in her chest.

'Oh, oh. That sounds…ominous.' Della added milk to her tea, her mind unhelpfully filling in the blanks. Was he flying home early as she'd teased that day they'd agreed to their fling? Given that she'd literally just decided to start a controlled exit, that shouldn't matter, but her stomach took a sickening dive nonetheless, telling her she was already in trouble.

'I think it's good news,' Harvey said, leading the way to two comfy armchairs in the corner of the staff room.

'What is it?' Della asked impatiently, taking a seat.

'I checked my work emails this morning.' Harvey settled into the chair next to her and placed his coffee on a side table. 'Dr Jones, one of my senior colleagues, has announced his retirement.' His stare met hers, so she saw a flicker of excitement there. 'They'll be appointing his replacement, if you're interested.'

His tone was casual, but Della stilled, her heart racing with both a surge of excitement and a greater sense of panic. Before Fiji, before she'd slept with Harvey again, before she'd seen the other side of him, a job back in her native Melbourne doing what she loved would have been a dream come true. But now…the idea of working in Harvey's department came with extra considerations. Could she see him every day and get over him, over this fling, at the same time?

'You don't like the idea,' he said, his voice flat.

'It's not that.' Della touched his arm. 'I'm thinking,'

she hedged, her mind racing as fast as her pulse. 'Has the job even been advertised yet?'

'Not yet,' Harvey confirmed, ignoring his coffee while he observed her intently. 'But there have to be some perks when you're sleeping with the head of the department.' He flashed her a cheeky wink. 'I'm giving you advanced warning, before the job goes public.'

'There's no guarantee I'd get it, of course,' she mumbled, unable to meet his stare. Maybe the fact that a big part of her loved the idea was reason in itself to be cautious. Yes, their time in Fiji had proved that when it came to their jobs, they could get along just fine. But that was with a set expiration date for the end of their fling. It would be a very different story if their physical relationship limped along back in Melbourne, until one of them—Della because she wanted more, or Harvey because he didn't—broke it off. And what then?

Could she continue to take the only part of him on offer, sex, knowing he was too scared to ever consider having a real relationship? Could she work in the same department as Harvey every day and watch him return to his single life? Could she see him socially with her family and still manage to keep her own feelings at bay? Because she could not fall for Harvey Ward. They wanted different things. She'd be humiliated again. Hurt. And she'd only have herself to blame for making the same mistake twice.

'Hmm…' she offered, 'perhaps I'm just too tired to think straight. We have been living on very little sleep for a week.' Della tried to smile, but it felt like a grimace. 'Perhaps we should sleep alone tonight and catch up.' She felt sick. Suddenly she had no idea what she wanted, but some distance, some time away from Harvey to think, might help.

'Of course…' he said, concern and guilt hovering in his stare. Then he frowned, glanced down at his hands. 'I'll be honest. I thought you'd be a little more enthusiastic about the job. After the hard time you gave me three years ago, I assumed moving back to Melbourne was still something you really wanted.'

'It *is* something I want,' Della said unconvincingly. 'I'm just considering all the implications.'

'What implications?' His frown deepened.

'You know…' Della squirmed. 'Us, working together.' There was a lot to think about. It wasn't a decision she could rush, not if she hoped to protect herself in the process.

'We've managed to do that successfully for over a week, Della.' Harvey shrugged, a flicker of hurt in his eyes. 'Why would Melbourne be any different?'

Della swallowed. That was exactly her point—it *wouldn't* be any different. With the exception of their fling being over, everything would be the same. Harvey would still be avoiding relationships, because on some level he was scared to be vulnerable after being abandoned by his mother and losing Alice. And Della wanted a relationship, but would still be terrified to pin all her dreams on another person in case she got it wrong again. But the fact that Harvey was suggesting them working together would be easy told Della exactly where his head was. For him, it was straightforward. The fling would be over, business as usual, no problem. Whereas Della already suspected she'd take longer to adjust, that her feelings, her desire for him, would take time to switch off.

Hoping the wild flutter of her pulse wasn't obvious, Della breathed through her fear and met his stare. 'It's not that we *couldn't* successfully work together, Harvey. It's just… It would be intense after…you know…everything we've shared here. It will take some time to adjust to going back to what we were before. That's all.'

She couldn't bring herself to call them friends. She had a sneaking suspicion that Harvey would always be tempting. She'd known going into this fling that it was temporary, but now that it was almost over, now that she understood him, now that she saw he might be too broken to allow himself to be happy, to believe he was loveable, there was a part of Della that couldn't help but wonder *what if*?

What if he could see that he was worthy of being loved? What if he overcame his fear and gave a real relationship a shot? What if she and Harvey *could* work?

'I think we could make it work,' he said, as if reading her mind. But where she was talking about a relationship between them, he meant them working together in the same department.

Della almost laughed at how out of sync they were, but instead nodded vaguely, her fatigue weighing heavily. Of course she was so much more invested emotionally than Harvey. He'd spent twenty years holding people away, whereas she wore her *heart on her sleeve*, as he'd said. Just because he'd told her about Alice and his mother didn't make Della special. He was still putting up emotional barriers, and if she wasn't very careful, she'd make a fool of herself and get hurt.

'I'd hate our fling to be the reason you didn't apply,'

he pushed, making it sound so easy, so cold and clinical. 'I know how much you miss being close to your family.'

Della nodded, her heart sinking. That was Harvey— his mind on the fling, confident that when it was over, he'd just slip back into his single life. But he'd warned her that he was no good at relationships. He'd abandoned messy emotions years ago, because they made him feel powerless. If she'd ignored the obvious signposts, that was *her* problem.

'Well, I'll definitely look out for the job ad,' she said. 'Thanks for the heads-up.'

'Great,' he said, sounding less certain than before.

Della swallowed the lump in her throat, glugged her tea and pasted on a bright smile she was far from feeling. He seemed merely worried about a bit of workplace awkwardness, given the amount of sex they'd had. He hadn't mentioned them continuing to see each other after Fiji, but then, what did she expect? And was she really going to miss out on her dream job again because of Harvey, when all she needed to do was put this fling behind her as easily?

'I might head back to the emergency department,' Della said, standing. 'See what's happening before I call it a day. You finish your coffee.'

He nodded, clearly bewildered, and she fled, needing some distance. As she walked, she gave herself a stern talking to. Clearly Harvey saw no problems with them working together, because he fully intended to return to his old life. It was only soppy, romantic Della who was overthinking it with improbable what-ifs.

Even if by some miracle, Harvey wanted a real relationship, when it came to commitment, he was beyond rusty. Della couldn't afford to carry him while he tried a relationship on for size. Nor, with time to build her dreams running out, could she afford to be wrong again about anyone, including Harvey.

Harvey walked into the ED, guilt and confusion still knotting his insides. Della *had* looked tired. Was his constant need for her selfish? Their time together in Fiji had been intense. Perhaps she was right. Perhaps a night in their own beds would help them both achieve some clarity.

So why did he feel so crushed, as if Della was already withdrawing from him, despite the fact they still had three nights of their holiday left? He glanced around, hoping to spy her, as if one of her smiles would settle the doubts coiling inside him. Her tepid reaction to his news of a job vacancy had completely swept his feet from under him. He'd assumed she'd be overjoyed to come home, not hesitant. But maybe she was right to apply the brakes. Maybe he should proceed with caution, too. After all, a job in his department represented a significant move for Della, and seeing her every day at work would be an adjustment for them both. Maybe Harvey was too invested in the idea of them working together long-term, whereas Della intended for them to return to the way they were. Maybe he was jumping the gun when he should be preparing himself for the end of their fling instead.

A growing sense of foreboding urged him onwards in his search. If he only knew what she was thinking… He found Della in resus with a patient, a boy around ten years old, and his father. His heart lurched at the sight of her as if they'd been estranged for years, not minutes.

As he approached, Della looked up with no evidence

of her earlier doubts. 'Dr Ward, this is Taito. He fell from his trampoline this afternoon. I was just explaining to Dad that he has a fractured femur.'

The boy moaned in pain. Harvey greeted the patient and his father, stepping close to Della to examine the X-ray on the screen, while a trickle of relief calmed his pulse.

'Mid-shaft, spiral fracture,' she said to Harvey, placing a butterfly needle in the crook of Taito's left arm before addressing the boy. 'I'm going to give you some more medicine for the pain.' She injected the painkillers slowly into the vein and then touched the boy's shoulder in comfort, her expression full of her signature compassion.

Harvey's pulse bounded as he watched her work. Della was such a caring person, that big heart of hers making her so hard to resist. No wonder he was struggling.

A fresh wave of panic struck him. He wanted more time.

'Skin traction will help with pain relief,' Harvey said, staring into her eyes, searching for her true feelings, desperate to know how she felt about him to help him understand what was going on inside his own head.

'I'll get that organised with Seema,' she said, holding his eye contact as if silently communicating something he was too confused to see.

'Want me to ring the on-call orthopaedic reg?' he asked, needing to be near her because she made him feel better, but also aware that she was nearing the end of a long day, and he could help out.

'Yes, please,' she said, flicking him a look of gratitude. 'I'll meet you in the office shortly.'

Harvey used the phone in the doctors' office to speak

to his orthopaedic colleague, making the referral. Taito's fracture would need internal fixation surgery, but he and Della could pass the case on. He'd not long hung up the phone when Della appeared.

'Long day...' she said, taking the seat beside his to add a note to the patient's file.

'How is Taito?' he asked, wishing he could massage her shoulders, run her bath and pour her a glass of wine. But they'd agreed to spend the night apart.

'He fell asleep as soon as the painkillers kicked in. His poor father felt so guilty.' She turned to face him, her stare full of uncertainty, or perhaps he was just imagining it.

Harvey reached for her hand and wrapped his fingers around hers. 'Why don't you go home, have a relax in the bath, a glass of wine and an early night.'

'Sounds heavenly,' Della said, her stare searching his so he witnessed her doubts. She sighed. Then, without warning, she leaned close and pressed her lips to his, her body sagging against his chest.

'What was that for?' Harvey asked when she pulled back, his hand cupping her face.

'No reason,' she said with a small frown, 'other than I wanted to kiss you. In a few days' time I won't be able to.'

Harvey's pulse thudded harder, the reminder that their time in Fiji would soon be over releasing another cascade of panic. Della leaned in again, slid her fingers through his hair and kissed him slowly and thoroughly as if she was memorising the feel of his lips against hers for when this was over. Harvey gripped her upper arms and kissed her back, more confused than ever but determined to take every scrap of her she would allow in the time they had left.

When they parted, each breathing hard, she blinked up at him. 'Come home with me,' she whispered. Her eyes were heavy, her pupils dilating.

Excitement energised Harvey's body, mocking his attempts to stay in control of his thoughts and how she made him feel. 'I thought you were tired.' He brushed the hair back from her face.

Suddenly he didn't care about preparing himself for the end of their fling. He wanted as much of Della as he could get until they left the island. Maybe by then, he'd have his conflicted feelings all figured out.

'I am, but I don't care.' She took his hand and dropped her gaze. 'It's just struck me that we only have a few nights left, and I don't want to waste a single second.' She met his stare, hers bold. 'I don't want to have regrets when I leave here.'

Harvey tilted up her chin and brushed her lips with his. 'Neither do I.' He would immerse himself in this relationship until the last minute. Surely by then, a way forward would present itself.

'Let's go,' he said, logging off from the computer. 'I'll run you that bath and pour you a glass of wine.'

'Harvey,' she said, reaching for his arm so he stilled. 'Thanks for thinking of me for the job. I will seriously consider it.'

He nodded, wanting to crush her in his arms and beg her to apply, but maybe Della could see pitfalls he hadn't even considered. 'You're welcome, Della.' Considering her for a colleague was no hardship, given he thought about her every minute of every day. And despite all the reasons for caution, he couldn't see that abating anytime soon.

CHAPTER TWELVE

TWO DAYS LATER, jittery with nerves, Harvey walked behind Della, his hands covering her eyes as he guided her into the luxury villa he'd booked for their final night in Fiji.

'Ready?' he asked, sucking in the scent of her freshly washed hair and her light floral perfume, his heart thumping with bittersweet excitement.

Della nodded, her hand gripping his arm. 'You'd better not have brought me to see one of those giant coconut crabs, because that's not funny.'

'Would I do that to you? You hate crabs,' Harvey said, his doubts building because romance wasn't his strong point. 'Now, keep your eyes closed until I say so.' He removed his hands from her eyes and stepped around Della, positioning himself so he could see her reaction. 'Okay, open them.'

Della blinked, quickly glanced his way and then took in the room, which was scattered with flickering tea light candles. The French doors opened to reveal their own private veranda with an in-ground infinity-edged spa pool that overlooked the sea views.

Her eyes widened, and her hands covered her mouth. 'Oh... It's so beautiful. This is so thoughtful of you,

Harvey.' She reached for him, her smile worth a hundred words.

Harvey snaked his arm around her waist, drawing her into his arms, relief flooding his system. 'We've had such a busy week, we deserve a treat on our last night. Do you want to have a soak in the spa before we eat?'

'Definitely,' she said, her eyes full of excitement and laughter as she kicked off her sandals and reached for the hem of her dress. Underneath, she wore the pink bikini he loved. While Della climbed in the spa, Harvey hastily tossed aside his shirt, poured two glasses of wine and then joined her.

The water was warm, the sounds of the sea and the Fijian insect life from the surrounding forest soothing background noise. But not even Della's obvious delight could chase off the hollowness deep at the centre of his chest. A huge part of him didn't want to go home. So many times this week, he'd almost raised the subject of them seeing where this relationship could go, and each time, he'd chickened out, kept his mouth shut, his doubts that he could form a committed relationship building. But his head couldn't seem to let the idea go.

'To two weeks in paradise,' Harvey said, making a toast to remind her how far they'd come in such a short time.

Della touched her glass to his, her eyes bright. 'Who'd have thought that being stuck with each other would turn out to be so…rejuvenating.' Before he could comment, she playfully sat astride his lap, resting her arms on his shoulders, leaning in to press a kiss to his lips.

Harvey savoured the contact, his heart thudding wildly. Della seemed to be handling their final night better than him, not that it was a competition. But where he was desperate to talk about the future, to voice his feelings and find out what she was thinking, Della seemed to be intent on keeping things light. It left him wondering if his instincts were way off. That if he tried to talk to her about them, she might dismiss him out of hand.

He swallowed hard as she pulled back, trying not to get lost in her stare. 'So, how do you want to play it?' he asked, his voice strangled with lust and confusion. Before he got too carried away by her touch, her kisses, that seductive look in her eyes, he at least wanted to address Jack's naming day in a fortnight, when they would definitely see each other again.

'Play what?' She shifted on his lap, the position putting her breasts in his line of vision, which was very distracting.

'Us,' he choked out, 'at Jack's naming day, with your family.'

Della tangled her fingers in his hair and tilted his head back, sliding her lips from his earlobe to his jaw, her touch speeding up his already erratic pulse. 'Well, given we agreed to leave *us* behind when we left Fiji, we'll find a way.'

His heart sank further. He closed his eyes, arousal a fire in his blood as she trailed her lips down the side of his neck. But his words, his yearning wanted an outlet before it was too late and they'd succumbed to this endless need for each other. 'But don't you think one of your family—probably Brody, let's be honest—will be able to tell something is different with us?'

It would be a miracle if Harvey managed to keep his eyes off Della when they next met, and if he looked at her, surely someone would be able to see what he was too scared to articulate—how he had feelings for Della he had no idea what to do with. But the two of them exploring more than sex felt ludicrous. An outrageous and risky fantasy. He'd been single by choice for twenty years, and Della... Della was a hearts and flowers romantic who deserved to have her every wish come true. How could a man like him ever be good enough?

What did Harvey know about long-term commitment? What would he have to offer this incredible woman? Even if she did want him, could he step up and be what she needed, or would he ruin everything if he tried, losing people he considered family?

'That's easy.' Della sat back, her expression transparent as she placed her wineglass on the edge of the spa. 'We'll throw Brody off the scent. I'll make a few digs at you, and you can goad me into an argument, perhaps over the wine. No one will ever know.' She chuckled, pressed her lips back to his, and writhed on his lap so he struggled to think of anything beyond how much he wanted her. But beneath the arousal, his stomach knotted.

He didn't want Della and him to revert to the strangers of old, bickering as if these two unexpected and passionate weeks hadn't happened. But Della was obviously happy to leave this, them, behind. Whereas Harvey...? He wasn't sure which way was up, but he was terrified that he'd never be able to switch off this physical craving. He'd found something with her here in Fiji. Nothing as mundane as friendship, more like an intense connection someplace way beyond friends. Mutual acceptance and respect and...obsession. There was no point trying to pretend. He thought about her all the time, wanted to be around her every moment of every day. For the first time in years, he'd developed deep feelings for a woman, a woman who didn't, *couldn't*, feel the same way about him. A woman he needed to protect from the kind of man he'd become, because she deserved so much more than he could give.

The familiar taste of rejection and failure burned his throat, so he held her closer, tighter. 'Do you think we can pull it off?' he asked, placing his wineglass beside hers. 'Not the bickering for Brody's sake, but…you know…the clean break?' His heart raced as if he was a teenager with a crush, asking for a girl's number. He held his breath balanced on the edge of a knife. Harvey had never been less certain of anything in his life or more out of control. But Della did this to him, left him powerless until he wasn't sure whether to run from the feeling or push through it to the brave new world on the other side.

Della stilled, staring down at him with a frown. 'I think we'll be okay. After all, we live in different countries.' She smiled, her fingers moving restlessly through his hair.

Was she making light of their split to protect herself or to let Harvey off the hook? Because they both knew he was in foreign waters here, wanting more than sex. He had no idea what more would even look like for them. He didn't want this fling to end, but nor was he certain he could make her the kind of promises he knew she wanted and deserved after so many years of shutting down his feelings. Was he simply being selfish by trying to hold on? Would he be the ultimate loser if he tried and failed?

'As easy as that, huh?' he asked, barely able to breathe, he was so confused and conflicted. And he hadn't missed the fact that she'd yet to confirm if she was applying for the job in Melbourne.

She frowned, her stare shifting between his eyes. 'It'll be an adjustment. I'll miss this.' Shifting her hips on his lap, she brushed his lips with hers.

Harvey's hands glided from her back to her hips, holding her still. Every move she made, her curves and softness filling his arms were torture to his strung-out body. He wanted to crush her to his chest and pleasure her over and over again until dawn when they needed to leave for the airport. Maybe then, he'd have worked her fully out of his system and everything would make sense. Maybe then, Della would look at him the way she had under the waterfall, as if he, broken, unworthy Harvey, might just be the answer to her dreams. But who was he trying to kid?

'I'll miss this too, Della,' he said, his throat raw with longing. *I'll miss you.* Gripping her waist, he buried his face against her breasts, over the beat of her heart. Now that their last night together was here, he wanted to rewind time. To go back to the start of their two weeks. Or better still, to go back twenty years and be a different man, one who'd overcome his grief and the ingrained belief that there was something unlovable about him and who deserved Della. One who understood that losing Alice, losing his mother's love, had nothing to do with him and everything to do with the unfair randomness of life and the selfish choices of others.

Della was right. He wasn't that powerless kid anymore. Except she made him feel that way, as if one wrong move would shatter the safe, predicable existence he'd clung to most of his adult life. He'd wasted so much time fighting his desire for this woman, when now it was all he could think about.

Della stroked his hair, and he held her tighter. He didn't want their last night to be only about desire. He needed to know Fiji had meant something to her, because it meant something to him.

'Would you have dated me when we first met?' he asked, looking up. 'If I'd been ready to ask you and you'd been single? If I hadn't been grieving and you weren't my best friend's sister?' Regret was pointless. Time travel impossible. But he needed to know that he hadn't been alone in imagining the shadow of what might have been between them all this time.

Della froze, her stare flitting. 'I… I don't know. Perhaps I would… It wasn't that I didn't fancy you, just that we've always wanted different things.'

Harvey nodded, too confused to explain that he wasn't sure what he wanted anymore. Somehow, it was easier to admit how he'd felt about her when they'd first met than how he felt now, tonight. But instinct told him Della was preparing to walk away, and he couldn't blame her. What did he have to offer? Just himself, as lacking as he was?

'I know the timing was wrong for us both, but part of me wishes I'd asked you back then,' he said, his voice thick with emotion. 'Who knows how life might have turned out differently if I had?'

Confused, her frown deepened, her fingers stilling in his hair. 'It's in the past. We can't change it.'

'Right. I guess I wanted you to know that I've always fancied you. I just wasn't ready for a relationship. And even twenty years ago, despite being a bit of a jerk, I was smart enough to know that hurting you would have cost me nearly everything I had—you, Brody, your mum and dad.'

'Harvey...' she whispered, resting her forehead against his, but somehow still seeing right through him. 'You know it wasn't your fault, don't you?'

Harvey froze, his pulse flying. Why hadn't he just seduced her instead of trying to verbalise the storm raging inside him?

'Not your parents' divorce,' she continued, 'or your mother choosing to leave, or Alice's accident.'

'I know.' Those events weren't his fault, but they had shaped him, made him someone who valued emotional control over all else. And look where that had led.

'And you have nothing to prove anymore,' she said, brushing his lips with hers. 'You're in control of your own life.'

The change of subject felt like a goodbye, a pep talk, a final note to see him on his way. Crushed by her emotional withdrawal, Harvey held her tight, pressing his face against her chest. He didn't want her to fix him. He wanted her to want him. To choose him over all men. But he'd seen the same look in her eyes when he'd encouraged her to apply for the Melbourne job. If he pushed for more than this fling, he might discover that he could never be what Della needed, that she wanted so much more than he was capable of. Could he live with that knowledge when he had to live with her in his life?

'Let's go to bed,' she whispered, tilting his head back, her lips finding his, parting, caressing, while her hips rocked on his lap.

Clinging to the distraction of her touch, he gazed up at her. Maybe she was right to remind him this was about pleasure. Maybe this was the only part of her he could have. Maybe once he was away from her, he'd move on as easily as she predicted. Harvey steeled himself against the pleasure her kisses always delivered, his hands cupping her breasts to coax out those moans he loved.

Della gasped, her eyes glazed with arousal as he thumbed her nipples erect. Because he was raw and exposed and ravenous for her, as always, he chased her lips with his. Their tongues met and duelled as their kisses deepened out of control. He might not be able to give her a ring, a family, that white picket fence dream, but he could give her this. Make tonight one she'd always remember.

Harvey slipped his hand between her legs, inside her bikini bottoms, and stroked her. Della broke free of their kiss to stare down at him, her pupils dilating with arousal. Emotions fluttered through her eyes. Arousal, uncertainty, perhaps even fear. But of course she would be scared to expect anything from him, scared to trust that he could be more than a good time, and she was right. The powerless feeling he detested returned. He couldn't let her down. He couldn't lose Della or the other Wiltons from his life. Better to let her go now and keep a part of her forever than to risk losing everything.

Harvey stroked her faster, one arm holding her around her waist. She rode his hand, her eyes on his and her arms braced on his shoulders.

'Kiss me,' he said, because he wanted to forget that this would be the last time he touched her, the last time he held her in his bed and awoke to the scent of her perfume on his pillow.

She whimpered, grasped his neck and lowered her

mouth to his. Her hips bucked. He stroked her faster, slid his fingers inside her and braced himself against her wild kisses.

'If you had asked me twenty years ago,' she panted after pulling away, 'I would have said yes.'

Triumph soared in Harvey's chest. He tugged down her bikini top and bent his head, captured her exposed nipple, sucking. She cried out her climax, her slippery body bucking against his under the water. Harvey held her close. Her heart thudded against his cheek where he'd crushed her in his arms. She whimpered and he slid his hand from between her legs, wrapping both arms around her, certain that he should never let her go in case it became the biggest mistake of his life.

Hours later, Della clung to Harvey as the dying cries of her orgasm echoed around the room. The moonlight shone through the window of their bure, streaking the sumptuous bed with surreal shafts of light. She kissed him, snatching breaths between surges of her tongue against his. The entire night, from the moment he'd excitedly collected her and her cases from the staff bungalow at the hospital to when he'd made love to her over and over again, carried a fantastical dreamlike quality. And Della was scared to wake up.

Harvey groaned, tore his mouth from hers and collapsed on top of her, his body racked with the spasms of his climax as he crushed her close, so close she almost lost her breath.

'We have to stop,' Della said, panting, pushing his sweaty hair back from his face. 'We have to stop before we kill each other like those horny mice.' Her plea was feeble, born of exhaustion more than a desire to stop. The night had been both endless and too short. Every time one of them dozed off, the other would reach for them again, their touch, their kisses quickly escalating as if they were both intent on outrunning the passage of time. But it was as if they'd missed their chance twenty years ago, and they both knew it.

Harvey slid from her body and rolled to the side, drawing her onto his chest. He pressed his lips to her head, his arms banded around her shoulders. 'I don't want to stop. I can't seem to.'

Della nodded, her eyelids heavy. 'Me neither.' But as the pleasure subsided, the heavy ache in her chest returned. Her flight to Auckland was leaving in four hours. She could sleep on the plane. If she closed her eyes now, if she fell asleep, their relationship would be over when she awoke, and a part of her never wanted that moment to come.

Harvey's words from earlier scratched at the closed door in her mind. They'd sounded like regrets. But surely Harvey hadn't changed his mind about staying single? He couldn't possibly want a relationship. He didn't do those. Perhaps Della was simply seeing what she wanted to see.

Scared that she was projecting her own feelings onto him, Della closed her eyes. She'd spent all week preparing for this night, their last, holding something back, refusing to rely on her intuition, focussed on the end goal: leaving Fiji and moving on from their fling. Because Harvey might have regrets—everyone did to some extent—but he still wasn't ready to change. Maybe he was too broken to allow himself to be loved. Maybe, because of his mother, he felt inherently unworthy of love. But Della needed to be strong. This time, she couldn't afford to be wrong or settle for a relationship with misaligned expectations. This time, she had to get it right.

'Can I call you from Australia?' he asked, his voice husky with lack of sleep. 'I won't just miss the sex. I'll miss you, too.'

Della's heart fluttered painfully at his words. It had been an intense fortnight. Adjusting to their new reality would feel strange for a while. But could she be Harvey's friend, knowing how close she'd come to falling for him? If they talked, their emotional connection would deepen, at least for Della. Could she then keep her feelings at bay the way she'd tried to every night in his arms this week, or would missing him, craving him, cause those feelings to overwhelm her? Wasn't a clean break the only sure-fire way to protect her heart? After all, she'd tried and failed miserably to wean herself off sleeping with Harvey.

'I don't know, Harvey.' She felt him tense, and her arms reflexively tightened around his chest. 'I'll be honest, I'll struggle to be your friend at the moment.' She felt the thud of his heart under her cheek and went on. 'There's just so much water under the bridge when it comes to us. If we talk, I may weaken next time I see you and end up seducing you again. You know how weak my willpower is.' The dash of humour was intended to soften the blow, but Della had never felt less like smiling, because every word was true and laced with fear.

'Would that be so terrible?' He pressed his lips to the top of her head. 'When we're not bickering, we're very good together.'

Della blinked, her eyes stinging. 'Of course it wouldn't

be terrible. But this time here with you has made me realise that maybe I am ready to start dating again. That husband I'm after isn't going to just land in my lap, so I probably need to get out there and find him.'

All Harvey was offering was another night in his bed. As tempting as that was, she'd want so much more. She'd want another night and another and another. Then she'd fall in love with him and want him to be the man of her dreams. Would he ever be ready for that? And could Della afford to put those dreams on hold again and wait around on the off chance that he might change his mind?

He'd told her to be uncompromising when it came to her next relationship, and he was right. If they tried to drag this physical fling out, she'd be forced to one day make the tough choice: amazing sex with Harvey or having it all with someone else. She'd hate herself if she reached her expiration date like all his other women. Because it would be so easy to allow herself to fall in love with the Harvey she'd come to know in Fiji. Maybe they were better off as friends, after all.

'I've had a wonderful time. I'll never forget it.' Gripping his face, she pressed her lips to his, ignoring the flicker of disappointment in his dark stare. She felt it too. It was hard to give up something so good. But Della needed to be selfish, to trust her gut and go after what she wanted, to have it all.

'Me neither,' he said hesitantly.

'And if I get the job in your department, we might end up working together again.' Maybe friends and colleagues were for the best. So why did it suddenly feel like a second-rate consolation prize?

He offered her a smile tinged with sadness she didn't want to acknowledge. 'I'd like that. I really hope you'll apply.'

Della nodded, the burn in her chest, the plummeting of her stomach leaving her to wonder just how she would work with Harvey every day and not want him. Tonight had almost broken her. Their out-of-control need for each other was so profound, she wondered how she would survive the sexual drought to come.

But survive it she must.

CHAPTER THIRTEEN

Two weeks later.

HARVEY SMOOTHED A nervous hand down the front of his polo shirt and yanked open his front door, his heart lurching at the wonderful sight of Della on his doorstep. His pulse galloped so fast he worried he might pass out.

'Della. You look…nice.' *Nice?* Two weeks away from her, pining and picking up the phone to call her, and stalking her social media accounts to see if she was dating anyone, and *nice* was the best he could do?

Before he could reach for her and kiss her, she stepped over the threshold, holding out a bottle of red wine like a shield. 'I brought you a lovely New Zealand Pinot Noir. If you don't like it, you can serve it to Brody. He'll drink anything,' she said, breezing past him without so much as a proper glance.

She headed for the kitchen, where her family were already gathered, leaving Harvey stunned and confused. He closed the door, his stomach in his shoes and his legs threatening to collapse. That wasn't the reunion he'd expected, the reunion he'd played out in his mind on a daily basis. The one where he kissed her, told her that *friends* wasn't working for him, that missing her had made him realise for the first time in twenty years he wanted a real relationship, with *her*, and then kissed her once more. All it had taken to bring about this massive realisation was a bit of physical distance. Without her body asleep next to his, the bed felt too big. Without her smile, her laughter, the challenge in her eyes, beautiful Melbourne seemed drab. Without Della to bounce ideas off, even his work seemed...mundane.

But clearly Della was still set on the charade for her family, acting as if Fiji hadn't happened. And Harvey could understand. He didn't want to answer any questions about them until he'd had a chance to talk to Della alone.

Cursing the wisdom of hosting a barbecue for the Wiltons the night Della had arrived from Auckland, Harvey joined them in his kitchen. He should have met her at the airport, taken her out to dinner instead, kissed her until her eyes glazed with passion and made love to her all night long just to prove that they could never be just friends. That colleagues alone wouldn't work either, because he wanted her more, not less, than when they'd been in Fiji. But what did Della want, and what if it wasn't him?

Thinking back to their reserved farewell kiss in Nadi Airport, just before he'd boarded one plane to Melbourne and Della another to Auckland, Harvey glanced her way. He understood that she'd been protecting herself on that final night when he'd tried to push for more. He was a big risk for someone who wanted lifelong commitment. But was that enough reason for them to completely give up on something so good? If she'd only give him a chance, he'd show her that his feelings were genuine. That he was ready to let her in and try to be what she needed.

Brody kissed his sister on the cheek, refusing to take

the bottle of wine Harvey set in front of him. 'Not for me. I'm a changed man.' He cast a nervous glance at his wife, who was conspicuously sipping a soft drink. 'Now that Dells is here,' Brody continued, 'we may as well tell you all—Amy is pregnant again. Jack's having a little sister!'

Jenny Wilton hugged her daughter-in-law, and Brody's dad, Graham, shifted Jack in his arms to embrace his son. Congratulations flew. But while Harvey was happy for his friend, his eyes were glued to Della's reaction.

She stood frozen, her eyes blinking rapidly as if she was fighting tears. Harvey's heart jolted in his chest. He'd never seen Della cry. His arms ached to hold her, to whisper how much he'd missed her these endless two weeks, to kiss her and make her a hundred promises that might put a smile back on her face. But what if his promises weren't enough? What if she stonewalled him again like she had in Fiji?

'I'm so happy for you,' she said bravely, snapping out of her trance to hug Amy and then Brody.

'It's early days,' Amy said, laughing, 'and we don't know if it's a sister or brother yet, but Brody seems to think he's telepathic.'

To give himself something to do beyond clearing the house of the other Wiltons so he could be alone with Della, Harvey collected a bottle of fizz from the fridge and popped the cork. 'Just a drop to celebrate,' he said, handing a grinning Brody a glass.

Harvey offered Della a glass of champagne, trying to catch her eye, but she was avoiding looking at him. Instead she declined, putting her arm around Amy's waist. 'I'll abstain in solidarity with Amy, seeing as Brody has no willpower.'

The excited chatter continued as the Wiltons drifted outside to the deck. Why wouldn't she look at him? Yes, they'd agreed to a clean break—he'd done what she asked and not called—agreed to act normal in front of Della's family. The last thing they needed were intrusive questions when their relationship was so...fragile. But how could she act as if that fortnight in Fiji had never happened, when a huge part of Harvey wanted to announce to the world that he wanted her in his life? Not as a friend or a colleague, but as a partner.

Harvey's stomach twisted with doubt. Maybe Della wasn't as sure about him as he was about her. Maybe she wanted more than she believed he could offer. Maybe if he pushed her again, he might ruin what they already had and lose her from his life. That wasn't an option.

'So, what did Harvey get up to in Fiji, sis?' Brody asked, flicking Harvey a knowing look. 'Any wild nights to report? Did he leave a trail of broken hearts scattered all over the islands?'

'Don't ask me,' Della snapped, avoiding Harvey's stare. 'Ask him. He's *your* friend.'

It was the kind of thing she might have said before Fiji, before they'd become lovers, before he'd opened up to her about his mother in a way he'd never done with anyone else. It was part of the act they'd agreed to, so why did Harvey feel as if she'd physically punched him in the gut?

'Oh, I have asked him,' Brody said playfully, completely missing the tension between Harvey and Della, 'but he's been uncharacteristically tight-lipped. There must have been someone, though. He hasn't had so much as a coffee date since he's been back. If I didn't know better, I'd say he'd met someone he actually cared about.'

Harvey's entire body tensed as he willed Della to look his way. He *had* met someone he cared about—*her*. He wanted her to want him, to fight for him, not disown him. He wanted to matter to her enough that she chose him, here and now in front of her family, people he also considered *his* family. But what if her apparent coldness wasn't an act? What if she'd easily reverted to her feelings of contempt now that their fling was done? What if everything he'd confided in her, everything they'd shared, meant nothing?

Feeling nauseous, Harvey shot Brody a warning a look. Normally he wouldn't care about being the butt of his friend's joke. But something seemed off with Della. Perhaps she was upset about her brother's announcement.

'Oh, I doubt it,' Della said, finally glancing Harvey's way. 'You know what they say—a leopard never changes its spots.' Her expression was another physical blow—confusion, anguish, a flicker of longing gone before Harvey could be certain of it. She turned back to Brody. 'But I was there to work, not to catalogue your friend's female cast-offs.' Spinning on her heel, she joined her parents, who were sitting with Jack on the grass. On seeing his aunt, Jack held out his chubby fists. Della swung him up into her arms, her face beaming with the first genuine smile of the evening.

Harvey's entire body sagged, his pulse thrumming with hunger. He wanted Della to look at *him* that way. He didn't want to play it cool. He didn't care about awkward questions. He'd rather announce to her family that he wanted her to move back to Melbourne so they could try and have a proper relationship.

Hearing how absurd and inadequate his solution

sounded in his head, Harvey deflated. How could Della and he, of all men, work out when she was already way ahead of him, looking for love, a husband, a family of her own? She'd rejected his attempts to start a conversation about them back in Fiji, as good as telling him he wasn't relationship material. He wasn't good enough for her. Felling utterly powerless, he glanced at Brody and winced.

'What on Earth did you do this time to upset Della?' Brody asked sheepishly, as if at last he was finally picking up on the tension between them, the weird dynamic that didn't quite ring true.

Harvey shrugged, his chest hollow, all the excitement of seeing Della again draining away. 'Just existed, I think, mate. Same as usual.'

Only there was one additional thing that wasn't usual—the way he felt inside, as if he'd explode unless he could convince Della to hear him out. With a sickening lurch of his stomach, Harvey realised he might already be falling in love with Della, and it wasn't going to be anywhere near enough.

Della stacked the final plate into the dishwasher, her head all over the place and heart aching. Outside, happy conversations and laughter of her family swirled around. Tomorrow, Jack's naming day would be a joyous occasion, but her smiles felt insincere, and she could barely look at Harvey, so strong was the desire to hurl herself into his arms and make him want her forever.

Della swallowed down the sense of panic. The past two weeks without him had been a living hell. She'd been wrong; the physical distance, the lack of contact, the clean break...*nothing* had helped her get over their fling. *Nothing* was back to normal. Her feelings, the ones she'd tried to deny and sweep under the rug in Fiji, were bigger than ever, especially now that she'd seen Harvey again. The hurt in his eyes when she'd tried to throw Brody off the scent had crushed her.

With a trembling hand, she closed the dishwasher and went in search of Harvey's bathroom. She needed a moment to herself in case she broke down in front of both Harvey and her family and told them exactly what had happened in Fiji. She'd almost spluttered when Brody had asked about wild nights, because there had been plenty of those. As for broken hearts, she'd naively assumed hers was untouchable, but Harvey had found a way to get under her guard, to make her fall for him, until she'd become the cliché she'd mocked other women for: past her expiration date, but left wanting more. So much more.

She'd stupidly fallen in love with Harvey, a man who couldn't love her back because he'd spent years shutting down his emotions and feeling unworthy of love. And that wasn't all. That morning, before leaving Auckland for Melbourne, she'd taken a pregnancy test, discovering she was pregnant.

Locking herself in the bathroom now, Della rested her hand on her stomach, choked with happiness. She was finally achieving one of her dreams. A baby. Harvey's baby. But it changed nothing. Of course she needed to tell him, and soon. How would he take the news? Would he be angry? Feel trapped? She had no doubt that he cared for Della and that, in time, he'd do right by their child. But that wasn't how she'd envisioned having a family. She wanted to be in love and loved in return.

She wanted to build a home with that love of her life. She wanted forever.

Della blinked away the sting in her eyes. Harvey had urged her to be uncompromising when it came to her dreams and desires, to reach for it all and never settle. Of course he couldn't have known that he'd become tangled up in those dreams. That she'd want to spend the rest of her life with *him*, have *his* baby. But Della couldn't make him feel something for her that he just wasn't capable of. Better to take what was on offer, his friendship and respect. Better for them to focus on being parents, separate but united for their child. This time, it was better to strategically settle than to risk losing a chunk of her heart she wasn't sure she'd survive without.

While she washed her hands, she splashed cold water on her face and avoided looking at her reflection in the mirror. She knew what she'd see. A woman in love. A woman who in fact, despite all her tough talk and Harvey's encouragement, *couldn't* have it all. A woman who'd made another mistake and fallen for a broken man incapable of loving her back. Because to Harvey, love was weakness. Powerlessness. A price too high.

Della emerged from the bathroom, reluctant to head back outside just yet. Distracted by the framed photographs lining the hallway, she took a closer look. She'd never really noticed them before, but they were pictures of Harvey with all the important people in his life. One of him and Brody in their twenties, dressed in tuxedos at some medic's ball. One of Harvey and Bill dressed in hiking gear on the top of Victoria's Mount Oberon. One of Christmas at the Wiltons', everyone wearing paper hats as they raised a toast to the camera.

Her family was Harvey's too. He loved them and they him. All the more reason for Della to tread with caution so neither of them lost what they valued. She spied herself in the last photo, struggling to identify which Christmas it was. But even then, all those years ago, some part of her had wanted Harvey, had been halfway in love with him. She would likely always have unresolved feelings for Harvey. But she'd survive that. What she wouldn't survive was loving him with her whole heart when he didn't love her back.

Della was just about to turn away, to head to the garden and tell her family she was calling it a night, when a pair of hands gripped her waist. 'There you are. I've been trying to get you alone all night.'

His warm breath tickled the side of her neck and she shuddered, his touch sparking her body alive as if she'd been in a coma for two long weeks. Della turned, bracing herself against how handsome he was, how it physically hurt to look at him because he could never be hers. His eyes danced with the excitement she'd waited two endless weeks to see.

'Come with me,' he said. She meekly followed, clinging to his hand as he tugged her into a nearby room, which turned out to be his home office.

He shut the door and pulled her into his arms. The force of wanting him almost buckled her knees, but panic beat at her ribs.

'Shouldn't we head back outside before they come looking for us?' she said feebly as he cupped her face and slid his fingers into her hair, tilting up her chin.

'Brody's taken Amy and Jack home,' he breathed against her lips. 'I think both your parents have dozed off sitting around the fire pit.' Without another word, he pressed his lips to hers and just let them sit there for a handful of seconds as he breathed in deeply. Della sighed, sagged against him, her entire body melting as if she was finally home. But he couldn't be her safe place. She needed to be strong for their baby and for her own stupid heart.

'God, I've missed you,' he said, pulling back to stare deep into her eyes.

Della saw longing and desire and euphoria in the depths of his eyes, but it still wasn't enough. She wanted more of him. She wanted all of him—the good and the bad and the broken. She wanted impossible things.

'Why didn't you tell me when you were arriving?' he said, wrapping his arms around her shoulders so her head rested on his chest. 'I'd have picked you up from the airport.'

Della shrugged, her heart so sore she could barely breathe. 'You were busy here, and how would we have explained that to the others?'

Harvey stiffened, rested his hands on her shoulders and peeled her away so he could look at her. 'Is everything okay? You've been avoiding me all night. I've been going out of my mind. I wanted to kiss you so badly.'

'I thought the plan was to play it cool,' Della lied. She'd ignored him because to be close to him was torture. Because she'd almost snapped so many times tonight and confessed that she loved him. Because the part of her that yet again had realised too late she'd have to compromise her dreams wanted him anyway, as she'd known she would.

Della swallowed, stepping back but wishing she was

still in his arms, where things made a twisted kind of sense. 'We don't need Brody and his intrusive questions. I swear Amy is a saint for putting up with my brother.'

'Can you stay?' he asked, reaching for her again. 'Here. With me, tonight? After everyone else leaves.'

Della rested her hand on his chest, felt the rapid pound of his heart, wished that it beat with love for her. 'I can't... We agreed.' Her throat ached with longing. Why had she ever thought she could be this man's friend? She'd known it had been impossible the first time she'd met him. Now, twenty years later, when she knew him better than ever, there was no hope. She loved him. She craved him. She wanted him. *Friends* was for the runner-up.

'Della... I've been thinking,' he said when she stayed silent, because she was desperately trying not to cry. 'I've missed you so badly since I arrived home.'

'Me too,' she said, her throat tight. She refused to cry. She didn't want to blurt out her irrelevant feelings or her news about the baby. She'd planned it all on the flight. She'd tell him tomorrow, after Jack's naming day party.

He smiled, and her heart cracked a little more. 'I really want you to apply for the job in my department. Us working together has to be better than this—missing each other, waking up alone, not to mention the abstinence.' He shot her a playful smile that two weeks ago she could have returned. But not now.

'I... I'm not sure, Harvey.' Della shook her head, looked down. She wanted more than sex. She wanted it all. She always had. The only change was that she wanted it with him—Harvey Ward.

'I know it's complicated,' Harvey rushed on, 'and I don't have the first clue what I'm doing, but if you move back here, maybe we could, you know, try dating. Each other, I mean.' He exhaled a sigh, as if speaking those words had left him exhausted.

Della's chest ached. Of course he would struggle with dating, but she could see how hard he was trying. That he genuinely meant what he'd said. That the first tentative step towards a relationship was a huge step for Harvey. But they'd always been too different when it came to commitment, and that hadn't changed. Della was miles ahead, a place where she was sure to get hurt. And what then? What about the baby?

'You know I haven't done this in a very long time,' he continued, misinterpreting her hesitance. 'I know I'm a risk, but it could work. *We* could work.' Before she could reply, he hauled her close, bringing her lips up to his, sliding his tongue against hers, filling her body with love hormones. Della surrendered, luxuriating in his kisses, which, after two parched weeks in the desert, felt like heaven. But the high faltered, her head intruding. She'd have to turn him down. She'd have to tell him why.

Because she was too scared to part with her secret just yet, because she wanted him, one last time, in spite of how ridiculously out of sync they were when it came to relationships, Della allowed herself the indulgence of his strong arms, his frantic kisses, the hot possessive surge of his tongue against hers. Oh, how she'd missed him, the breadth of his smile and the playful glint in his eyes. The feel of his strong arms and the beat of his heart. The way he believed in her and the way he made her feel. She panted, preparing to stop this. To walk away before any more of her heart was eroded, but her fingers flexed in his shirt, her head falling back so he could ravage her neck, her moans encouraging.

'That was the worst two weeks of my life,' he said, hoisting her onto the desk. One of his thighs slotted between her legs as he pressed kisses over her face, her neck, the tops of her breasts and back to her lips. 'Every day I wanted to call you. The only reason I didn't call was to give you the space you wanted, to pretend that we could be friends. But it's not working for me.'

As his lips parted hers once more, his hand cupped her breast through her dress. Pregnancy hormones had made her sensitive, but his touch set her alight, inflamed her from head to toe. She twisted his hair in her fingers and rubbed the hard length of him through his shorts. Just one more time... Then, at the end of the weekend, she'd tell him about the baby and fly back to Auckland, where she could patch up her bruised heart away from this temptation.

Reaching for his fly, she dragged her kiss-swollen lips from his. 'Hurry,' she said, 'I want you.' If this was the only part of him she could have, she'd take it and worry about the price later.

Harvey didn't argue. While she undid his shorts and pushed them over his hips, taking him in her hand, he lifted her dress and shoved her underwear down her legs, his tongue in her mouth.

Della spread her thighs, making room for his hips, casting the closed office door a nervous glance. But she was too far gone to care about interruptions, too high on the decadence of Harvey's touch to voice caution. Too lovesick to protect her battle-worn heart. She would love him with her body, silently say goodbye. Then she'd walk away from one dream and focus on being the best parent she could be.

Dragging his mouth from hers, Harvey dropped to his knees, shoving her dress up her thighs. 'I locked the door,' he said before covering her with his mouth.

Della closed her eyes against the intense wave of pleasure. Dizzy with it, she braced one hand on the desk behind her and tunnelled the other into Harvey's hair, holding on for dear life.

'Harvey,' she gasped, looking down at him. His eyes were dark with desire and determination, his hands on her thighs, gripping her tight. Pleasure built and built, the sharp ache only a fraction of the pain she'd endured these two weeks without him. But she couldn't keep him. She had to put the baby first. Put herself first.

Her moans grew. She released Harvey's hair and covered her mouth, bit the back of her hand to hold them inside. As if he knew her body, knew how close she was, Harvey jerked to his feet, gripped her hips and slowly pushed inside her. Della clung to his shoulders, wrapped her legs around his hips and dragged his mouth down to hers. Harvey bucked into her, his pace as frantic as the beat of her heart, his kisses as deep as his possession of her body, his passion for her almost enough to make her change her mind. Almost.

Della wanted more than passion. More than really great sex. She wanted him to love her as desperately as she loved him. She wanted them to raise their baby together in that house with the clichéd white picket fence. She wanted him to feel the terrifying fear and powerlessness of love and want it anyway, with *her*. But those dreams belonged to Della, not to Harvey.

Her orgasm ripped through her, and she sobbed his name. Harvey crushed her in his arms and groaned, joining her, his fingers and his whispers in her hair.

'I missed you,' he said, his breath see-sawing in his chest. 'I missed you so much.'

Della hid her face against his neck, blinking the sting of tears from her eyes. That had been a big mistake. 'I'd better go before my parents come looking for one of us.' She pushed him away, slid from the desk and scooped up her underwear from the floor. She needed to get away from him before she begged him to love her.

'You're leaving?' he said, confusion clouding his handsome face as he tucked himself back into his shorts. 'Just hang around until they leave. Stay the night. I'll make you breakfast, and we can go to Jack's thing together.'

'I can't, Harvey. I—' she broke off, realisation dawning. She couldn't wait any longer. She had to tell him now. He deserved to know about the baby, and her confession, the knowledge that he was going to be a father, would put everything back into perspective for him the way it had for Della that morning. She wanted him like oxygen, but this was no longer just about her desires.

'Did you see the job's been advertised?' he pressed, a desperate look in his eyes. 'You should apply. They need someone to start as soon as possible.'

'Harvey, we need to talk.' She straightened her dress and folded her arms across her waist, holding her fractured pieces together.

'Okay, come and have a drink. Perhaps your parents have already left.'

Della shook her head. 'No. I don't want a drink. I just want you to listen.' Just like they had when they'd left

Fiji, it was better to make a clean break of it now. The sex was over, as great as it had been. Now there were bigger issues to work on than if they should be colleagues or whether or not they could make a relationship work.

'Okay. I'm listening.' He reached for her hand, and she paced away. If he touched her again, she'd mess this up, say the wrong things, beg him to love her or worse, settle for only a part of him, not the whole.

'I didn't want to tell you until tomorrow, after the party,' she began, a chill spreading along her bare arms, 'but I'm pregnant, Harvey.' She looked up, saw the flash of disbelief in his eyes and rushed on. 'We made a baby in Fiji. Probably that time in the waterfall.'

Confusion shifted in his stare. He opened his mouth to speak. Closed it again. Shook his head, as dumbfounded as she'd been that morning, seeing those two pink lines.

'I know I reassured you that I was on the pill,' she rushed on, 'which I was. But obviously I must have missed one or something. And I know that you never wanted kids. I know this—' she placed her hand on her stomach '—is my dream, not yours. But I want you to know that you don't have to feel responsible. You don't have to do anything or say anything or be anything you're not ready to be. I understand.'

Poor Harvey. He'd only just decided that he might want a relationship, and now he was going to be a father. Talk about life in fast forward… At his bewilderment, she winced, hating herself for her lack of willpower. If she hadn't slept with him again, maybe she could have kept her secret until a more appropriate time. 'I know it's a lot to take in. You're probably angry and upset—'

'I'm not angry,' he said, his jaw clenched as he

scrubbed a hand through his hair, glancing down at her flat stomach. 'Are you…okay?'

Della nodded, brushing aside his concern. If he carried on being wonderful and thoughtful, she was going to cry. As it was, this baby would probably be born holding a box of tissues, she'd cried so much over Harvey this past fortnight.

'Obviously this weekend is about Amy and Brody and baby Jack,' she said, also reminding herself that she couldn't be properly excited yet and tell anyone else. 'I know we'll need to explain about us eventually, but I think it's best if we keep this to ourselves for now and figure everything else out later. I'll, um…call you from Auckland, and we can talk everything through.'

Harvey's frown deepened, his helpless expression hardening. 'Wait,' he said, stepping forward and reaching for her arm.

Della stepped back, ducked out of his reach. She couldn't let him touch her again or she'd break down.

'You're going back to Auckland?' he asked, incredulous, his stare carrying pain and accusation.

Nausea swirled in her stomach. 'Of course, Harvey. I live there. My home is there. My job.' She couldn't just drop everything. She needed time to think.

'So you're not going to apply for the job here?' He gripped the back of his neck and paced back and forth. 'Where we could raise our baby together?'

A wild flutter of hope bloomed in her chest. Could she do that? Move home, work with Harvey, have his baby and hope that in time, he might fall in love with her? Could she settle for so little when she wanted it all? If it worked, it would be everything she'd ever dreamed. But if it failed, would she survive? Maybe if she hadn't fallen in love with him, she could return and just see what happened. But it was too late for what-ifs.

'I'm not sure yet,' she whispered, fear and guilt and loathing forcing her stare from his. 'I'll certainly think about the job. But like you, I'm in shock. I only found out about the baby myself this morning, and now I have to think about things like maternity leave...' Della swallowed hard, wishing dreams were that easy. She knew from experience that reaching for it all, pinning her hopes on a man who wasn't sure what he wanted, could backfire. She couldn't make that mistake again, not when there was their baby to consider. She needed to trust her instincts.

He came to a standstill and stared her way. 'So, if you're not sure about the job, you're even less sure about me, about us having a relationship? And yet you let me prattle on about dating, knowing you were going to turn me down.'

Della pressed her lips together, her throat raw with emotion. 'I'm sorry. I wasn't thinking straight.' Had she selfishly used him again? 'I just know that I need to put the baby first. *We* need to put the baby first. This isn't about us anymore, and you and I still want different things.' Dating wasn't enough, not when she loved him so desperately. She'd overreached before, pushed for more and lost. It was better to forget about love and focus on the baby.

'I get it.' Harvey nodded, his stare bleak. 'I'm fine as a sperm donor, I'm fine for sex, but I'm just not up to scratch when it comes to relationships.'

'I didn't say that,' she said, looking away from the pain

in his eyes. 'I want us to do this, the baby, together. I just haven't figured out all the details yet.'

'It's okay. I understand,' Harvey said, heading for the door. 'You'll have my baby, but good old Harvey couldn't possibly be anything serious, least of all a husband, right, not when there's probably a better option out there somewhere?'

He left the room, left Della with the echo of his pain and resentment. Rather than face her parents, rather than hurt herself or Harvey any more tonight, Della slipped out of the front door and escaped.

CHAPTER FOURTEEN

HARVEY PRESSED HIS lips to the top of Jack's head and breathed in his clean baby smell, his stare glued to the door of the party venue for a first glimpse of Della. He'd arrived early at the trendy restaurant near Brody and Amy's suburb, which had a small function room for events. His house was too big and too quiet now that he knew not only that he was going to be a father, but that Della wanted nothing more to do with him beyond some depressing shared custody arrangement.

She'd rejected him, as much as told him he wasn't good enough for her to risk her heart, that she could never love a man like him. And he couldn't even be angry, because maybe she was right.

'Are you nervous?' Brody asked, reaching for his son.

Nervous? He was bereft. Della might as well have ripped his heart out of his chest last night and looked down on it with disappointment. He wasn't enough for her, even after everything they'd shared, even when he'd offered to give her everything he could, even when they'd made a child together.

'I'm not nervous,' he reassured Brody, chilled to the bone, because he was so gutted by her rejection he couldn't even be properly excited by the news of his baby.

'I'll be fine.' If *fine* meant desolate, inadequate, helpless like never before.

'The others are risking being late,' Brody said about Della and Mr and Mrs W, looking slightly harassed. He bounced on the balls of his feet to keep the baby happy.

'Should I call Della?' Harvey asked, tension tightening his shoulders. 'Find out where they are?' Maybe they were having car trouble. Maybe Della was ill or there was something wrong with the baby. He'd give her two more minutes, and then he was going to look for her.

Brody scoffed, handing the baby his phone to stop him fussing. 'You calling her would only make her grumpy. We don't want bickering today of all days.'

Harvey rubbed a hand down his face in frustration. Was his friend truly that blind? Why had he never noticed the way Harvey felt about Della? The way he'd *always* felt? Was Harvey that good at hiding his feelings? Because now, when it was over between them, when he'd finally realised that he'd fallen deeply in love with Della in Fiji, he could finally admit that those feelings had always run deep inside him, waiting for the timing to be right. Except nothing was right without Della.

'Haven't you ever stopped to wonder why Della and I are always at each other's throats?' he snapped, taking his frustration out on his clueless friend.

Brody shrugged, distracted. 'You're just too different, that's all.'

'That's not all.' He couldn't do it any longer, pretend that he wasn't crazy about her, that he just wanted sex or friendship or some depressing co-parenting situation. He wanted Della. 'This might be hard for you hear,' he said, past the point of no return, 'but I've always fancied your sister.'

Brody looked up, startled.

'When I first met her,' Harvey continued, 'I was in such a bad place, I knew I couldn't act on it without hurting her or messing up our friendship.'

'My sister?' Brody gaped in disbelief.

Harvey nodded and gripped the back of his neck, his panic mounting. 'I'm in love with her,' he said in a rush. '*She's* the one I care about. *She's* the reason everything has changed for me.' *She* was worth this sickening feeling of fear and inadequacy that made him feel eight years old again.

Brody's eyebrows shot up, and then a slow grin spread over his face. 'Harvey Ward finally falling in love, and it's for my little sister?'

Harvey shook his head and paced away in disgust. 'I shouldn't have told you,' he muttered foully. This was serious. He loved her and he'd lost her because she couldn't believe in him, couldn't want him, couldn't choose him.

'Don't be like that,' Brody said, sobering. 'Does she love you too?'

Harvey shot his friend an incredulous look. 'Don't be stupid. She's an intelligent woman. She could never take me seriously, and she's probably right not to. I don't know the first thing about committed relationships. And I don't want to let her down or hurt her. She's been through enough.' Della was scared, too. Scared to trust her instincts, scared to be hurt again, scared to want her dreams. Why would she take a chance on a beginner like him, especially now that they had their baby to consider? But he'd keep that part of the story to himself for now.

'That bickering you two always do, you know that's two-sided, right?' Brody said, as if he'd completely missed the point Harvey was trying to make.

'Yeah, so?' Harvey checked the time, frantic now for Della to arrive so he could ensure she was okay.

'Duh…' Brody said, as if reverting to a teenager. 'Della's always had a bit of thing for you. I used to tease her about it. I never told you, obviously, because…you know…she's my sister.'

Harvey shook his head, in no way comforted. Just because she'd always fancied him, just because they were great together physically, didn't mean she was ready to trust him, of all men, with her massive heart. She wasn't even ready to be his colleague, to raise their baby with him, to give him a chance to forge a proper relationship. She didn't want him, and there was nothing he could do to change that.

'It doesn't matter,' Harvey said, too heartsore to explain the details. 'She wants us to be friends.' To raise their baby together but nothing more.

Brody frowned, sceptically, realisation seeming to dawn. 'You haven't told her, have you? That you're in love with her.'

Harvey winced, his chest too small for his lungs. 'I tried…last night…' But he hadn't been able to get the words out. A part of him, the part that had shut down any emotional connection for the past twenty years, still worried he was unworthy of love, especially the love of a woman as amazing as Della.

'Seriously?' Brody asked, inching closer and lowering his voice. 'Don't try, just tell her.'

Harvey curled his hands into fists. Would she care

when she'd already decided a relationship with him wasn't enough? Was he setting himself up for another slap of rejection if he told her his true feelings? Was he at risk of not just losing Della, but also of their chance to be parents who got along and respected each other?

'Don't be stupid, man,' Brody pressed. 'She's flying back to Auckland tonight. If you don't tell her today, you might regret it.'

Harvey nodded numbly, his brain firing normally for the first time this weekend. Of course he would regret it. He loved Della, and she needed to know. Even if she could never take him seriously or love him back, he should tell her how she'd made him believe in love again.

'I'm going to find her,' he said, heading for the exit without waiting for permission.

'Don't be late,' Brody called after him. 'My son is counting on you.'

Graham Wilton pulled into the last available parking space outside the restaurant where Jack's naming day party was taking place and turned off the engine.

Della's stomach lurched with despair and anguish. How would she face Harvey today and not completely break down? She'd hurt him last night. Thrown his offer of dating back in his face. Rejected him, just like his mother.

'Can you give us a moment, darling?' Della's mother said to her husband from the passenger seat. 'I just need a word with Della.'

Della shifted in the back seat of the car, checking her watch. 'We're cutting it pretty fine, Mum.' The last thing she needed when she was feeling so bereft was her mum digging around in Della's head.

'This won't take long,' Jenny said, popping her seat belt and turning to face her daughter. 'Especially if you just come out and tell me what's wrong instead of denying it.'

Della sighed, glancing down at her hands twisting in her lap. Of course her mother would pick up on her mood. 'Nothing's wrong,' she started, scared that if she began the story, she'd cry and ruin Jack's photos with her blotchy red face. She looked up, met her mother's sympathetic stare. 'I'm pregnant, that's all.'

Jenny's hand gripped Della's. 'That's wonderful news. I'm so happy for you. Are you feeling okay?'

Della nodded robotically. 'I'm fine. It's very early. Obviously it's Jack's day, and I don't want to tell anyone else yet.'

Jenny nodded, her astute expression turning curious. 'Who's the father?'

Della dragged in a deep breath. This was the tricky part. The risk of breaking down and confessing to her mother that she'd stupidly fallen in love with Harvey Ward. 'It's Harvey.'

Her mother's eyes widened. 'Our Harvey?'

'Of course, Mum. I don't know any other Harveys.' Now that she'd told him her news, now that she'd protected her heart and put the baby first, now that she'd relied on her instincts and refused to settle for less than she deserved, she was supposed to feel better. But if anything, she felt worse. She'd barely slept a wink last night, replaying that last conversation over and over until nothing made sense. Reliving the hurt in Harvey's eyes. The rejection and the heartbreaking acceptance, as if he'd been expecting it all along.

'Oh, my...' Jenny said, with a flash of respect. 'I didn't know you two were—'

'We're not,' Della said flatly. 'It happened in Fiji.'

Jenny nodded, knowingly. 'Of course. Well, he's always liked you.'

Della looked up, her heart withering a little more. If only he could do more than like her. If only he wanted more than a *try it and see* relationship. If only he could love her. 'Yes, well, I just want to get through today, so if you could not mention it to Dad or Brody or Amy, and maybe stop looking at me like that.'

'Like what?' Jenny asked innocently. 'Like I'm about to ask what your plans are?'

'Exactly.' Della sighed as Jenny waited for her to elaborate. 'My plan is to go back to New Zealand and have a good long think,' she said, caving to pressure. 'My plan is to focus on raising my baby, with as much input from Harvey as he wants, obviously.'

'And what about you and Harvey?' Jenny asked, a flicker of sympathy in her eyes. 'What about having a relationship?'

'Come on, Mum. This is Harvey,' Della said, glancing out of the car window to stop herself from crying. 'He's not really ready for a relationship, not that I can blame him. But the most important thing for all of us, him, me and the baby, is if we're...friends.'

Jenny frowned, her eyes full of questions. 'But you're in love with him.'

'I am.' The admission should have filled her with joy.

'How is that going to factor into your *friendship*?'

Della ducked her head in shame. 'Obviously it's not. I'll get over it. I'll put the baby first, and I'll be fine.'

Jenny nodded in agreement. 'Yes, you will. But you won't have everything you've ever wanted. Does Harvey know that you're in love with him? Have you told him how you feel? Because if you really love him, it's not just going to go away, and he deserves to know something so important.'

Della shook her head, her eyes burning. 'No. I... I didn't think it was relevant. We still want different things.'

Except what had Harvey meant when he'd said 'good old Harvey couldn't possibly be anything serious, least of all a husband'?

'Harvey thinks he wants to try and have a relationship,' she went on, more confused than ever, 'but I can't be his trial run, putting my feelings on hold, loving him but waiting around to see if a relationship is what he genuinely wants. I just can't.' It would destroy her.

'But if you haven't told him how you feel and what *you* want, you haven't really given him a chance to step up, have you?' Jenny tilted her head, seeing way too much for Della's liking. 'What if he needs to know that you love him? What if he loves you too?'

Della glared, her heart in her throat. Of course, Harvey needed to be loved as much as the next person, perhaps more so after everything he'd been through. She shook her head even as hope rushed through her like an electrical storm. 'He can't love me. He's spent most of his adult life shutting down, keeping people out.'

Jenny smiled sadly. 'And you're still scared to want it all in case you make another mistake.'

Della swallowed, sick to her stomach. Had she written

Harvey off too soon, because she was still scared to trust her judgement, still settling for less than she deserved? Still terrified to reach for all of her dreams? Had she unfairly judged him, rejected him the way his mother had, when in reality, she loved and wanted every inch of him, even if he didn't love her back?

'You've always been scared to fail,' Jenny said, squeezing Della's fingers. 'I blame myself and your father. We inadvertently created a very competitive household. But your drive is your strength. Don't let one relationship failure hold you back from having everything you want. Tell Harvey how you feel and give him a chance.'

Della nodded numbly, feeling stupid. A small, building sense of panic was choking her. Her mother was right.

'Come on,' Jenny said, opening the passenger side door. 'We'd better go inside. The ceremony is about to start.'

Della slammed the car door and rushed inside the venue. Was she too late to undo the damage she'd inflicted last night when she'd hurt both Harvey and herself with her fear? Her mother was right. Harvey deserved to know that she loved him, even if he couldn't return her feelings. To know that, of all men, Della chose *him*.

CHAPTER FIFTEEN

HARVEY HADN'T MADE it to Della in time. Just as she and her mother had walked into the room, her eyes meeting his for an electrifying beat, the celebrant had announced it was time to start. All throughout the naming day ceremony, as together they'd promised to guide and support Jack, he'd struggled to take his eyes off her. She looked beautiful, her simple blue dress matching the colour of her eyes, and her hair casually pinned up to expose her neck. It had been torture fighting the urge to drag her aside and tell her how he felt about her, but somehow he'd managed to put Brody, Amy and Jack first temporarily.

Outside in the garden at the side of the restaurant, Harvey's cheek muscles twitched from the pressure of maintaining a semi-fake smile. But he didn't want to ruin Jack's photos.

'And one last smile, please,' the photographer said, snapping the final photo—Amy and Brody in the centre holding Jack with Harvey and Della at either end.

The minute the photographer checked the shot in the digital display, Harvey moved to intercept Della, panic like ice in his veins. But his patience had run out.

'Della, we need to talk,' he said as Amy and Brody wandered back inside with Jack.

'Yes, of course, we do,' she said, blinking up at him. 'Harvey, I'm so sorry about last night.' She reached for his arm. 'I was all over the place. I'd like to blame my hormones, but I think that would be a lie.'

Harvey shook his head, cutting her off, drawing her deeper into the shade of a tree out of the sun. 'No. *I'm* sorry.' He took her hand from his arm and squeezed her fingers. 'I was stupid, Della. I was so excited to see you after these past two weeks that I stepped in my own way, and I forgot to tell you the most important thing.'

He gripped her arms, wishing they were somewhere more romantic than a garden so he could convince her that he meant what he was about to say. But he'd just have to risk that this, here and now, would be enough. 'I love you, Della. I fell in love with you in Fiji, and I should have told you as soon as I realised.'

She blinked, her eyes wide with confusion and doubt.

'I was scared,' he rushed on, his hands skimming her upper arms, because he couldn't not touch her. 'Scared that I'm not enough for you, because I'm a forty-two-year-old man who's never been in love before, not like this.' He pressed a fist to the centre of his chest, where it burned the most. 'Scared that you deserve someone better at relationships. That if I tried to be what you need, I'd fail and let you down, and I never want to be a man who lets you down.' He shook his head, the idea abhorrent.

'Harvey…' she whispered, her eyes shining with unshed tears. 'You *are* enough.'

But the pressure to say what he should have said last night was overwhelming. He slid his hands down her bare arms and gripped her fingers. 'I know I'm a big risk for you, and I know that you're scared. I know that we wanted different things in the past, and that you've been hurt and let down before. I know that we can't afford to mess this up, because we're already a massive part of each other's lives. But I've half loved you for twenty years, Della. I was just too scared to fall all the way in case I discovered that there was, in fact, something unlovable about me. Something that meant you could never choose me.'

Della shook her head, tears landing on her cheeks. 'No, there isn't, and I do.'

'But I'm not scared anymore,' he said, only half hearing her as he cupped her face and wiped a tear away with the pad of his thumb. 'Well, that's not strictly true. I *am* scared. I'm terrified. But mainly about losing you, or having to live without you. So if you'll just give me a chance, one chance, at our relationship, I promise that I'll try and give you everything you've ever wanted. I'll try every day to be what you deserve. I'll never stop trying to make us work, because I'll always love you.'

Della laughed through her tears, throwing her arms around his neck. 'Harvey, you are already everything I want. You, us, the baby.'

'Really?' he asked, the lump in his throat so big he thought he might choke. But he was smart enough to grip her tight in case she changed her mind.

Della nodded, standing on her toes to press her lips to his. 'I'm sorry that I made you doubt yourself. It wasn't that you weren't enough. It was that *I* was still scared to trust my instincts and go after all of my dreams. But you showed me that I didn't have to settle, that I can have it all, as long as I follow my heart. And my heart leads to you, Harvey. I love you, too.'

Harvey held her close, his heart thudding wildly. 'Don't

say it if you don't mean it,' he choked out, overcome. He was willing to hold on to her forever in the hopes that one day she might love him in return. As long as it took.

'I do mean it,' she cried, cupping his face. 'I want to move back to Melbourne and work with you, and raise our baby with you, and grow old with you, although I can't promise that we won't bicker from time to time.'

Harvey grinned, his heart soaring with hope. 'What's a little bit of harmless bickering when we're so good together in all other areas?' Before she could answer, he hauled her into his arms and slanted his lips over hers, kissing her with everything he was. Their tongues glided together, her fingers twisting his hair as her body shifted restlessly against his, seeking more.

Harvey pulled back, panting hard, her face gripped between his palms. 'You really love me?'

She leaned back and looked up at him, her emotions shining in her eyes. 'Of course I do. I almost told you last night, but then I thought you couldn't love me, and so I left first. I sabotaged this before you could hurt me, but I'm done being scared. I'm done putting my dreams on hold. I want us to build a life together. I want it all, and I know you can be everything I need, because you already are. I choose you, Harvey.'

Dragging her close again, Harvey kissed her until his head swam from lack of oxygen. 'Can we get out of here yet?' he asked, drying the rest of her tears. 'I want to take you home to bed before you fly back to New Zealand.'

Della laughed, rubbing at her smudged mascara. 'I think my brother might never speak to us again if we did that.'

Harvey shrugged, willing to risk it if she was, but they

owed it to Jack to be present, not that the cute little fella would ever remember their sacrifice.

Della sobered, searching his stare. 'How do you feel… about the baby?' she asked with a frown of concern. 'I know it wasn't planned, and you're going from being alone to being in a relationship *and* being a father. That's a lot.'

His hands held her waist, but he wanted to drop to his knees and press a kiss to her stomach, where their baby grew. 'I feel like the luckiest man alive, Della. I love kids—tiny cute humans. I always have. They were just something else I denied myself because I was so used to holding back my emotions. But I don't know, something happened in Fiji. I kept seeing a different side to you and then another and then another, and I found myself help-less to letting you in. I found myself telling you things I've never told anyone else.'

She nodded. 'Me too.'

'But how are *you* feeling? Any morning sickness? You look a little tired?' Guilt for the way they'd left things last night crawled over his skin.

'I'm okay. I didn't sleep well last night,' she said, press-ing her lips to his with a breathy sigh. 'But it's my own fault. I met this gorgeous man in Fiji and had the best sex of my life, the best holiday fling, and then I fell in love. But when I saw him again, I bottled it, despite being crazy about him, despite choosing him of all men.'

Harvey grinned, his ego inflating. 'The best sex, huh? Tell me more.'

Della rolled her eyes. 'Of course that's the thing you focus on.'

Laughing, he wrapped his arm around her shoulders

and pressed a kiss to her temple as they headed back inside to the party. 'That first day in Fiji, you said it wasn't that great, so I'm just clarifying the details.'

Della nudged him with her elbow, tilting her face up for another kiss. 'Don't gloat.'

'I'm afraid you can't stop me.' He paused in the doorway and cupped her face, brushing his lips over hers.

When he pulled back, she looked up at him, slipping her arm around his waist, her other hand gripping his fingers on her shoulder. 'What will we tell them about us?'

She meant her family, the Wiltons, and Bill too, who'd been invited to join the celebration. Harvey smiled, never more certain of anything in his life than he was about Della. 'We'll tell them the truth. We'll tell them I fell in love with you in Fiji.'

Della shook her head, that familiar spark of challenge he loved in her eyes. 'No, we'll tell them *I* fell in love with *you*.'

'Okay, you win.' He winked, chasing her lips with his in a final kiss before they pushed open the door to the restaurant and stepped into their future.

EPILOGUE

Two years later.

DELLA'S PAGER SOUNDED, summoning her to theatre. Her next patient must have left the surgical ward. She silenced the device, which was clipped to the pocket of her green Melbourne Medical Centre scrubs, and took the stairs. She was just about to turn the corner into the operating suites when Australia's hottest surgeon appeared in her path.

'Well, fancy meeting you here, Dr Wilton,' Harvey said, his stare travelling her body with a look that was way too indecent for the workplace.

'Are you following me again, Dr Ward?' she said, her breath trapped in her chest at how handsome he was and how, after almost two years of marriage, she was still crazy in love with him. 'Because you seem to be every-where I look—in *my* bed, at *my* work, father to *my* chil-dren.' Pointedly, she glanced down at her pregnant belly, resting a hand over their growing son. 'If I didn't know you better, I'd guess you were my husband or something.'

They'd married in an intimate ceremony with family and friends four months before the birth of baby Lily, their daughter.

Harvey grinned, glanced along the corridor and then opened the nearest door, dragging Della into a utility room, the shelves of which were stacked with folded clean bed linens. 'Man, I missed you,' he said, hauling her as close as the baby bump would allow.

Della kissed him back, finally pulling back with a chuckle. 'Since this morning?'

'Yes,' he said simply, his expression sincere. That playful glint came into his eyes, doubling Della's pulse. 'Believe it or not, being married to you is the best thing that's ever happened to this old reformed bachelor. And the sex...' He rolled his eyes closed and groaned. 'Don't even get me started on how good that is. Some might say the best of their life...?'

Della laughed, too happy with his smug confidence to pull him up on his arrogance. When it came to accepting her love, trusting in it and giving her everything in return, her husband had risen to the top of the class during the past two years.

'I have to go,' she said, kissing him swiftly once more. 'I have a man who came off his motorbike yesterday about to arrive in theatre.'

Harvey gripped her waist, blocking her escape. 'One more kiss to get me through the afternoon,' he begged, sliding his lips up the side of her neck so she shuddered against him with desire.

As she did every day, Della tangled her fingers in his hair and kissed him properly—her lips parting, her tongue sliding against his, her body shifting restlessly as she tried to manage how much he turned her on.

'Wow,' Harvey said when they parted, looking a little dazed. 'That was some kiss.'

'I'm softening you up,' she said, running her fingers through his hair in order to make him look presentable for his patients. 'Do you want day care pickup or dinner?'

Harvey groaned half-heartedly. 'Come on... I made dinner last night.'

'Perhaps you prefer both,' she said, playfully digging in her heels. 'My surgery will probably run over anyway.'

'Fine,' he said with a mock sigh, 'I suppose I'll pick up my adorable daughter from nursery and make my pregnant wife a delicious, nutritious meal for when she gets home from work.' Finally turning serious, he cupped her face and kissed her one last time. 'Leave it to me—the best sex and the best husband you've ever had.'

Della laughed, loving his competitive streak as much as she loved the rest of him. 'Don't forget the best father to our children,' she said, reaching for the door handle. Just before she left the glorified cupboard to sheepishly make her exit, hoping no one would see, she turned back. 'I love you.'

She never tired of saying that to Harvey. Nor had she ever grown used to the hint of bewilderment she saw in his eyes every time she did, as if he couldn't quite believe it was true.

'I love you too, Della.' He reached for her hand and squeezed her fingers. 'See you at home.'

She opened the door and was about to duck out when he pulled her back. His lips found hers, his hands gripping her face so tight, she forgot to breathe as he kissed her. When he pulled back, he rested his forehead against hers and whispered, 'Do you have everything that you've ever wanted?'

Dazed from the passion and desperation of his kiss and awash with love hormones, Della nodded, lost for words.

'Good,' Harvey said. 'Because that makes two of us.'

* * * * *

The Rebel Doctor's Secret Child

Deanne Anders

MILLS & BOON

Deanne Anders was reading romance while her friends were still reading Nancy Drew, and she knew she'd hit the jackpot when she found a shelf of Harlequin Presents in her local library. Years later she discovered the fun of writing her own. Deanne lives in Florida, with her husband and their spoiled Pomeranian. During the day she works as a nursing supervisor. With her love of everything medical and romance, writing for Mills & Boon Medical is a dream come true.

This book is dedicated to all the medical staff
who volunteer their time at our local clinics, schools,
and with our local disaster teams.
Thank you for your service.

PROLOGUE

EXCITEMENT VIBRATED THROUGH Brianna Rogers as she followed the office manager, Sable, into the crowded conference room. With her arms loaded down with boxes of donuts, Brianna looked across the table at all the people she'd soon be working with. She'd done it. In just a few months, she'd be working as a certified nurse midwife. The opportunity for a residency at Nashville's Women's Legacy Clinic was one that she'd never imagined receiving. It was known as the premier women's clinic in the city, so the experience she'd receive here would be priceless.

As the door opened and a silver-haired man with kind blue eyes came in, the room went quiet. Bree rushed to her seat. She had only met the founder of the clinic, Dr. Jack Warner, once during an interview, but she admired the practice he'd built and especially the home for pregnant women in need of a safe place to stay that he had founded.

He took his seat at the end of the table then reached for the tablet Sable had told her contained the itinerary for the meeting.

"First off, I'd like to welcome two new colleagues. I

hope you've all met our new resident midwife, Brianna Rogers. She's a recent graduate of Vanderbilt and came to us highly recommended."

A man yelled, "Go Commodores," from across the room, taking the attention off her, something she appreciated. One of the midwives, Sky, waved at her from down the table. Bree waved back. Even with the unwanted attention, she was already feeling at home here.

"Also, I want you to welcome Dr. Knox Collins, who will be filling in for Dr. Hennison, who, I'm sure you all know, just welcomed another baby boy."

Bree's heart skipped a beat and her arms and face prickled with tiny pinpricks. No. It was impossible that he could be there. A roaring in her ears started as her eyes scanned the room, stopping when she saw a man with laughing gray eyes and a devilish smile that should have come with a warning.

Never in her wildest dreams would she have imagined herself stuck looking across the table at the man who had broken her sister's heart and left Bree to pick up the pieces. Especially since one of those pieces had been a newborn baby. She'd never forget the first time she'd heard that name. It had been when her phone rang. She hadn't spoken to her sister in months and was so happy to see her name on the display.

Suddenly, she was back there, eight years earlier. Brittany, her voice overflowing with a happiness Bree hadn't heart in years, laughing as she told Bree the news. "It's a girl, Bree. A beautiful baby girl. I have a daughter. You're an aunt."

Stunned, Bree didn't know what to say. Brittany had been pregnant? How was that possible without Bree knowing about it?

"Well, aren't you going to congratulate me?" her sister asked.

"Of course," Bree said, recovering from the shock of her sister's words. "Where are you?"

Bree listened closely as her sister explained how she'd gone into labor early and the baby was still in the hospital.

"Who's the father?" Bree asked, unable to hold back the question any longer. Brittany had been known to hook up with some less than desirable types in the past.

"It's Knox Collins, Gail and Charles Collins's son. But you can't tell anyone. Me. This baby. We mean nothing to him. He's messed up, Bree. He drinks and parties all the time. I don't want that for my daughter. Promise me you won't tell anyone, Bree. Promise me."

Bree had no choice but to agree. If Brittany thought the man would be a bad influence on her daughter, she had no choice but to believe her. She'd ask for more information the next time her sister called her.

But the next call she received wasn't from her sister. Instead, it was from the hospital. She could hear the woman's voice. "I'm sorry, Ms. Rogers, but there's been a terrible accident."

She told the woman that she was wrong. She'd just spoken with her sister only hours earlier. Her sister couldn't be gone.

She remembered holding her niece in her arms for the

first time, knowing it should have been Brittany standing there to take her baby home. Not Bree.

Overwhelming grief had threatened to overtake her then, but she pushed it back. Just like she had when she'd realized she was suddenly responsible for her sister's newborn baby. There was no time for grieving. Because if she let it take hold of her, she'd never climb out of the dark pit of it. She'd never be able to take care of the child who had no one else. Just like Bree had no one else but that child.

The noise of the room rose, bringing her back to reality as everyone around her stood up to leave.

Looking down the table she saw Knox accepting the greetings from the clinic's staff. How was it that he stood there, smiling and happy, going on with his life while her sister's life was cut so short?

Bree shook her head. No. She wouldn't let herself go there. Ally had to be her first priority. The little girl had given Bree a reason to keep on going for years now, to keep pushing to better herself so that she could provide a good life for her niece. And there was no way she was going to let some hotshot rebel doc like Knox Collins get in her way.

CHAPTER ONE

BRIANNA ROGERS WAS trying to ignore them. All of them. The giggling nurse with bouncy honey-blond curls Bree would give her already strained credit card to have, the anesthesia nurse whose toothpaste-ad smile could blind someone, and the drooling surgical tech whose no-nonsense attitude had turned disgustingly mushy. But most of all, she was trying to ignore the man in the middle of all three of them, Knox Collins.

From the moment Bree had attended her first staff meeting at Women's Legacy Clinic, she'd made it her priority to avoid Knox. For three months she had accomplished the impossible by managing to dodge the man whom she'd considered enemy number one for the past eight years. It looked like her luck had run out now, and the only thing she could do was pretend that he wasn't there.

Her teeth ground against each other when the blonde nurse giggled again at something Knox had said. She forced her eyes back to the computer screen in front of her and did her best to block out everyone else in the room.

Should she have turned down the opportunity that

Dr. Warner, Jack, had given her when she'd found out Nashville's own bad boy turned doctor was going to be there? Maybe, but how could she? With the amount of student loans she had and the cost of raising her niece, she was lucky to get the chance to do her midwife residency at the clinic. There was no way she could afford to turn down the opportunity. Not having to leave Nashville or change her niece's school had been a blessing and reduced the stress that always seemed to be right around the corner waiting to overwhelm her. Oh, she'd been tempted to pack up Ally and skedaddle out of town, but where would she go? It would have taken months to get set up with another clinic. Months of falling further and further behind financially.

So instead, she'd convinced herself that if she was careful and kept her head down, she'd be able to avoid Dr. Knox Collins. And it had worked. Until now.

"Need some help?" A deep voice came from right behind her, causing her to jump then grab for the coffee mug as her hand knocked against its side.

"What?" she asked, the word ending with a squeak that made her sound like the mouse her sister had always accused her of being. Looking around, she saw that the other staff members had finally left the room. Clearing her throat, she tried again. "I'm sorry, do you need something, Dr. Collins?"

"I just noticed you staring at the screen," he said, his hand waving toward her computer, "and I wondered if you needed help charting something in the delivery record. One of the nurses was just telling me that it was a difficult delivery you and Lori just attended. Sometimes that complicates the charting."

It had been a difficult delivery with the baby being much larger than expected and its face turned up. It had taken everyone working together to get him out. But with Lori, her midwife preceptor beside her, Bree had been in control of the situation. "No. There's no problem."

"Good. I know Lori's your preceptor, but if there's anything I can do, or anything you have a question about, just ask. I know I'm just here temporarily, but I want to help if I can," Knox said before moving back to his own computer.

Once he wasn't looking over her shoulder, Bree's body relaxed, at least a little. He was still too close and his words just made things worse. Because the biggest surprise she'd had since the day they'd first met was that Dr. Knox Collins didn't seem like the coldhearted, self-absorbed man that her sister had made him out to be. He seemed to be truly interested in the patients and the staff at the clinic.

Or was the overly nice doctor he presented to the staff just an act to make people like him? Didn't the man ever wear something besides a smile on his face? Didn't he ever have a bad day? Maybe if you were the only son of mega-rich country music stars you didn't have bad days.

But no matter how nice the man appeared to be, she had to keep her defenses up around him. The last thing she needed was to have him focus that charm of his on her.

"Why? Do you need more members in your fan club?"

she asked, the sarcasm as thick as the butter on a country biscuit.

Had she really just said that?

Way to keep yourself off his radar, Bree.

"I keep getting the feeling that you have something against me. Do you want to talk about it? Clear the air? Is there something I did?" Knox said, the sincerity in his voice setting her teeth to grinding again. Didn't the man ever get mad?

And what would he say if she told him it was definitely something he'd done? He'd gotten her sister pregnant and then ignored her. Bree couldn't blame him for her sister's death—that had been the result of her sister taking a curve around a mountain too fast—but that didn't mean Bree could forgive him for his part in her sister's last days. For not being a man her sister wanted to help raise her daughter.

She knew she couldn't say any of this. Not if she wanted to keep her promise to her sister. And not if she wanted to protect her niece. Instead, she had to find a way to put some distance between them.

"I'm sorry, Dr. Knox. I appreciate your offer to help. It's just been a long day."

The silence in the room was deafening. She knew he wasn't buying her excuse. She'd spent the past three months avoiding him and apparently he had noticed. Had she been that transparent?

"Hey guys, what's up?" Lori asked as she entered the room. Bree released a slow, steadying breath. She'd known from day one that she and Lori were going to make a good team. Though only a few years older than she was, Lori had been with the practice since she had obtained her midwifery certification. She'd taken Bree in as if they'd been friends for a lifetime, and she shared all her experience and knowledge. Lori was someone people knew they could trust the moment they met her. More than once, Bree had started to spill all her secrets with the midwife.

"I'm almost finished with the charting if you want to look it over," Bree said, turning toward the doorway, glad to end the conversation with Knox.

"Sure," Lori said, looking between the two of them, her eyes seeing more than what Bree wanted her to see. Her preceptor was smart and observant.

"I heard that the two of you had a challenging delivery," Knox said, turning his attention to Lori.

"Posterior delivery, but Bree handled it perfectly," Lori said as she took a seat next to Bree. "She's going to make a great midwife."

"I was just telling her that the staff was saying she did great today," Knox said.

"She did," Lori said. "I'm very proud of her."

Bree ducked her head as her cheeks warmed with a blush that would make the freckles on her nose stand out even more.

Where her sister had thrived on the applause and praises of the press and audiences when they were young, it had always made Bree feel uncomfortable and awkward to have others compliment her. It was one of many reasons she had protested when her sister and their agent had decided it was time to take their duet to the next level in the country music scene.

"I still have a lot to learn," Bree said, making herself lift her eyes and look at her coworkers.

"Dr. Collins, they're ready for you in the OR," Kelly, the nurse who'd been giggling with Knox's group earlier, said from the open doorway.

Once Knox left the room, Bree could feel Lori's eyes on her. "What was that about?"

"What?" Bree asked, pretending not to know what Lori was referring to. Unable to hold Lori's gaze, Bree looked back at the computer screen, pretending to study it.

"There was something going on between the two of you. I could feel it."

"It was nothing." All Bree wanted to do was finish her charting and get out of the room before Knox returned.

But the experienced midwife was not going to let it go. Reaching over, Lori shut the door. "I might believe that if this was the first time I'd noticed the change in you when Dr. Collins was around. Has he done something? Anything to make you uncomfortable?"

It seemed that would be the theme of the day. She was too tired to go through another review of all the things Knox had done again.

Still, she knew Lori was concerned that he had done something inappropriate, and Bree couldn't let her think that. "No. He's been nothing but helpful to me since I came to the practice."

"So, what is it, then? I know we were all worried that

he'd be this stuck-up rich kid, but I haven't found him to be that way at all."

Neither had Bree, which had thrown her off, leaving her feeling a guilt that she hadn't expected. Which led her back to the possibility that the man might have truly changed. What if he wasn't the selfish, ego-obsessed man Bree had assumed from her sister's description? And even worse, what if he had never been that man?

No. She wouldn't even consider such a thing. Brittany might not have always been up-front when it came to getting what she wanted, but she never would have made Bree promise to keep her daughter away from her father if she hadn't had a good reason for it. Bree, herself, had looked into his background after Brittany had called her and told her about the baby. Knox Collins had been a troubled teenager who'd been kicked out of more than one private academy. Reports of his partying his way through college were all over the local media.

"Of course, if it's something more personal, I wouldn't blame you. The man is certainly nice to look at. I think half the staff is in lust with him." Lori gave Bree a wicked smile. "It's nothing to be embarrassed about. He's not my type, but I get it."

Bree looked over at Lori. The midwife had a natural beauty that came from her generous smile and kind eyes. "What is your type?"

"I'm not quite sure," Lori said, her eyes looking off into space before returning to Bree. "I'm stuck somewhere between wanting a Mr. Darcy and a Jamie Fraser."

Bree hadn't ever cared much for Mr. Darcy, too stuffy,

but she had watched every season of *Outlander* and couldn't help but think that Knox, with his thick light brown curls that fell almost to his shoulders, would make a great Jamie Fraser.

"Really, Lori, there's nothing like that going on." No matter how good-looking the man was, she would never let herself be attracted to him.

Lori studied her a little too long before finally shaking her head. "Okay, but if there is something that's bothering you, I want you to know you can talk to me. No matter what it's about, but especially if it's something that could affect your work."

Bree bit back words that would spill the secret she had worked so hard to keep for the past eight years. She trusted Lori, she did, but there was too much at stake. If the truth came out about who was Ally's father, Bree could lose the child she loved as her own. Let the other midwife think that Bree was harboring some deep longing for Dr. Collins. Better that than she know the truth.

"If you're good, then, I'm going to let you finish up rounds. We don't have any new labor patients, but there is a day-two postpartum on the floor who needs discharge orders put in. You remember Kristina? It's her third baby. No complications. Just look in on her and make sure she doesn't need anything before discharge. You can meet me back at the office when you're finished."

As soon as Lori had shut the door to the physician's work room, Bree dropped her head to the desk. Why did life have to be so complicated? It had always been her sister who had loved drama. Not Bree. She took in a big breath then let it out, along with all the pent-up stress of the past few minutes, and made herself look on the bright side of things. Dr. Collins had only a few more weeks before his ad-locum contract would be finished and he'd be moving on.

She'd managed for weeks to keep her head down around him. And if luck was on her side, she'd be able to continue to avoid him. But then again, when had luck been on her side?

"I'm not sure I understand," Knox repeated for the third time. "I thought Lori was Bree's preceptor," he said to Dr. Warner.

"I'll still be her preceptor," Lori interjected. "I just think that it would be a good thing for her to get an opportunity to do some work in the county women's clinic. You've been saying you need more volunteers to help. This will work out perfectly," Lori said.

There was something about the way that Lori was looking at him that set his warning bells ringing. It reminded him of the look his momma got when she was about to set him up with her newest matchmaking victim.

"Lori's right," Dr. Warner said as he looked at the two of them from across his desk. "Brianna needs to get some experience in a women's clinic like the one run by the county. There is no telling where she might find herself in the future. Our clinic is lucky enough to have fancy equipment with all the bells and whistles. If she ends up in one of the more rural parts of our state, she might not have those."

Jack was right. The older man had built Legacy Women's Clinic into one of the best clinics in the state during his career. And though he'd stepped back and let his son take over a lot of the running of the clinic now, Knox respected the man and couldn't deny that Jack wanted only the best for all his staff. Unfortunately, that meant Knox was going to have to agree with him. With the shortage of obstetricians nationwide and the rural areas of Tennessee depending on the certified midwives to fill in where they could, Bree would be welcomed in one of the rural areas.

"Okay. Fine. I'll work with her. But I need to know her proficiencies as well as her weaknesses. I don't want to put her in a position she's not comfortable with." It was bad enough that she seemed to have taken to immediately disliking him, something that he still didn't understand. There was even the possibility that Bree would refuse to work with him.

There was a soft knock on the door before Bree stuck her head inside. "You wanted to see me?"

Knox could see the hesitancy in her expression as she entered the room and looked around. When her eyes met his, all the color drained from her face. At that moment she looked so young with her strawberry blond hair pulled back in a tight braid that was a little lopsided. There was an innocence in her green eyes that sparked a sudden, unexpected need to protect her. Just how innocent was she? He hadn't missed the fact that she'd actually blushed when Lori had complimented her earlier that day. When had he ever seen a woman do that? Had he ever?

His attitude concerning Jack and Lori's request to allow the young midwife to work with him at the county clinic made a U-turn. Bree needed to get out into the real world. It had certainly been an eye-opener for him. And one that had changed his whole career. It would be interesting to watch her interact with the women he saw there. Women who didn't have the resources for the kind of care they received at Legacy. Women down on their luck and needing help.

"Come in, Brianna," Jack said, then waved her to the seat next to Knox. "We were just discussing with Dr. Collins the possibility of you helping him out at the county clinic for a few hours a week."

Knox wouldn't have thought her face could have gone any whiter, but it did. For a moment she just stared at Jack, then she turned to Lori. "Is there a problem with me working with you?"

"No, not at all," Lori reassured her. "You are doing beyond what I could have hoped for at this stage of your training. But Jack and I think that you could be an asset to the county clinic while increasing your experience. Here we have a controlled atmosphere where we see our patients on a schedule so we can prepare for our day. At the clinic, you will see more of a variety of patients, including more gynecology patients. It's also something that will look good on your résumé. More importantly, you'll be helping women who need your care."

"I've helped out at Legacy House when I've had the time," Bree said. "And I have...other responsibilities. I don't have a lot of free hours."

"We wouldn't expect you to work any more hours. If Dr. Collins agrees to this, you'll be able to get your clinic hours at the county two days each week in exchange for two days in the clinic here."

When they all turned toward him, Knox felt the tension in the room soar. While Jack's eyes seemed confident that Knox would agree, and Lori had one eyebrow lifted in challenge, Bree's eyes were round as saucers with a fear he could not understand. Had he somehow intimidated her? Was that what all this tension he felt around her was all about? No, the comments she'd made that morning, ones he'd chosen to ignore, showed that she wasn't afraid to speak her mind with him.

Maybe it was because of who his parents were. That, he was used to. A lot of people were overly impressed by his parents' fame. But somehow he knew that wasn't it, either. This was something different. And for some irrational reason, while it should have irritated him, it intrigued him. He wanted to know what it was that had her bristling every time he came into the room.

"I think it would be a great learning experience for Bree, and I could certainly use the help," he said. Neither of those statements was a lie. The clinic was chronically short on staff. He was only filling in for a friend for a few weeks, but he could use the help, even if it was temporary.

Then Bree did something he wasn't expecting. She

pulled back her shoulders and sent all of them a confident, though a little wobbly, smile. "Okay, then. It's settled. I look forward to working with Dr. Collins at the county clinic."

The tremble of her lips as she said the words betrayed that she did everything but look forward to the next month of the two of them working together. Was he the only one in the room who could see she was most definitely not excited about working with him at all? From the smiles on Lori's and Jack's faces, he was afraid that he was.

It had been a long time since he'd had this amount of interest in a woman. Bree Rogers was a mystery, one that he couldn't wait to solve.

"Is this about this morning?" Bree asked as soon as she and Lori were alone in Lori's office.

"Of course not," Lori said and then sighed. "Okay, maybe a little. The truth is Jack mentioned the idea to me and I thought it might be good for you to take this opportunity, not just to learn more about how to work in a county clinic, but also to learn to work with coworkers that you might not like."

"I don't not like Dr. Collins. I just don't…" She'd talked herself into a corner now. How did she explain to Lori her feelings for Knox without spilling all her secrets? "I don't find him particularly likeable."

Lori rolled her eyes at Bree's contradictory statement. "Like I said, Jack—Dr. Warner—came up with this idea. To be honest, I think there's a possibility he has heard some of the office chatter suggesting that you have a problem with Knox. I'm not the only one who has noticed how you have a habit of avoiding our ad-locum doc."

She should have known she couldn't keep her feelings toward the doctor hidden in such a tight-knit group as the one that worked at Legacy Clinic. Did that mean they were talking about her behind her back? Did they, like Lori had, think she had some schoolgirl crush on him?

"Look at it this way. There's only a few more weeks to Dr. Collins's contract here. Do a good job and learn everything you can at the clinic. He's a good doctor. You might be surprised how much he can teach you. He might not have been a doctor for very long, but he's worked some places so far back in the mountains that the nearest hospital was over an hour's drive away."

Bree had heard that Knox had even done some work off the grid up in the Smoky Mountains, which in spite of herself she wanted to hear more about. And like Lori had reminded her, Knox's contract would be over soon and he would be moving on. She just had to hold it together till then. She'd kept her sister's secret for eight years. She could do it a few more weeks.

That thought had her feeling better, until a few hours later when she arrived to pick Ally up from her after-school care program. Seeing her little girl surrounded by her friends as they worked on a craft project made all her protective instincts kick in. Just eight years old, Ally was already showing signs of being a people magnet like her mother. Unlike Bree, who'd been shy most of her childhood, her sister Brittany had always had a way with people. Ally's friendly smile and quick laughter helped her make friends wherever she went. She was sweet and innocent and Bree would protect that little girl with the last breath in her body. She would never allow the man whom her sister didn't approve of take Ally away from her. Never.

"How was your day? Did you deliver any babies?" Ally asked.

Bree flipped a pancake over before turning to her niece. The last thing she wanted to do was talk about her day, but she couldn't ignore the question.

When Ally had started school and Bree had her own classes along with two jobs sometimes, it had become hard for Bree to spend the quality time she wanted to with Ally. Most nights dinner had become fast food or boxed mac-'n'-cheese, so Bree made the effort to make the middle of the week meal fun and a chance for the two of them to spend time together. Since Ally's favorite meal was breakfast, Bree had deemed Wednesday night as breakfast night.

"I did deliver a baby. A really big one with adorable chubby cheeks." Bree turned around and puffed her cheeks out, making a face that had Ally laughing. "What about you? Did the teacher like the picture you drew?"

Ally's laughter stopped and her eyes filled with tears.

"What's wrong? Did something happen to the picture?" While Ally's picture, one that showed Bree and Ally in front of the small house Bree rented, wouldn't have won any awards, she had worked hard on it, and Bree knew Ally's teacher had to have seen that.

"Holly asked me why I didn't have a mommy or daddy," Ally said, before wiping her eyes with her shirt-sleeve.

This wasn't the first time someone in Ally's class had asked her that question. Bree had struggled with the decision of whether to tell Ally about her mother or whether to let her grow up believing that Bree was her mother. To Bree, Ally had been her little girl from the moment the nurse had put her in her arms.

Still, no matter how much Bree loved Ally as her own, it was important that she knew about her mother. In some ways, Ally helped to keep her sister's memory alive for both of them.

Bree knew grief. She and Brittany had lost their parents within a few months of each other. It had been hard, but she'd still had her sister. They'd shared everything from a womb to a room for the first eighteen years of their lives. Not having her sister left a hole that ate at Bree. It was only in the middle of the night, after Ally was safely tucked into bed, that Bree allowed herself to let the grief of losing her sister take over. But the next morning, she pasted on a smile and went back to living, for her sister as much as for her niece.

After taking the pancake from the griddle, Bree went around the island and hugged the little girl. "I'm sorry. I know it makes you sad when someone asks you questions about your mommy."

As always, she avoided the question of Ally's daddy,

something she knew she wouldn't be able to do for too much longer. Till now Ally had been satisfied with Bree's explanation that there had been an accident that had taken her mother away, but it was only a matter of time till the child became more curious about her father. And what was Bree going to do then? She'd found it hard each time she had to explain to Ally how her mother had died; explaining that her father hadn't been in the picture when she'd been born would be even harder.

Ally snuggled closer against her and Bree's arms tightened around her small frame.

For now, all Bree could do was give Ally all the love she had and hope it would be enough to shield her from that and all the other heartbreaks she was bound to encounter. Bree knew she'd always appreciated having her parents to lean on when she'd faced her own heartaches. Of course, that was before the cancer had taken her momma and the bottle had taken her daddy. And then the search for fame had taken Brittany into a whole different place in life than Bree had wanted to go, taking Brittany completely out of Bree's life.

"How about we eat a bunch of pancakes until our tummy hurts and then we can snuggle up together with a couple books till bedtime?"

"Not schoolbooks?" Ally asked. Bree knew she was remembering the months, no, years, that Bree had spent studying for her nursing degree and then her nurse practitioner and midwifery degrees.

"Not schoolbooks," Bree said, though she did have some community health studying she'd planned to do to start preparing for whatever she might encounter with Knox at the clinic. The more she knew, the fewer questions she'd have to ask him.

But later, after their meal and dishes were done, Bree noticed that Ally wasn't paying attention as she read the little girl one of her favorite wizard books. "Do you want us to read something else?"

"I don't feel much like reading. I thought maybe you could tell me a story about my mom instead?"

Bree wasn't surprised at her request after their discussion earlier that night. Bree had been telling Ally stories about Brittany since she was around three. If Bree added a bit to the stories sometimes, it was always for the little girl's benefit. The truth was there were a couple years when Brittany had cut Bree out of her life, which was something Bree would never tell Ally.

"Well, let's see. Where do you want me to start?" Bree asked, though she already knew the answer.

"Start where you and my mom came to Nashville and sang on stage at the Grand Ole Opry," Ally said, snuggling farther down into her covers. "When the two of you were famous."

Bree laughed. "I don't think the two of us were exactly famous. There just weren't a lot of eleven-year-old twins playing guitar and singing Loretta Lynn songs back then."

"Loretta who?" Ally asked.

"Never mind." She'd hold the history of country music lesson till later. "Okay, so you know we'd won a contest at the county fair and made the papers. And then one morning our momma got a phone call inviting us to come sing a couple songs on stage in Nashville. Of course she agreed, but our daddy thought it was a hoax…"

"A what?" Ally asked.

"It's what they used to call scams. Anyway, he called the Opry and asked to speak with the manager, who told him no, it wasn't a hoax. They had seen the article in the paper and they had invited us. It was a good thing it wasn't a scam, too, because our momma was so excited that she had already left the house to pick us up early from school." Bree could still remember the way her momma's eyes had shined when she'd had the principal pull them out of class to tell them. She didn't think she had ever seen her momma so happy. Then Brittany had squealed loud enough that the teachers had stuck their heads out of their classrooms to see what was going on. Before long, the whole school was caught up in the celebration. No one seemed to notice that Bree wasn't celebrating with them. Not even her mother or her sister.

"Tell me about the dress my momma wore," Ally said.

"I've showed you pictures," Bree said, unable to keep the grumble from her voice. She had hated those dresses with the yards of ruffles and bows. The fact that they had been pink, her sister's favorite color, not hers, had nothing to do with it, either. "It was awful. It had all those ruffles and too much lace. It was way too girly."

Ally giggled. "I think it was pretty."

"So there we were, Saturday night, out on the stage, when Loretta Lynn herself came up to your momma and told her that she was 'just the prettiest thing I ever saw.'"

"But you weren't there because you were sick in the dressing room," Ally said.

It had been one of Bree's most embarrassing moments. She'd been throwing up so hard her eyes had watered, and one of the women who worked backstage had to help her clean herself up before she could go on stage. "No, but my momma told me all about it."

"Then the two of you sang that song about being from the country and one of the people there offered y'all a lot of money to sing for them."

"Something like that." Bree was too young to know anything about the money side, but it was the night they got their first agent. Their first in a long line for the next eight years as Brittany and her parents chased their dream for fame and fortune, despite Bree trying to explain to them that she wanted something different for her life.

"I bet if my momma was here right now she'd be a big star. Then I could draw pictures of the three of us up on stage together." Ally yawned and rolled over on to her side, her eyes closing as the long day caught up with her.

"I bet she would," Bree whispered, though in her heart she wasn't so sure. Bree's and Brittany's thirty seconds of fame had been long gone by the time Brittany had died. Brittany had blamed Bree. It had caused a rift between them that Bree had hoped someday to mend. She liked to think that the two of them were moving toward that after the call she received from Brittany before the car crash.

Bree sat there for a few moments until she was sure

that the little girl was asleep, then went to her own room to spend a few hours studying. She had no idea what she might encounter at the county clinic but she was going to be as prepared as possible.

Later, when her eyes refused to read another case study, Bree put her books away and climbed into bed. Somehow, she'd managed to avoid the dreaded conversation about Ally's father once more. But for how long? There was going to come a day when she wouldn't be able to avoid that question. And what was she going to say then? How did she tell a story that she didn't really know herself? All she'd been told by Brittany was that she and Knox had been involved and that he'd left her and had no interest in a child. How did you tell a child that her father hadn't wanted her?

And how did Bree know if that was still the way Knox felt now? Brittany's words had been so cryptic that she wasn't even sure if Brittany had ever told him about the pregnancy. There were so many questions she'd never been able to ask her sister. She was having a hard time believing the man she'd watched interacting with the staff today wouldn't want to know his daughter. And if he did? What would that mean for Ally? For Bree?

Since the moment she'd been told by Dr. Warner and Lori that she would be working with Knox at the clinic, Bree had felt a sense of impending doom. As a midwife, she knew that when a patient felt that way, you never ignored it. There was always some reason, some instinctual knowledge, for that intense feeling that something bad was about to happen.

Even as she slipped into sleep, she acknowledged that everything in her life was about to change and all she could do was ensure that she protected her niece no matter what it cost her. Because after losing everyone else in her family, she would not lose Ally.

CHAPTER TWO

KNOX WATCHED AS Bree entered the aged county building where the small women's clinic where he was filling in for a friend was located.

"Good morning," he said, startling the young midwife as she reached the top of the first set of stairs that
would lead to their second-floor office. She looked up
at him with her bright green eyes that he always found
appealing. Then there was that long strawberry blond
hair and those freckles that dusted her nose. She wasn't
striking and she didn't fit the trendy idea of beautiful.
What was it about her that kept his mind returning to
her over and over again?

He shook his head at his early-morning musings. He'd
only had time for one cup of coffee so far and it would
take a couple more before he'd be ready for clinic hours.

"I have to say that I'm surprised to find you working
at one of the city's free clinics," Bree said as she looked
around the worn floors and walls that were in deep need
of new paint. She didn't seem to be judging the building
as much as she was judging him.

"I ran into a friend from college who works here and
he needed some time off. The clinic is only open two

days a week. It's not really any different from the work that I do when I'm working up in the mountains. I'd already planned to take the temporary position with Legacy, so why not help him out?"

"I wouldn't think you'd have the time. It almost sounds like you don't do anything but work. Which doesn't make sense."

Knox wasn't surprised by her comment. A lot of people figured that with parents as rich as his, there wasn't any reason for him to work. What they didn't get was that he enjoyed his work. Especially work like he got to do in the rural communities in the mountains. "Both jobs are temporary. And both are very different. You won't see the same clientele here that you've been seeing at the Legacy Clinic. A lot of these women don't have insurance or even money to cover high copays. Some of them don't trust the state health care system. And some of them won't trust you, either. Getting someone to trust you after they've been let down by the system is a major accomplishment. You'll find trust in short supply here. You might not even like the work. It can be very repetitive, mostly yearly exams, medication refills, STD testing, that type of thing. But I can guarantee that it will open your eyes to the needs of the community."

"I'm here to learn as much as possible. Dr. Warner and Lori think this will be good for my training, and their opinions are important to me. I've worked in a labor and delivery department with patients from all backgrounds so that won't be a problem."

This was probably the longest conversation they'd ever

shared. Fortunately for the two of them, there was none of the sarcasm she'd been so happy to share with him the week before, which made him feel better about bringing her in to help out. Maybe having a week to adjust to the idea of working with him had been good, though he still didn't understand what it was about him that caused her to go on the offensive every time she was around him.

"That's good," Knox said as they headed up the second set of steps. He liked the fact that Bree wasn't afraid to stand up and say what she thought. He'd had too many coworkers who treated him differently either because he was a doctor or because of his parents. Bree didn't seem to be impressed by either. "I wanted to show you around the building before we went upstairs to the office since when the doors open I won't have the time. Most of the first story takes care of the county clerk business, but the second floor is mostly used by the health department. At the end of the hall is the children's clinic, which you might need to know to refer some of our patients with children there. And before that, on the right, there is a dentist office and health records departments. There is a substance abuse center across from there. Unfortunately you will need to make referrals there, too."

He watched as she studied the areas he pointed out. When she didn't make any comment, he continued. "Any OB patients get referred out. The health department has a separate program for them."

Turning left, he led her to the set of offices where they'd be working together. The simple block letters that read Women's Clinic was the only thing that set itself apart from the other line of doors down the hall. Opening the door, they were met with the one thing that made the clinic possible, its no-nonsense, but still empathetic, office manager.

"Bree, I'd like you to meet the real boss of this joint, Ms. Lucretia Sweet. Don't be fooled by the name. She's only sweet when she wants to be."

"And I'm certainly not sweet till I get my brew in the morning. Hand it over."

Knox did as he was told and handed the special order coffee to the woman who had won his heart the first day he'd shown up to work there.

"Bree's a midwifery resident at Legacy and is going to be helping for the next few weeks so don't run her off," Knox said. "And if you can show her around while I start a pot of real coffee, I'd appreciate it."

"Me run off good help? Especially when it's free? Not going to happen. Come on in here, Bree. Is that short for Brianna?"

"Yes, ma'am. Brianna Rogers, but please call me Bree."

Knox listened to the women's exchange as he started the coffee in the small corner that also provided snacks and water for their patients. After his first good swallow of the dark-roasted drink, he returned to find Lucretia questioning his resident like a military drill sergeant.

"Have you ever worked in a clinic like this? Because I want you to understand that while we might not agree with some of these women's choices, we treat each one of them as equals."

"I did a rotation in the county jail during my masters in nursing degree. I plan on doing my doctorate dissertation on the need for more women's care in the correctional system."

"I didn't know you were planning on getting your doctorate," Knox said as he leaned against the doorjamb and studied the woman. She was gutsy and driven. He liked that. She'd do well as a midwife wherever she went.

"I'm sure there's a lot you don't know about me," Bree said, then squeezed her lips together as if she wanted to take back the words.

"A woman of mystery. Well, you give me time and I bet I'll learn all those secrets you're keeping," Lucretia said. "Now, let me take you back to the exam offices so I can show you how I set up the supplies. Mind you, don't be wasting them. They don't grow on trees and the budget's tight for this place."

Knowing that Bree was in good hands, he left them to it and went back to top off his cup of coffee. The two women had just met, but already Bree was talking with Lucretia like the two of them were old friends. It seemed she was only prickly with him. So what was it about him that made the woman's back go up every time he was around? Was it because of who his parents were? He'd met a lot of people who were intimidated by his parents' fame, but he still didn't think she was one of them.

The door to their offices opened and he heard Lucretia welcome their first patient of the day. It looked like the mystery of Midwife Bree Rogers would just have to wait.

* * *

By lunchtime, Bree understood immediately why Knox had referred to Lucretia as the boss. From the time the first patient came through the door until when they took a thirty-minute break to swallow down some takeout, the woman had kept the line of patients that filled the small rooms organized and constantly moving.

Lori had told her that she would be starting off working one-on-one with Knox, but by the time they'd seen the first ten patients, Knox had assigned her one of the exam rooms as her own and told her to let him know if she needed him. It had felt good that he had confidence in her skills, even if she shouldn't have cared what he thought. Since then, she'd seen another six patients on her own and after figuring out the computer system for ordering lab tests and pharmacy prescriptions, she'd not had any trouble. She'd discovered quickly that most of the women the clinic saw were young and seeking an inexpensive way to obtain birth control or to be tested for STDs or pregnancy, all things that she'd been well trained in at the Legacy Clinic, though she'd quickly learned that giving these women a prescription didn't always mean the women could afford it.

When one woman she saw explained that the reason she had returned after being seen the month before was that she couldn't afford to get the birth control prescription filled, Bree had gone into the storage closet and taken out a six-month supply for the woman, along with a handful of condoms that she stuffed into the bag before the woman had left. The look on Lucretia's face when the woman walked out told Bree that the boss knew exactly what she had done and would be watching her. Giving the *boss* a guilty wave, Bree had slinked back into her assigned exam room to see her next patient. Yes, she knew they were working on a limited supply of samples of medication, but how much more wasteful would it be if the woman had to return every month? It would still be the same amount of samples given.

By the time they had stopped for their break, she was prepared to support her argument in case she was called on the carpet by either Lucretia or Knox.

"So, any issues?" Knox asked her as he handed her a canned drink and sandwich.

"No, it's all been good," she said, looking over at Lucretia. When the woman didn't say anything to the contrary, Bree figured she'd been worrying for nothing.

"I know this work isn't as exciting as delivering babies, but some of the women who come here have no place else to turn for basic care. My friend Dean, who runs this place, spends almost as much time working to get financing for supplies as he does seeing patients. I don't know exactly what his salary is, but if it's anything like what I receive when I'm working out in the small rural areas, it isn't much."

She'd only been working there a few hours, but already she could see that there was a true need in the community. How could one clinic that was only open two days a week provide for the needs of a city the size of Nashville?

"If you like the work, I know he would be happy to have the extra help," Knox said.

"I don't know what I'm going to do when I finish my residency. I have to pass my boards and then…" Had she really been about to say she had a little girl to take care of? "I just have a lot on my plate."

"I understand," Knox said, shrugging, before looking away. Bree had a strange feeling that she had disappointed him somehow.

"I'm sorry. I just can't commit to anything right now. I've been going nonstop for several years now and… I have other responsibilities that I need to take care of."

"It's okay, Bree. I didn't mean to put you on the spot. I just noticed that you seemed to be enjoying the job, and the patients seemed to be comfortable with you. But then I hear you've always been great with the patients at the clinic. You know I've helped start clinics like this one in the rural mountain towns where I've worked. I've even left some of them with a midwife in charge."

"Really?" she asked. "I'm surprised you could do that."

"The state of Tennessee allows midwives to work on their own without a doctor present. Of course, they all have doctors as resources and can refer out as needed. And not all the clinic services are free. If a patient has insurance, the clinic can file for reimbursement. A lot of their patients do have funding, they just don't have anywhere to go without traveling more than an hour."

"That sounds like an interesting job," Bree said. She could imagine herself living in a rural area someday.

A place where Ally would have plenty of room to run and play.

"If you ever decide you're interested, get in contact with me. After watching you today, I think you might enjoy the work," Knox said.

Bree could feel the blush creep up her face with the compliment. Why did this man have to keep being so nice to her? She didn't want him to be nice. She wanted him to be...well, she didn't know what she wanted him to be, but she didn't want him to be like this. His being nice just increased the guilt and fear she had that everything she'd believed about him wasn't true. And that wasn't something she could consider.

Because if you've been wrong all this time, if this man would have been a proper parent for Ally, how are you going to live with the fact that you didn't contact him after Brittany's death? And what do you do about Ally then? Can you live with the guilt that you knew he was Ally's father and never told him? Or her?

It had been easy to keep silent about Ally when her father had been some undeserving sperm donor. But now, actually getting to know the man herself, she couldn't conceive that the man her sister had made sound so cold and uncaring was the same man sitting across from her. The same man who went across the country starting clinics for underserved communities.

And it wasn't just that she had taken Brittany's word. Bree had done some investigating herself. There was no doubt that Knox had gotten into trouble during his teenage years. It had been small things, but she knew those things usually grew to bigger things when a teenager got older. There were also reports of him going to rehab more than once. Had he really changed his life that much? From everything she had seen since meeting him, it seemed that he had.

Bree's hands began to shake as she lifted the sandwich toward her mouth. Her stomach protested at the thought of taking another bite. What was she going to do? Tell him about Ally? She'd promised her sister that she would keep her secret. How could she ignore her sister's last request?

"Are you okay?" Knox's hand reached out across the table, just stopping before it covered hers. "You look a little pale."

Looking up, her eyes met his and she bit back a groan when she saw the concern there. "I'm fine. I'm just tired."

Her eyes remained locked on his and the guilt she'd felt earlier changed to something more disturbing. As she realized how close the two of them were, her unsteady stomach suddenly seemed to be filled with happy little butterflies performing an unfamiliar dance. Looking down, she saw his hand, strong and steady, so close to her own. She was shocked to find that she wanted to reach out her own hand and cover his. She wanted to feel that connection of skin to skin. She wanted to feel the warmth of his fingers slipping over hers. She wanted to find some comfort from this mess she'd made and the consequences she had to face.

"I hate to hear that," Lucretia said from the doorway, causing the both of them to jump, "because I've got a pregnant woman that just walked in saying she's having contractions, and I don't know nothing about delivering babies."

The two of them jumped up, with Knox beating her to the front of the office where a woman who looked not far from a full-term pregnancy was bent over at the waist.

"I tried to get her to sit down, but she won't budge," Lucretia said.

Even with her limited experience, Bree could see the woman was deep into laboring. She and Knox looked at each other. Gone was the intimacy she'd felt before. They were back to business. Thank goodness.

"Lucretia, call 911 and tell them we have a woman in labor," Knox said.

"What's your name?" Bree asked, putting her arm under the woman's to help support her when her pregnant body relaxed in relief as the contraction ended.

"Elena," the woman said, her dark brown eyes looking up at Bree. "My name is Elena. The pain, it's so hard."

"It's okay. There's an ambulance coming that will take you to the hospital where they can help with that. How many weeks are you?" Knox asked as he looped his arm around the woman's other side.

"The baby...he is due next month," the woman gasped out as another contraction started.

Half lifting, half dragging, they helped the woman into the first exam room, pausing when another contraction hit, causing her to double over with the pain.

Bree squatted down in front of her and took her hands. "Breathe with me. It will help."

Eyes drowning with the pain met Bree's, searching for help. "Let's get you up on the exam table so Dr. Collins can check to see how dilated you are."

Knox lifted the woman up while she gripped Bree's hand with a strength that seemed inhuman.

"Next contraction, we'll breathe together." As the next contraction hit, Bree coached the woman into deep breathing through it, Bree's eyes demanding the woman's dark brown ones to focus on her, as Lucretia and Knox helped set up for examination. "That was great. You are doing so good. You said the baby was a boy?"

"A boy, yes. A son," Elena said.

"The contractions are less than two minutes apart. That ambulance better get here fast," she said to Knox before another contraction hit her patient.

"Look at me," she told Elena, trying to keep the woman's focus centered on breathing.

"I don't think it's going to matter how fast the ambulance goes," Knox said. "Lucretia, get me some blankets and the emergency box."

Knox's words and the worried look in his eyes told her that something was wrong. As he mouthed the word *feet*, Bree's heart rate spiked and her hand tightened on the young woman's. A footling breech delivery was difficult and dangerous in the best of settings. Here? Where they had no anesthesia, no NICU nurses, no option except to deliver vaginally? This was the worst possible situation.

Lucretia rushed into the room carrying a box labeled emergency delivery and a stack of white hospital blankets.

"Elena, your baby is coming, but he's coming out with

his feet first. I'm going to need you to listen closely to Dr. Collins so we can get him out safely. Can you do that for me?"

Elena nodded her head, fear replacing the pain in her eyes. Bree wanted to watch Knox work, to see what was happening. There were so many things that could go wrong. A prolapsed cord. Entrapment. Elena's baby was in real danger, but Bree knew she couldn't let her worry show. It was too important that Elena stayed in control. It could determine the baby's survival.

"Okay, Elena, you're going to feel a lot of pressure. I need to maneuver the baby the rest of the way out, but I don't want you to push. Just pay attention to Bree. She'll help you."

Bree's hands tightened on Elena's while placing her face inches from the other woman's. "You've got this, Elena."

"But the pressure..." Elena's voice broke on a groan.

"Look at me. You are going to pant with me now," Bree said, using her momma voice that told Ally she had better be listening to her. Elena's eyes returned to her and the two of them began to pant, their sounds filling the room.

"Come on, little guy, help me out here," Knox said, before Elena gasped, then collapsed back on the exam table.

"He's out!" Lucretia shouted from the end of the exam table as the sound of a faint cry, followed by a very loud, pissed-off wail, filled the room.

"He's okay," Elena said. "He's really okay?"

"He's fine," Knox said, holding up the screaming baby. Bree noticed that the baby was on the small side, but his color was turning a beautiful, healthy pink with his crying.

Her eyes met Knox's and at that moment something passed between them as they shared the joy of a new life coming into the world; something unlike anything she had ever experienced. It was as if pieces of a puzzle slid into place, bonding them together right then and there. She didn't want to look away, knowing that she would lose this shared moment when she did.

Voices came from the office entrance. The ambulance had finally arrived.

Minutes later Elena, with her son held tightly in her arms, was loaded up on the stretcher for their trip to the hospital. As soon as they left the exam room, Knox sank to the floor, his back pressed up against the exam table. Unable to stop herself, Bree followed him down.

"I was so afraid you wouldn't be able to get him out in time," she said.

"Me, too," Knox admitted, removing the gloves he still wore and dropping them on the floor. The room was a mess, but cleaning it could wait.

"I couldn't tell. You seemed so calm."

"We were lucky that the baby was small and it wasn't her first. The fact that we didn't have a prolapsed cord was a miracle. I don't know what I would have done if you hadn't been there to keep Elena in control. You were great with her. We made a great team, didn't we?"

"We did," she said.

Bree liked the fact that he included her, making her feel as if her part in helping to get the little one out was just as important as his.

"I'm a likeable guy, if you give me a chance."

Bree was afraid he was right. Even though she didn't want to admit it.

Lucretia rushed back into the room and stopped, seeing the two of them on the floor together. "What do y'all think you're doing? If you think the two of you are just going to lie around for the rest of the day, you better start thinking again. We've got a hallway of women waiting for me to open the door. We ain't got no time for the two of you peacocking around because y'all delivered a baby."

Turning, the woman headed out the door, calling back, "You got two minutes, then I'm letting in the horde."

"You're a tough taskmaster, Lucretia," Knox called after her.

"And if you make me stay after five you'll be paying me overtime," the woman called back.

The two of them looked at each other and Bree realized just how close they sat together. Close enough for her to see that there were little flecks of brown scattered throughout his light gray eyes that seemed to match the light brown hair that curled around his face. Her breath caught. He was a beautiful-looking man. She looked away, hoping he hadn't noticed her staring at him.

"I guess we had better get back to work," Knox said, standing and then offering her a hand.

Bree looked at the hand he held out. Something had

changed between the two of them over the past few minutes. Working together to deliver Elena's baby had torn more chunks out of the wall of bitterness she had constructed to keep Ally and her safe from him, creating even more confusion inside her. A part of her wanted to build back those walls, to hold on to the anger and bitterness that Brittany had passed on to her. She needed to ignore everything she was beginning to learn about him. The other part of her knew she had to discover the truth. Was he really the kind, caring man he appeared to be? Had he changed so much from the man Brittany had described to her? How was she supposed to discover the real Knox Collins? Maybe working with him was a good idea after all. Maybe it was time she gave him a chance to prove that he could be a good father to Ally.

Looking back at his hand, they both knew that if she took it she would be acknowledging that things had changed between the two of them. Somehow, she knew there would never be any going back after this.

Swallowing down the fear of where accepting the friendship he offered would take her and how that could affect her and her niece's lives, Bree reached for his hand.

CHAPTER THREE

KNOX HAD JUST gotten home when his phone rang. Some part of him, some crazy part he needed to ignore, had hoped that it was Bree calling. Instead, he saw that it was his mother making her daily check in with him. Why his mom felt the need to make sure he was taking care of himself now, he didn't know, though he couldn't deny that a part of him still craved his mother's attention. Still, he'd tried to explain to her that he was a grown man who didn't need his mommy checking on him every day. She'd pushed back, telling him that if he had a wife she wouldn't feel the need to call every day. He'd dropped the argument, knowing he'd been outmaneuvered. His mother was an expert at that. They both knew that there had been a time when his parents had been so busy with their country music careers, that they hadn't given him the time or the supervision he'd needed. It wasn't a coincidence that the daily calls had started after his best friend had died from a car accident that he could easily have been in. Thad's death had affected all of them.

"Hi, Mom," he said as he opened the door to the fridge.

"Hello, darling, how was your day at the clinic?" His

mother's voice warmed that part of him that went cold with memories of his friend.

"Interesting and very unexpected," he answered. "We delivered a baby on our lunch break."

"A baby? At the clinic? I thought this was a community clinic, not an OB clinic."

"Well, today we changed the rules." Knox stared inside the fridge. What was it he had been looking for?

"We? You mean the manager you told me about helped? I hope she wasn't traumatized. That's not what she signed up for, I'm sure."

"It was unexpected for all of us, but no. I meant the midwife who was working with me." Knox grabbed a bottle of water and shut the refrigerator door. "It was a difficult delivery. I don't know what I would have done if Bree hadn't been there to help keep the mother in control."

"You didn't tell me you had more staff. Tell me more about this Bree. Is she married?" The hopefulness in his mother's voice set off all his warning bells.

"No. At least I don't think so." Bree didn't really talk much about anything outside of work, at least not around him. But there hadn't been a ring on her finger. He knew because he'd checked not long after they had met. Not that it had done any good. It had only taken a couple of weeks at the Legacy Clinic for him to realize the woman did not care for him at all. And that was putting it mildly. She'd shut him down the first conversation he'd tried to start with her, and things had only gone down from there.

"What's wrong? Is it this Bree woman?" his mother

asked. He wondered sometimes why scientists hadn't been able to discover just where a mother's intuition was located. He had no doubt that it did exist.

"I don't understand her at all," Knox said before realizing the giant hole he'd left open for his mother's inquisition.

"Imagine, a man that doesn't understand a woman. I take it this isn't a work thing. You said she helped you with the delivery?"

Knox thought about the way she'd eyed his hand before she'd reached out to him. It had been just a friendly gesture, one that he would have offered to anyone. But with Bree, the way she'd studied it, it had felt like more. And then there'd been the feel of her hand in his. There'd been nothing friendly about the way his heart rate had spiked from the touch of her soft hand sliding inside his. If he'd held on for just a second too long, he didn't think she had noticed.

"No, not exactly work, it's just…" Knox didn't know how to describe the way Bree had reacted to him from day one. "She acts like I've done something to make her mad at me. Or as if somehow I've let her down. But it doesn't make sense. I'd never met her before I started working at Legacy."

"Are you sure of that?" his mother asked. "Women tend to remember more when it comes to, let's say, romantic interludes."

There had been a time when he'd been wild and reckless, and there were a lot of women who had come and gone in those days. But none of them had been Bree.

He was sure of that. He'd remember her. Besides, Bree wasn't the kind of woman who ran after the town's bad boy that he'd been then. She was smarter than that.

"I'm sure. Don't worry about it. It could all be my imagination," Knox said, though he knew it wasn't. "Tell me about Dad. Is he still obsessed with his new golf clubs?"

As his mother talked about his father's golf swing, as well as the new putting green he was insisting they have put in, Knox found himself thinking again about the way Bree had sat so still as she'd studied the hand he'd held out to her, as if she feared taking his offer of help. But it had been more and he'd known it. He'd been extending a hand in friendship.

And even though she'd taken his hand and he knew something had changed between the two of them after working together in the clinic, he couldn't help but think whatever it was she was holding against him was going to come out eventually.

Bree turned around as her name was called from across the bar. Waving to a customer she'd been dodging for the past fifteen minutes, she shouted over the noisy crowd, "I'll be right there."

Was the place exceptionally loud tonight, or was it just that she was getting too old for the job? There was a time, when she was young and just beginning college, that working at The Dusty Jug in downtown Nashville on a Friday night had been the perfect job. Now, after ten years of slinging beers and dealing with the occasionally rowdy tourist, she could do the job on autopilot, something that she found herself doing more and more lately. Being a single mom, a midwife resident and fill-in bar staff was getting to be too much for her. The lack of sleep was beginning to wear on her.

But what were her options? She had food, rent and childcare to pay for and the tips at the bar were good on weekends. If she could just hold on for a few more months, she'd be able to have a normal schedule. Well, as normal as a midwife's schedule could be.

"Is that guy bothering you?" Mack asked from behind the bar.

"He's just another guy who's partied a little too much this weekend. I can handle him." Bree had been handling men like him for years now. The best way to deal with him was to serve him his beer with a smile, then walk away as fast as she could. The place was so busy tonight that she wouldn't have to worry about him following her through the crowd.

Bree delivered an order, then went over to the table where the man who'd waved her down sat with three of his friends, all of them in different states of inebriation. She'd bet her tip money on the three of them being college students who were celebrating the end of the semester. They'd all regret it in the morning, but there wouldn't be any convincing them of that tonight. "What can I get you?"

"How about your number?" the young man asked, then elbowed his friend when he started to laugh.

"Sorry, not tonight," she said. "But I will give you the

number to a car service as there is no way any of you are driving home tonight."

"I've got one," one of the other men stated, waving his phone up in the air toward her.

"Okay, then," she said, turning to leave, only to have the one closest to her grab her arm.

"One more round?" he asked, giving her a smile that made him look even younger.

She looked down at his hand pointedly, and he immediately let go.

"Sorry, ma'am," he said, his eyes dropping from hers.

"One more, then you call for a ride," she said, then pointed over to Danny, the bouncer on duty. "I'm telling him to keep an eye on y'all and make sure you get a safe ride home. No more bars, either. You all go home."

All four heads turned toward the man standing at the door. Six feet five and over two hundred fifty pounds, Danny had played offense for the Vanderbilt Commodores back in his college days and now coached football at one of the local high schools. He was all muscle, and wearing a skintight T-shirt, he proved he was not afraid to show it off. Anyone who thought they'd act out at the Dusty Jug changed their mind when Danny looked their way.

Heading back to the bar for their order, she was stopped when Sara, one of the other waitresses, flagged her down. "Mack said the band is running fifteen minutes late and he wants you to cover for them."

"That's the third time this month. Mack needs to do something about them." It wasn't that Bree minded entertaining the crowd. She'd been doing it for years and Mack would make sure the band gave her a share of their tips. And even when the bar was busy like tonight, it wasn't the same as getting up on a concert stage where those huge blinding lights kept you from seeing the people you were supposed to be performing for. "Can you take care of the group at table twenty? Tell Mack they only get one more round, he knows what they're drinking, and then they're out of here."

"Got it," Sara said, rushing back to the bar.

After stopping to give Danny a heads-up on the group of young men in case they tried to sneak past the bouncer, she headed back to the staff lounge where she kept her guitar stashed for times like this. She stopped by a mirror and couldn't help but remember that first time she'd gone on stage, dressed up in that ridiculous pink dress, with her sister beside her. Life hadn't turned out the way any of them had expected then. Her dreams and her sister's had been so different. Her sister loved the stage from the moment they'd walked out in front of those glaring spotlights, while Bree had only wanted to run off stage and hide in their dressing room until it was all over.

She couldn't help but ask herself if things would have been different for Brittany if Bree had just gone along with her sister's plans. Yes, Bree wouldn't have been happy with a life in the spotlight. But would that have been so bad if it meant she would still have her sister?

Thinking about Brittany as she climbed up on the small platform that acted as the bar's stage, Bree ran her fingers over the guitar strings, making adjustments before picking out a song she'd written one night after her sister had died. She'd never sung it in public, it wasn't a bar kind of song, but when her fingers played the intro to the song she had written so long ago, she began to sing.

Knox hadn't been crazy about a night of bar hopping. He'd left that scene years ago and had never looked back. But it was his cousin's bachelor party; his attendance had been demanded. Now, after two hours of going from one overcrowded bar to another, he was already planning his escape. He'd spent too much of the first years of his college life at bars, something he was still trying to live down. With his reputation as a doctor always on the line, he was now aware of everything he did. He never wanted to be thought of as Nashville's rebellious bad boy again.

As he followed his cousin and his friends into the next bar on their list, he felt a change in the atmosphere. The Dusty Jug was packed, but instead of the normal rowdy crowd of the other bars, the place was almost silent except for the voice of a young woman singing. Unable to see the stage from where he stood at the entrance, he weaved his way through the crowd, drawn by a voice so sweet and pure, yet for some reason familiar.

Finding a place against the bar, he craned his neck to the side to see a young woman with a guitar in her arms, playing a song whose words spoke of a deep pain of loss. Just the sound of her voice made you want to weep.

"You left me with an angel to heal my heart." The woman sang the chorus, then started on another verse. "When you got your wings, you left an angel with your eyes, your laugh. You left an angel so that I'd always have you with me. As long as your little angel is with me, I'll always have an angel to heal my heart."

As the woman played the last notes then looked up at the crowd, Knox's breath seized in his lungs, his heart stuttering from shock. The crowd's enthusiastic cheers jerked him back to reality and he sucked in a breath. Sitting on the stage, Bree Rogers smiled and thanked everyone before standing as a group of musicians began to take the stage.

Her hair was pulled back into a ponytail, the same way she wore it at work. But with her white T-shirt, cutoff jean shorts and white tennis shoes, she looked too young to even be allowed in the bar, let alone old enough to be delivering babies.

Then he remembered the pain he'd seen in her eyes as she sang. A pain he knew spoke of a heartache she was definitely too young to have experienced. He recognized that pain. It was the pain of loss. He had carried the weight of that pain since the unnecessary death of his best friend. It had been almost nine years and it hadn't gotten any easier.

He watched as she moved toward the bar, then stopped when she spotted him. For a few seconds neither of them moved. None of this made sense. What was the midwife doing here entertaining a bar crowd? He'd never heard anything about her being able to sing like that, either. Not that there weren't thousands of people who had come to Nashville to get a break into the country music world. But he couldn't believe Bree was one of them. Just the little bit he'd worked with her proved that her dedication was to midwifery.

"What are you doing here?" she asked, suspicion in her eyes. Did she think he was stalking her?

"Bachelor party," he said. "What about you?"

She looked down at the T-shirt she wore that displayed the bar's name. "It should be pretty obvious that I work here."

She moved past him and said something to the bartender before turning back to him. "I've got to get back to work. Enjoy your party."

He watched as she walked off, her head held high as she balanced a tray of drinks. He spotted his group at the back of the bar where they'd managed to find a table and went to join them. The mystery of Brianna Rogers just kept getting bigger and bigger. He knew he should let it go. Bree deserved her privacy. But he couldn't seem to do it. The more he learned about her, the more he wanted to know.

It wasn't that hard to figure out that she had to be working at the bar to pay the bills. He didn't know anything about her past. He'd had rich parents to support him while he was in school; most students didn't. But the music, the voice, that was the surprise. Instead of waiting tables, she could have been singing anywhere in Nashville with that voice.

"I saw you talking to that waitress. You know her?" his cousin said, leaning over toward Knox while the other men were busy with a conversation about their golf game that day.

"I thought I did, but now I'm not so sure." But he would. Somehow, someway, he would find out everything there was to know about Brianna. Then maybe this obsession with her would end.

He studied the drink in front of him, refusing to let her catch him studying her. He didn't want her to think he really was stalking her. She might not have accused him of it, but the look she'd given him had spoken of a mistrust. Was it possible that she had a history of being stalked? That would explain a lot about her behavior, not only here, but also at the office. Maybe a bad experience had her keeping her distance from all men.

"I don't know what the two of you have going on, but some guy over there seems to be giving her a hard time," his cousin said, starting to stand.

Knox looked up and saw a young man slam his empty drink glass down on the table then stand. Knox put a hand on his cousin's shoulder and pushed him back into the chair before standing. "Your momma will kick my butt if you get in a bar fight and mess up your pretty face tonight. I've got this."

Most of the crowd was settled around the stage where the band played, making it easy for Knox to cross the room to where Bree was arguing with a kid who had plainly drunk more than he should. He looked over to where the bouncer on duty was busy dealing with three other guys about the same age. They all looked like they were about to fall over. Knox could still remember those days of being old enough to drink legally, but not smart enough to know when to stop.

"Is there a problem?" he asked as he approached. With Bree's hands on her hips and her eyes shooting fire, Knox was glad he wasn't the one in her sights.

Without looking at him, Bree waved him away. "Cooper doesn't want to leave with his friends. For some reason, he thinks I have to serve him a drink even though I've already told him he was cut off."

Knox took in the relaxed way she stood. She wasn't really intimidated by this guy. She was just looking out for the kid and he was too drunk to see it. "Well, Cooper, it sounds like it's time to thank your waitress for her service, leave a big tip for her trouble and head home before you do something that you'll regret in the morning."

When the boy turned, swinging wildly, Knox's arms came up instinctively while he moved himself in front of Bree. The boy's swing met air and the rest of his body followed through, sending him sprawling on to the bar floor.

The sound of Bree's whistle carried over the band and both the bartender and the bouncer headed their way. Within minutes, the kid was off the floor and headed outside with the bouncer, who had assured Knox that the kid and his friends would be tucked into a car from a local service.

"Are you okay?" he asked Bree, once the bar doors closed behind the bouncer.

"I'm fine. I've seen worse," Bree said, then glanced up from where she was gathering empty glasses from the table. "How about you?"

"Unfortunately, I've seen worse, too.' He tried to keep

his voice calm, but he couldn't help but think about the night he and Thad had been out drinking in a bar not much different than this one. Who knows, they might have come to this bar that night. They'd both been too young and dumb to know when they'd reached their limit then. Maybe if someone like Bree had stopped Thad from stumbling outside and getting into his car, his friend would still be here. It had only been the fact that Knox had run into a group from his parents' band that had saved him from joining his friend.

"You sure you're okay?" Bree asked. She'd moved in front of him, dipping her head down until her eyes met his. There was worry in her eyes now. Worry for him.

"Sorry, just memories from long ago when me and my friends thought we knew everything, too," he said. She moved back from him and picked up her tray that she'd loaded with glasses. She started to walk away, back toward the bar, and he tried to find a reason to stop her. "Thank you for looking out for that kid. I wish there'd been someone like you that night."

Turning, she gave him a quizzical look. "What night?"

They stood there, standing in the middle of a bar, and for some reason Knox couldn't stop himself from spilling his guts. "Me and my friend went out partying one night, though we should have been back at the dorm studying for exams. Thad said we'd cram the next day. I was young and stupid. I had dreams of medical school, but I was messing them up. I agreed with him. There was plenty of time for studying. I didn't even try to talk him out of going out. I'd spent most of that year partying instead of studying. I still don't know how I graduated that year."

"What happened?" she asked.

Knox looked around, before looking up at Bree. "You had to have heard all the reports of the wild son of Charles and Gail Collins."

From high school to the day Thad had died, he'd given his parents nothing but trouble. All in the name of a "good time." Back then, if there was a bar fight in downtown Nashville, he had probably been in it. That had been what he thought was a good time.

He didn't want to think about those times. He didn't want to remember that last night when Thad had thrown his arm over Knox's shoulder and told him he'd see him the next day. He didn't want to think about letting his friend walk out, knowing that his friend was as drunk as he was, and never making a move to stop him.

"I let my best friend, as drunk as those kids who just left, walk out of the bar, knowing that he was going to drive himself home. He never made it there."

He saw the shock in her eyes, then the pity that followed. He didn't need her pity. Didn't deserve it.

"Anyway, thanks for watching out for guys like Cooper. I hope someday he realizes he owes you a thank-you." Knox turned and walked back to the table where he could see his cousin's friends were finishing their drinks and getting ready to move on.

He felt raw from the memories and irritated at himself for letting his guard down in front of Bree. He was Dr. Collins now. Her mentor. She needed to trust his guidance. He didn't need to dig up all his past sins for her to see. He'd fought too hard to turn his life around. His memories were of a past he had tried to bury. So why did it feel so important that he share them with Bree?

CHAPTER FOUR

WHEN BREE WOKE up Tuesday morning, she was surprised to find that she was looking forward to a day at the community clinic. Not that she didn't still have reservations about working with Knox; after their conversation at the bar she was more confused than ever. No matter how much she wanted to ignore it, the Knox Collins she was getting to know was not the same one that her sister had known.

But how could someone change that much? Oh, she could understand that Knox had changed his ways as far as being totally centered on partying while he was in college. A lot of kids went down that road before waking up and discovering life wasn't all partying. Bree had no doubt that her sister had been right there in the partying crowd. It was probably where Brittany had met Knox. But there was something else that bothered her. Bree knew Brittany's thirst for fame had always been her sister's driving force. She'd always wondered if Brittany had really just run across Knox at a bar one night, or had she sought him out knowing that Knox's parents could help her in her drive for her career? It was a terrible thing to think about her sister, but Bree had personally seen the things Brittany would do for her career. She had to be honest with herself.

But did it really matter what Brittany's reasons were? Her sister was gone. It was only Ally who mattered now. Her niece would someday look at her and ask about her daddy. And what was Bree to say then? That she'd promised Ally's mother that she'd never tell her father about her? Was it really fair to the child for Bree to hold back information that would affect her whole life? Was it fair to Knox? She knew the answer to both questions. She knew she had to do the right thing for both Ally and Knox. She just didn't know if she had the courage to do it.

Bree was still struggling with her thoughts when she walked into the clinic and was greeted by Lucretia.

"Well, what are you doing coming in here looking like your best friend just died?" Lucretia asked when Bree entered the office with none of the excitement she'd felt that morning. Instead, she felt the weight of years of keeping a secret that she never should have been forced to keep.

"What's wrong?" Lucretia asked, all her teasing gone now.

Bree's mouth refused to move as her throat tightened and her eyes began to water. She looked around the room, beginning to panic. The last thing she needed was for Knox to find her having a meltdown in the waiting room.

"Come on," Lucretia said, then gestured for Bree to follow her back into one of the exam rooms.

"Sit. You've got five minutes to tell me what's wrong.

I can't have you bringing problems here that might affect your work," the woman said as she pointed to an old plastic chair against the back wall. While the woman's words could have seemed cold, her eyes were full of concern.

Bree looked at the chair then back at Lucretia, who stood against the door and Bree's only escape. At that moment Bree realized why she'd come to like the woman so much. Lucretia's take-charge attitude reminded her of her momma's. But while her momma had become blinded by the glitz of the country music world and her dreams for Bree's and Brittany's music career, Lucretia was only looking out for her and the patients at the clinic.

"It's nothing. I'm here to work. I just have some things on my mind." Even as she spoke the words, she wished she could say more. She'd kept her sister's secret for so long. And for what? Everything her sister said wasn't true now, which left Bree with a terrible burden that she didn't think she could carry any longer. "I've done something, something that I thought was the right thing at the time. I kept a secret that I shouldn't have. Now I think I was wrong. Now I have some hard decisions to make because what I've done has affected other people's lives."

Bree swallowed, then forced herself to continue. "And the truth is I'm afraid."

There. She'd said the two words she'd refused to admit even to herself. She was afraid. Afraid of breaking a sacred promise she'd made to her sister just days before Brittany had been killed. Afraid of confronting Knox with the news that he had a daughter. Afraid of telling Ally that she'd had a father her whole life who didn't know about her. But most of all, she was afraid of losing a child that was as much hers as she was Brittany's and Knox's. Whether it had been the right thing to do or not, Bree had raised Ally as her child. And the thought of losing her scared her most of all.

Looking up, Bree saw Lucretia's eyes soften. "Girl, being afraid is part of living. And sometimes it's part of doing the right thing. We don't know each other that well, but I don't think you would have done something to hurt someone. At least, not on purpose."

Bree shook her head. "Just because it wasn't on purpose doesn't mean it won't hurt them."

"Which will hurt them more? Admitting to them that you made a mistake? Or continuing to keep a secret they have the right to know?"

Bree knew the answer to Lucretia's question. She'd already made the decision that she had to tell both Ally and Knox the secret she'd promised never to tell. She had to do the right thing by both of them. Now she just had to figure out how.

"Lucretia? Bree?" Knox's voice called from down the hall. "Where is everybody?"

Bree knew that there was no way that Lucretia could know that her secret involved Knox, but the sound of his voice sent warning signals to her brain while at the same time she felt the heavy weight of guilt in her chest. "Please don't mention any of this to him."

"Anything I hear in these office walls is privileged information, isn't it?" Lucretia asked, then winked at her before the exam door opened and Knox stuck his head inside.

"Is there an office meeting I wasn't notified of?" Knox asked, his voice light and teasing.

"No," Bree said, rushing past the two of them to escape. In a matter of minutes, Lucretia had helped her narrow down the answer to her problem to the simplest of answers. She had to do the right thing, no matter how scared she was.

But first, she had to come up with a plan. It wasn't every day that a man learned he had an eight-year-old daughter. Would he be happy? Angry? He'd certainly be angry that Brittany, and then Bree, hadn't told him about the pregnancy, because the more she got to know Knox, the more she was convinced that he had never known about Brittany's pregnancy. She could understand that he'd be angry with her and she deserved his anger. But no matter how angry he was, they would still have to work together. And they'd have to figure out a way to tell Ally.

They'd have to do that together, too, she decided as she went into the second exam room, pretending to organize the supplies, though she had no doubt Lucretia had seen to that earlier.

Finally, the first patient arrived and her busy day began. Putting her personal problems aside, she focused all of her energy on her patients. Avoiding Knox wasn't a problem. The two of them were kept too busy to even stop for a break.

After seeing twice the number of patients that she

saw in a day at the Legacy Clinic, she'd thought her day over when Lucretia found her in one of the exam rooms setting up for their next clinic day. "There's a girl, she can't be eighteen, that has been pacing outside the office for the last thirty minutes. I tried to talk to her, but she ran off. Now she's back. Can you talk to her and see what she needs?"

Looking at her watch, Bree saw that she was due to pick up Ally in less than an hour. She couldn't be late getting there, again. It seemed she never had enough time anymore.

Both she and Knox were scheduled at the Legacy Clinic the next day, as Lori had rearranged Bree's office and call schedule around Knox's so that Bree could continue to work with her two days a week. And while Bree was happy that she was getting the experience she needed, it was getting harder and harder for her to manage her work at the two clinics, her job at the Dusty Jug and make sure Ally was given the attention she needed.

"She looks scared, Bree. And she's very skittish. I don't want to scare her away again." Bree had only known the office manager for a couple days, but she had already learned to trust Lucretia's instincts.

"I'll try to talk to her. Maybe I can get her to come back next week when we are open." Bree said, before heading to the small office waiting room where she could see the shadow of someone outside the frosted glass front door.

Not wanting to scare the girl, Bree opened the door slowly then stepped out into the hall, shutting the door quietly behind her. The girl, looking closer to seventeen than eighteen if you ignored the heavily made-up face, was thin. Too thin.

The girl's eyes met Bree's and Bree knew the girl was about to make a run for it. Stepping in front of her, Bree tried to stop her, holding out her hands to the girl. "Wait. I just want to help you."

But Bree could see that the girl wasn't listening. As the girl rushed past her, pushing Bree over as she passed, Bree caught a glimpse of big brown eyes that were filled with terror.

Bree had never seen anything like the look on the girl's face, and on instinct she had pushed away from the wall and started after the girl when the office door opened and Knox rushed out, Lucretia following right behind him.

"What's going on?" he asked, grabbing a hold of Bree's arm to steady her.

"I'm not sure," Bree said, though her mind was flooded with a hundred scenarios, none of them good. "There was a girl, a teenager, but she ran as soon as I tried to talk to her."

Bree looked up into his eyes. "She's in danger, Knox. I don't know what kind, but she's afraid of something. Or someone."

"Maybe she came to the clinic for birth control or because she thinks she's pregnant and she's afraid her parents will find out. Let me see if I can find her," Knox said, then let go of her arm and headed down the hall toward the stairs at a jog.

While Lucretia went back to shut down the office, Bree waited for Knox to return. When she saw him coming back down the hall, alone, her hopes that he had caught up with the girl died.

"She had too much of a head start for you to catch her," Bree said when he walked up. "I've dealt with the teenagers at Legacy House and others while I was working in the hospital as a nurse. I haven't ever had one react that way. Not with that amount of fear."

She had been more likely to get attitude from her teenage patients, at least at first. It usually took a while before you would figure out that it was mostly fear of what their bodies were going through or how their lives were about to change that was responsible for those attitudes. But she'd never seen such a hopeless fear on anyone's face as she'd seen on that young girl's.

"Maybe she'll be back Tuesday, when the clinic is open again," Knox said, though he looked as worried as Bree. "There's nothing we can do about it now."

The phone alarm on Bree's watch went off, reminding her that she had to leave then or she'd be late for after-school pickup. Silencing it, she saw that Knox was studying her.

"You're not working a shift at the bar tonight, are you?" he asked. "You have to be back at Legacy Clinic tomorrow."

Was she imagining the censorship in his voice? Was he suggesting that she shouldn't be working at the bar when she had to be at the clinic the next day? "I only work at the bar when I have the next day off, but that's really not any of your business, is it?"

"I'm sorry. You're right. I just think working at the bar while you're doing your residency could be a problem. You need to be at your best, especially if you have a labor patient."

Bree chose to ignore the concern in his eyes. What right did this man have to judge her? She felt the anger at his words as it boiled out of her. She'd worked her butt off getting to where she was. She'd spent years juggling a child, school and a job. To suggest that she would do anything to jeopardize her career, or more importantly a patient, was insulting.

"You don't know anything about me, Knox." The heat in her face and the dangerous rate of her heart told her that she was about to go ballistic on the man. The anger drove her to take a step, then another. She was so close now that she would swear she could hear the beat of his heart. Or was that sound the beat of her own racing heart? Her breaths came faster as her eyes met his. Her hands came up to rest on his chest. They both stood there a minute while her anger warred with something else. Something more dangerous than her anger. For a second she couldn't remember where she was or why she was angry. All she knew was something changed in her, in him, when their eyes met. When his eyes dropped lower to rest on her lips, she felt herself sway toward him. Was he thinking about kissing her? She was surprised to find that she wanted him to. She wanted Knox to kiss her. It didn't make any sense, but she couldn't deny it. She was attracted to the last person she had these feelings for.

No. She couldn't do this. That was wrong. Nothing had changed between them. It was just something she had imagined. This was just a flood of hormones that had been brought on by her anger.

Her hands fell away from him. Her back stiffened. She forced her eyes away from him. She was too strong, too smart, to let a bunch of hormones take control of her like this.

Turning, she walked back into the clinic and grabbed her backpack, passing him where he still stood in the hallway. Refusing to look at him, she started toward the stairwell. She'd only gone a few feet before she heard him call after her.

"You're right. I don't know you, Bree," he called out behind her, "but I want to. I want to know everything about you."

Bree's feet faltered as her heart stuttered for a second. What did those words mean? And did she really want to know? She made her feet continue down the hall. While Knox might not know it, soon he would know more about her than he had ever dreamed possible. She just hoped that what was left between them when he did learn the truth about what she had done wasn't the nightmare she feared.

Knox knew that Bree was back to her old ways of avoiding him the next day. He'd hoped after the time they'd spent at the clinic, and after their talk at the bar, that things had changed between the two of them. Of course, it was probably his stupid confession that he wanted to get to know her better that had changed things. They'd just begun to get into a nice rhythm working together at the clinic, so why had he gone and ruined it? Maybe because it was the truth? Maybe because as they'd stood together in that hallway, with her hand pressed against his chest, all he could think about was wanting her to stay there, touching him. When she'd moved away from him, he'd felt the distance between them as acute as having a part of himself ripped away.

Bree Rogers not only fascinated him in a way no woman had ever done before, she also made him feel a longing he didn't know was possible. She was more pretty than beautiful, more sweet than sophisticated. In other words, nothing like the women he normally found himself attracted to. There was something special about her that he couldn't describe. And when she looked into his eyes it was as if she could see into his soul. He just wished he knew what it was she saw. Was it the boy he'd been who had never thought of others or of the consequences of what he did? Or was it the man he'd worked so hard to become? From the way she seemed to avoid him, he was afraid it was the former instead of the latter. Would he ever be able to put his past behind him?

"Do you have a moment, Knox?" Jack called out to him as Knox passed the senior Dr. Warner's office.

"Sure. I'm just headed over to the hospital to check on a postsurgical patient before I leave for the day. What's up?" Knox said, stepping into the older man's office.

"I know that you only have a few more weeks before your contract is up and Dr. Hennison returns. I just wanted to touch base with you and see what your plans were."

Knox took the seat in front of Jack's desk. "I've had some requests from some of the general practitioners up in the Smoky Mountains for me to return. I've been thinking of starting a type of travel practice where I can set up a home base in a central location, but still travel to some of the outlying areas where it's hard for people to get down to an office for a visit."

The two of them discussed the shortage of OB/GYN practices in the rural parts of the country for several minutes and what more the government could do to help encourage practitioners to move to those areas. Both of them agreed that a solution needed to be found for the women who didn't have access to the prenatal care they needed, due a lot to the cost of liability insurance.

"And what about Bree? How is she doing at the county clinic? I know she wasn't happy at first about the opportunity, but I thought the two of you would make a good team there. I hope you've been able to change her mind."

Knox was pretty sure that he'd destroyed the teamwork that they had been developing by admitting his interest in her, but he wasn't about to discuss that with Jack. And he knew she was mad at him over his questioning her about her need to work at the bar. He wasn't even sure if the practice was aware that Bree was working outside her commitment to them. But as he had been told, it wasn't his business. "She's doing well. The patients like her and she has a lot of empathy for their situation. Not everyone does."

"Well, that's good to hear. From everything I hear from Lori, she's going to make a good midwife," Jack said as his phone rang. Looking at the number, he shook his head. "It's my son. Always worrying I'm working too much."

"I have a mom for that. It's nice to know someone cares, isn't it?" Knox laughed, then stood and started out the door before Jack waved him to wait after telling his son to hold a moment.

"If you change your mind and decide to stay in town, let us know. We'd be happy to have you join the practice permanently," Jack said.

"It's a tempting offer, sir. Maybe one day I'll take you up on it. But for now, I think I'm needed in the mountains." He'd wondered if he'd get an offer from the practice and he hadn't been sure until that moment what he'd do if it came. Living close to his parents was tempting. His mother reminded him constantly that he wasn't getting any younger and needed to settle down. But just talking to Jack about the opportunity to make a difference in the rural communities of the mountains got him excited. That was where he was truly needed.

"I can't blame you for that. If I was twenty years younger, I think I'd join you. The mountains are beautiful this time of year and the work you're going to be doing will make a lot of difference for those communities," Jack said before returning to his call.

Knox stepped out the office door, only to find Bree standing in the middle of the hall.

"You're leaving?" she asked, her look intense and her tone demanding. "When?"

"I didn't know you cared," Knox teased, then stopped when he realized she was seriously upset. "I'm not leaving today. Jack just wanted to know my plans after I finish my contract here. What's wrong?"

Bree wasn't sure what was wrong. Knox's leaving was the answer to all her problems. If he wasn't there, the guilt she felt every time she looked at him would go away. Except, that wasn't true. She'd told herself that she was going to be honest with him. She was going to tell him about Ally. His leaving would complicate that in a lot of ways. The worst way being if he decided that he wanted to fight for custody of Ally and wanted to take her away with him, something that she hadn't considered until now. Her stomach protested at the thought, her insides doing a somersault. She couldn't face the possibility of Ally being taken from her.

But she couldn't explain any of this to Knox. Not yet. "I just need to know if I'll be working with you at the clinic for the next three weeks like we had planned."

"Like I said, I'm not leaving till my contract is over."

"Good," she said. She sounded like someone with only two functioning brain cells. "I mean, it's good that you'll be there to work in the clinic."

"Are you okay?" Knox asked, his eyes studying her too closely. "You look tired."

"Well, thank you for that. That's just what every woman wants to hear." After another night of tossing and turning, she hadn't been surprised to find the dark shadows under her eyes. She'd told herself that she wasn't sleeping because of her decision to tell Knox about Ally, but she'd awakened more than once from dreams about Knox that had her pushing the covers off her overheated body. She couldn't forget the way she'd felt when Knox had brushed his finger down her cheek. The way her body had responded when he'd just looked at her lips. If he'd kissed her at that moment, she would have gone up in flames.

"I'm just concerned about you. You're doing a lot between the clinic and working at the bar," said Knox, his eyes lingering on those shadows.

The concern in his voice just made her feel worse about her deception. Guilt was eating her up inside. She had to move forward with her plan to tell Knox about Ally. She had to ignore all other feelings she had for Knox and concentrate on the fact that he was her niece's father.

And the first thing she had to do was to introduce him to Ally. "Are you going to be at the cleanup day at Legacy House this weekend?"

"I'm planning on it," Knox said. "I think everyone that isn't on call is coming. It seems to be a big office project."

"That's good. It sounds like they'll need all the volunteers they can get," she said, then began walking backward, away from him. "I guess I'll see you there, then."

"Okay, it's a date," he said, giving her a smile that sent her libido into overdrive. Then the evil man winked at her before walking away, leaving Bree in shock as she stood and watched him go.

What had just happened? Was the man flirting with her now? He wasn't serious. He'd just been joking. Hadn't he? He didn't really think she'd been trying to get a date with him.

Slowly, she walked away, her mind filled with scenes of Knox Collins and his dangerously wicked smile.

CHAPTER FIVE

BREE HELPED ALLY pull the wagon they'd filled with small tree limbs the two of them had picked up from the backyard of Legacy House. She had told Ally that she wanted to introduce her to the doctor she worked with at the clinic, hoping to somehow smooth Knox and the little girl's introduction before she revealed to the two of them that they were father and daughter. Now the little girl asked every few minutes if "that doctor" was there yet. Bree was starting to think that she had been stood up, which was crazy. It wasn't a real date. Knox had just been teasing her. Still, she caught herself looking up from their work every time a new car drove into the driveway of the home.

They'd been working for almost an hour, when a dark blue truck stopped in front of the house and parked. Her breath caught when a jean-clad Knox climbed out. Dolly Parton's song about a man with a cowboy hat and painted-on jeans showing up to tempt her started playing in Bree's mind. Knox was every bit tempting as any man she had ever seen. He'd pulled his hair back into a tiny tail at the back of his head, giving him the look of a young rogue in one of her historical romances.

"Aunt Bree, who's that guy? Is he your doctor?" Ally asked from beside her.

That question got her full attention. If someone had told her six months ago that she would be standing there, about to introduce Ally to the man who was her father, Bree would never have believed it. Knox's finding out about the little girl was a nightmare that she would have run from. But now, after getting to know him, she knew she was doing the right thing.

Not that she was going to tell either of them about their relationship yet. She had to go about that more cautiously. First, she wanted them to meet. She wanted Knox to see that Ally was a happy girl and that Bree was taking good care of her. Then she would tell him. After that, she'd see where they went. She thought that it would be best if Bree and Knox told Ally together, but that would all depend on how things went with Knox first. There was a probability that Knox would want to get a DNA test before he accepted that Ally was his. And while Bree had no doubt that Brittany had told the truth about Ally being his child, she couldn't blame him for wanting proof.

"He's not my doctor. He's the doctor I work with at the clinic downtown. The one I told you about. Do you want to meet him now?" Bree asked the little girl, who was studying Knox as he greeted one of the other volunteers. She watched as he opened the bed of his truck and began to remove bags of soil, throwing two of them over his shoulder before he headed their way.

"Sure," Ally said, then headed off to where some of

the other children were helping to pull the weeds out of a flower garden that ran the length of the front porch. It seemed Ally wasn't as impressed as Bree was by Knox's arrival.

She knew the moment he saw her, their eyes meeting and his lighting up as he gave her a grin before handing the bags of soil over to the man next to him and then returning back to the truck where he opened the back door. She watched as he reached into the backseat and came out with a small pot containing a beautiful royal blue orchid. Turning, he looked back at her, smiling as he headed toward her.

"I'm not usually late for my dates," he said, holding out the ceramic pot with the beautiful flower. "This is for you."

Bree looked at the potted plant, then back up at his smiling face. Had the man been serious when he'd called their meeting together today a date? Or was he still teasing her?

Guilt flooded through her system, as a nasty knot formed in her chest. What was she doing? She'd thought that getting to know Knox would be a good way to help her decide what to do about her niece, but the more she got to know him, the more she liked him. Now she thought of him as more than Ally's father, and more than just a work colleague. Now she was venturing into a place that could turn into a nightmare. The sooner she told Knox about Ally, the better for both of them. She just needed to give them time to get to know each other first. And she needed to build a relationship between her and Knox so that when she did approach him with the truth, he would be more open to listening to all the reasons she needed to remain as Ally's guardian.

Using that excuse, she reached out and took the plant, her hand brushing against Knox's, sending a tingle of awareness through her.

"What's that, Aunt Bree?" Ally asked from beside her, startling her. "Are you going to plant it in the flower beds?"

"Not this one," Bree said. "It's an orchid. We have to keep it inside and take good care of it."

"Well, hello," Knox said. "What's your name?"

Bree's heart expanded with something she refused to name at the kindness in Knox's eyes as he bent down to the little girl's level. Ally and Knox's first meeting would forever be a bittersweet memory that she hoped she would never feel the need to regret.

"I'm Ally. Are you Aunt Bree's doctor?" Ally asked, her face studying Knox's with a seriousness beyond her years.

"I'm one of the doctors your aunt works with," Knox said.

"Okay," Ally said, before turning to her aunt. "Is he the doctor you wanted me to meet?"

Knox stood and looked up at Bree, one eyebrow lifting as his lips turned up in a teasing smile. "Am I the doctor you wanted her to meet?"

Bree chose to ignore his teasing. "This is Dr. Collins, and yes, he's the doctor I've told you about. The one I work with at the clinic where the women come in for help."

"You didn't say he was pretty," Ally said, cutting her eyes to look over at Knox. "Don't you think he's pretty, Aunt Bree?"

Now the two of them were teasing her, surprising, since Bree had never known her niece to be teasing like this before. She was even more surprised to find that both Ally and Knox shared the same expression on their face. Both expectant. Both waiting to see what she was going to say next.

"Well, look at that," Bree said, adopting their playful manner, "I've never noticed before, Ally, but I think you might be right. He is kind of pretty."

Knox laughed and Ally giggled before running off to where one of the volunteers had started to help some of the kids spread the soil in the beds that they were preparing to plant flowers.

"I didn't know you had a niece," Knox said as they stood there together with Bree feeling awkward now that Ally wasn't there between them.

"I told you that you didn't know everything about me," Bree reminded him.

She could just blurt out the truth. Just spit out the words "Yes, I have a niece and she's your daughter," but she knew now was not the time. So instead, she changed the subject to something more comfortable. "I think we've finished cleaning up all of the backyard. Jared and Sky just hauled a truckload of limbs and leaves away. We just need to edge the sides of the driveway now."

Walking away, she grabbed a hoe one of the volunteers had brought out and began to work on one side of the driveway while Knox grabbed another tool and started on the other side. Together, they worked in silence. Soon, they were joined by some of the other staff members who had finished in the backyard. By the time they completed edging the drive, Jared and Sky were back and everyone began to fill the truck with the last of the yard trimmings. The junior Dr. Warner, Jared and his fiancée, Sky, left a few minutes later with the last truck full of leaves and limbs.

"I have to say I'm impressed with all the work that was done today," Knox said as he joined Bree as she headed to the backyard where the Legacy House mom, Maggie, had taken the volunteers' kids to play on the new equipment that had been donated for the children who sometimes came to stay with their moms.

"I'm impressed with Legacy House in general. Nashville is lucky to have a place like this. It's nice to see that not only the office staff, but the community comes together to help the women here, too." Legacy House was truly a community project. There had been hundreds of women over the years who had found a safe haven there until they could find a permanent home.

"The news is so filled with the negatives of society, but I think that most people want to help others if they can. I see it a lot when I'm working in the rural areas up in the mountains. Neighbors help their neighbors, but most of them are just as willing to help out a stranger." Knox stopped and took a seat at an old picnic table that was in need of a coat of paint, something that one of the volunteers had mentioned needing to tackle on their next cleanup day at the house.

"It sounds exciting to work up in the mountains, never knowing what you are going to encounter, but what is it really like?" She was stalling, not wanting to leave without him getting to spend more time with Ally, while at the same time she'd wanted to ask him about his work in the mountains since the first time she'd heard of his work there.

"It's not like the TV shows. I'm not riding a horse up the side of the mountain every day, though I did ride one once with a local doctor who had an elderly woman that he wanted me to see. Her son had taken her down to the local clinic one day and when the doctor had recommended that she have surgery for a prolapsed uterus, she'd left swearing never to come see him again. He thought maybe with a second opinion, she'd change her mind. Needless to say, she took one look at the two of us and slammed the door."

"Well, that had to be discouraging," Bree said. While she'd worked with some difficult patients, she had never had one refuse to at least listen to what she had to say.

"It happens. Besides, I got a nice horse ride through some of the most beautiful country in the world," Knox said.

"You got to ride a horse?" Ally asked.

Bree hadn't realized the girl had come up beside her and was listening to their conversation. As Ally was getting older, Bree knew she needed to be more aware of what she said when her niece was around.

"I did. He was a really nice horse, too," Knox said as Ally came to sit beside him.

"Can I ride him?" Ally asked, moving closer to Knox.

"You can't ride that horse. He's not mine. Besides, he lives a long way from here. But my parents have several horses at their ranch. If your parents are okay with it, maybe me and your aunt Bree can take you to see them."

"I don't have parents. I have Aunt Bree," Ally said before turning toward Bree. "Can we go see the horses?"

"We'll have to see," Bree said. Ally had always had a fascination with horses, even though she'd never been around one except for the ones at the county fair. And while she was happy that Knox and Ally had something to bond over now, taking Ally to Knox's parents' home? That came with complications she hadn't even considered. Not that she had anything against the couple. Bree had met them as a child. They both had been nothing but kind and encouraging to Bree and her sister when they were just starting out in their music career. But there was always the possibility that they would recognize Bree as one of the Rogers Sisters, wasn't there? Bree didn't think so. They'd only been twelve and she had changed a lot over those years. No longer was she the long-limbed, awkward little girl she'd been on those big, imposing stages. Still...

"That always means no," Ally said solemnly to Knox.

"I didn't say that..." Bree said, though the girl was right. Usually, it did mean the answer would be no.

"How about the three of us get something to eat together and we can talk about it then?" Knox asked, his eyes studying Bree.

Bree started to refuse; she could see that he had questions about Ally. He had to have figured out that she was raising Ally on her own. And the fact that she had never mentioned having a niece whom she was responsible for probably seemed strange, as if she had been hiding that fact. Of course, she had been. But explaining why might bring up questions she wasn't ready to answer. Not yet. She needed more time.

But still, this was an opportunity for them all to get to know each other. Wasn't that what she wanted? Didn't she need to see how Knox responded to having a child around?

"I think that would be great," she answered, surprising herself as much as her niece. "Where did you have in mind?"

Knox watched as Ally, Bree's niece, finished off her glass of chocolate milk. When the little girl looked up at him, a ring of chocolate circling her mouth, Knox thought she had to be the prettiest thing he had ever seen. With her aunt's strawberry blond hair and bright green eyes, Knox could have taken the child to be Bree's.

He couldn't understand why Bree had never mentioned that she was raising a child. Wasn't that something people just talked about? All the parents he knew couldn't talk about their children enough. He knew if he had a child, he'd probably be one of those parents, too.

Was it because Bree wasn't the child's mother? He didn't think so. He'd observed Bree in her interactions with their patients at the clinic. She had always been warm and caring. So why did it seem that she had been keeping Ally a secret until today? She had told him that he didn't know everything about her. He had known that. After all, they'd only known each other for a short period of time. Still, this was something he thought would have come out at some point in their conversations together. If not at work, at least when they'd met at the bar. It would have explained one of the reasons she was working there. Supporting herself and a child while in school would have been tough.

"Can I have some money for the jukebox?" Ally asked.

Before Bree could open her purse, Knox pulled out his wallet and handed her a five-dollar bill. "Do you want me to ask the lady at the register for change for the machine?"

"No, thank you. I can do it. I am eight years old, you know," the little girl said before turning and walking over to the counter where the waitress who had served their pizza stood.

"A little touchy about her age?" he asked Bree.

"Apparently, eight is the new twelve. At least, that seems to be what her and her friends think," Bree said, then sighed. "She's determined to grow up as fast as possible, while I just want the time to slow down so she can enjoy being a child for as long as possible."

"Weren't you like that? Eager to grow up? I know I was." It was just too bad that he had wasted so much of his life while he was growing up, making decisions that he wasn't old enough to make. He'd spent most of his teenage years rebelling against parents who had been too busy with their career to notice. He could only hope Ally wouldn't waste her childhood that way, because it was only later, when you grew up and looked back, that you realized what you had lost. But then Ally didn't have parents who were always gone on the road. It was easy to see the way that Bree interacted with her niece that the two of them were close.

"I guess I was," Bree said.

He watched as she stared into her half-empty glass. Was she thinking about mistakes she had made, just as he had? He knew so little about her, something that had never bothered him about other women. But whatever this fascination he had for Bree, it made him want to know everything. Even the tiny things. What was her favorite color? Her favorite movie? Did she even like movies? Maybe she preferred books. There was so much he wanted to know. "How did you end up with Ally? Did something happen to her parents?"

She looked at him for a moment, before her eyes dropped back to her drink. "Her mother, my sister, was injured in a car accident not long after Ally was born. She didn't survive. I've had Ally since she was a newborn."

"I'm sorry. That had to be hard." And explained so much, like the pain he'd seen in her eyes the night she'd sung at the bar. And that song. It had to be one she'd written about losing her sister. "So you've been raising her by yourself for eight years? It has to have been hard balancing school with raising a baby."

And Bree didn't have just school to worry about. She'd had to make a living, too. He knew she'd worked as a labor and delivery nurse; all midwives did at some point. Had she also been working at the bar then, too? "Where is her father? Doesn't he help you?"

"My sister..." Bree stopped midsentence and Knox could tell this wasn't something that was easy for her to talk about. He shouldn't have pushed her like he'd done.

"I'm sorry. It's none of my business. It's just that the thought of a man not supporting his daughter or the woman who had chosen to take care of his child, seems inexcusable to me."

"It's not like that," Bree said quickly. "It's complicated. My sister... Well, that's complicated, too."

"You don't have to tell me," Knox said. He didn't want Bree to feel like he was pressuring her to tell him all of her secrets, even though he wanted to know every single one.

"No, it's not that. I need to tell you this." Bree looked over to where Ally was picking out songs on the old-timey jukebox. "Ally's mother, my sister, she didn't feel that it would be a good thing for Ally's father to be involved in her daughter's life when she was born."

Knox didn't like the sound of that. "Was he abusive?"

"No, she never said that." Bree's voice sounded strange and he looked down to see her fingers had turned white as she gripped the table. "She just told me that he wouldn't want a baby and he would be a bad influence."

"So she never told him about the baby?" That didn't seem right to him. Didn't the man have a right to know? Even if he wasn't in a good place then, was it possible that knowing he had a child might have given him the encouragement to change?

"Look, I know it has to be hard talking about this. Your sister was young when you lost her, right?"

"She was my age," Bree said. "We were twins."

Twins. As an only child, he couldn't really appreciate what losing a sibling would be like, but it had to be hard. Losing a twin, someone you'd shared your whole life with, had to be even harder.

"Is it possible, then, that she might have changed her mind about Ally's father? Maybe they could have worked things out?" he said. "It just doesn't seem fair that he wasn't given that chance."

The small restaurant filled with music from a well-known pop star as Ally rushed back over to them, cutting their conversation off.

Knox could see that Bree's niece was a happy, well-adjusted child, even after what had to be a rough start to her young life. He had no doubt it was because Ally had been lucky enough to have someone like Bree to take care of her.

And though it seemed wrong that Bree's sister hadn't told Ally's father about the pregnancy, it wasn't any of his business. It sounded as if the mother had been looking out for her child. What more could a parent do?

"Are you two talking about horses again?" Ally asked as she flung herself into the seat beside her aunt.

"No, we weren't. But if the invitation is still open, I think it would be a great idea for you to go see his parents' horses."

Knox was surprised by Bree's about-face on his invitation, but he wasn't about to lose the chance to spend more time with the two of them, as he was discovering that Ally was almost as enchanting as her aunt. "Are the two of you by any chance free tomorrow?"

That night, as Bree climbed into bed, she looked over to where a picture of her sister sat on her nightstand. Was she doing the right thing? Did she have a choice? She couldn't continue living with the knowledge of how her promise to her sister had affected Knox and Ally.

She picked up the picture of Brittany and a wave of grief hit her. How many nights had she cried herself to sleep while she was holding this picture? How long was she going to put herself through this? It was time to do the right thing for both Ally and Knox. And it was time to let go of the grief and guilt that she'd felt ever since Brittany had died.

She would always love and miss her sister. And even though they'd grown apart, Bree knew that Brittany had still loved her. Her sister wouldn't want her to keep going through this pain, night after night.

"I love you, Brittany," she said before setting the picture down, "and I'm sorry I have to break my promise to you, but I can't keep doing this. Ally deserves to know her father and Knox deserves to know his daughter."

Bree wiped away the tears from her eyes and took a

shaky breath. "I will never forget you. You will always be my sister. But from now on, I'm going to concentrate on the good times we had, instead of what we lost. Because I deserve to be happy, too."

CHAPTER SIX

BY THE TIME Bree had gotten Ally ready for their trip to Knox's parents' ranch, her mind had come up with a dozen ways that what she was about to do could go wrong. What if Knox was so angry at her that he went to Dr. Warner and had her thrown out of the practice? What if his parents called one of their lawyers and had Ally taken away from her?

The doorbell sounded. It was too late to cancel now. Ally checked the door monitor as she'd been taught before skipping away to let Knox in. Bree rubbed her damp hands down her jeans. She had to make herself relax. She was doing the right thing.

Now that she'd cracked open a can of worms, she knew that it could be thrown wide open for the whole world to see by the end of that day. Scared of what might follow, she wanted to take her niece and hide in her closet. But she'd made her peace with her decision the night before. It was time for her to face Knox and tell him the truth.

Squaring her shoulders, she pasted a smile on her face as Knox walked inside, Ally beside him with her mouth going a hundred miles an hour.

"Sorry, she's been like this ever since she got up this morning," Bree said. "Ally, run and get your backpack."

As the girl ran off, twin pigtails flying behind her, Knox laughed. "She has a lot more energy than me at this time of the day."

"Me, too. Would you like a cup of coffee?" Bree asked, turning away from him and heading to the kitchen. She was finding it hard to look Knox in the eyes, something that didn't bode well for the rest of the day. She had to calm down. Trying to anticipate what his reaction to learning about Ally would be was too much. She just needed to take this one step at a time. The first thing to do was to get it over with, but there was no chance at that while Ally could interrupt them at any moment.

Right then, the little girl flew into the room. With eyes bright with excitement, she reminded Bree so much of Brittany right before she performed. It was pure, innocent joy on Ally's face, and Bree was so afraid she was about to destroy all of that if she didn't handle this right.

"Can we go now?" Ally begged, pulling on the leg of Knox's jeans.

"It looks like I'll need that coffee to go," Knox said, looking down at Bree's little girl, his own face just as happy-looking as the child's, before he looked back up at her.

With that one look, Bree's stomach unknotted and her body relaxed. Knox didn't even know that Ally was his child, yet Bree could see how much he enjoyed being around her. No matter how Knox took the news, as long as he loved Ally, it would be okay. Even though she knew that Bree and Knox's relationship would never be the same, it would all be worth it for Ally and Knox to have the life they deserved.

"Are we almost there?" Ally asked as Knox turned his truck down a small lane that led to his parents' ranch. She'd been asking the same question for the past thirty minutes, her excitement increasing with each mile.

"Almost. Keep looking over on your right and you might see a horse or two in the field," Knox said, then looked over at Bree. "I'm afraid of what she might do when she finally sees one of the horses."

"We had a talk about behaving around the horses this morning when she got up, but it would probably be a good idea for you to tell her, too." Bree wasn't really worried about Ally's safety. She knew that Knox wouldn't let her niece around any of the horses that were dangerous.

"I will. And I talked to the ranch manager, Rodney, about bringing the two of you out today. He was going to pick out a pony for Ally. I wouldn't take a chance with either of your safety."

"I know that," Bree said, and knew there was truth in his words. No matter what her sister had thought of Knox when he was younger, he wouldn't do anything to hurt Ally. Not intentionally at least.

Ally let out a squeal and began hopping up and down in her seat. "I see one, I see one."

Bree looked over to where her niece was pointing and saw a pretty brown-and-white horse standing in the field.

A few minutes later, they came to a halt in front of a

large red metal barn. Before Bree could get out of the car, Ally had freed herself from her seat and was running toward it.

"Whoa, there," Knox said, catching up to Ally and stopping her, before taking a knee in front of her. "I know your aunt Bree told you that you needed to be careful around the horses. Running up to them is not being careful. You could spook one of them and they could hurt you or themselves."

"I don't want to hurt the horses," Ally said as her chin began to tremble, and big fat tears rolled down her cheeks.

Knox looked up at Bree with something akin to horror in his face. "I didn't mean to make her cry."

The man could handle all kinds of emergency situations in the operating room, but one little girl's tears scared him like this?

"It's okay, Ally. We know you don't want to hurt the horses. Knox just wants to make sure you are safe. And we did discuss no running around the horses this morning, didn't we?" Bree asked her niece.

"Yes, ma'am," Ally said, using her shirtsleeve to wipe at her face before turning toward Knox. "I'm sorry, Dr. Knox. I won't run and scare the horses. I promise."

"That's okay," Knox said, standing and holding out a hand to Ally. "Let's go see some of my parents' horses. And then I have a surprise for you."

When Ally took Knox's hand, then looked up at him with eyes full of trust, Bree's heart was filled with so much love that she felt as if it might burst out from her chest. She realized then that it wasn't just Ally she was feeling that love for, it was also for the man who held her niece's hand. How had her feelings for him changed so much, so fast? It was as if everything in the universe had thrown them together at just the perfect time.

"You coming?" Knox asked, looking back at her, then stopping as he studied her face. Did he see how much his simple act of taking her niece's hand in his had affected her? Could he see how much her own reaction to him was changing? Did he feel this way, too?

Not that it mattered. She couldn't make this about her and Knox. She had to remember that her focus had to be on Ally and Knox's relationship, not the way that her heart sped up every time he looked at her, just like the way he was looking at her now.

"Come on," he said, holding out his other hand to her. Was it wrong for her to wish everything could be different between them? That she could take what he offered her, the friendship and maybe more, without knowing that soon he might hate her for all the years of his daughter's life that she stole from him?

Unable to help herself, she reached out and took his hand. Its warmth calmed her. And for the next half hour she held on to it, wishing she would never have to let it go as he took them through the horse stables, pointing out one horse after another. Ally's excitement grew with each new horse they saw, but she stayed close to them as Knox had instructed her, while staff members went about their work hauling hay and cleaning the stalls.

"And this is where we keep my mother's ponies," Knox said when they got to the end of the stalls.

"Isn't your mom too big to ride a pony?" Ally asked as they stopped by an older man who was saddling up a small black pony.

"Mrs. Collins keeps the ponies around so that when little girls like you come over, you will be able to ride them," the man said, then removed his hat, exposing a bald head that was sporting a fresh sunburn, as he held out a hand for Bree to shake. "I'm Rodney, ma'am."

Letting go of Knox's hand, she took the man's hand, noting its rough callouses that reminded her of her father's. "It's nice to meet you, Rodney. I'm Bree. And this is Ally."

"It's nice to meet you both. This here is Sammy. He's a nice little pony that likes little girls. Do you want to pet him, Ally?"

With a nod from Bree, Ally approached the pony slowly, before placing her hand on the top of its head like Rodney showed her.

"I think it's love at first sight," she whispered to Knox when he stepped closer.

"I think so, too," he said. But when she looked up at him, she noticed that it was she he was looking at, instead of her niece. Her hand shook when his hand reached down for hers again. She let him take it. Why couldn't she enjoy a few moments before everything came crashing down around her?

They stood and watched Ally get her first lesson on how to saddle the pony before Rodney helped her up onto the pony's back and led her out of the barn and into an adjoining paddock.

"There you are." A loud feminine voice came from behind them. Turning, Bree saw Gail Collins approaching. The years since Bree had seen her had been good to her. Though there was a little gray in the woman's long dark blond hair, her face carried very few wrinkles. Dressed in jeans and sporting a rhinestone belt buckle, she still looked like the Country Music Queen she'd been all those years ago when Bree had met her.

"Bree, this is my mom," Knox said as the beautiful woman stretched up on her toes and planted a noisy kiss on his cheek. Instead of shrugging off her attention, Knox wrapped his free arm around her. "Mom, this is Bree Rogers. She's the midwife who has been working with me at the county clinic."

"It's nice to meet you, Bree," Knox's mother said before stepping back and studying Bree. "Have we met before?"

Bree knew that this time would come. She was bound to meet Knox's mother someday. Yet, she still hadn't decided on how to handle it. With the exception of telling Knox about Ally, she had always stuck to the truth. It seemed best to do that now. "Yes, ma'am, but I doubt you'd remember me. I was only twelve years old at the time. My sister and I used to perform when we were kids. We were known as the Rogers Sisters."

"I remember now. The two of you were twins, not identical, though you did look similar."

"It was the hair and eyes," Bree said, shooting a look

over at Knox, waiting for him to put the two things together. Hadn't Brittany told him about her childhood
career?

"And you're a midwife now?" the woman said, still
studying her.

"Yes, ma'am. I'm just finishing up my residency now."

"And your sister?" Knox's mother asked. "Did she
leave the business, too?"

"Mom, Bree's sister was killed right after her daughter, Bree's niece, was born," Knox said, cutting into what
was starting to feel like an inquisition. "That's the little girl, Ally, that I told you I was bringing to see the
horses. We were just about to walk outside so we could
watch Rodney work with Ally. He has her on Sammy."

"I'm so sorry, Bree. Please excuse me from asking
so many questions. It's just so rare for Knox to bring
a woman out here to meet us. I just want to know all
about you. And it's so interesting that we met when you
were a child."

Bree looked over at Knox and caught him rolling his
eyes at his mother's statement. His mother changed the
subject to ponies and horses, then circled back to her
hopes that someday she would have grandchildren to
teach to ride all the horses she'd collected. Bree wanted
to laugh at the woman's not so subtle hints that Knox
needed to get busy in the baby-making department.

But once they reached the paddock, the woman
stopped talking and just stared where Ally sat on the
pony, listening carefully to every word Rodney said.
Never had Bree seen her niece look so serious.

"She's beautiful, Bree," Knox's mother said from behind her. "And a natural in the saddle. Look how perfectly she's seated. She'll make a great rider."

Bree didn't know what to say to that, so she just stood there, still holding Knox's hand, and watched as her niece took one more step away from her into a life that Bree would never be able to give her.

Fifteen minutes later, she could see that Ally was getting tired. Fortunately, Gail Collins could see it, too. "Let me go get her back to the stable."

When Bree started to follow her, Knox pulled her aside. "I'm sorry if my mother upset you with her questions about your sister. She didn't mean to."

"I know that. She had no way of knowing," Bree said, wanting to say so much more. She suddenly needed to get all of this off her chest, once and for all. Both Knox's and his mother's kindness was just too much. She didn't deserve any of it.

She pulled her hand from his, feeling the loss immediately. Then she wrapped her arms around herself, unexpectedly cold while in the warmth of the summer sun.

"I need to talk to you. Privately." The words sounded more ominous than she'd meant them to and the whole mood of the day changed as Knox looked at her, his eyes worried.

"I asked my mother to have a picnic fixed for the two of us. I thought I could show you some of the ranch and I know my mom would love to spend time with Ally. That is, if you would like that," Knox said as they walked back into the stable where they were greeted by a smiling Ally and Knox's mother.

"Ms. Gail says I can come to her house and see her horse collection," Ally said. "They aren't real horses, but she says some of them have pink and purple ribbons I can braid in their hair."

"That sounds like a lot of fun. But you have to be careful and not break them," Bree told her niece.

"I'll run in and get the food. Then we can go down to the pond," Knox said. "Or you can come up to the house with me if you would like."

Bree followed him out of the barn where she could see the two-story house that stood to the north. It was a beautiful house. And just one more thing to remind her that Knox and his parents could give Ally so much more than she could.

Around her, the fields of grass swayed with the summer breeze. Even with the voices of the workers in the stables, there was a calming quietness there that she needed. "No, I'll wait here."

She strode over to a fencerow and placed one boot-clad foot on the first fence post she came to, welcoming this short period of time she had alone with her thoughts. She was going to do this. She had no other choice. Even without seeing her niece walk off, hand in hand with the grandmother she had never known, Bree knew coming clean with Knox about Ally had to be done now. Her and Ally's time alone together was up.

It was only a few minutes before she heard the sound of a small motor headed her way. She turned to see Knox driving an all-terrain cart toward her, a basket sitting beside him.

"Climb in," Knox said when he stopped and moved the basket to the back floorboard.

Bree took the seat beside him, buckling herself in before Knox started down the drive. He then took a right turn down a worn path through an open field running beside another paddock, this one larger with a taller fence.

She grabbed a handle above her as they drove over the rocky path at a speed that at first scared her, then became thrilling. By the time they had arrived by a large pond, they both were laughing.

For a moment, Bree forgot that she was about to spill a secret that would change all their lives. When Knox bent his head toward hers, she knew she should stop him, but she couldn't find the strength to turn her head away. As his lips brushed against hers in a gentle kiss, she closed her eyes and made a wish for her and Knox to someday get a second chance. When she opened her eyes, she found Knox's face still close to hers. Her hand cupped his cheek, the day's stubble rough against her skin.

"Something's bothering you, Bree. Is it those questions from my mom? She didn't mean to bring up bad memories," Knox said, his eyes watching her with an intensity she'd never experienced. It wasn't the first time she'd seen him like this. It was as if he was memorizing everything about her in that moment. As if he wanted to sink into her soul and know all her secrets.

And now he was about to learn more than he could ever have imagined.

"It's not that, not really. I've decided that instead of thinking about those bad memories, I need to concentrate on the good ones. Over the years, I've let the loss of my sister define our relationship, and I shouldn't have. Does that make sense?" She didn't know why she was telling him this, but it seemed important that he understand that she was making changes in her life. Looking at things differently. Just like she was looking at him differently now.

"It makes a lot of sense. Everybody handles the grieving process in different ways and in different time frames. But if that isn't what's bothering you, what is it?"

"Can we have just a few more minutes before I tell you?"

"Of course we can," Knox said, moving away from her and reaching over for the basket. When she joined him, he took her hand and led her down to where a weather-beaten wood pier had been built across part of the pond. When they got to the end of the pier, he put the basket down, then sat down beside it. Hanging his feet over the end of the pier, he offered Bree a hand and she took a seat beside him before looking out at the lake with its mirror-smooth surface. It was the calm before the storm.

Opening the basket, Knox pulled out sandwiches and drinks, laying them between them, along with some fruit. Her stomach was queasy, but she forced herself to unwrap a sandwich and take a bite. She wasn't sure if her stomach was reacting to her nerves about what she was about to do or if it was because of the kiss they'd just shared.

They ate in silence as they both looked out across the water. A fish hit the top of the water startling Bree and causing her to jump and let out a nervous laugh. The hollowness of it seemed to echo across the lake.

"I don't know where to start. I know I should start at the beginning, but I can't say I even know where this all began. Maybe you can help me with that."

"I'd be glad to help you if I can," Knox said, turning toward her, laying his sandwich down. "Maybe if you tell me what's wrong, the two of us can fix it."

Bree looked at him sitting there beside her. He was so calm. So reassuring. It was hard to believe he was the same man that her sister had been so adamant that he wouldn't be good for her child.

Bree had made such a big mistake all those years ago, not giving him a chance to prove that he would be a good father.

"I'm going to tell you everything I know, and then maybe you can help fill in some of the blanks for me. You see, before my sister died, I hadn't heard from her in over eighteen months even though we lived in the same city."

"I'm sorry to hear that. Families can be so complicated," Knox said. "But I don't know where I come in."

"I know you don't. And that's my fault, not yours. I should have told you this months ago." She looked away from him then, seeking the calm she'd felt from their surroundings earlier, but it didn't come. Maybe she didn't deserve it. Maybe she deserved all the sleepless nights, and guilty nerves she'd suffered for the past few weeks.

"No. That's not right. I should have told you this years ago. But I didn't know you then. And I'd made a promise I didn't think I could break."

When Knox started to interrupt her, she rested a hand on his chest. "Do you even remember my sister?"

Knox stared at Bree. She was talking in circles, making it impossible to figure out what it was that she was trying to tell him. Her sister? Why would he remember her sister?

"She had dyed her hair, it was more red than blond the last time I saw her, but she would still have had my eyes. She still went by her first name, Brittany. But she had changed her last name to Moore. She didn't want people to remember her from our childhood performance."

The name was vaguely familiar, but why? Then it hit him. "She was working at one of the recording studios as a backup singer. I remember her. She hung out with some of the music crowd I knew. I didn't know her that well…" A memory surfaced then. Red hair. Beautifully haunting green eyes. It was the night he and Thad had been out partying. She had been with the group of his parents' band members whom Knox had stayed back with when Thad had left the bar. As it always did, thoughts of Thad brought back all his old grief and guilt. He talked a good talk with Bree about grieving, but he was still struggling himself with the loss of his friend.

And the girl? He remembered meeting her at the bar that night, and then the two of them sharing a car ride. Later, at his place, they had shared more. Was that what this was all about? Did Bree know that her sister had spent the night with him? "She went by Britt," he said. "I guess like the way you go by Bree, instead of Brianna."

"She did go by Britt, sometimes. It was usually only with people she was close to, though," Bree said, her eyes looking at him expectantly, like he had the answer to a question he didn't know.

Or was she just waiting for him to admit that he had slept with her sister? His life then had been so different. He'd lived it one day at a time, never thinking about the consequences. That is, until the night Thad was killed.

"I don't know what your sister told you, but back then, when I met your sister, I wasn't the same person I am now. I was young and reckless. There are a lot of things I wish I had done differently then. I'm sorry if the night I spent with your sister upsets you. It's not something I'm proud of." Revisiting that night was a nightmare. He and Thad had started partying early that day and hadn't had the good sense to stop. If it hadn't been for who his parents were, he was sure the bars would have thrown them out on the streets.

But then, if his parents hadn't been who they were, he might not have acted out the way he had. It hadn't been until he reached rock bottom that he and his parents had realized how unhealthy their relationship had become. Thank goodness they'd been able to work things out then, before there was any more damage to their relationship.

But that night had been before he'd come to his senses. He could barely remember the girl he now knew as

Bree's sister, offering to get him home. It wasn't until that morning when he'd received the call that Thad was in the hospital with little hope of surviving, that Knox had finally sobered up. He'd left Bree's sister in his bed without an explanation and hadn't returned until the next night. He was ashamed to say that he hadn't given Brittany another thought, until now.

It was like all his sins were coming back to revisit him when he looked over at Bree. How did he tell her that he'd known her sister, but all she'd meant to him was one night of drunken pleasure?

"I don't know what your sister told you about me. I can tell you that I'm not the man I was then and I'm ashamed of the way I acted that night. I wish I could say that there weren't any more women like her, one-night stands with women I barely knew, but I can't. I can use my youth as an excuse, but I don't want to make excuses. I learned the hard way that you have to take responsibility for your actions and face the consequences. I did that many years ago, but sometimes those consequences last for years."

"I don't understand. Are you saying that Brittany was just a one-night stand? Because that isn't how she acted. She acted like the two of you had been together and it had ended badly. I took it to mean that the two of you were involved."

Knox looked over at Bree. Her face was pale, her pupils almost pinpoint. She looked as if she was in shock as she stared at him. Gone was the warmth he was used to seeing in her eyes. She looked like she'd seen a ghost.

The ghost of her sister? Because right then he felt like Brittany was standing there between the two of them.

How did he fix this without making it look like he was calling her sister a liar? Had he said something that would have made Brittany think that there was more between the two of them? How could that even be possible when he'd never seen her again?

After Thad's death, he'd applied himself to finishing his exams. And when the guilt and depression from Thad's death had threatened to send him back into his bad ways, he'd checked himself into a rehab. He'd cut all ties then, only taking calls from his parents until he'd found the help he needed to get his life onto a path he was proud of.

"I'm sorry, Bree. I don't want to hurt you or suggest that Brittany wasn't truthful, but the only thing that me and Brittany shared was one night together. That was all."

Knox started to gather the leftover meal wrappers. This was not the way he had planned for the two of them to end the day. When Bree's hand closed over his as he reached for the last of their mostly uneaten meal, he looked up at her, expecting to see anger, disgust, or the coolness she'd treated him to the first months they'd worked together.

But there was none of those things. Instead, there was sorrow and regret. "But that wasn't all you shared, Knox. The two of you shared Ally."

CHAPTER SEVEN

THERE WAS NO laughing on their ride back to the ranch house, as Knox shot off question after question at her. Bree couldn't blame him for the anger she could see brewing in his eyes.

"How is that possible?" he asked, then shook his head when she didn't answer. He was an OB/GYN; he knew how pregnancy happened as well as she did.

"Okay, let's say I am Ally's father. Why wouldn't Brittany have told me?" he asked, then answered the question himself before she could answer. "She would have found out about the pregnancy when I was away in rehab. I didn't have my phone with me. Only my parents knew how to contact me. But after? When Ally was born? I would have been out then. She should have called then."

"I told you I had a lot of blanks I needed you to fill in. I only talked to her the once in eighteen months. She hadn't told me anything about the pregnancy. I don't have any proof of this, but I've always thought that she might have been considering giving up Ally. Maybe that's why she didn't tell either of us? Maybe it wasn't until Ally was born that she decided to keep her. We've both seen that happen before."

Knox swerved around a rock in the middle of the path, causing Bree to grip the over-the-head handle even tighter.

"Maybe we should stop." He'd been driving full throttle since he'd insisted that they get back to the ranch as soon as possible. He was upset. Shocked. But so was she.

Learning that her assumption that Brittany and Knox had been involved in a relationship was wrong changed everything. What if Ally wasn't even Knox's child? She hadn't been able to say those words out loud, but he had to be thinking them, too.

Was it possible? Could it be that Brittany had made that part of her story up, too? The answer to that question tore Bree in two. On one hand, if Knox wasn't Ally's father, Bree could let go of the guilt she'd felt at assuming that he wasn't fit to be. And if Knox wasn't Ally's father, she wouldn't have to worry about losing Ally. On the other hand, that would mean that there was another man out there who could someday challenge Bree for her niece. A man who wouldn't be as kind and caring as Knox. A man who might not be good for her niece.

Being honest with herself, Bree knew that Ally having Knox for a father would be good for her. And she had to admit that it would be best if her niece's paternity was settled sooner instead of later.

Knox stopped the cart, but he didn't look at her. "We need a plan. We can't tell my mother this. And I know we can both agree that we can't tell Ally until we know for sure that I'm her father. There's places in Nashville that can run a paternity test in a day. We need to get that done first." He turned his head to her, his eyes somber now. "And then we need to have a long talk, no matter what the results."

The rest of their time at the ranch seemed to fly by as Knox did everything but rush them out to his truck. She started to stop him and ask if he thought she was going to just blurt out the news that Ally was his child to his mother or if he just couldn't stand to be around her anymore, but she was afraid to hear his answer.

He was angry and confused. She got that. She was, too. Just like him, she wanted to know the truth about her niece.

And she was also afraid. Only this time it wasn't the fear that she'd spoken to Lucretia about, the fear of losing Ally. This was a new fear. Something she was ashamed to admit because it was so selfish of her. What right did she have to fear that what she and Knox had begun to feel for each other had been destroyed when he was now faced with the fact that he had trusted her and she had betrayed him by not sharing Brittany's secret with him?

By the time Knox dropped her and Ally off at their home, Bree had come to accept that there was little hope that Knox would forgive her, even if Ally wasn't his child. There had to be trust in any relationship, especially one as new as theirs. She could try to make excuses for her actions all day long, but the man who'd driven them home without even looking at her once was not going to listen to them. And she couldn't blame him.

* * *

The new week started off with a stop by a local lab where Bree could pick up a DNA paternity test. She had asked Knox to let her explain to Ally, but Bree still didn't know how to do that. While Bree believed in being truthful, she didn't think her niece was old enough to understand DNA or what it was used for. She'd finally decided in the middle of the night that it was best, for now, to just tell Ally it was a test she needed.

The rest of the day had gone by quickly with Bree and Lori attending two deliveries, one of which Bree was primary. The good thing about being busy was that it didn't give her a lot of time to think about her own problems. She'd only seen Knox once in the clinic hallway, but they'd both been too busy to stop and talk.

It wasn't until the next day, after she'd carefully swabbed Ally's cheek then dropped her off at school, that Bree had time to worry about the outcome of the paternity test. When she walked into the county clinic, she went straight to the back office and took the safely packaged test from her backpack. Knowing she could trust Lucretia not to snoop, she put the test in a paper bag and added a note to let Knox know it was for him.

A few minutes later, Knox stopped by Lucretia's desk where she and Bree were discussing supply list changes. After nodding his head toward the exam rooms, Bree followed him. He handed her the paper bag that contained the test, and she slipped it into her pocket. She couldn't help but smile at the way they were treating this.

"I feel like I should have a hat and fake mustache.

Maybe a trench coat, too," Bree said, hoping that she could lighten up the situation.

"I'd like to see you in a trench coat," Knox said, surprising Bree with the teasing comeback before turning serious again. "How did it go with Ally? She ask anything about the test?"

"Not at all. I admit I was surprised. I wasn't sure what I was going to say if she asked me what the test was for. I've always been honest with her about everything, but sometimes you can't tell someone everything you want to. Sometimes things are more complicated than the simple truth."

"If you are talking about your not telling me about Ally, I know there were reasons you didn't tell me. You made a promise to your sister, and then she passed away. But I don't understand how, after you met me, after you saw that I wasn't a bad person, you didn't tell me then. Why, Bree? Didn't you think I deserved to know if Ally was my child?"

How could she make him understand the weight of her sister's secret that she had carried for years? How could she expect him to forgive her for not telling him? "It was the last thing I told her, Knox. The last thing I said to my sister. I promised her that I wouldn't tell anyone about who was Ally's father."

She walked the length of the small exam room, then turned and started back to him. "Until this weekend I had never broken that promise. I had held my sister's secret deep inside and never dreamed of telling anyone the truth about Ally. Until I met you. And though I'm not proud of it, if you had been the type of man Brittany had accused you of being, I wouldn't have told you then. The only person I had ever considered telling Brittany's secret to was Ally when she got old enough to make her own decisions about the information her mother had given me."

"So, what? When she was eighteen or nineteen, she'd have suddenly showed up on my doorstep? Would that have been fair to either of us?" Knox asked, coming to stand in the path where she had been pacing the floor.

"Nothing about this situation is fair to any of us," Bree said, stopping in front of him. "It wasn't fair that Brittany was killed in an accident before she had the chance to raise her child. Who knows? Maybe once she had Ally at home, she would have changed her mind. But we'll never know that, will we?"

"You're right," Knox said, running his hands through his hair where it had fallen down in front of his face. "This hasn't been fair for anyone."

Bree heard a door shut and then Lucretia talking to someone who would be their first patient of the day. Holding the brown paper bag up in front of her, she nodded at Knox. "But at least with this we will have the truth."

Because until they found out if Knox was really Ally's father, there was no way for them to move forward.

Bree rushed back to put the test in her backpack before following Knox to the front of the office to greet their patient. By the time Bree got there, other patients had begun to file into the waiting room. The little office was soon full again, as it had been every day that Bree had been there. While Bree was glad to be busy, she hated that there were so many women who couldn't afford to get care. They provided what they could, but it wasn't the same.

For her last appointment of the day, Lucretia brought back a woman in her midthirties, along with an elderly woman whose eyes darted around the room, taking everything in. "This is Leah and her grandmother."

"It's nice to meet you both. What brings you to the clinic today?" Bree asked, still watching the older woman who was acting uneasy.

"My grandmother, Camila, she doesn't speak English. She has a knot, a lump, in her breast. I don't know where to take her to get this looked at. My sister says she needs a mammogram, but where do we get this?" The younger woman looked at Bree with worried eyes and Bree instantly understood her concerns.

Bree had lost her own mother to breast cancer. If her mother had gone to get her yearly exam, the cancer would have been caught earlier and her mother might still be alive today. "If it's okay with you and your grandmother, I'd like to give her an exam. That way we can make sure there isn't any other issue that we need to investigate. Then I'll get a mammogram scheduled."

After giving the woman a thorough exam, Bree left them in the exam room while she went to find Lucretia. She knew that there were programs run by the local hospitals to help women get their yearly mammogram, but she wasn't sure where the information was.

"I'm glad you're here," Lucretia said when Bree stepped into the reception office. "There's someone outside the office pacing back and forth. I think it's that young girl. The teenager from last week."

Bree stepped into the waiting room and looked out the door. She could see the shadow of someone outside the frosted door, standing against the back wall of the hallway. It was possible that it was someone waiting for a patient to finish, maybe another grandchild of Camila's, but Bree didn't think so. She'd waited all day for the frightened girl who had run away to come back. Bree was pretty sure that she had.

Bree went over to the reception window. She didn't want to let the girl get away before she could talk to her, but she also didn't want Leah or Camila to think she had forgotten about them. "Can you find the information for the free mammogram programs at the hospital and make an appointment for the patient in my exam room? Her granddaughter has all her contact information. It could be benign, but there is definitely a large mass in her right breast that needs to be seen to immediately. I'm going to ask Knox to recommend a surgeon who will work with them on finances once we get the results of the mammogram back."

"I can do that," Lucretia said. "What are you going to do?"

"I'm going to see if it's our returning patient. If it is, I'm not going to let her get away this time." Bree started toward the door. "Don't let anyone else out this door until I tell you to."

"Maybe we should call the police? What if she's dangerous? She pushed you over last time she was here," Lucretia said, leaning over the reception window.

"She's not dangerous. She was just scared."

"Wait," Lucretia said, holding out a pack of peanut butter crackers, "take these."

"You're the best," Bree told Lucretia, taking the crackers and heading back to the door. Maybe if she couldn't talk the girl into coming inside, she could bribe her.

She opened the door and stepped into the hallway, leaving the door open for a second while she waited to see what the girl's reaction was. Bree had denied to Lucretia that the girl was dangerous, but what did she really know about her? Fear made people do things that they normally wouldn't do. It had certainly caused Bree to make some bad decisions.

When the girl didn't run, Bree closed the door behind her, then held out the crackers. Once again, Bree noted the fear in the girl's eyes. "We thought you might like these."

The girl stared at the simple package of crackers like it was steak and lobster before looking at Bree with suspicion. "It's okay. They're for you."

"What do I have to do for them?" the girl asked, her young face transforming from that of a child's to a hardened adult in seconds. Bree had no doubt now that this girl was being abused in some way.

"You don't have to do anything," Bree said, coming to stand against the wall across from the girl. She wanted to take the girl into her arms and promise her she'd keep her safe, but that would only frighten the girl more. "You don't even have to talk to me if you don't want to."

When the girl reached for the crackers, Bree leaned forward toward her, then moved back away from her again. She wanted to cry when she saw the girl rip open the package of crackers and stuff the first one into her mouth. She wanted to go inside the office and get more for the girl to eat, but she was still afraid the girl would bolt on her.

When the girl finished the crackers and didn't run, Bree decided to take a chance. At some point someone was going to have to come out the office door and she didn't know how the girl would react. "Do you want something to drink? We have all kinds of bottled drinks inside. I can get you one if you don't want to come inside."

The girl's head shot up at the mention of a drink, her eyes coming to rest on the office door. Bree could tell that she wanted to go inside. The girl had come there for help. Bree just had to find a way to make her feel safe. "My name is Bree. I just started here as a midwife in training, but I can tell you that this is a safe place. No one is going to make you do anything you don't want to do here. But if you need help, you've come to the right place. We help people with all kinds of problems and we keep everything confidential. It's what we do."

"I'm Christine," the girl said, barely above a whisper, her voice sounding raw as if she hadn't used it in a while.

"Well, Christine, do you want to come inside with me? I don't mind talking in the hallway, but our office would be more private." When the girl didn't move, Bree continued. "I know you're scared. That's okay. I've been scared, too. Sometimes trusting someone is the scariest thing of all."

The girl pushed away from the wall, then stood staring at Bree. They stood there looking at each other for almost a minute, before big fat tears began to run down the girl's face and her body began to shake. "My name isn't Christine. That's the name the people who took me told me to use. My real name is Megan. Megan Johnson, and all I want is to go home. Can you help me?"

Knox walked out of an exam room where he had been speaking with the police officers that had been called when Bree had come inside with a sobbing teenager who had begun to spill her story. It had only taken a few minutes for him to realize they were dealing with a victim of human trafficking and they needed more help than he and Bree knew how to give. Once Megan had gone into the back with Lucretia, who had been happy to play momma hen to the young girl, they'd made the call to the police.

"They've contacted Megan's mother in Memphis and she's headed to the downtown Nashville police station," Knox said when he pulled Bree into the hallway.

"I know. I talked to her mother after Megan talked to her. She needs to be taken to a hospital for an exam, but I haven't been able to bring myself to mention that yet. She's so fragile right now, Knox. Her mother says this was the first time she had run away. The first time she's done anything like that. They had a fight about a boy who had been hanging around the park where she skateboarded." Bree took a deep breath before she looked up at Knox with what could only be described as murder in her eyes. "The boy was a twenty-two-year-old man who was hooked up with other human traffickers. It was all a setup."

Knox's arm came around Bree as her whole body shook with anger. "She's only seventeen. She should feel safe to go to the park and skateboard."

Knox was afraid that the young girl might never feel safe again. "From what the officers told me, it sounds like Megan's mother will make sure she gets the help she needs."

One of the officers came out from where she had gone to talk to the young girl and handed both him and Bree a card. "We're going to take Megan downtown to meet with our human trafficking officers. She's got a lot of information that they will find helpful. She's willing to talk with them, but she wants Ms. Lucretia to go along with her. The team might have questions for you, too."

Knox, along with Bree, offered to help in any way they could. While Bree went to say goodbye to Megan and help Lucretia gather her things, Knox pulled the officer over to the side. "Is there any chance that someone followed her here? Do I need to worry about the safety of the office?"

"That's one of the reasons I gave you my card. From what Megan says, she was sent here by one of the traffickers to obtain birth control pills. If you see anything suspicious, please call."

The officer's words made Knox feel sick. He hoped that the information Megan had would help to put the traffickers away, where they belonged. If not, there'd be another girl, in another park, and that one might not have the courage to do what Megan had done.

The young girl came down the hall, Lucretia following close behind her. When the girl hesitated at the door, one of the officers got in front of her while the other followed behind them. Bree pressed a note in the girl's hand before the officer opened the door and they walked out.

"What was that?" he asked.

"I gave her my number, in case she needs something. Or if she just wants to talk." A beeper on Bree's phone went off. "I'm running behind. Ally went home with a friend today, but I don't want to be late picking her up."

Knox watched her reach into her pocket and pull out the bag holding the paternity test. "Can you drop this off for me?"

Knox reached for the bag and Bree's hand closed around his.

"I can't imagine what Megan's mother is feeling right now. She's been going through hell for two weeks wondering if her daughter was even alive. I know we have a lot going on right now, but the most important thing is Ally is safe. And I know no matter what happens with these results, she'll still be safe."

"You're right. No matter what happens with these results," Knox said, "there is nothing more important than that Ally stays safe."

CHAPTER EIGHT

BREE LISTENED TO Ally chatter about her day at school as she began to mix the pancake batter. With only two more days left before summer break, Ally and her friends were getting more and more excited with plans for their time off. Bree, on the other hand, was already worried about how she was going to get someone to watch Ally on the nights she and Lori took call at the hospital. But most of all Bree was worried about the email that she had received from the lab that afternoon with the results of the paternity test.

"Is Knox going to be here soon?" Ally asked again. Ever since Bree had told her niece that she had invited Knox over for pancakes, the little girl had run back and forth from the front window to the kitchen.

Bree looked at the clock on the stove; she was getting anxious, too. Knowing that the information in the email could change both of their lives, she kept glancing over at her laptop as if the thing could open itself and spew out the information. Not that she was ready for the results on the paternity test.

While she wanted to know the truth about Ally's father, Bree knew that it could change everything about her and Ally's life. Knox had made it clear that his priority was Ally, but what did that really mean?

Bree looked around the tiny house that she had made into a home for her and Ally. It wasn't even theirs. She had been renting it month to month, not knowing where she would be settling once she got her midwifery certification. Would Knox see all the work and the love for Ally that she had put into the home? Or would he see the tiny, outdated place as something not good enough for the granddaughter of Gail and Charles Collins? He'd been brought up on a ranch that was bigger than the whole suburb where Bree had grown up.

Ally had just rushed back into the room when the doorbell finally rang. Jumping up and down with more energy than she should have had that late in the day, her niece raced back toward the door. "I've got it."

Bree forced herself not to run to the door alongside her niece. She told herself that she was anxious to see Knox because she was anxious to read the email with him. But she had been just as excited to see him every time they had passed in the halls of the Legacy Clinic that day. Something had changed between them since the day she had shared with him the truth about Ally. For the first time there had been no secrets between the two of them. She'd admitted her guilt and her fears and he'd admitted his own struggles when he was younger. If the two of them didn't have the results of the paternity test hanging over them, Bree thought that maybe the two of them might have had a chance to find something deeper.

But those results could be the very thing that destroyed that chance.

"Look what Dr. Knox brought," Ally said as Knox followed her into the kitchen carrying a large carton of chocolate milk, along with a bottle of wine.

"Is the chocolate milk for me?" Bree asked him, then looked down to Ally.

"He said it's for me, but you can have a glass," Ally said, reaching for it.

Bree turned back to the stove and began to pour the batter on the griddle. "It will definitely go with your dinner."

"It's Wednesday, so it's pancake night. Do you like pancakes?" Ally asked as she and Knox took a stool at the counter.

"I love pancakes. My mom's cook, Ms. Jenkins, makes them for breakfasts whenever I spend the night at my parents' house."

"You don't live with your mom?" Ally asked before jumping down and running over to where the dishes were kept.

"No. I have a house of my own. Like your aunt Bree."

Ally came back with the dishes and then ran back to get the utensils, explaining, "It's my job to set the table. Aunt Bree says we have to share the chores."

"That sounds like a good plan. Sharing is important," Knox said, his tone as serious as her niece's.

"So I guess the two of you can share these pancakes," Bree said as she took two plates and put a pancake on each of them. She placed bacon from the pile she had cooked earlier on each plate then brought them back to the counter. "This should get you started."

Bree listened to their conversation as she finished, then went to sit beside them at the kitchen counter that also acted as their dining table. Occasionally, she would join in, but mostly she just listened, enjoying the sound of her niece's laughter and the patience in which Knox answered all the little girl's questions.

It would have been a perfect meal if she didn't have the DNA test results weighing on her. She forced each bite of pancake down to her nervous stomach, until it protested.

"I'll do the dishes," Knox said when the last pancake had been eaten.

"You don't have to do that," Bree protested. "You're our guest tonight."

"And sometimes guests help with dishes. It's sharing, right, Ally?"

'I can help, too," Ally said as she started to take the dishes off the counter and carry them to the sink.

"Me and Knox will do the dishes. You need to go take a shower and get ready for bed," Bree said, preparing herself for the child's nightly complaints when it came to bedtime.

"Can we read tonight?" Ally asked.

"We'll see. Remember last night you took too long in the shower and we didn't have time to read." And Bree had felt guilty because it had been she who had been too tired to read that night, not Ally.

It seemed every day was getting shorter and shorter.

Each night she climbed into bed making a list of everything she needed to accomplish the next day, but it didn't seem as if she ever caught up. Between working at the two clinics, taking care of Ally and then working weekends at the bar, she never had a moment free. Add in the sleepless nights where she went from scared of what would happen with the results of the paternity to fanciful dreams of Knox kissing her again, and she was emotionally and physically drained.

"She'll be in there a while if you want us to check the email," Bree said, taking a plate from Knox and adding it to the sink.

"How about we wait until after we get these done?" Knox said as he picked up a towel.

"It's okay if you're nervous," Bree said. "I know I am."

"I'm not nervous, I'm terrified," Knox said. "Part of me wants to know the truth, while the other part worries that I'm not ready for it."

"Why is that?" she asked, though she could understand how he felt. She wanted to ask him then what his plans would be if Ally was his, while at the same time she didn't want to know what he would say.

Because unlike Knox, she was already convinced she knew what the results would be. Her sister might have changed over the last years while they'd been apart, but she didn't think Brittany would have lied about her baby's father. Why would she lie to Bree? It wouldn't have made sense.

"I'm just afraid of messing things up. My parents weren't always the best. They had a lot going on with their careers when they had me. I felt I was just an afterthought sometimes. They mostly hired staff to take care of me instead of spending time with me themselves. I'm not blaming them. The music business is rough to break in to, as I'm sure you already know. Once you get to the top, it's even harder to remain there. They did the best they could, I'm sure..."

While he said the words convincingly enough, she wasn't sure how much of it he truly believed. Families were complicated. She and her sister were a good example of that.

"I think fame and fortune change people. I know my mom changed her whole focus on life from being my mom to being me and Britt's manager. I would never want that for my child. I missed the mom I had before, the one who cared more about my everyday life than about whether I'd sung that note perfectly in practice." Bree paused with a half-washed dish in her hand, then let out a short laugh. "Don't I sound so high and mighty. The truth is, it's a struggle every day to keep my focus on Ally. I've spent most of her life working weekends to pay the bills and attending classes during the week. Some days I wonder if it was worth all the time I've missed with her. Even when I had a couple years of working in the hospital before I started midwifery school, I was working extra to pay off my college loans."

"I've seen how the two of you get along. Ally knows she's an important part of your life. You two are like a team. That's something special. I wish I'd had that with my parents. I think that's one of the reasons that my mom wants grandchildren so badly. She wants to do it right this time. And if I'm Ally's father, I want to do it right the first time. I don't want to look back like she does and see I did all the wrong things. I'll already be starting out behind."

"When Ally was born, I was only twenty-one. Suddenly, I had a baby to look after and a funeral to plan. I was drowning in grief while also trying to figure out my new life. But then one night I looked down at Ally and saw her looking up at me. I promised her then that I would be the best aunt I could be. I haven't been perfect, Knox, I know that. But I want you to know that I've always done my best."

She turned off the water and dried her hands. "I don't know how this is going to work out. If you aren't Ally's father, I will have to decide if I want to pursue finding out who is. I'll be honest. I don't think that's something I'm going to do. At least, not until she's older."

"But is that fair to Ally or to her father?" Knox asked.

Bree headed to the small sitting area where she had left her computer. "I don't know. I didn't have a choice in telling you. Not with the information I had from Brittany. And not now after I got to know that you aren't the person I thought you were. I told you about Ally as much for her sake as for yours. I promised that I would be truthful to her, and keeping this from her isn't the right thing for me to do."

She opened the laptop and began to sign in to her email account. "But I'll be honest. If you had wanted to walk away after I told you about Ally, I would have been okay with that."

He looked at her and she could already feel the crack forming on her heart. Because she knew the man Knox was now. He wouldn't walk away no matter how much more simple it would make both their lives.

"Open the email, Bree. I'm not going anywhere."

Knox sat down beside Bree as she opened the email from the lab. This was it. His life could change forever at this moment. Looking over at Bree, he had to admit to himself that his life had already changed. Bree had opened up the possibility of a new world to him. One that he hadn't known he wanted. Already he was trying to figure out how he was going to fit a little girl into his life as a traveling doctor, always moving from town to town. And every time he pictured his new life with Ally, Bree was always there, too. Right beside him. And that was just one more thing that scared him. He knew she was scared. She'd raised Ally alone for eight years and now he was there threatening the life she'd made for them.

"Okay, here it is," Bree said as she hovered over the results, her finger hesitating before tapping it.

As the email opened, Bree reached for his hand, the connection to her soothing in a way he couldn't explain. She had made it sound like the two of them were adversaries, but still, she wanted him beside her. He tightened his grip, hoping to give back some of the comfort she so readily gave to him.

They read the email silently, but together. When they

had both finished, Bree shut the laptop, then turned to him. "My sister might have had a lot of faults, but lying wasn't one of them."

Knox just nodded his head. He was so full of emotions that he couldn't speak. He had a daughter.

The sound of little bare feet slapping against the wooden floors seemed to be the only sound in the house. Bree let go of his hand and moved away just moments before Ally ran into the room, her damp hair flying around her face. She dropped down on the couch between him and Bree, the smile on her face disappearing as she looked between the two of them. "What's wrong?"

"Nothing is wrong," Bree said, before looking at Knox. "It's just as it should be."

The words struck Knox like a battering ram, opening his eyes to what was really there before him. Ally was his daughter. His daughter. Wow. His mother was going to need sedatives when she got the news.

And when was he going to tell her? It wasn't right not to share the news, but didn't Ally need to be told first? And how were they going to tell Ally? Because it had to be both of them telling her. That, he knew.

"Why don't you tell Knox good-night and go get your book out for us to read?"

"Can Dr. Knox read the book with me?" Ally asked, looking from her aunt to him. His chest was suddenly tight as emotions he'd never felt before began to surface. His little girl wanted him to read to her? Was it possible that she felt the connection between the two of them without being told? Was that even possible? The two of them had gotten along well since the moment Bree had introduced the two of them. Knox didn't know everything about Bree's life before they started working at the clinic together, but wasn't it more likely that Ally just hadn't had many men in her life? Bree was very focused on Ally and her career. It could be that like him, she hadn't had time for a serious romantic involvement, and having a man at their home was just something different.

"If he'd like to do that, it's fine with me," Bree told her niece before looking over at him.

Knox didn't miss the pool of tears that were forming in her eyes. While he'd been there processing what being Ally's father meant for him and his family, what had Bree been feeling?

"Please?" Ally asked, hopping up and down on the seat next to him.

This was the first thing his daughter had asked of him. Looking into Ally's brilliant green eyes that reminded him so much of Bree's, he knew he couldn't disappoint her. "Sure, but you might have to help me with the big words."

"I can read most of them, but Aunt Bree has to help me sometimes. She can help you, too," Ally said, her face all serious with not a hint of a smile.

"I think the two of you will be fine without me," Bree said, giving her niece a watery smile. "And I've got some work to do on my computer before I go to bed."

Knox gave Bree a smile, unsure what else to do as Ally took his hand and began to pull him down the hall to her room. He and Bree had a lot to talk about, but it would all have to wait until Ally went to sleep.

A half an hour later, after reading a total of four pages before Ally had fallen asleep, he returned to the living room only to find her aunt with her own eyes closed, her hands resting on the keys of her laptop. Carefully, he removed the laptop before taking the seat next to her. Bree shifted and her head came to rest on his shoulder. But instead of waking, she seemed to settle into sleep even deeper, her lips curving into an innocent smile, so much like his daughter's.

Like his daughter's. Wasn't it weird how that thought seemed to come so easily now? An hour ago the thought of having a child was something foreign and frightening. Now it just felt…right.

Bree's eyes blinked open and she looked around the room, slowly sitting up. "Ally?"

"She was asleep before the wizard had his first dance at the ball," Knox said, staring down into Bree's sleep-drugged eyes.

"She'll be disappointed in the morning. It's one of her favorite scenes," she said, stretching and moving away from him. "Thank you for doing that."

"Thank you for letting me," he said. "Thank you for everything. I don't know how I can ever repay you for taking care of Ally all these years. I don't want to think about what might have happened to her if you hadn't been there for her."

When Bree stiffened beside him, he realized he had said the wrong thing. "I don't mean to insult you. I know she's your niece and you've taken care of her because you love her."

"She's not just my niece, Knox. She's my child in every way except that I didn't give birth to her. We're all the family the two of us have had. Until now," Bree said as she moved away from him, then let out a deep sigh. "I know we have a lot to discuss, but I think it would be best to wait until another day. We're both tired and there's a lot for both of us to take in now that we both know the truth."

"Bree, I don't want to make this hard on you," Knox started, then stopped. Of course this was hard on Bree. That test had changed her life, too. But not all change was bad. In his way of seeing things, this could be a good thing for both of them. He just had to give her time to see that.

Pulling her feet up onto the couch and curling into a protective ball, she looked so small and defenseless. He tried to think of something to say. It was as if all the tension that had existed between the two of them before they had begun to work together had suddenly resurfaced. They'd come so far and now it was more important than ever that they got along.

But she was right, it was late and they were both expected at the clinic the next day. Standing, he looked down at her. "We'll talk tomorrow."

"Tomorrow," Bree said, nodding her head. "We can both talk tomorrow."

CHAPTER NINE

WHILE KNOX TRIED to catch Bree between patients the next day, they were both busy from the start of the day until Lucretia put the closed sign out on the office door. Bree had mentioned earlier in the week that there were only a few days left before school was out for the summer break. He expected things would be hectic till then, but he wanted to discuss when, and how, they were going to let Ally know that he was her father. It was the *how* that worried him the most. He wasn't equipped for a "how I met your mother" type of conversation with an eight-year-old.

He'd just finished seeing his last patient of the day when Bree stepped out from the exam room with her own patient. He waited while she handed the patient a prescription along with some samples before he joined her.

"And this is Dr. Collins," Bree said, introducing him to a young woman who looked to be about Bree's age. "This is Kelly. She's just moved to town and needed a refill on her birth control until she can get set up with a primary doctor."

"It's so great that this clinic is open for walk-ins.

There's nothing like this where I'm from and my insurance doesn't start for another two weeks. I've got three little ones at home. I didn't want to take a chance on adding to that number."

While Bree and Kelly discussed things from potty training to the best time to change from a bottle to a cup, Knox listened. He'd missed both of those steps with Ally. He'd missed all the firsts. First steps. First words. Even the first day of school. He couldn't blame Bree for any of that; she had only been looking out for his daughter. But still, he wished he'd been there. He was sure Bree would be glad to share baby pictures, but it wasn't the same as being there. He'd just have to make a point of being there for all the other things, though how was he going to do that? He'd spent the past few years traveling from clinic to clinic. He and Bree had a lot of things to discuss.

"Well, that's the last one," Lucretia said, locking the door behind Bree's patient. "I think we might have set a record today. I know Dr. Reynolds will be impressed when he returns and sees the numbers. We've been able to see almost twice as many patients since you brought Bree here. Maybe he'll be able to get some other midwives in to help."

Knox had kept Dean Reynolds up-to-date with the running of the clinic through regular text messages and when he'd mentioned bringing a midwife resident in, the other doctor had thought it a great idea. Neither of them had expected it to be this successful. Knox had especially been concerned after the way Bree had initially reacted to Dr. Warner's suggestion that she spend time at the clinic.

* * *

"I'll mention it to my preceptor and my nurse counselor at the college," Bree said. "I've enjoyed the work here and I've gotten a lot of experience I wouldn't have gotten otherwise. I'm sure there are more midwives that would be interested."

"I don't guess I can talk you into staying," Lucretia said.

"I don't know what I'll be doing once I finish my residency. But if I'm in Nashville, I'll certainly try to volunteer a couple times a month," Bree said. The alarm on her watch went off, and she slid the straps of her backpack on. She was about to make her escape before they had a chance to talk.

"Do you have a moment to discuss...a few things?" Knox asked, aware that Lucretia would overhear anything that he said to Bree.

"I'm sorry, but Ally's class is having an art exhibit this afternoon at the school and I promised I would be there."

Knox was surprised at the hurt her words caused. Shouldn't he have been invited now that Bree knew for certain that he was Ally's father? He decided then and there that he wasn't going to miss another day of his daughter's life. "I'd love to see Ally's artwork. We can talk on the way there."

While Bree hesitated, Knox headed for the door. The hurt he felt from not being invited was turning into anger, something that was very rare for him. He fought against it as they exited the building as neither of them said a word. Bree's car door had barely shut when he let go of the words he had been holding back. "Why didn't you tell me Ally had something going on at school? I thought I made it clear that I wanted to be a part of her life."

"It's just a bunch of pictures drawn by a class of eight-year-olds. I didn't think you would be interested," Bree said, her eyes fixed on the windshield in front of her as she started the car.

"But it's my eight-year-old's pictures," Knox said, then realized he sounded like an eight-year-old himself.

Bree looked over at him then; her bright green eyes held none of the sparkle he was used to. "I'm sorry. I didn't think about inviting you. Like I said, it's just a bunch of pictures that they've drawn throughout the year."

"Is it a big deal to Ally?" Knox asked, knowing the answer. "I remember all the school activities that my parents missed while they were out touring. I remember the disappointment of not having anyone there for me."

"Ally isn't you, Knox. I've been to almost every activity she's had at school for the last three years." She looked at her watch, then turned off the car. "I realize this has all been a shock to you. We both have a lot to process. I promise that I'll be better at communicating with you while we work things out, but you using words like *my daughter* isn't going to help. Ally is mine, too."

"Of course, Ally is yours, too," Knox said, his hands instinctively running through his hair. He was messing all of this up with Bree. He didn't want things to be this way. Not for Ally. And not for him and Bree, either. They both wanted what was best for Ally. They needed to be united or this could turn into one of those ugly battles adults get into over their children.

And maybe that meant giving them both some time to come to terms with what this new reality would mean for the two of them was a good idea. "I'll admit that finding out Ally is my daughter has brought up some old feelings I probably need to deal with. I know you've been there for Ally and I shouldn't compare my childhood to hers."

"How about, for now, I promise to include you in Ally's life while we sort out things between the two of us?" Bree asked. "We can enjoy today and then I think we need to deal with things between the two of us before we move forward with telling Ally anything."

"I can live with that. I think seeing us together more would be good for Ally, too. It would give her more security when we tell her about me being her father. Get her used to me being around on a regular basis. Does that work for you?" He wanted to move forward with telling Ally about him, but he understood that he and Bree had to do it together. He'd have to be patient.

And he'd enjoyed spending time with Bree and Ally before he'd even known about the possibility of being Ally's father. Now spending time with them would mean even more. He also hoped that working out things between them would also include more kisses like the one they had shared at the ranch. He had to believe that her response to him that day meant she had felt the same magnetic pull that he had felt almost from the moment he'd met her. That wasn't magically going to go away just because of the results of the paternity test.

"I can work with that," Bree said, restarting the car. "The most important thing is for us to make this as easy on Ally as possible. That means both of us taking into consideration what is best for her in whatever decisions we make."

Was she unknowingly answering Knox's thoughts about her words and the situation that they were both in now? Was that her way of telling him that they needed to ignore what had been building between them? If so, he would have to make it a point to change her mind. Because just like things would never go back to the way they were before he learned he was Ally's father, he didn't want things to go back to the way they had been before he had found Bree.

Bree watched Knox as he went from picture to picture with Ally pulling him down the line of drawings that had been hung on her classroom walls. He smiled and commented on each picture as if it were hanging in a New York City museum. It should have surprised her, and it would have two months ago when she had thought of him as a spoiled rich kid who had gone through life ruining young girls' lives, just like she had imagined that he had done to Brittany. But now that she knew him? No, it didn't surprise her at all. What did surprise her was the way her heart hammered every time he turned to look at her and gave her that wicked smile of his that sent shivers running up her spine and heat settling in places where it shouldn't be. How could she have such a response to a man whom she'd given the power to take away the child she'd raised? Shouldn't her heart see the danger it was in? Well, maybe her heart did, but her body wasn't listening to anything it had to say.

"Look, look! Those are my pictures there," Ally said, dragging Knox down to where her pictures hung. Bree recognized one of them as being the picture her niece had drawn of her family. "That's a picture of me and Aunt Bree in front of our house. And this is a picture of my mommy in heaven. My teacher helped me draw it because my friends asked me why I didn't have a mommy or daddy and I didn't know what to say."

Bree pushed back against the pain of seeing an eight-year-old's idea of what her mother would look like as an angel. Sometimes she felt very inadequate in filling her sister's place as Ally's mom. It was something she had dealt with from the first moment she'd held Ally in her arms. Mostly, she had learned to ignore the feeling that she wasn't enough. It wasn't that she wanted to replace her sister. There would always be a place in both Ally's and Bree's hearts for Brittany. But looking at the picture of a stick figure woman with hair the color of Bree's and eyes that matched hers, too, Bree could feel the loss Ally felt and she had never known how to fill it.

As if Knox understood that this was something she was sensitive about, he reached back and took her hand, pulling her up beside the two of them. Then he did something that was totally unexpected. Taking out his phone, then smiling at Ally's teacher, who had been hovering around the parents and students, he waved her over to the three of them. "Do you mind taking a picture for me?"

Ally's teacher took the phone as Knox turned Bree toward the camera while draping his arm across her shoulder and positioning Ally between the two of them. If Bree's smile was a little watery when the teacher handed the phone back to him, he didn't comment.

"This is Aunt Bree's boyfriend, Dr. Knox," Ally said, introducing him to her teacher.

"I...ah..." Bree tried to get the denial out of her lips, but the words were jumbled up inside her brain as she tried to recover from her niece's words. Looking over at Knox for help, she watched as he introduced himself and shook the woman's hand, never once denying Ally's statement. By the time Bree could form a half-witted sentence, the teacher had moved on to another student.

When Knox suggested that they stop at the same pizza place they had visited before, Ally immediately set to getting Bree to agree. It was easy for Bree to see why Ally thought of Knox as her *boyfriend*. Bree had spent more time out with Knox in the past three weeks than she'd spent with any other man since she'd had Ally.

As they ate, she watched as Ally and Knox laughed at a show on the screen above their table. She had never noticed before, but the two of them had a similar laugh. One of those whole-body laughs where their grins were wide and their eyes crinkled in the corners. She couldn't help but laugh, too, even though she wasn't watching the show. She only had eyes for the two of them as they clowned around with each other. With everything in her heart, she wished she could freeze that moment. There were so many things that would be changing soon, for all of them. But she didn't want to think about that tonight. Tonight she was going to just enjoy them being together like this. If a part of her was pretending that the three of them were just a normal family out for the night, who did that hurt?

When Knox looked over at her, his eyes shining with happiness, she picked up her glass of wine and took a sip before giving him a smile. He was a good man. An honest man. A caring man. One that worked in underprivileged communities when he could work in any OB/GYN clinic in the country. And it was already clear that he loved Ally just as much as she did. What more could she ask for as a father for her niece?

That was why after he carried the sleeping little girl into her bedroom and helped Bree get her tucked into bed for the night, she decided that he deserved some one-on-one time with his daughter.

"I've got the early-evening shift at the bar Saturday night. Would you like to watch Ally for me?" she asked as they stopped at the door.

"Of course, I'll keep Ally. What time do you want me here?" Knox said. It almost hurt Bree to see how happy her request made him. It was like giving a starving man a piece of bread. He'd been like this since the moment he'd found out Ally was his.

"If you could be here at four-thirty I can make it in by five. I'm only working till eleven. I take the early-evening shift so my usual babysitter isn't too late getting home. She just lives across the street, but she's older and her husband doesn't like her out any later than midnight." Bree had always thought it was more that Fran's husband couldn't sleep himself until his wife came home. Not that she minded. She knew that she had been lucky to have so many people to help her out with Ally over the years.

"I'll be here," Knox said. He opened his mouth to say something else, then stopped.

"What is it?" she asked. "If you have something else planned, it's okay."

"No. I'm not on call this weekend. There's nothing I'd rather do Saturday night."

He stepped closer to her and placed a light kiss on her lips, lingering there for only a second, resting his forehead against hers. Before she could react, he'd stepped away. "Thank you for this evening."

She watched as he made his way to where a car waited for him and she wondered what he would have said if she'd had the nerve to ask him to stay the night instead of taking a hired service back to the office to get his own car. If the look in his eyes before he'd left was any indication, she was pretty sure he would have stayed. And she would have been glad to let him.

CHAPTER TEN

KNOX LOOKED AROUND what had been Bree's orderly living room. He hadn't known what to expect, but the stack of books and pile of games that lay open around the room wasn't it. Though Ally had never appeared to be a low-energy child, she'd been more energetic than usual. Maybe it had been the ice cream he'd brought for dessert. Or the sprinkles that they'd added when Ally had shown him where her aunt hid them.

Looking at the clock, he knew he had only moments to get the mess cleaned up before Bree arrived. He didn't want to give her the impression that he couldn't handle taking care of his eight-year-old daughter. He needed her to see him as a capable parent. He had a lot to make up to both Bree and Ally. He didn't know how he was going to do it, but he would spend the rest of his life trying.

As the front door opened, he stacked the last of the board games together. Turning, he saw that the smiling Bree that had left just hours ago now looked like she couldn't take another step. The laughter that had been in her eyes when she'd been warning Knox of all the ways Ally would try to escape her bedtime was gone. Her mascara was just smudges under her eyes now and there was nothing left of the pretty pink lipstick that he'd been thinking about since the moment she'd walked out.

"Hard night?" he asked. He hadn't made it a secret that he didn't like her working as much as she was, but he knew she wouldn't appreciate his concern. He would have to be very careful when he approached the subject.

"It was bachelorette party central tonight. There had to be at least ten of them that came in. The place was packed," Bree said, landing on the couch before slipping her shoes off.

Knox watched as she wiggled her toes back and forth as if trying to return the circulation to them. He sat down on the rug in front of her and pulled off her simple white socks and began to massage the pale pink polished toes.

"What are you doing?" Bree asked. He looked up to see her eyes closed, and the muscles of her tired face relaxing.

"My father used to do this for my mother when they'd had a long night on stage. She said it helped her unwind. Is it working?"

Instead of answering, she let out a moan, then stretched her legs out farther, arching her back and burrowing into the couch. Something inside him awakened with that sound. His mind went to places he'd been avoiding since the day they'd kissed at the ranch. When she arched her back and burrowed deeper into the couch, he forced himself to concentrate on what he was doing. Then his hands moved up to the calves of her legs and the tension in her body disappeared. His hands reached the backs of her knees and he looked up to see Bree watching him, her eyelids barely opened. When she didn't tell him to stop, he continued.

Unfortunately, his own body was tightening with each stroke of his hands across her soft skin. Desire ran through his system, the heat of it flooding his veins. His heartbeat drummed to a different beat in his chest, each beat becoming faster and faster. What had started as a way to comfort Bree had turned on him. His body was now as tight as a guitar string. He didn't know when he'd ever been this aroused.

Then his hands slid higher, brushing against the tattered hem of her denim shorts, and Bree let out a gasp before arching her back again.

"Do you want me to stop?" he asked as he came up on his knees, his eyes even with hers.

"No, please don't stop," she said, her hands tentatively coming up to rest on his chest. She bit her lower lip then looked up at him, an innocence and trust in her eyes that had his body going into overdrive. Bree had always been a woman of secrets to him, always holding back something even as she smiled and laughed and looked so innocent. He wanted to know all her secrets tonight, especially the ones her body held.

He moved over her and slowly lowered himself until their lips touched. She tasted of sunshine and honey and when her tongue welcomed his, he couldn't resist the pleasure there. They tangled, released and then tangled again, his mouth wanting more and more as it caught each moan she gave him.

When her hands reached for the hem of his T-shirt, he scooped her up off the couch and carried her toward the bedroom. Her green eyes seemed to shine in the darkness as they left the light of the living room and headed down the hall. When her mouth moved up his neck, he had to stop and lean against the wall. "If you don't stop, we won't make it to your bed."

"Really," she said, surprise and a sweet, sexy smile dancing across her swollen lips before they returned to torturing him as they moved down to his collarbone.

"Behave," he said as he gritted his teeth and forced his feet to start moving again. Only the presence of his daughter in the room down the hall kept him moving forward.

He made it to the door of her room, pushed it open and unceremoniously dumped her in the middle of the bed. He finished stripping his shirt off and then paused at the sight of Bree staring at him. When she came up on her knees and put her hands on his belt buckle, his whole body went rock-hard.

"I don't know exactly how to do all this, but I think I can handle it," she said. Her hand began to undo his belt while her lips trailed soft kisses down his chest. What was she saying? That she was innocent? That couldn't be; she was only four years younger than him. He was suddenly out of his depth.

"Are you saying that you're a virgin?" he asked, his head swimming from the possibility.

Bree's hands stilled and she sat back on her heels. "Is that a problem?"

There was a vulnerability in her voice that shook loose every protective instinct in his body. "No, sweetheart, it's not a problem. It's a privilege. I just need to know. I don't want to hurt you."

"Okay," she said, her hands less sure as they fumbled with his belt now. His hands covered hers and he bent down to kiss her. The desire that had almost consumed them earlier returned as he nibbled at her lips until she was moaning again.

While this would be a first for Bree, it would also be a first for him. The women he'd been involved with before had always been as experienced as him. Even his first lover, one of his parents' crew members and a few years older, had been skilled in the art of making love. He wanted to make this special for both of them, but especially for her. He knew in his heart that this was a memory he would always treasure. He wanted to have a memory just as precious as she was.

When Bree finished removing his belt, he let her unzip his jeans, but stilled her hand when it closed around him, wrapping his around hers. Her grip tightened and he moaned as he locked her eyes onto his, his hips rocking against her hand. "This is what you do to me, Bree."

As his control began to crumble, he removed her hands and raised them over her head. "Stay like this."

He thought she'd protest, but she kept her arms up as he peeled her T-shirt off her body, uncovering a pale pink bra that displayed softly rounded breasts. Her skin was a pale pink that reminded him of peaches and cream and he knew it would taste just as sweet. Unable to help himself, he bent and licked the top of each breast. The shiver that ran through her body, transferring itself to him… His body shaking, he held himself in check. He removed her bra, his mind taking in each curve. He laid her down and undid her shorts, while his lips sprinkled kisses over her breasts then down her abdomen. Time stood still for a moment as he spread her legs. When he looked into her eyes and saw not only desire, but trust, too, his heart filled his chest with an emotion he had never shared with another person.

"Do you know how special you are, Bree Rogers? Do you have any idea what you have done to me?" he asked.

"I just know that I want you," Bree whispered back to him. "Is that enough?"

He didn't answer her back. For now it would have to be enough. But when he bent his head and tasted her most private places, he knew that this night with Bree would never be enough for him.

Bree's mind tried to wrap around the reality of the moment while her body flooded with sensations that it had never experienced. Finding Knox waiting for her when she'd come home had seemed so right tonight. And when his hands had begun their lazy exploration of her legs as he'd massaged each aching spot, she'd been overcome with a desire for more as every nerve ending in her body called out to be touched by him. She'd arched into his touch as her body had cried out for more. Just more. But of what?

When his lips had touched her, she'd thought, *This is it. This is what I need.* But still, that hadn't been enough.

Now, as she lay there with all her innocence exposed to him, the desire for something more was almost painful. He lowered his head and gently kissed the inside of her thigh, and her body almost bucked off the bed. Never had her body been so sensitive. She bit her lip as his lips lazily moved inside her thigh. And then his hands parted her and her breath caught as his tongue raked across her center.

Her hands clutched his head, her fingers tangling in his curls, and her body came off the bed as she was suddenly inundated with sensations that wanted to overwhelm her. It felt like every nerve ending she had was too sensitive. Knox's hands joined her mouth as he left no part of her unscathed as he tormented her with a pleasure that built until she wanted to scream. She tried to tell him it was too much, but the words died in her throat as the pleasure inside her body began to build. As the orgasm hit her, she grabbed on to it, embracing it. Her world shattered and she knew everything about her had suddenly changed.

When her mind righted itself, she opened her eyes to find Knox staring down at her. With her brain still jumbled, she could only get out the most important of words. "More."

"Are you sure?" Knox asked, his face set in hard lines,

his body hard against hers, his breaths coming just as fast as hers.

"Please," she said as she lifted a hand to his cheek. He wouldn't understand that she had never been with another man because there had never been one she'd wanted to share her first time with, until now. "I want this. With you."

Even as relaxed as she was, her body tightened as she watched him roll on a condom he'd produced from his jeans. He was as beautiful a man undressed as he was dressed. Uncertainty filled her, along with fear that she'd disappoint him. Of course, she knew the mechanics and she'd read enough on the subject to know what to expect.

But when he entered her, so gently, she found a new desire as he filled her. If there was pain, the pleasure overrode it. And when he began to move inside her, she let her body respond, holding nothing back from him.

As a new climax, this one even stronger than the one before, began to build inside her, she opened her eyes and found his eyes fixed on hers. A scream tore through her and his mouth sealed over hers as they both rode the orgasm out together. Yes, her world was definitely never going to be the same again.

"I have to go," Knox whispered in Bree's ear, brushing her hair aside as he applied a soft kiss to her neck.

Bree opened her eyes and saw the clock. It was almost five. Her mind tried to remember the day. Was she at the clinic or the hospital today? No. She'd worked the night before. Before…

Her eyes popped open and she took in her surroundings. She was in her bed. The sun had begun to come up, casting shadows between the dark curtains on her windows, and she could see a pile of clothes scattered across the wooden plank floors.

She'd worked last night at the bar and when she'd come home Knox had been there. More memories of the night returned, explaining why she was in her bed and why Knox was bending over her.

She'd slept with Knox. She wouldn't regret it. It had been perfect. Knox had been perfect. Not that she was really surprised. The attraction between them, though she'd tried to ignore it, had been growing for a while.

But still, he was the father of her niece: the one person who could take her away from Bree. How would it affect Ally if she ended up involved with him? And shouldn't she feel some kind of guilt for the fact that her sister had once been, though shortly, involved with Knox? It was a complication that they didn't need in a relationship that was already complicated both emotionally and legally. It was just too bad that her body and her heart hadn't come up with that information before things had gotten this far.

There was so much between them that had to be settled before they could address any of this. But instead of sitting up and facing all of it, she closed her eyes and pretended to fall back off to sleep. When Knox kissed her forehead before leaving, she curled deeper into the bed covers. Maybe if she buried herself deep enough, she could just this once enjoy her memories of the night before she had to face the consequences that would come with the day.

CHAPTER ELEVEN

MONDAY MORNING, Bree walked into Legacy Women's Clinic cautiously. She'd never had the experience that other women talked about as far as the awkward mornings when you saw someone you'd slept with. There'd been no walks of shame for her. While the other college girls had been hooking up with guys, she'd been raising her niece. She didn't know how to handle things like this. She didn't want to embarrass herself or Knox by making too much of the fact that they had slept together. But how did she do that when what they'd shared had been earth-shattering to her? How did she act all nonchalant when she knew just seeing him would bring up memories of the night they had shared?

When the first thing she saw was Knox where he stood deep in a conversation with Sable, the office manager, she did the first thing she could think of. She ducked into the first door she could find. It wasn't until she heard someone clearing her voice that she realized it was Lori's office. Turning, she found her mentor, along with the practice's other midwife, Sky, staring at her.

"Sorry, I just..." Bree tried to think of some excuse that would have her interrupting the two of them. Before her brain cells supplied her with anything that sounded plausible, Sky went to the door and cracked it open.

"Well, well," Sky said, shutting the door behind her and giving Bree a questioning look before looking over at Lori. "Since I'm thinking it would be very unlikely that you are trying to avoid the office manager, it seems our new midwife is avoiding Nashville's famous bad boy."

"That's not who he is anymore," Bree said, realizing too late that taking up for Knox was the last thing she should have done. "I mean, I don't think it's fair to judge him by what he did when he was a kid."

"Oh, she's got it bad, Lori," Sky said.

Bree felt the blush as it crept up her face. Bree knew she was only teasing her, but the midwife had hit too close to the truth.

"Stop teasing her, Sky. It wasn't that long ago that you were mooning around over Jared."

"I never," Sky said, then stopped. "Okay, maybe I did."

When Lori's eyes turned back to her, Bree wanted to slide under the door and take her chances with being cornered by Knox even though she still didn't know she'd feel uncomfortable seeing him there after what they'd shared. How did people do this? It wasn't that she was embarrassed that they'd had sex. Or that she felt they'd done something wrong. They were both consenting adults. It had just seemed so intimate. And he knew she had been a virgin. She'd bared so much of herself to him. Been so intimate when she normally held back so much. Maybe the word for what she felt was *shy*?

"When me and Jack set it up for you to work at the clinic, you were very adamant about not wanting to work with Knox. I think your exact words were 'I just don't find him particularly likeable.' I take it that has changed? Did the two of you kiss and make up?"

Bree's face got even hotter. There had been a time when she and her sister had teased each other unmercifully like this. She missed the closeness that she'd shared with her twin. It had been years since she'd had someone to tease her.

"Oh, my goodness, you kissed him?" Skylar said before busting out laughing.

"Sky, stop it. You're embarrassing her," Lori said before turning to Bree. "Please tell me you didn't kiss him."

When Bree didn't answer her, Lori dropped her head onto the desk. "It's all my fault. I feel like I threw you to the wolves."

"Okay, the two of you need to stop," Bree said.

"I'm sorry," Lori said, lifting her head. "We shouldn't have teased you. But in all seriousness, I don't want you to be hurt. I know Knox has changed a lot since he went into medicine. The work he does in the rural areas is tremendous. But what do you really know about him?"

Bree almost laughed. The two of them had no idea. Not that she could explain all of that to them. His being Ally's father would eventually come out. There would be no way to keep that news private. It was even possible that it would be reported in the media at some point because of his parents, which could bring up the story of Brittany's death. She and Knox would have to find a way to protect Ally from the attention if that happened. Just one more reason to make sure they told Ally about her mother and Knox carefully. The child had lost her mother suddenly; it didn't seem right that she should suddenly be faced, while unprepared, with a daddy, too.

"I'm a big girl. I can handle it," Bree told the two of them, turning toward the door. And for the first time since Knox had left her bed, she felt like she could handle it. She could handle all of it. The way her and Knox's relationship was changing, the need to find a way to explain Knox's sudden presence in his daughter's life to Ally, and even the fact that Knox could now have more rights to her niece than Bree did. Knowing him now, she felt safe that the two of them could work together to make all this work. And yes, she was even beginning to believe that she, Knox and Ally might be able to find a happy ending together.

That thought put a smile on her face that lasted throughout the day. After that, the hours went by fast as she and Lori saw mostly obstetric patients and then attended a late-afternoon delivery, which left a smiling new family with a healthy baby girl. It wasn't until she was rounding on their last postpartum patient that she saw Knox. She started toward him, then saw that he was in a deep conversation with one of the anesthesia nurses. When the woman smiled at him, Bree remembered her toothpaste-ad smile. A feeling came over Bree that she had never felt before. Possessiveness? Jealousy? A mixture of both? It wasn't a feeling she liked. While she had no claim over Knox, she also knew he wouldn't have slept with her if he was involved with someone else. That thought calmed the green-eyed monster that had wanted to come out. Instead, she managed a smile and wave as she passed the two of them in the hall, then continued to her patient's room.

She wasn't surprised when she came out to find Knox waiting for her. She'd known in her heart that he would want to see her as much as she wanted to see him. It seemed like days since she'd seen that smile of his, and seeing it made her smile, too. Why had she been so concerned that things would be awkward between them? There was no awkwardness now. Instead, there was an openness, an honesty, that had always been missing. She liked the way things were between them now better than the way things had been when she'd been keeping secrets.

"I'm glad I caught up with you. I kept missing you at the office," Knox said when he saw her. "I'd thought we'd share lunch, but you were tied up with Lori."

"It's been a busy day. Do you have a patient delivering?" she asked.

"No, I've just finished a Cesarean section. A patient with a complete previa came in bleeding," he said, falling in beside her as she started back down the hall toward the exit.

"The mom and baby?" she asked, though she knew they had to be okay or he wouldn't be standing there all relaxed.

"Both doing good, though mom is receiving her second blood transfusion now. I was going to see if you'd let me take you and Ally out to supper, but I think I'd better stay here. She's still having more bleeding than I would like. I wanted to spend some time with y'all, though."

Looking down at her watch, she saw that there was only a few minutes before her alarm would go off and she'd have to be on her way to pick Ally up at the local athletic center, which provided summer day care. "I understand. I'm about to head out to pick up Ally now. Maybe you could call later tonight?"

"I will," he said, then turned when one of the labor and delivery nurses came rushing toward him, calling his name.

"That doesn't look good. You better go. Just call me later," Bree said, waving him away when he looked back at her. She watched as Knox jogged toward the nurse then started giving orders. She heard *OR* and knew his patient wasn't doing well. There had once been a time when she'd wanted to be the doctor standing there giving orders. Tonight she was glad that it wasn't her.

Bree rushed into the county clinic pulling a slow-moving Ally by the straps of her backpack behind her.

"There you are. I wondered if you were going to show up today. I know this is your last week but it's not the time to be slacking," Lucretia said with her usual big-dog bark and her puppy-dog bite. Then Ally peeped from behind Bree. "Wait. Who is that?"

"This is Ally, my niece," Bree said. "And Ally, this is Ms. Lucretia. She works with me and Dr. Knox."

Ally gave the woman a little wave, then looked around the room. "Don't you have a TV in your waiting room?"

"When we got to Ally's summer care program there was a note that they had a water pipe burst and would be closed till it was fixed. Knox said it was okay for me to bring Ally to work. I thought maybe she could hang out in reception with you?"

"Of course, she can. I can always use a helper," Lucretia said.

"Did I hear my name?" Knox said, coming in from the back of the office. "Hey, Ally. How do you like the clinic?"

Bree watched as Ally's disappointed face changed immediately. Running across the room, the little girl threw herself against Knox. Hugging Ally, he looked up at Bree. Even with her limited experience with it, she knew that it was love she saw in Knox's eyes. But when he looked down at Ally, Bree couldn't help but wonder if all that love had been for his daughter or if, maybe, some of it had been for her.

Which was a ridiculous thing for her to even be worrying about. Why did her mind constantly go to the negative where Knox was concerned? Was it the uncertainty of where the two stood after the night they'd spent together? Probably. She lay in the bed last night waiting for his call, the whole time wondering if she was making too much of that night. And then she'd remember how happy he'd seemed when he'd seen her at the hospital before he'd rushed off to an emergency, and she'd felt better.

But when the hours without a call from him had continued to tick away, she'd been left feeling forgotten and alone. Was this what her sister had felt like?

She realized then that Ally had been talking to her. "Can we, Aunt Bree?"

Bree looked from Ally to Knox. "I'm sorry, can we what?"

"I was telling her that my mother had invited the two of you back to the ranch this Saturday. I know it's Jared and Sky's weekend on call, so you and Lori should be free." There was something in Knox's voice that said this wasn't a simple invitation. He seemed to be holding his breath as he waited for her answer. Her mother's instinct was warning her that something was up.

"How about we talk about this later? We'll have patients coming in any minute and I want to get Ally set up with some of her toys in the reception office." Bree was prepared for the disappointment and the whining that came from Ally as she began to bargain in order to secure Bree's agreement to the trip. What she wasn't prepared for was the disappointment in Knox's eyes. But when he turned and walked away, she knew that they would be discussing this later.

But when the morning rush hit and Bree went from patient to patient performing everything from Pap smears to treating abscess infections, she didn't have the time to worry about the fact that both Ally and Knox weren't happy with her. Between every patient, she checked on Ally. While she might not have been happy with her aunt, the rest of her behavior couldn't have been better. Lucretia had put her to work stapling together the handouts they supplied to the women they see to find other resources to help with housing and food. Not for the first time Bree thought how lucky she was that she'd been able to provide for Ally over the years. It hadn't been easy, but her little girl had never gone to bed hungry and she'd always had a safe place to live.

She'd just checked on Ally and was headed back to see a new patient when Knox waved her into an empty exam room.

"Can we talk for a minute?" he asked, the seriousness in his voice so different from his usual joking manner.

"I have a patient waiting," she began.

"There will always be a patient waiting. It won't take but a moment." Knox opened the door wider and she walked in.

"I wanted to talk last night, but by the time I left the hospital it was too late." When he offered her a chair, she took it. If he wanted her to be seated, he had already decided that she wasn't going to like whatever it was he wanted to say.

"The patient with the previa? How is she?" Bree asked, mainly because she had worried about the patient when she'd left the hospital, but also so she could stall Knox from saying whatever it was that she knew would change things between them.

"There was no stopping the bleeding. I had to perform a hysterectomy," Knox said. "It was their second child and they had wanted more. I hated it, but it was either that or she was going to bleed to death. I went by to see them this morning and they both know they made the right choice."

"I'm sorry that it ended that way, but I'm glad she's okay." Of course they made the right choice. The only choice they really had. Sometimes the hardest choices are the ones where there really isn't a choice. Telling you that you have a choice is just someone's way of giving you some power over the situation, when truly your power has been taken away. Bree had faced those choices in her own life. Right now she felt that she was about to face another one of them.

"I wanted to talk to you about Ally. I think she's ready for us to tell her that I'm her father." When Bree started to interrupt him, Knox stopped her. "Can you honestly tell me that you will ever think she's ready?"

Bree looked at Knox. She knew he was right. She'd had Ally all to herself almost from the time she was born. She knew it was selfish to want to hold on to her this way. And Knox wasn't asking for her to give Ally to him. He was just asking for her to share her niece with him. And he was right; she'd never think Ally was ready for this news. How could you prepare a little girl for something like this?

"I'm Ally's father, Bree. The longer we keep this from her, the worse it feels. She has the right to know."

"But what if she isn't ready? How do we tell her she had a daddy all this time and I didn't tell her about him?" Bree felt the tears begin to flow, but there was nothing she could do about it. "What if she hates me for keeping you from her? She's too young to understand that her mother had reasons that she thought Ally shouldn't know you.

"And what about the promise I made to my sister? I've already broke that once. I feel like I've let everyone down." Bree felt Knox's arms come around her. Laying her head on his shoulder, she spilled her last secret. "What if she grows up and realizes how much of this was because of my promise to her mother and how much of this was because I wanted to keep her all to myself?"

"It's going to be okay. We'll talk it out among the three of us. I'm not saying it's going to be easy. There's a lot that we need to figure out together. But we need to move forward, Bree." Knox moved away from her then and tipped her face up to his. "Ally loves you. Nothing that happens after this will ever change that."

Knox bent down toward her, his lips just grazing hers when a voice came from behind them. "Have the two of you forgotten that we have patients in the office? If you're going to be doing all this lovey-dovey stuff, you need to at least shut the door."

"I thought..." Knox began.

"We didn't mean to..." Bree said, then stopped when she saw the amused look on Lucretia's face. "Can you let my patient know that I'll be right there?"

"I can, but there's someone else you need to see first. That little girl, Megan. The one that those horrible human traffickers took. She's here with her mother."

Both Bree and Knox followed Lucretia out of the room to where a young girl who barely resembled the Megan they had met sat in the waiting room. There was no trace of makeup on the young girl's face and her hair had not only been washed, but had also been cut into a neat shoulder-length bob. Her clothes were clean and she looked like she'd gained some weight. Bree was sure that there would always be trauma left from her experience, but it was easy to see that she was on a good track for recovery. Beside her sat a woman not that much older than Bree. She was pretty like her daughter, but Bree recognized the fatigue and stress in the woman's eyes. The woman had gone through hell while searching for her daughter.

"We wanted to bring you these," the woman said, standing when they entered the room. "Megan helped make them. She wanted to thank you and the police officers for everything you did for her."

"Thank you. We were glad that we could help." Bree knew that they'd only offered the girl food and a phone call, but it was those two things that had gotten the girl off the streets and back with her mother. What wrong turn Megan and her mother had made didn't matter now. All that was important right now was that they were back together. With help, hopefully the two of them would work things out and be okay.

While Knox and Megan's mother talked, Bree went to look for her own little girl. Seeing the teenager who had once been in so much danger made it seem all the more important that she hold Ally close. She knew that Knox wasn't going to take Ally and run away with her. She knew Knox would never endanger his daughter in any way. But after all the years of providing for Ally all by herself, it was hard for her to think of giving some of that control up to Knox.

When Bree found the reception office empty, she began to go through the exam rooms. When she got to the one that held her patient, the only one left in the office, she listened at the door, thinking Ally had probably gone in to talk to the woman while she waited, even though she'd been warned to stay out of the occupied rooms. But when she entered, she found that her patient was there alone. Excusing herself again, with the promise that she'd return as soon as possible, Bree went to the bathroom at the end of the hall. There were only so many places where Ally could be in the small offices. Knocking on the bathroom door, then opening it to find it empty, the panic that had begun to rise inside her burst out. "Ally? Ally? Where are you?"

Bree rushed back through each room, calling out for her little girl. When Knox met her in the hallway, she was shaking so badly that she could barely get the words out of her mouth. She had experienced this once when she and a three-year-old Ally had been shopping and the toddler had decided to hide in a clothes rack where Bree couldn't see her. There was no way to describe the fear you felt when your child was suddenly gone.

"What's wrong? Where's Ally?" Knox asked, taking Bree's shoulders and steadying her.

"She's gone. Ally is gone."

Bree's words made no sense to him. His daughter had been there just minutes before, playing with her Barbie dolls on the floor by Lucretia's chair. Leaving Bree, he rushed to the receptionist office to see the dolls lying on the floor. He started back toward the other rooms when Bree stopped him. "I've already looked everywhere. She's not there."

"What's happened?" Lucretia said, coming from the waiting room where she had gone to show Megan and her mother out.

"I can't find Ally. Was she with you?" Bree asked.

But Knox could see by the shock in Lucretia's face that she didn't know where the little girl was. "I'll call the security guard and have him start looking for her."

Knox took Bree's hand as Lucretia rushed to the office phone. "We'll start on this floor and work our way down."

"But what if she went outside? Oh, God. What if she was taken?" Bree pulled her phone out. "Lucretia, call 911. And call me or Knox if you find out anything."

Knox led Bree into the hallway, looking both ways, but seeing nothing. "She couldn't have gone very far."

"I don't understand why she would have left the office at all. We talked about this. She knows not to go anywhere without an adult. I don't even let her be outside our house without me with her."

Knox tried to think of some reason Ally would have left the office and where she would have gone. "Maybe she's just playing with us. Kids don't understand that sometimes playing like that can be dangerous."

He stopped at the first office they came to and looked

around the room. "I'm sorry to interrupt, but have you seen a little girl? A blonde? Green eyes?"

"She was wearing jean shorts and a pink-and-purple plaid shirt," Bree said, her body trembling when she joined him in the doorway.

When the woman in the office shook her head, they moved on. They had visited each office on the floor, looking closely at the children in the waiting room at the county pediatric clinic. But Ally wasn't there.

They had started down the stairs when Bree's phone rang. "Hello? Ally?"

Knox tried to listen to the person on the other line but they spoke too quietly. When Bree hung up and her legs went out on her, Knox caught her and lowered her to the nearest step. Her face was paler than usual and then she began to cry.

"What is it?" Knox asked, holding Bree by the shoulders. "Tell me."

Knox had been through many tragedies in his life. He'd lost friends and loved ones. He'd held babies that had never taken a breath. He'd held the lives of patients and their babies in his hands during emergency surgeries. He'd even been in danger himself at times when he found himself up on a mountain, driving around their hairpin turns in snowstorms or torrential rains. Nothing scared him like the look in Bree's face at that moment.

"They found her. She's in the security office downstairs," Bree said, her voice shaking with each word.

Then she lost it, there on the steps of that old, run-

down county building. All Knox could do was hold on
to her as the tears began to run down his face, too.

They made it to the security office as soon as they got
themselves together. But when they walked in, Knox
was surprised to find a solemn Ally that made no move
to run to them.

"Oh, Ally, you scared me so much," Bree said, not
seeming to notice that the little girl didn't hug her back.
"Why did you leave the office? You know that you can't
go anywhere without an adult with you."

"I don't want to talk to you," Ally said, pulling away
from her.

"What? What's wrong, sweetheart? Is this about the
trip to the ranch? I told you that me and Dr. Knox needed
to talk about that. Being mad about that isn't a reason to
run away and scare us like that."

Knox could see that Bree's fear of losing Ally was beginning to dissolve. She had moved on to wanting answers and he had an idea what those answers would be.
Bending down so that he was on his daughter's level, he
met her eyes. "Ally, did you listen in on a conversation
between me and your aunt?"

The girl only showed the slightest hint of guilt before
she put her chin up in the air. "You said that you were
my daddy and Aunt Bree doesn't want me to know."

Knox heard Bree catch her breath, but he didn't look
up. "Me and your aunt were having a private conversation. If you heard us say something that you didn't understand or that made you angry, you should have let us

know you were there. Running off wasn't the right thing to do. You scared us badly. If you ever hear something that scares you or that you don't understand, I want you to tell one of us so we can explain it to you."

He didn't want to scold his daughter. She'd heard something that she shouldn't have overheard and she was probably as much confused as she was scared. That was on him and Bree. But he also couldn't allow her to think that running away would be the answer when she was angry or scared.

Bree bent down and joined them. "I'm sorry that you overheard us. We were both trying to find a way to tell you, but I wanted you to have some time to get to know Dr.… I wanted you to get to know your daddy before we told you. I know you have a lot of questions and we're going to try to answer them the best we can."

Ally looked from him to Bree, then back to him. "Are you really my daddy?"

Knox looked his little girl in the eye. Green eyes, so unlike his own, but still there was something in the stubborn glint of them that reminded him of his mother. "Yes, Ally. I'm really your daddy."

CHAPTER TWELVE

WHILE BREE TALKED to the police officer and the Children's Services officer, Knox took Ally over to a corner where they could talk. "Do you have any questions for me while your aunt Bree is talking to the officers?"

"Did I get her in trouble?" Ally said, biting her lip in the same cute way Bree sometimes did.

"Your aunt can take care of this. Just like she's always taken care of you."

"Does your being my daddy mean that I won't live with her anymore?"

Right when Knox thought he was prepared for anything his daughter could ask, she surprised him. He'd thought she'd have questions about how he and her mother had met. How was it that he didn't know that she was his daughter? Questions that he'd have asked. Instead, she'd asked something that was much more simple. At least it should have been. "Me and your aunt are still trying to work out the details. How do you feel about it?"

He knew these were things that he and Bree should be discussing with her together, but the choice of time and place had been taken away from them when Ally had overheard them talking.

"Don't you like Aunt Bree?" Ally asked.

"Of course, I like your aunt a lot." He wasn't about to try to explain the crazy emotions Bree made him feel to his daughter. He was still trying to understand them himself.

"Do you want to kiss her?" his daughter asked. "My friend at school, Danny, says his parents kiss because they love each other."

Knox was going to have to find out who this Danny kid was and why he was talking to his daughter about kissing. He looked over to where Bree spoke with the officers. There was nothing he'd like more than to kiss away the worried look on her face right then. "Yes, I want to kiss her."

"Then why can't we all live together?" Ally asked, her face turned up to him.

How did he explain to her how complicated adult relationships were? But did it really have to be that complicated? Wasn't the simple truth that his feelings for Bree had grown into something much more than those he should have for his daughter's aunt or for the midwife he worked with? Hadn't his fascination with her freshness, her spirit, the way she stood up to him, started long before he even knew about his daughter? Hadn't he felt something forming between the two of them the day they'd delivered the baby at the clinic when she'd smiled at him and it had suddenly felt like the two of them were the only two people in the world, and he was okay with that?

And then there was the night they'd spent together.

He'd never felt so whole, so complete, as when he'd held Bree in his arms that night. It was like pieces of the puzzle that had been his life that he'd scattered recklessly had suddenly come together. He couldn't imagine his life now without his daughter. He didn't want to imagine his life without Bree beside him.

He looked down to see his daughter staring at him with such faith in her eyes. Such faith in him, trusting that he would make everything right, when all along it was Ally's innocent reasoning that pointed him toward what he had wanted since the day her aunt had accused him of having his own fan club. If he'd ever had a fan club, there was only one person he would want in it. And that was Bree.

Bree sat beside Knox as he parked his truck in front of his parents' house. Facing Gail and Charlie Collins today wasn't something that she wanted to do today, but she knew she would have to face them at some point.

"So Ms. Gail is really my grandmother?" Ally asked for the hundredth time since they'd left their house.

"She's my mother and that makes her your grandmother," Knox said once more, with a patience that he should have won an award for.

But then again, he wasn't about to face his parents while trying to explain why they had never been told about their granddaughter before now. Knox had given them the news over the phone and he said that they had taken the news well, that both of them were excited to learn that they had a grandchild even if they'd lost the first years of her life. Now it would be up to her to explain just how she had kept them from their only grandchild.

"It's going to be okay," Knox said, taking hold of her hand.

He'd been quiet most of the ride there, answering Ally's questions easily, but saying almost nothing besides that. He'd even seemed nervous when he'd arrived to pick them up. The kiss he'd given her when Ally had run to get her backpack had been little more than a peck between friends. He seemed to be somewhere else. And considering what they were about to do, she needed him to be there with her. "Are you sure they won't run me out of town the moment they see me?"

"I can almost guarantee you that by the time the day is over they will be the happiest people in the state of Tennessee," Knox said, though she noticed his eyes didn't meet hers.

Ally, tired of waiting for the adults, undid her seat belt and opened the truck door, hopping down and running toward the house before Bree could make a grab for her. By the time Bree and Knox made it to the door, Ally was already opening it and running in as if she owned the place.

"Ally, stop. You didn't even ring the bell," Bree called from behind her. The Collinses were going to think she'd raised their granddaughter as if she lived in a barn. Of course, their barn was actually nicer than the house Ally lived in.

"That's okay," an older man said as he came down

the stairs. With hints of gray shooting through the same light brown hair that matched his son's, Charlie Collins had aged well. His skin was tanned and a little weather beaten, but as he walked toward them, she could see that he still had that swagger that had sent screaming women falling out into the aisles when he'd performed. His eyes were the same light gray as his son's, too. And right then he only had eyes for one person.

Ally stood staring up at him, her eyes studying him. "Dr. Knox, he's my daddy, he says that you are my grandpa. Are you okay if I call you grandpa or will it make you feel old? My friend Josie says that she doesn't call her grandmother Grannie because her grandmother says it makes her feel old. I can call you something else if you'd like me to."

Charlie Collins looked down at the little girl before he broke out in laughter as loud as if he had a mic hidden in the beard running down his chin. "I think I'd like to be called Grandpa. And what shall I call you?"

"My name is Ally. Ally Rogers. And this is my aunt Bree. You can call her Bree, though, because you're an adult."

"It's nice to meet you, Bree," Charlie said, nothing but politeness in his tone.

"It's nice to meet you, Mr. Collins."

"There she is," Gail Collins said, coming down the stairway behind her husband. "How are you doing today, Ally?"

Ally ran up the stairs and met Gail. "I'm fine. You're my grandma."

"So I've been told," the older woman said, taking Ally's hand as she continued down to where Bree waited. "Charlie, why don't you take Ally down to the basement to see the playroom? If I remember correctly, our granddaughter likes to play those video games you have down there."

"Can I go?" Ally asked Bree. When Bree nodded, Ally let go of her grandmother's hand and grabbed hold of Charlie's.

"I thought I'd saddle up a couple of horses for me and Bree. I'll be right back," Knox said, giving Bree an encouraging smile before heading back out the front door.

Bree watched him retreat, leaving her alone to face his mother. "I guess I owe you an explanation about why I didn't tell you about Ally when we were here."

"Let's sit down a moment," Gail said, moving over to where four leather chairs faced a large fireplace. "Knox has explained most of everything, at least everything he knows."

"I've told him everything that I know myself. I wasn't in Brittany's life at the time so I can only say I think she had reasons for the way she handled the pregnancy. Maybe if she hadn't been killed, she would have changed her mind. I don't know."

"If it's not too painful, do you mind me asking why you and Brittany weren't communicating? Knox said you didn't even know she was pregnant until after Ally was born."

"When I look back, it was stubbornness on both of our parts. Brittany wanted a life in country music. I wanted to go to college and then medical school. She felt that my refusing to perform with her had ruined her chances of that life. I didn't think so. I still don't. Don't get me wrong, she had a beautiful voice, but there are a lot of beautiful voices in Nashville."

"I'm glad you got to go into medicine, but midwifery? That wasn't in your plan, was it? But then I'm sure raising Ally wasn't in your plan, either. You had to have considered telling Knox about her at some point. You had to know that you could have gone on to medical school if he'd taken Ally."

Knox taking Ally from her had never crossed her mind. She'd done her best to honor her sister's promise, until she'd had proof for herself that her sister was wrong. "Ally's not just my niece, Mrs. Collins. She's my child in every way. I never thought of giving her up to anyone. I did what was asked of me by my sister. Neither of us knew that within a few hours she would be dead."

"I'm sorry. I don't want to upset you. I have no doubt you did what you thought was best for Ally. I could see the love you two share when Knox first brought the two of you to the ranch. I thought then that maybe Knox had finally found someone that he could have a steady relationship with. Then I find out that it wasn't you that he was interested in, it was Ally. It's taking me a few moments to believe that."

They both stood when Knox came into the room. "Ready?"

"Yes, but is it okay if Ally stays here?" Bree asked Knox's mother. Their whole conversation was confusing to her. She couldn't tell if the woman was angry at her or if she truly was trying to figure out how all of this had taken place. And Bree had to admit, her saying that Knox was only interested in Ally had hurt, even if Knox's mother hadn't meant for it to.

"Of course. This is her home now as much as it is Knox's. Besides, I have an interior decorator arriving soon to help us make one of the rooms here just for Ally."

Not knowing what to say to that, Bree followed Knox outside. He helped her mount a sweet, gentle mare before he climbed up on his own horse. "I haven't been on a horse in a while. When I was young, me and Brittany took lessons. It's one of the few things I regret not being able to give Ally."

"I don't think you need to worry about that now. We'll make sure she gets lessons," Knox said, leading the way across a field that ran behind the house.

"Are you okay?" Bree asked. "You've been quiet all day."

"I'm fine," he said. "There's a path I want to take you up to on that hill. Then we need to talk."

His words had an ominous tone to them. What had happened since the two of them had talked last that would have made him change so much? And what had he meant when he said that *we* would make sure that Ally had riding lessons? Did he mean the two of them, together? Or was he talking about him and his parents? Anytime Knox had brought up helping Bree pay for Ally's support, she'd shut him down. She knew that at some point she'd have to accept that Knox had the right and the responsibility to help with Ally's expenses, but it was hard to take money from someone when she'd worked so hard to support the two of them on her own.

And what had his mother meant by having a room decorated for Ally? Did she think that Ally would be moving in here? Was that what Knox wanted?

And then there was the comment of his mother's about Knox being just interested in his daughter. Had he not told her that the two of them were involved? Or was that all in her own imagination? She knew that people had sex and then moved on; wasn't that what her own sister and Knox had done?

Was that it? Had she been just as naive as her sister, thinking that she and Knox were building a relationship together?

By the time they got to the top of the hill, Bree was beginning to fall apart. Had she really fallen for a man so devious that he would use her to get his daughter?

That thought stopped her in her tracks. Or in her horse's tracks. No matter what she might think, she knew that Knox Collins didn't have a devious bone in his body. If he did plan to take his daughter away from her, which she had to admit was his right as Ally's father, he would never do it backhandedly. He'd tell her gently, letting her down as easy as possible.

Yeah, he'd do something like take her on a horse ride in the country.

"Stop!" The sound of her own voice startled her as it echoed into the hills.

"What's wrong? We're almost there," Knox said.

"If you're going to tell me that you're going to take

Ally away from me, I'd rather do it before we go any farther," Bree said.

Knox jumped down off his horse and came back to her. "What are you talking about?"

"I don't want you to try to sugarcoat this. Just tell me the truth. Are you going to take Ally to live with you?"

"Yes, I want Ally to live with me. That's something I wanted to talk to you about," Knox said, then reached up and pulled her out of the saddle and into his arms. "And before you start imagining the worst, though I have the feeling that you already have, maybe you should listen to me."

Bree pushed against him until he placed her down on her feet, then started up the path, leading her horse behind her. "How can I not imagine the worst when you've barely said ten words to me today and you have a mother who's right now making plans to decorate a room for Ally?"

"I haven't felt like talking because I've been trying to find a way to talk to you about this. But you've already jumped to the conclusion that I would just take the child that you have raised like a daughter away from you. Does that really sound like something I would do to you? Is that really what someone who loves you would do to you?"

Bree stopped, her horse bumping against her, making her lose her balance. Sitting there in the dirt, she looked up at Knox. 'You love me?"

"Yes, I love you. I was hoping that you loved me, too. I had this great speech I had been working on. A fancy one where after I've taken you to the top of this hill, I tell you about how all of this will be mine one day, but none of it would mean a thing if you weren't there beside me." Knox sat down beside her. "Stupid, huh?"

"Maybe a little bit. You know that I don't care about any of this stuff. I care about you and Ally. The two of you are all I need, too." Bree leaned against him then, putting her head against his shoulder. Leaning forward, she took his face in her hands and kissed him. "I love you, Knox Collins."

When they pulled apart, Knox stood and offered her a hand. "I might have brought a blanket and some wine in my saddlebags, if you want to climb up this hill with me."

Bree put out her hand, knowing that when she took his hand her whole life was about to change. "Knox Collins, nothing would make me happier than the two of us climbing this hill and every other one that life puts in front of us, together."

EPILOGUE

"IS THAT it?" Knox asked her for the third time. She'd told him when he rented the trailer that it wouldn't be big enough for everything she and Ally needed to take with them.

It had been three months since they'd told his parents that they were all moving in together. It had only been two weeks that Knox had gotten the call about a building he had been looking at to start a new clinic, one that both he and Bree could work at together now that she had passed her examinations and received all her certifications.

"Did you get Maggie's blanket?" Ally said, carrying her new puppy that her grandparents had insisted she needed if she was going to be moving away from her friends. They might just as well have bought their daughter a pony by the looks of the curly-haired dog's enormous paws.

"Her blanket and her bowls are in the back of the truck. Why don't you climb in and get her settled." Bree helped Ally up inside the truck then turned to the friends who had come to see them off.

"I had really hoped the two of you would settle down here in Nashville," Sky told her as they hugged.

"We'll be back next month for your and Jared's wedding," Bree said, wiping at her eyes.

"And then you'll be coming back for your own wedding this Christmas," Lori said as she shared a hug with the two of them.

Bree looked down at the diamond that glittered on her finger. It was a beautiful ring, but it was the question that Ally had asked when she and Knox had shown it to her little girl that had been the brightest moment of the night. "Because you are marrying my daddy, does that mean you will be my mommy now?" It had been a night of laughter and tears, and she would remember it always.

"You ready?" Knox asked, shaking Jared's hand before climbing into the truck. Bree turned back to look at the little house where she'd worked so hard on her own to make a home for her and Ally.

But now she wasn't alone. She and Ally had Knox. They'd gone from two to three, and they were even talking about adding a fourth one to their numbers, though they hadn't shared that with Ally yet.

Climbing into the truck, she looked over at the man she loved, the one she wanted to share all her new adventures with. "Yes, I'm definitely ready."

* * * * *

MEDICAL

Life and love in the world of modern medicine.

Available Next Month

Melting Dr Grumpy's Frozen Heart Scarlet Wilson
Neurosurgeon's IVF Mix-Up Miracle Annie Claydon

....

Brooding Vet For The Wallflower Sue MacKay
Family Of Three Under The Tree Traci Douglass

....

Nurse's New Year With The Billionaire Karin Baine
Resisting The Single Dad Surgeon Louisa Heaton

Keep reading for an excerpt of a new title
from the Western series,
THE MAVERICK'S CHRISTMAS KISS by Joanna Sims

PROLOGUE

Tenacity Elementary School
Tenacity, Montana
December 2006

IT WAS TWO weeks until Christmas Eve, and eight-year-old Marisa Sanchez had just performed in the Tenacity Elementary holiday show. Like many of her peers, she had auditioned for the holiday show, but only she had won the coveted spot of the star on top of the singing Christmas tree. Her mother was a seamstress by trade and, with materials that she had been provided by the school, she had designed and sewn the costumes.

Dressed as a puffy, bright yellow five-point star with a small hole in the top point for her face, Marisa was now standing in line to greet the music teacher, Mrs. Jankowski, who had produced the holiday show. Her parents and her brothers, Julian, Diego and Luca, along with her sister, Nina, stood beside her. Marisa's face was flushed and her dark brown eyes were shining from her triumphant performance. Yes, it was difficult for her to wait, but the wait was totally worth it to spend a moment with her favorite teacher.

Before taking her turn with her teacher, Marisa tugged on her mother's hand to get her attention.

Her mother leaned down and asked, "Yes, *mija*?"

"Remember how scared I was?"

"I do," her mother said.

"Guess what?"

"What?"

Marisa smiled up at her mother. "Once I got onstage, I wasn't scared anymore. I was the very best Christmas star I could be."

This made her mother laugh. "Yes, you were, *mija*. A perfect Christmas star!"

When it was *finally* their turn, Marisa threw herself into Mrs. Jankowski's arms and hugged her tightly.

"My beautiful little star!" The music teacher returned her hug. "You were the perfect topper for our Christmas tree!"

"Thank you, Mrs. Jankowski," Marisa said with a happy grin.

"You are welcome, precious one." Mrs. Jankowski gave her one last big squeeze before she turned her attention to Marisa's parents, shaking hands first with her father and then her mother.

"Mr. and Mrs. Sanchez, thank you so much for coming," the music teacher exclaimed. "I hope you all enjoyed the show."

"We loved the show," Nicole said. "We didn't know that Marisa could sing just like a pretty little songbird."

That made Mrs. Jankowski's smile broaden. "Your daughter is very talented. She has a beautiful voice and she is picking up the piano so quickly."

"Thank you so much for everything you have done for our daughter," Will said while Marisa basked happily in the praise of her teacher.

"Of course!" the teacher said with a nod before she added, "And thank you, Mrs. Sanchez, for making our costumes. The Kindergarten Christmas show never looked so good!"

"I was so pleased to be able to help," Nicole said, putting her arm around Marisa the Five-pointed Star.

"Well," Will said, glancing at the parents and students waiting to greet the teacher. "We'd better let you go."

As her family moved on, Mrs. Jankowski had one final had one final word for her parents. "Please consider getting music lessons for Marisa. I would start with voice and piano, as she is really quite gifted."

Marisa waved goodbye to her teacher as she walked with her family to the parking lot. As expected, the older siblings held the hands of their younger siblings, and because it was her special night, Marisa walked between her parents holding their hands and swinging every couple of feet. Marisa was feeling so happy, but there was something bothering her. When Mrs. Jankowski had mentioned lessons, a dark cloud of worry had passed over her parents' faces. Their house was full of love and family and laughter, but money was always tight. Even at her tender age, Marisa was aware that, even though they were rich in the love department, they were considered poor when it came to money. Many times when she asked for something that she saw other kids in school had, her mother, with a deep sadness in her eyes, would tell her that they would have to wait. Her father worked on a ranch and rented land to farm, growing hay for the animals. Will also regularly took on odd jobs to make ends meet while her mother sewed nearly seven days a week.

Once their family of seven was seated in her father's van, her mother met her husband's eyes. "Lessons. Can we manage that?"

Will was silent for several seconds, then he broke the gaze with his wife and stared out of the windshield that had a small crack in the center, his hands gripping the steering wheel so tightly that his knuckles had blanched white.

"We will figure it out, my love," her father said. "Somehow, someway, we will get our sweet angel those lessons. You heard her teacher—she is talented."

"I can take on more sewing," her mother said with a nod and a look of determination on her face.

"And I can take on more handyman jobs," her father agreed, his jaw set.

"She can have our mowing money," Julian said, and her brothers Diego and Luca nodded their agreement.

Will Sanchez looked back at his boys. "Thank you. You make us so proud."

Little Nina piped up and said, "Marisa can have my birthday money."

"My lovely Nina," her mother said, "you are such a sweet thing."

"Wait a minute! Am I going to take music lessons?" Marisa asked, her eyes, wide with hope, dancing between her parents' faces.

Her mother smiled at her. "We will have to see what Santa left under the Christmas tree for you."

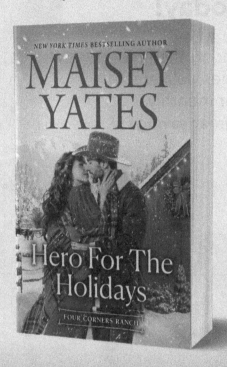

Subscribe and fall in love with a Mills & Boon series today!

You'll be among the first to read stories delivered to your door monthly and enjoy great savings.

WE SIMPLY LOVE ROMANCE

Subscribe and fall in love with a Mills & Boon series today!

You'll be among the first to read stories delivered to your door monthly and enjoy great savings.

WE
SIMPLY
LOVE
ROMANCE